"A unique take on paranormal romance."
—Sherrilyn Kenyon
on *A Hunger Like No Other*

The "awe-inspiring" (*Romantic Times*)
New York Times bestselling author
KRESLEY COLE
Winner of the 2007 RITA Award
for Best Paranormal Romance

The critics love her "devilishly passionate"
(*Romantic Times*)
series The Immortals After Dark

CKED DEEDS ON A WINTER'S NIGHT

it to the awe-inspiring Cole to dish up a combustible sorcery and passion. One for the keeper shelf!"
—*Romantic Times* (Four and a half Stars; HOT)

NO REST FOR THE WICKED

ng sex and high-stakes adventure are what's on nega-talented Cole's sensational new paranormal . . . one nonstop thrill ride. Brava!"
—*Romantic Times* (Top Pick)

Dark Desires After Dusk

"What a fabulous story! I can hardly wait to get my hands on the next one in the series."

—Bella Online

"Oh, wow! Kresley Cole writes another spine-tingling, adventurous, and passionate romance. . . . I recommend readers grab a copy of Kresley Cole's *No Rest for the Wicked* today. It's a definite keeper."

—*Romance Reviews Today*

A *HUNGER LIKE NO OTHER*
2007 RITA Award Winner

"With intense action, devilishly passionate sex, and fascinating characters, *A Hunger Like No Other* leads readers into an amazing and inventive alternate reality. . . . Hot stuff!"

—*Romantic Times* (Top Pick)

"Unquestionably an awe-inspiring romance!"

—*Reader to Reader Reviews*

"Not just another romantic read . . . it's a powerful experience!"

—*The Best Reviews*

"A unique romance—it truly stands on its own!"

—Sherrilyn Kenyon, *New York Times* bestselling author

And her gripping historical romances featuring the MacCarrick brothers

IF YOU DECEIVE

"With power and passion, Cole completes her MacCarrick brothers trilogy with a bang. . . . You'll be held fast in Cole's grip and utterly satisfied with every aspect of her story."

—*Romantic Times* (Top Pick)

IF YOU DESIRE

"Cole steams up the pages and keeps you coming back for more. . . . It's impossible to resist these heroes and their stories. Savor every moment of another passionate tale from a queen of adventure romance."

—*Romantic Times* (Top Pick)

IF YOU DARE

"Filled with heated passion and wonderful repartee."

—*Romantic Times* (Reviewers' Choice Award Winner)

"Cole's voice is powerful and gripping, and *If You Dare* is her steamiest yet!"

—*New York Times* bestselling author Linda Lael Miller

"A deliciously entertaining read that kept the sexual tension high!"

—Romance Designs

"[A] classic romantic adventure that will leave you breathless!"

—*New York Times* bestselling author Julia Quinn

Books by Kresley Cole

The Sutherland Series

The Captain of All Pleasures
The Price of Pleasure

The MacCarrick Brothers Series

If You Dare
If You Desire
If You Deceive

The Immortals After Dark Series

A Hunger Like No Other
No Rest for the Wicked
Wicked Deeds on a Winter's Night
Dark Needs at Night's Edge
Dark Desires After Dusk
Kiss of a Demon King
Pleasures of a Dark Prince
Demon from the Dark
Dreams of a Dark Warrior

Anthologies

Playing Easy to Get
Deep Kiss of Winter

Kresley Cole

Dark Desires After Dusk

SIMON & SCHUSTER

London · New York · Sydney · Toronto

A CBS COMPANY

First published in the USA by Pocket Books, 2008
First published in Great Britain by Simon & Schuster UK Ltd, 2011
A CBS COMPANY

1 3 5 7 9 10 8 6 4 2

Simon & Schuster UK Ltd
1st Floor
222 Gray's Inn Road
London WC1X 8HB

www.simonandschuster.co.uk

Simon & Schuster Australia
Sydney

A CIP catalogue record for this book is available from the British Library

ISBN: 978-1-84983-416-2

Printed in the UK by CPI Cox & Wyman, Reading, Berkshire RG1 8EX

For Richard
Because you're like Rain Man with numbers,
and you don't laugh at me 'cause I'm not.

Jag älskar dig för alltid.

Acknowledgments

My heartfelt thanks go out to the Gibson Hall Grid. You know cryptography, so I don't have to. And much love to the usual suspects: Gena, Boo, Beth, and Rocki. All fabulous authors and amazing friends.

Glossary of Terms from *The Living Book of Lore*

The Lore

". . . and those sentient creatures that are not human shall be united in one stratum, coexisting with, yet secret from, man's."

The Valkyrie

"When a maiden warrior screams for courage as she dies in battle, Wóden and Freya heed her call. The two gods give up lightning to strike her, rescuing her to their hall, and preserving her courage forever in the form of the maiden's immortal Valkyrie daughter."

- Take sustenance from the electrical energy of the earth, sharing it in one collective power, and give it back with their emotions in the form of lightning.
- Possess preternatural strength and speed.
- Without training, they can be mesmerized by shining objects and jewels.
- All first generation Valkyrie are half sisters.

The Demonarchies

"The demons are as varied as the bands of man. . . ."

- A collection of demon dynasties. Some kingdoms ally with the Horde.

- Most demon breeds can *trace* like vampires. Some breeds are bound to obey summonses.
- Those that can emit poison from their fangs, horns, or claws are more vulnerable to others' poison.
- A demon must have intercourse with a potential mate to ascertain if she's truly his—a process known as *attempting.*

The Rage Demons

"The one who controls Tornin controls the kingdom. . . ."

- A demonarchy located in the plane of Rothkalina. Castle Tornin is their capitol. King Rydstrom III is their deposed monarch.
- Rage demons were the guardians of the Well of Souls, a mystickal font of power located within Tornin.
- The sorcerer Omort the Deathless seized Tornin, and thus Rydstrom's throne.

The Vessel

"To be chosen is to be doomed . . ."

- At the cusp of each Accession, a chosen female will beget a child who will become a warrior of either ultimate evil or of ultimate good—depending upon the father.
- Of the last seven Vessels, six have spawned evil.
- Some factions seek to assassinate the Vessel to prevent any birth. Others battle to possess her and control her offspring.

The Vampires

- Two warring factions, the Horde and the Forbearer Army.
- *Tracing* is teleporting, the vampires' preferred means of travel. A vampire can only trace to destinations he's previously been or to those he can see.
- *The Fallen* are vampires who have killed by drinking a victim to death. Distinguished by their red eyes.

The House of Witches

"*. . . immortal possessors of magickal talents, practitioners of good and evil.*"

- Mystickal mercenaries who sell their spells.
- Strictly forbidden to create personal wealth or grant immortality.

Revenants

"*The dead robbed of eternal rest, forced to serve a dark master . . .*"

- A corpse raised from the grave and reanimated, most often by a sorcerer or necromancer, who controls it.
- Can't be slain until the one who commands it is killed.

The Talisman's Hie

"*A treacherous and grueling scavenger hunt for magickal talismans, amulets, and other mystickal riches over the entire world.*"

- The rules forbid killing—until the final round. Any other trickery or violence is encouraged.
- Held every two hundred fifty years.

Wendigo

". . . corpse-eaters insatiable for flesh, ravenous for blood. They feed and feed, but can never be sated."

- Found in the boreal forests of cold and northern lands. Distinguishable by their long, knifelike claws, and bodies that are forever emaciated.
- Will dig up graves for flesh.

The Accession

"And a time shall pass that all immortal beings in the Lore, from the Valkyrie, vampire, Lykae, and demon factions to the phantoms, shifters, fey, and sirens . . . must fight and destroy each other."

- A kind of mystickal checks-and-balances system for an ever-growing population of immortals.
- Occurs every five hundred years. Or right now . . .

"A lot of people fear change. And traveling. And disarray. Sidewalk crack avoidance is more common than one would suspect."

—Holly Ashwin,
Tulane math instructor,
PhD candidate with an emphasis on formal and computational cryptography

"The first rule of being a mercenary? Find out what the client wants, then convince him that, a) you can get it for him, and, b) you're the only *one who can get it for him. Second rule? Lie. Often. The truth rarely serves you well in this business."*

—Cadeon Woede, mercenary,
second in line to the throne of the rage demons,
a.k.a. Cade the Kingmaker

Prologue

Rothkalina, the Kingdom of the Rage Demons
In ages long past

Cadeon Woede came upon the headless bodies of his foster father and brothers first, the three slain in a desperate defense of their home.

Their remains littered the ground near a demolished section of the barricades around their farmstead. Cadeon recognized the merciless slaughter as the work of revenants, corpse creatures dispatched by Omort the Deathless, their kingdom's most dreaded enemy.

He shuddered in stunned disbelief, his mind refusing to accept this . . .

The girls—

Like a shot, he charged up a hillock to the smoldering shell of the family's house. His foster sisters might have escaped into the forest. Heart thundering, he searched the ruins, praying to find nothing within. Sweat rolled down his face and into his eyes, mingling with the swirling ash and soot.

In the area where the hearth used to be, he found what was left of his younger foster sisters. They'd been burned, and while they were still alive. Their muscles had contracted in the heat, their little bodies curling up on the floor.

He lurched outside, retching until his throat was raw. No one had survived.

Running his forearm over his face, he staggered to an old oak, sinking down against it. In the space of a day, everything he'd loved in the world was dead.

The threat of Omort had hovered idly over the land for decades, yet the dark sorcerer had chosen this time to attack. Cadeon feared he knew why.

Mine own fault. He buried his head in his hands. *All of this is my doing.*

To most who knew him, Cadeon was a simple farmer, with few cares. But he'd been born a prince and was his brother's sole heir to the throne. He'd been ordered to return to Castle Tornin to defend the capitol.

Cadeon had disobeyed. *The one who controls Tornin controls the kingdom. . . .*

Cool steel suddenly pressed against Cadeon's neck. He glanced up without interest. A demon had hidden behind the tree, and now had drawn on him. A rage demon.

"My master said you would return," the swordsman said. By the look of his weapon and tunic, he was an assassin dispatched by Omort. A traitor to his own kind.

"Be done with it," Cadeon whispered as a stream of blood welled at the edge of the sword. He had no cares now. "What do you await—"

Without warning, an arrow embedded itself into the assassin's neck; he dropped his sword to futilely claw at it, ripping at his skin while Cadeon watched dispassionately. As the bastard slumped to his knees, still digging at the arrow, a troop of cavalry neared.

The leader, clad in light armor, wore a fearsome black

helmet—a notorious one. It was King Rydstrom, leader of all the rage demons. Cadeon's true blood brother.

Rydstrom removed the helmet, revealing his battle-scarred visage. Most saw this sight and grew weak with fear.

Resentment boiled in Cadeon's veins. His mind flashed to the last time he'd seen Rydstrom—when Cadeon had been only seven. As his brother's heir, he'd been separated out of the royal family twelve years ago, sent to live hidden in anonymity far from the oft-targeted Tornin.

The memory of his banishment rushed over him. . . . As Cadeon's carriage had rolled away, Rydstrom—who'd once been more like a father to him—had stood with his shoulders back, his face expressionless.

Cadeon remembered wondering if his brother had cared at all that he was leaving.

Now the king wasted no breath on greetings to his younger brother, nor did he bother to dismount. "I'd commanded your presence at Tornin."

To sit as regent while Rydstrom had journeyed off to defend against the aggressing Vampire Horde.

"Yet you refused to return with my guard?" Rydstrom said harshly. "And then you evaded them like a coward?"

Cadeon hadn't evaded the guards out of cowardice. His foster family had his first loyalty, and they'd needed his help. Because he could read and write and teleport, Cadeon was the natural choice to go afield and seek help for the blight on the area's crops.

And no one had ever suspected that Omort would truly attack. "Have you come to kill me for that?" Cadeon asked, his tone indifferent.

"I should," Rydstrom said. "I've been advised to." Cadeon's gaze flickered over Rydstrom's trusted officers, staring down at him with thinly veiled hostility. "You've been branded a coward. And not only by our enemies."

"I'm no coward. It wasn't my life—I hardly know you or that family."

"None of that mattered. It was your duty to be there," Rydstrom said. "The castle had no leader within. Omort seized on that and launched his rebellion, sending this scourge across the country. He has wrested control of Tornin. He possesses my crown."

"I did not lose your crown because of one decision. 'Tis not so simple a thing," Cadeon said, though he suspected otherwise.

"It *is*. The tides of war can be swayed by a word, an act, even the absence of a leader in the stronghold of a kingdom."

If true, then Cadeon's loved ones would still be alive.

"Let me explain this to you," Rydstrom bit out. "A childless king goes off to defend a surprise attack, and his sole heir, the last male of their line, repudiates his responsibilities. We couldn't have signaled our vulnerability more clearly."

Cadeon swiped at the blood on his throat. "It was not my crown, nor my concern."

With his fangs sharpened in aggression, Rydstrom dismounted. He drew his sword as he strode toward Cadeon, raised it—and seemed surprised when Cadeon refused to back up.

But his brother didn't understand; Cadeon should've died here. He had nothing to lose.

Cadeon didn't flinch, didn't blink, when the sword

sliced down. A flicker of interest arose in Rydstrom's eyes as he beheaded the assassin behind Cadeon.

"Do you want to avenge the deaths of these people, brother?"

Rage filled Cadeon's chest at the idea, determination welling inside him. He grated, "Yes. I want to kill Omort."

"How do you expect to do that without training?"

Cadeon's peaceful existence had left him ill-prepared for war. "If you train me, I won't stop until I have his head," he vowed. "And once I do, I'll pluck your crown from it and return it to you."

After a lengthy silence, Rydstrom said, "A life driven by revenge is better than a life driven by nothing." He turned for his horse, saying over his shoulder, "We camp in the forest this eve. Tend to your dead, then find me there."

Cadeon would, because he wanted to destroy Omort. But he also wanted to atone for his failure.

Because of his decision to turn his back on his blood kin, Omort controlled Rothkalina—and Cadeon's foster family was dead.

Revenge and atonement. Cadeon couldn't do one without the other.

Yet as Rydstrom mounted his stallion, his soldiers gazed at Cadeon with an expression of hatred, tinged with disgust. They clearly thought Cadeon should die.

I had best get used to that look, he thought. Even at his young age, he knew he'd be seeing it for the rest of his life.

Or until I get that crown back. . . .

1

New Orleans
Present day

"Stupid . . . safety lock," Holly Ashwin muttered as she fiddled with the nozzle of the pepper spray in her bag.

With her free hand, she pushed up her glasses, casting another nervous glance over her shoulder. She'd thought she heard footsteps behind her in the night. Was she being followed—or paranoid?

For months, she'd had the sense that someone was watching her. Yet strangely it hadn't bothered her before. She couldn't explain it, but there had been an almost soothing quality to the presence she'd felt.

Tonight, all that had changed.

She sensed raw menace, and wished she hadn't made the walk from the parking lot to Gibson Hall by herself. Usually her boyfriend escorted her to class, but Tim was at a symposium presenting their latest paper—alone, because her condition made it nearly impossible for her to travel.

The manicured lawns on the way to her classroom were unusually empty. No doubt there were widespread parties tonight celebrating the full moon, which hung heavy and yellow in the black sky.

There was enough light that she could see the bushes

behind her trembling. In a growing panic, she broke off the nozzle of the spray.

"*Crap*." She hastily abandoned her one weapon, tempted to snag one of the pill bottles in the pocket beside it for a dose of relief. Instead, she increased her pace toward her destination, the math building, brightly lit like a beacon.

Almost there. Her heels clicked along on the sidewalk—though they never landed on a crack, even in her rush. Apparently, obsessive-compulsive disorder was panic-proof. . . .

She checked her watch. She was on time, of course, but she was late enough that her Remedial Math 101 students would be in the classroom already.

A few yards left. Almost to safety. . . .

Once she'd made it up the six stone steps to the doors, she exhaled in relief. Inside, the hall was ablaze with fluorescent light. *Made it*.

Her class was in the second room on the right and would be filled with thirty-three very large and very loyal Tulane football players. Anyone thinking to frighten her would soon learn how a tackle dummy felt at season's end.

Holly's colleagues believed she'd drawn the short straw to have to teach Digits for Idjits, as some of the instructors called it. But Holly had actually volunteered for jock duty.

If she was to teach math, then why not instruct the ones who had exponentially more to learn?

And in truth, they were on their best behavior ninety-nine percent of the time. Though each Tuesday and Thursday night, some of the players always got there early to scribble sprawling messages for her on the blackboard. A fellow instructor had related to Holly that "the boys"—who were all of five or six years younger than she was—enjoyed watching her erase things in "those skirts."

Holly wore old-fashioned pencil skirts with hemlines past her knees. Would she never catch a break?

She wondered what she'd be erasing tonight. Some of the past offerings included "Got it bad, sooo bad, I'm hot for teacher," "I've been a naughty boy, Ms. Ashwin," and "Professor + Ginger = Holly Ashwin." They'd crossed the *l*'s to make them *t*'s.

So far she didn't think any of them had noticed her need to erase every millimeter of writing on the board, or to arrange the chalk in the tray into perfect trios, even breaking a stick to achieve a multiple of three. . . .

Outside the door to her room, she took a calming breath and smoothed her tight chignon. After ascertaining that the clasp of her strand of pearls was directly in the center of the back of her neck, she tugged each sleeve of her twinset sweater until the ends perfectly hit her wristbones. She checked the backs of her earrings, then opened the door.

Empty. Every chair sat empty.

CLASS IS CANCELED was scrawled across the board. They'd gone too far this time.

Or maybe it wasn't them? She swallowed, whirling around.

Rough cloth covered her face, reeking of fumes, drowning out her scream.

Just as her eyelids slid shut and her body went limp, she heard the unholy roar of a man in the distance.

* * *

Rogue demons have my female.

As Cade's old Ford truck tore through traffic to yet another demon lair, he grappled to control the rage his breed of demon was known for.

They've taken Holly. . . .

Almost one year ago, Cade had crossed paths with Holly Ashwin and had recognized the human as his own fated female. Unable to claim a mortal, he'd had to content himself by following her, guarding her.

Which was the only reason why he'd been there when a group of demons had traced her, teleporting her to gods knew where. But they'd hunted on the campus; surely their lair would be near.

Why would they want *her*? Because she was an innocent? Then they'd picked the wrong virgin—Cade would hang them by their own entrails and watch them dance if they touched so much as a hair on her head.

His phone rang just as he surged past a visibly drunk driver. When drunks drove slowly, it was exactly like they whispered—noticeably.

"What?" he barked in answer. Tonight he was supposed to receive the details of his latest job. It'd be the most important one he'd had since becoming a mercenary centuries ago.

"I've just left the meeting," his brother Rydstrom said. "I have the information we need."

Riding the bumper in front of him, tempted to give it a tap, Cade asked absently, "So who's the pay?"

"The client is Groot the Metallurgist."

Normally that would have had Cade raising his brows. Groot was the half brother of Omort the Deathless. "He intends to help us against Omort?" Cade's truck overtook another car, nearly trading paint with it.

"Groot's crafted a sword that can kill him."

Then it would be the only one in existence that could. Omort the Deathless didn't come by his name without reason. "What's the job?"

"He wants us to find the Vessel and deliver her to him before the next full moon."

The Vessel. Every Accession, a female from the Lore would come into sexual maturity. Her child would be a warrior of either ultimate evil or of ultimate good—depending on which way the father leaned.

A car weaved in front of Cade. "Son of a—"

"What are you doing?" Rydstrom demanded.

"Traffic." He didn't want his brother to know anything was off. Cade had told him that he would stop watching Holly. Though they both suspected she was his female, a future with her was impossible.

Humans were forbidden to demons. Because they never survived the initial claiming.

But Cade hadn't been able to stop himself from watching her from afar, studying her, growing more and more fascinated with the young mortal. Becoming more convinced that she was his.

He knew it was ridiculous. He was an ancient immortal, a brutal mercenary, head of a crew of soldiers of fortune. And yet Cade looked forward to nothing—except seeing her.

Holly went through her life having no idea that she was the highlight of a millennium-old demon's disappointing existence. . . .

This new job was supposed to be the last chance for him and Rydstrom to reclaim the crown. If Rydstrom found out Cade wasn't "on," the two of them would be heading for another of their infamous house-killing brawls. Cade used to enjoy working off his anger. Now the idea wearied him.

"How are we supposed to find the Vessel?" Cade asked.

"I was told it's a Valkyrie this time around."

"Handing over a Valkyrie for the use of an evil sorcerer—you're not worried about our alliance with them?"

"I'm going to take a page from your book and say that what they don't know won't hurt them."

"They will know. Nïx will be able to see this." Nïx, the half-mad Valkyrie soothsayer, had helped Rydstrom and Cade in the past. In fact, she'd put together this deal, though she'd given them no indication who they'd be working for.

Cade had talked to her less than a week ago about Holly. Nïx had revealed nothing about tonight.

"If Nïx didn't see that the Vessel would be one of her own before, she might not now. Besides, it can't be helped," Rydstrom said. "Nothing is more important than this job. It was Nïx herself who vowed this was our last chance to defeat Omort."

"Do you have a location on the target?"

"Groot's oracles have been searching for her. As expected, she's here in this city."

The coming Accession was already pushing and pulling all the factions together in mystickal hotspots like New Orleans.

"And we're not the only ones who want her," Rydstrom added. "Oracles, witches, and sorcerers are all scrying for her."

Cade could imagine. "You got a name?"

"No name on her. But we have her last known whereabouts, a place called the Hall of the Son of Gib. I know it sounds like typical soothsayerese, but it's a lead."

A chill slithered up Cade's spine. *No. No way.* The Hall of the Son of Gib. Or Gibson Hall—the mathematics building on the Tulane campus.

Holly wasn't a Valkyrie; yet those demons might have seen her in the predicted location and mistaken her for one. She had the right delicate features and slight build. They could have assumed she was the Vessel.

Only one local demon faction would have had the resources to determine the Vessel's location before Cade and Rydstrom—the Order of Demonaeus.

"We go for the Valkyrie tonight," Rydstrom said. "I'll be back at the house in two hours. Meet me then."

Two hours. Even if Cade was tempted to ask his brother for help with the Demonaeus, there wouldn't be time to wait for him. "Yeah, will do." Click.

The wide wheels of his truck screeched as Cade cut across three lanes of traffic, careening over the median to speed back in the other direction.

He knew where the Order of Demonaeus was located, had been forced to convene with their kind on more than one occasion.

Cade had even seen their ritual altar. Was the sweet, impossibly innocent Holly stripped atop it even now?

The steering wheel bent under his grip.

2

She woke.

Her eyelids were too heavy to open, and she didn't know if she wanted to see anyway. A quick mental survey of her body revealed terrifying things.

She was lying on what felt like a stone slab, naked except for her jewelry, and with her long hair hanging down over the end, snagging on the rough edges. The stone seeped a deep chill into her body, so cold her teeth were chattering.

They'd taken her glasses from her face, ensuring that everything within ten feet would be a blur.

Deep-voiced chanting sounded all around her, in a bizarre language she'd never heard.

Holly finally cracked open her eyes. No man had ever seen her completely naked before. Now a dozen indistinct figures leered down at her.

One pinned her arms, another her legs. With a cry, she struggled against their grip. "Let me go!" *This is a dream. A nightmare.* "Release me! Oh, God, what are you doing?"

The meds were messing with her brain. Surely she was hallucinating.

When they didn't answer, only continued their chanting, she pleaded, "Don't do this," but she didn't know exactly what "this" could be.

Though no electric lights were on in this dank chamber, black candles sat all around and moonlight shone through a skylight of some kind. She squinted around her and could see that the men were wearing robes and . . . *costume horns?*

In their chanting, one word seemed to be repeated: *Demonaeus*. This must be some kind of sicko, demon-worshipping cult.

Yet they weren't wearing masks to conceal their identities. She was certain that meant one thing—they didn't plan to let her out of this place alive.

"My family will be looking for me," she lied. Her parents were dead. She had no siblings. "I'm not the one you want for this . . . this sacrifice." Tears pooled, then spilled down her temples. "I'm not special in any way."

A couple of them gave harsh laughs at that.

"*This isn't happening*," she whispered to herself, trying to stem her panic. "*This isn't happening.*"

She gazed up at the glass dome above her. The moon had risen almost directly over an unusual etching in the center of the glass, depicting what looked like the face of a horned demon.

The shadow from the etching would slide directly over the altar, over her, when the moon hit it. It was a gnomon, a shadow maker, like that of a sundial.

The men seemed to await the shadow's advent, glancing up every so often. Await it for what?

As the moon continued to ascend, their chanting grew louder. She struggled harder, kicking her legs and thrashing her arms.

Lightning flashed across the sky. She vaguely noted that the more she strained to get free, the more frequently the bolts flickered overhead.

The largest of the men slid between her spread legs. When he removed his robe, comprehension hit her. She couldn't see below his waist but knew he was naked. "*No, no, no . . . don't do this!*"

The whites of his eyes were . . . flooded with black? He clamped her thighs, dragging her over rough stone to the edge of the altar.

She shrieked. All hell broke loose.

The men slapped their hands over their ears; the glass above them splintered into ominous forks through the etched demon's face—then the whole of it shattered, raining heavy shards all around the untouched altar.

A lightning bolt jagged down through the opening to spear her squarely in the chest, tossing the men away.

She screamed from the impact, arching with her fists clenched. The bolt was a physical force continuing on and on.

Unimaginable heat sizzled through her veins. Her two rings melted off her fingers, her earrings from her ears. Her necklace and watch were seared to liquid, dripping from her body.

She was unharmed—because her skin was somehow hotter than the boiling metal.

The pressing weight of the electricity filled her with power, with . . . comfort. When it ended, Holly was changed. She didn't feel alone in this place.

Punish them, a voice seemed to whisper in her mind. *They dared to hurt you. . . .*

Her earlier terror was strangled by a fresh rage. Her fingers were suddenly tipped with razor-sharp claws. Her eyesight was keener than it had ever been even in the darkness. Fangs grew in her mouth.

Though she felt no ill effects from the lightning, the

demons looked dazed, blinded. They were bleeding from the falling glass.

But they quickly regrouped. She rose, crouching on the altar, waiting as they stalked closer. One had a club—her eyes fixed on it.

A club. To beat her unconscious so they could continue their sick ritual.

Red covered her vision. When one lunged for her, she snatched him by the horns. They were . . . attached to his skull. Not a costume. Which meant *real* demons?

Which meant hallucination. This couldn't truly be happening. She laughed as she twisted the demon's head, assured this was some kind of nightmare.

And in her nightmare, the instinctive drive to kill with her new strength and fury overwhelmed her.

When the others attacked, Holly was unafraid.

She knew *how* to kill them as if she'd been hunting and slaughtering them for thousands of years. She knew to wrench their heads from their necks, to slash out with claws that would rend through skin and arteries as they would tissue paper.

Punish . . .

When the blood began to spray, lightning scored the sky above her as if in encouragement.

"I understand," she murmured as she aimed for one's jugular and severed it. "I see." *Yes, their last sight on earth should be my laughing face.*

"*Easy, female,*" Cade soothed as he crept closer to where Holly huddled naked in a corner.

She was covered in blood. But had it come from her, or the twelve demons she'd apparently slain?

Her eyes were . . . *silver*, glowing in the shadows. Which meant Valkyrie. Somehow she was no longer a mere human.

A Valkyrie at Gibson Hall. Holly was indeed the Vessel.

She had her knees drawn up to her chest and was trying to cover her breasts while baring her little claws at him to ward him off. She was trembling with fear and shock, and tears coursed down her blood-splattered face.

It was killing him.

"Easy," he murmured. "I don't want to hurt you."

Her eyes darted from his horns to those on one of the heads lolling on the stone floor.

"Yeah, I'm a demon, too," he said. "But not at all like them. My name's Cadeon Woede."

How far had they gotten with her before she'd turned and attacked? Though the carnage looked to have been done some time ago, Holly still had gashes on her arm from the claws of one of these demons.

She might have been turned to a Valkyrie, but she hadn't yet been granted the accelerated healing and immortality of one. Which meant that she was still incredibly vulnerable to harm. Like a human.

Humans die so easily.

"Did they injure more than your arm?"

She finally shook her head.

"Hurt you anywhere? Do I need to get you to a hospital?" he asked, even as he knew that wouldn't work.

Other factions were searching for her. He would be surprised if they hadn't already scried the lightning he'd seen from a distance. Power still sizzled from her and throughout the chamber. New power was easily traceable.

She whispered, "They d-didn't hurt me."

"Good. I want to help you, Holly."

She frowned at his use of her name, studying his face.

"We've met before," Cade said, but she was in no way calmed—lightning continued to strike in constant streams. Lightning gave Valkyrie strength, but it also mirrored their emotions.

When he began unbuttoning his shirt to cover her, she gave a cry, and bloody claws swiped out at him. Then she stared in horror at her fingertips.

Just hours ago, she'd been living as a normal human—or near normal with some eccentricities. Now she had become something he never could have predicted. A Valkyrie. Or half one. He hadn't known she'd possessed this latent potential. The shock of the ritual must have triggered the transformation.

If not for this power, she would have been brutalized, her womb offered to the dark god this order of demons worshipped.

When he removed his shirt, she bared her small fangs and hissed, then looked aghast at her reaction.

"There, now, a good hiss never hurt anyone." He crouched beside her, fighting the urge to clasp her to his chest. "I'm going to put this on you. *Easy* . . ."

She gazed up at him with eyes wavering between silver and the intense violet he recognized. "Wh-what's happening to me?"

"You know all those creatures you thought were myths?" When she shakily nodded, he said, "Well, they're not. And you're changing from a human to an immortal."

Which meant it had become possible for Cade to claim her for his own.

And you've just become my target—the Vessel. The means to pay for a sword to kill our enemy.

She equaled the crown he'd worked for nine hundred years to reclaim—the unyielding pursuit that had given him a reason to go on living.

Never had it been so close. . . .

All he had to do was use and betray the woman he'd waited just as long to possess.

3

Holly turned and hunched to button the shirt, peering over her shoulder to keep this Cadeon in sight.

She remembered meeting him before. As if she could ever forget those stunning green eyes. She recalled his accent as well—it sounded like some type of British colonial, and he spoke with an unusual intonation.

Months ago, he'd approached her on campus. Initially he'd been cocky, then grew tongue-tied, stammering, even as he'd boldly studied her figure.

She'd found him weird. And that was before she'd known what had been hidden beneath the hat he'd worn.

Now she could see what had been covered by his shirt as well. His bared chest was rippling with muscles, and he wore a wide gold band just above his bulging bicep.

He was as massive as the others, admittedly one of *them*. She shuddered, trying to block out the sight of the corpses all around her.

But he looked different as well, his facial features appearing more human. His horns ran back along his head through his tawny hair, instead of jutting forward.

How can I see this well without my glasses? "Why should I t-trust you?"

"Because it's my job to protect you. More will be coming—I'll explain everything later."

When she still hesitated, he said, "These twelve were just the first round intended for you."

"First round?" she cried.

A creaking door sounded from somewhere on a floor above them. He shot to his feet. "Come with me if you want to get out of here alive."

"Wh-where are we going?"

"We're going to run for it. I'll keep you safe, but you'll have to trust me." He held out his big hand to her.

Seeing no other choice, she took it, and he pulled her up. She was surprisingly steady on her feet, all things considered. Never relinquishing her hand, he led her out of the chamber, then down a murky stone corridor.

When the passageway intersected with an alcove, they spied a group of three males, robed like the ones before, speaking that same odd language. Cadeon pulled her back against the wall, then whispered directly at her ear, "Don't make the smallest sound. You stay here until I return for you. Clear?"

She nodded, and he turned back. As he prepared to attack, the broad muscles in his back grew before her eyes. His horns straightened and blackened.

Her lips parted when he lunged for the others. His speed was mind-boggling, and his roar shook the room, paining her sensitive ears. He snatched the horns of one demon and twisted its head until an audible pop sounded.

As he faced off against the other two, his upper and lower fangs shot longer. He used them like an animal as he bit and clawed.

Had she looked that overcome with rage when she'd killed? Her earlier fearlessness disappeared. When his eyes flooded with black like the other one's had, she shuddered, backing away.

Had she thought him different? *I just want to go home. Forget this ever happened.* Why should she trust him? *I can find my own way out.*

Clear of the fray, she hastened in the direction they'd been traveling, eventually stumbling into an open gallery.

More bizarre symbols were stamped into the wooden chairs and stone floor. Ancient-looking tapestries hung on the walls. On a display shelf were skulls that looked human, but they had horns and upper and lower fangs.

Then she saw what appeared to be double doors to the outside. If she could get outside, she could find a car or hide—

Rapid gunshots exploded the plaster just feet to the right of her. She sucked in a breath and dared a glance as she ran to her left. Men aimed machine guns at her with deadly intent.

A second man began shooting from the other direction. Bullets riddled the wall on either side of her, closing in. She darted right, then left once more, blocked each way. The sweep grew closer . . . closer.

A foot away on each side. She froze with terror.

A bellow sounded over the gunfire. Cadeon hurdled the line of bullets to get to her. Scooping her up in his arms, he tucked her against his chest. Just as the shots reached them, he pressed her against the wall until his body covered every inch of hers.

He gritted his teeth when the first bullet hit him, unable to turn to run without risking her. She burst into tears. Two bullets, three, four . . .

He stared down at her, those jet eyes seeming to consume her, and grated, "No more . . . running from me. Yeah?"

"Y-yeah," she whispered brokenly, crying harder every time his big body jerked from the impact.

Over his shoulder, he roared at them, a furious warning growl, and she whimpered. His voice a harsh rasp, he said to her, "*No, no, female. Shh.*" He petted at her tears with huge fingers tipped with short black claws.

The shots abruptly stopped. Holly peered over Cadeon's shoulder. The robed demons were attacking the gunmen.

As the others clashed, Cadeon sprinted toward those double doors with her in his arms. He turned in midstride, hitting the doors with his bullet-riddled back, bursting them from their hinges.

Charging out into the night, he made for an older truck parked off to the side of the manor. After opening the groaning cab door, he tossed her inside on the cracked vinyl seat and followed her in. He pinched the key and turned. Nothing.

"Is the battery dead?" she asked, shaking off some of the shock and fog. "Does this thing still run?" Wrappers and crushed cans littered the floorboards.

"Hey, hey, no disrespecting The Truck. She's gotten me out of a lot of scrapes." He finessed the gearshift up and back. "I just need to make sure . . . she knows we're in neutral." Holly thought she heard a click. "There."

The engine roared to life. He cast her a patronizing glance as soon as they were tearing up the shell drive.

She peered back at the manor. From the outside, the residence was stately, the grounds immaculate. She would never have guessed what beings lurked in the bowels of that place.

And now she was with another of their kind. She turned to him, studying this being—this . . . *demon.*

He had blond stubble on his tanned face, and his hair was thick and straight, reaching past his masculine jaw. Uneven strands looked lightened by a life in the sun.

The gold band he wore on his right arm appeared to be permanent, as if he'd have to cut it to get it past that bulging bicep. And those horns . . .

When they'd straightened earlier, they'd become much larger and darker. Now they were smooth, the color of a shell, lying close to his head. With his hair tousled over them, they probably wouldn't be easy to discern.

"How am I measuring up?" he asked, his voice deep and rumbling.

She flushed. "I've just never seen . . . horns before tonight."

"Figured you'd be in for a shock."

"Where are we going now?"

"I've got to get you out of town," he said. "This place is too hot for us to stay."

She noticed blood on the back of his seat. "How are you still moving with all those bullets?"

"With a lot of fucking pain, Holly."

She gasped, his foul language grating on her like nails on a chalkboard.

"Oh, come on, halfling! My language's only going to deteriorate from here."

"I . . . it's just habit. Are you going to be okay?"

"I should be able to shed them." When she frowned, he

explained, "My skin should push them out when I heal."

Holly couldn't scarcely wrap her mind around that. "What did those men want with me? Who were the ones shooting?"

"The gunmen were leeches. Vampires."

"Vampires," she said softly, but her mind was screaming, *This is insanity!*

"They must know you haven't turned fully immortal yet. Our kinds never use guns, as evidenced by their shite aim."

She winced at the vulgarity, but managed not to gasp this time. "Again, why?"

"Because you just became the most popular girl in town."

"What does that mean?" In the stern tone she usually reserved for her students, she added, "This isn't the time for cryptic answers, Cadeon."

"This isn't the time for questions whatsoever, Holly."

Headlights met them on the drive. An SUV blocked the gated exit.

"Fuckall," he snapped, wheeling around, spraying up shells. "More vampires."

She clamped hold of the dashboard to brace herself. "Where are we going now?"

"Only one other way off this property. Into the swamp."

"How would you know?"

"Been here before." At her look, he said, "I've met with the demons here on occasion. As a representative of my breed."

"You . . . you *fraternized* with those animals? Does your 'breed' kidnap women as well?"

"Kidnap women? I can hardly keep the chits off the jock as it is, pet."

Eyes wide, she said, "*Chits? Pet?* Are you from the nineteenth century or just trying to be misogynistic?"

"I'm from medieval times, and I never have to *try* to be misogynistic." He slammed on the brakes, and cranked the four-wheel-drive gear, peering at her hard. "It just comes to me natural, like a gift." Stomping on the gas once more, he sent her flying back into the seat as they lurched forward, racing over pristine greens.

"Why did they want to hurt me? I've never done anything to deserve this!"

"It's not what you've done—it's what you are."

"A math instructor?" she said in a strangled tone.

"You're a Valkyrie now. And a special one at that. Your mum must've been one."

"Valkyrie! My mom was a pie contest winner! And she was *human*. She died two years ago."

"Then your biological mother must have been one."

She was shocked into silence for a moment. How had this demon known she was adopted? "I didn't even know her." Holly had always imagined her as a scared teenager who'd had the incredible good sense to leave her baby on the most wonderful doorstep imaginable. Now this demon was saying that her mother was a Valkyrie? "What exactly *is* a Valkyrie? And how did you know I was adopted?"

"Questions later. Right now we've got to get through the swamp."

The dark line of brush loomed. "I don't see a road!"

"There's a service trail," he said, then added in a casual tone, "It might be a shade grown over."

"A shade! Are you certain there's no other way to get out?"

He nodded. "The property's surrounded by bayou and swamp."

"What are the odds that we'll make it through?"

"I give us one in fifteen."

Her eyes went wide. "I wouldn't take those odds!"

"You would if there's *zero* chance otherwise."

"Oh, God," she muttered, feeling around the seat. "Where's the seat belt?"

"Broke a few years back."

"And you didn't get it fixed?" she snapped.

"Don't usually ferry around mortals, then!" he thundered back.

Struggling for calm, she said, "Cadeon, I do not see even a hint of a trail."

"Demon senses. I can find it." But he pressed his straightened arm over her chest as they closed in.

"Y-you're not really going in there?"

"Trust me."

This being had saved her life, had even taken bullets for her, and yet there was something so markedly *untrustworthy* about him. . . .

He flashed her a rakish grin with barely noticeable fangs. "Though if you're the praying type, now might be a choice time."

4

Holly catapulted forward against his arm as the truck burst into the brush.

Leaves and branches slapped the windshield as the cab bounced. They smacked something that left feathers and squawked an angry retreat.

She turned, clutching the seat-back to scan behind them. "They're just going to follow us, trap us back here!"

"Their nice, fancy SUVs are lower to the ground than older trucks like mine. With a little luck, they'll bottom out. At least before we do."

Over the sound of their wholesale destruction of native flora and fauna, she asked, "Why are you helping me?"

"I'm a mercenary—my current gig is to keep you alive."

"A *mercenary?* Who's paying you? Who would know to hire a demon to protect me from a demon threat?"

"There were also the leeches."

"How could I forget?" She pinched her forehead. "Who paid you?"

"We'll talk about it later."

"At least tell me why those demons chose me. I am the most boring person you have ever met!"

He met her gaze. "Not anymore, halfling."

She glanced behind them again and saw headlights. "They're coming."

Biting out words in a language she'd never heard, he sped up even more.

"Cadeon, is it safe to go this fa—"

Shots rang out, plugging the back of the truck and her side-view mirror. His big hand palmed the top of her head and shoved her down, making her slump in the seat.

When shards from the mirror speared at her window, she shrieked.

All around them, the glass shattered; he gave a roar of pain. Cracks forked out over the windshield before it exploded as well, raining glass chips against them.

"Mind the shrieks, pet!"

"How did I do that?" she cried, frenziedly brushing glass off herself.

"Nature of the beast," he grated. "Valkyrie shrieks crack glass. Lesson learned, yeah?"

When she spied blood trickling from his ear, she bit her lip and brushed glass off him as well.

He seemed shocked by her care. "Now, there's a sweet halfling. But a little lower and to the right would be sweeter—"

"Watch out!"

The trail was gone. Murky black water covered at least a three-meter-long span of it.

"Hold on!" He yanked her upright, his arm crossing over her again.

"Why are we going *faster* toward it?"

"So we don't bog down!" he said just before they hit.

She flew against his arm once more. With the windshield gone, water sprayed over the hood, shooting against their faces.

The front of the truck dove down. Water poured into

the cab. Mud, lily pads, and several crayfish were scooped up as though with a net. The engine roared with effort as they chugged through to the other side.

Back on semisolid ground, Cadeon shook his hair out like a beast. "I can't fuckin' believe we just made that!"

Holly dragged her soaked hair from her eyes, then swiped the end of the shirtsleeve over her wet face, clearing the spattering of blood from earlier.

He grinned at her. She gaped at him.

Headlights on their trail again. Those vampires were dogged. They must think that the demons had already had their way with her. They couldn't risk that all good or all evil would be in the form of a demon. "Bugger me."

She shrieked again.

"The language? Is that it? 'Cause—"

Like a shot, Holly launched herself into his lap, whimpering.

He swallowed, intensely aware that she had her knees spread over his groin and wore nothing under the shirt. At any other time, he'd be loving their position, might have manufactured a scenario to get her just like this. But he could barely see around her bobbing head.

"It's only crayfish!"

"N-no, not only—"

The truck dived sharply into a gulch before rearing up. Then down into another and another. Cade grabbed for her waist; she listed to the side. "Watch your knee with the goolies, pet—"

He'd cupped her between her thighs.

As he felt her soft flesh, giving and hot again his palm, he growled low. The engine was clamoring, the truck bouncing, and they still met eyes. Hers grew wide as she shoved his hand away. But she still didn't get off him. "Not only crayfish!" she cried.

"Then what is it?" he snapped.

"Th-that!" She pointed down to the sloshing pool of water covering the floorboard.

A small water moccasin was along for the ride, swimming dazedly among the crushed Red Bull cans, looking as freaked out as she was.

Cade dared a quick snatch for it, but it slithered under the seat. He'd never thought he'd say this, but . . . "Off me, Holly. Back to your seat. Just keep your legs up."

She shook her head. "Not until it's gone!"

"Then you're going to have to drive."

"Okay," she said shakily, taking the wheel as he edged under her.

His hand shot under the bench. "Come here, you little fuck."

"Cadeon!"

"Ah, come on, halfling!"

The truck began to slow. He jerked upright, facing backward, and was blinded by the nearing headlights. "What in the bloody hell are you doing?" he barked at her.

"Something moved in the water down there!"

"Holly, you slam that pedal down or you die! Clear?"

With a visible shudder, she stretched her leg far down, barely reaching the pedal, tamping it down with her toes. Each time she was jounced in the seat, the gas let off, but she doggedly kept at that pedal.

He snared the moccasin. Knowing that his female would have to see it to believe it, Cade held up the snake as it merrily envenomated him. "Here, look. Visual confirmation." He tossed it out the window hole. "Now, move your little ass over here, and let's lose these miserable pricks, yeah?"

"Yeah?"

When she shimmied over his lap, he resisted the urge to plant her there, then took the wheel. As they crested a small rise and started back down, he spied another washout. He sped up, yanking her into his side. "Hold on to me."

She wrapped her slim arms around his torso, burying her face against him. Tension shot through him, desire for her eating at him, even now.

He was holding her. *Forty miles per hour.* His female. *Forty-five.* He tightened his arm around her as the frame of the truck vibrated, sounding like rocks rattling in a tin can multiplied by a thousand.

The truck hit the washout at nearly fifty miles per hour, plowing through the water. Midway through, the engine strained, sputtering. *Water in the exhaust.* He floored the gas.

"Come on, baby," he muttered. He smelled incongruous smoke. Churning, churning, and then . . .

The old girl surged out the other side. When he glanced back and saw the trailing SUV bottom out, he couldn't resist a pat on the cracked dashboard.

"We lost them. Truck's not so bad, then, is it?" he said. "Holly?" He frowned down at her in confusion. She was still holding his torso like he was a tree in a storm. As if she needed him for comfort.

Cade couldn't remember the last time anything had felt a fraction so good.

5

"Little busy here, Rydstrom," Cade snapped when his brother rang again.

"What's wrong with your phone?"

"Got wet."

"Are you back at the house yet?"

"On my way," Cade answered. "I'm fifteen minutes out. Where're you?"

"An hour from the city." He paused. "You sound excited. You sound . . . not miserable."

Discerning Rydstrom knew him well. For so long, Cade had wanted Holly from afar, and now he was with her, talking with her, *touching* her. . . . "Naff off, Rydstrom."

"Something's up with you. Whatever it is, lose it. We've got work to do."

Cade glanced down at Holly still latched onto him, then back at the road. Switching to the demon tongue, he said, "Don't think you want me to lose this. I've got the Valkyrie."

"How the hell is that possible? We didn't know who she was—"

"She's my female. Did you know she was one and the same as the target?"

"That's impossible. Holly Ashwin's human."

"Not anymore."

"You're sure? And you're certain she's the Vessel?"

"The hall you described is where she teaches math. And she'd already been taken by the Order of Demonaeus. We just got free of them. There were vampires in play as well. They're trying to kill her."

Rydstrom exhaled. "I didn't know the Vessel would be yours. But the fact is—this changes nothing. We're out of options."

When Cade didn't answer immediately, Rydstrom said, "Just last week, Nïx asked if you would give up your female to get the kingdom back. You said you would. Did you lie?"

"I'll do what I have to do."

"If we can't kill Omort, we lose Rothkalina forever."

"Even I can remember that!" Cade snapped. "I've had nine centuries to get that into my thick skull."

"Good. Now, the airports are hot. We'll have to drive her out of the city."

"To where?"

"Groot's compound."

"Where the hell is that?"

"We don't have the end destination," Rydstrom said. "There will be three checkpoints in different parts of the country. Each will render information about the next until we have the final directions to the compound. I've only got the first checkpoint."

"Why the hassle?"

"Groot wants the Vessel, but he doesn't want his fortress discovered. He's taking extra precautions to make sure no one follows us."

"You have no idea where it could be?"

"Somewhere obscure, difficult to get to, with a lot of land. I've heard tales of the Yukon. Maybe even Alaska."

"I wonder that he trusts us with this at all."

"Though your means are questionable, you complete jobs. Hard ones. And he knows how badly we want that sword."

"Why doesn't he meet us?"

"He never comes out of hiding. Omort would destroy him. Groot's the only one who has the means to kill him. At least that we know of."

"What's that supposed to mean?" Cade asked, but he knew what his brother was alluding to. They'd had a lead, a vampire who knew of a way to kill the sorcerer. But to save that leech from certain death, Cade had accidentally taken the life of the vampire's Bride. A young human named Néomi.

Unbidden, the memory arose of his sword slipping into Néomi's body. . . . He blocked it out. Cade was the master of blocking out unwanted realities.

Even if they had captured the vampire and tortured him for the information, there was nothing they could inflict worse than losing a Bride. That lead had been extinguished.

Cade's fault again.

"Omort probably already knows our intentions," Rydstrom said. "He won't take this lying down—he'll send out everything he's got to prevent us from getting the Vessel to Groot."

"Little ironic that just when I find out my female's no longer a forbidden human, I have to turn her over."

"You can't be certain that she's yours. And even if she is, you have to think of your responsibilities. The last time the kingdom depended on you . . ." He trailed off. "Now you have to do what's right."

At the reminder of his failures, the guilt emerged

again, and Cade nudged Holly away from him. She shot upright, seeming embarrassed that she'd still been holding on to him.

"No need for me to drive back to the house, then," Rydstrom said. "Just meet me at the gas station north of the lake at eleven o'clock—we'll start from there."

"I'll be there at eleven."

After hanging up with Rydstrom, Cade called Rök—his second-in-command and flatmate. In Demonish, Cade told him, "Tried to ring you for backup earlier. Just before I stormed the Demonaeus lair all by my lonesome."

"Did you?" Rök asked in a bored tone. "I was getting a leg over."

"When are you not? Need you back to the house."

"What's doing?" Rök asked, then shushed a female voice murmuring, "Come back to bed."

Cade quickly relayed the developments, ending with: "Just be there in ten minutes."

Once he'd hung up, Cade glanced over at Holly, staring dazedly out the window frame. Her hair had begun drying in unruly reddish-blond curls. He'd been waiting more than a year to see her hair freed from that tight bun she always wore and had imagined it loose a thousand times.

He hadn't thought it'd be curly. She must hate that—seeing it as another aspect of her life she couldn't control.

She looked so lost, and his hand fisted as he stopped himself from touching her again. But he had to resist. It wouldn't do for Cade to get even more attached to her.

All these months watching, he'd become increasingly fascinated with her. While sitting atop the roof of the building neighboring hers, he'd observed her strictly regimented day-to-day activities. Among them: an hour for swimming laps in her private rooftop pool, three hours a day for her doctoral work, an hour in the morning and another at night to clean her already spotless loft.

In the beginning, Cade had scratched his head at the odd little mortal's repetitive behavior and obsessive cleaning. Now he just shrugged. It was part of what made Holly unique.

On campus, he'd seen her sitting lost in thought, running her strand of pearls against her lips or tapping away at her laptop in bursts of furious inspiration.

And Cade had watched her with her *boyfriend,* feeling a savage thrill every time she'd denied her lips to that tosser, instead turning to give him a cheek. That male had never spent the night, and she'd never stayed with him.

Which was why the human still lived.

Cade had thought he had learned so much about her, but he hadn't known she would be so brave. Not many females could blindly stick a foot in a pool of water when there were snakes about—much less take down a dozen demons.

But this silence from her made him uneasy. For all her quirks, she wasn't a shy one, nor was she hesitant to speak her mind. "You, uh, got more questions?"

Without hesitation, she asked, "Can this change in me be undone?"

He frowned. "What would you want that for? You're quick to give up immortality." Granted, her introduction to the Lore had been harsh, but still . . .

"I don't want to be like this. I want to go back to how I was."

As a mercenary, his primary job was to identify what someone desired. Then he had to convince the client of two things.

That he could get it for them. And that he was the *only* one who could get it for them.

Holly had just given him the key to her. Which was good, because he had to tell her something that would ensure her cooperation, something other than the truth: *To score a weapon, I have to give you to an evil sorcerer who will likely ensorcell you to sleep with him. Once you've delivered a child of ultimate evil for him, he may let you go.*

"There might be a way to reverse the change." Of course, there was absolutely no way to reverse the change.

She gazed over at him with hope in her eyes. If he were less of a bastard, that look would really bother him. As it was, he hardly noted it. Hardly at all.

"How? How's it possible?"

"Listen, I don't want to speak out of turn and overpromise you," he said. "Right now I'm going back to my place to pick up supplies before we leave town; then we're going to meet my brother, who'll know more about all this. Just bear with me till then, and we'll figure out a way to make everyone happy."

At length, she nodded. "I have to go by my loft and pick up some clothes and things—"

"No way. They'll be watching your place."

"But I need my . . . my medications. They were in my shoulder bag."

"What kind of meds?" he asked, though he knew about her disorder, had been studying it. He just wanted to see if she'd admit to it.

She raised her chin. "They're for OCD. Obsessive—"

"—compulsive disorder. I've heard of it." She was going to *love* his place.

"So you understand why I have to get them."

"Will you die without those pills? Because you sure as shite will die to get them. Your building is going to be crawling with assassins."

Her brows drew together. "You said *building*. How did you know I don't live in a house? And how did you know where to find me tonight?"

"We've been doing background on you. I was trailing you tonight and saw them take you."

"Tell me—who hired *you* to protect me?"

This was going to get sticky if she pressed. "Don't know exactly. I just got the job details instructing me to keep you safe and the payment scale. Anything else is of no matter to me."

She was quiet for a moment. "Background on me?" she finally asked. "You mean spying."

"I'm not apologizing for it—not when the outcome was that I saved your life."

"And what did you find out about me?"

How to answer her? Every time he thought he had Holly figured out, she surprised him. Over the last several months, he'd deemed her a math geek, a campus feminist, a tease, a tree hugger, and a closet sexpot.

He'd eventually figured out why he could never get a handle on what she was like—because she didn't have any kind of handle on herself. Even she didn't know who she was.

"You're twenty-six, an only child, adopted," he finally said. "Your adoptive parents both died of natural causes in the last two years. They left you a fortune. . . ." He slanted a glance at her.

Her face held no reaction. "Go on."

"You've got two master's degrees under your belt, and you're about to complete your PhD in mathematics." *You've got the confidence of a woman who knows she's smart, and that's arousing as hell.*

"You like to swim." *Your body in even your modest swimsuit puts this demon to his knees.*

"You've got a steady boyfriend, also in the PhD program." *Tim's a ponce loser and a hypochondriac.*

"You teach football players fun with numbers or something." *With every sexual comment those jocks make about you, they routinely tempt death by demon bite. . . .*

"You like things to be . . . clean." *You like blues rock and prepackaged foods.*

"All true," she said. "And yet I know nothing about you except that you're a demon mercenary who has at least one brother."

He stifled a harsh laugh. *That's all there is to know about me*, he thought bitterly, but he said, "That's probably good. The less you know, the better."

6

Long moments after he hung up the phone with Cade, Rydstrom was still uneasy.

This is bad.

Groot's emissary had insisted on meeting three hundred miles from the city, and Rydstrom was still more than half an hour from the gas station where he would join up with Cade.

He accelerated even more, his Mercedes McLaren flying along an old ribbon of road, built up levee-style through the bayou. He was cruising at an easy hundred and forty miles per hour—so smoothly that the car seemed bored and sullenly quiet.

Rydstrom had to get to his brother before he did something impulsive. He didn't think even Cade comprehended how much he wanted that female.

This is bloody bad. Because he wasn't certain that Cade wouldn't just run off with Holly now that he could have her.

Did Rydstrom suspect the female was Cade's mate? Yes. But clearly, it wasn't meant to be.

Before, she wasn't attainable because of her mortality.

Now she would be the difference between Rydstrom reclaiming his kingdom or not.

Reclaiming Rothkalina . . . His heart beat faster at the

idea of liberating his country, working to see his people prosper for the first time in a millennium.

Omort had been brutal to them, any rebellions crushed, the offenders sadistically punished.

But right now, their freedom was resting in . . . *Cade*'s hands. Which was a tenuous position to be in.

Cade frustrated the hell out of him. Rydstrom was a male who worshipped reason, the rare rage demon who never lost his temper. Except with Cade—who knew how to push his buttons like no one else. And in return, Rydstrom was hard on him. Some said too hard.

Yet after every one of their infamous fistfights, just when Rydstrom was ready to part ways permanently, he'd remember his brother as a towheaded pup of seven, still with his baby horns, following him around, hero-worshipping him. Rydstrom would feel some flicker of hope that Cade could still pull back from the brink and make something meaningful of his life.

But if he didn't do the right thing now, that hope would be forever finished.

Recalling the day Cade had first seen Holly, Rydstrom increased his speed. . . .

A little less than a year ago, Cade had taken on a job to retrieve a highborn demon's son from the Tulane campus. The son wasn't merely experimenting at passing as a human. The young male had actually been living the lifestyle, cutting off his horns, filing his fangs down, refusing to teleport.

The horrified parents wanted him brought home, without the "shameful secret" getting out to their friends and business associates.

Cade hadn't agreed with the parents' view—one of his mottos was *To each his own*. However, his overriding outlook was more along the lines of *Another day, another dollar*. The job had won out.

Rydstrom had accompanied him to the campus to make sure the extraction went smoothly. On the way to the son's dorm, they'd passed an auditorium with a sign announcing *Mathematics Awards Today!*

Cade had been amused, ready to ridicule. "Geeks on patrol, yeah?"

Though he'd been schooled in the basics of writing, mathematics, and languages, Cade still had a chip on his shoulder that he'd never been educated like other royals because he'd been fostered out. For him, there'd been no higher learning in subjects like philosophy, astronomy, or literature. And even after all these centuries, he felt lacking.

Over the years, Rydstrom had often found books on subjects like those among Cade's possessions. His brother, the cutthroat mercenary, was secretly educating himself. . . .

Then Cade had seen Holly Ashwin up onstage receiving a first-place math award. "Now, that's a fine bit of grumble and grunt, yeah?" Rydstrom could swear that Cade made his lower-class accent even lower just to screw with him.

At the time, he hadn't understood Cade's attraction. The girl was pretty, no doubt of it, but she'd been buttoned-up, with glasses, no makeup, and her hair pulled back in a tight bun. She'd been brimming with a quiet confidence and was obviously smart—definitely not like Cade's typical fare of brazen and empty-headed.

"Come on, Cade, it's not as if we blend in," Rydstrom

had said. Both of them stood over six and a half feet tall and wore hats.

But Cade had waited until the crowd adjourned. When she'd exited the auditorium, he'd called to her, "Come here, little bit. Got a question about the beauty pageant you just dominated."

She'd turned to him with her eyes narrowed, pushing up her glasses with the tip of her forefinger.

Rydstrom had leaned against the corner of the building, watching in grim fascination, like a bystander who saw the train coming and knew the track had been blown out ahead.

Cade's easy grin had charmed female after female, and he no doubt expected this one to heed him. Instead, she'd stood her ground and looked down her nose at him. "Can I help you?"

Flummoxed, Cade had crossed the distance to her as if helpless not to. "Ah, yeah. What's, uh, doing in there?"

She'd repeated, "What's *doing*?"

Taken off guard because she wasn't receptive to his flirting, Cade had stared, flushing at his own stammering attempts to talk to her. At one point, he'd blatantly peered around her to check out her figure again as if he couldn't help himself.

Just as Cade had reached forward, looking for all the world like he intended to undo her hair, and she'd looked as if she'd slap him soundly for it, Rydstrom had broken up the interaction.

Without a word, the girl had pivoted on her heel and started away.

As Rydstrom dragged him in the other direction, Cade had looked back over his shoulder. In a crushed tone, he'd said, "She didn't glance back at me. Not once."

In the months to come, Cade had discovered everything there was to know about her. Just last week, Rydstrom had caught him kicked back on a downtown roof with a flask of demon brew, spying on her swimming. Even at a critical time like this.

Yes, she was likely the only female he could ever be whole with, have offspring with, know real happiness with, but Rydstrom still couldn't understand it. The kingdom always came first.

He would die for his people. Why wouldn't Cade—

Eyes stared back at him in the headlights. Not an animal, a woman.

He slammed on the brakes and swerved, the McLaren skidding out of control. Just when he was about to right the vehicle, a bridge abutment seemed to appear from nowhere; he careened into it.

When he'd finally stopped moving, he grasped his head, shaking off dizziness.

Staggering out to survey the damage, he crunched over cement littered with glass, chunks of ruptured tire, and even bits of the frame.

At the sight, he whistled in a breath. *Totaled.* The right side of his car was completely shaved off. *So where is the woman?*

Flashes of her arose in his mind—eyes wide with fear, long red hair whipping as he'd just missed her.

He lumbered back in the direction he'd come. "Is someone here?" he called. "Are you hurt?"

No answer. The closest gas station was at least twenty-five miles away. He fished out his cell phone from his jacket.

Out of area, the screen read. "Bugger me."

When he glanced back up, he caught sight of her farther along this deserted stretch of road, standing alone.

What the hell is she doing all the way out here by herself?

Their eyes met. At that moment, he caught her sultry, feminine scent.

The night began to feel dreamlike, surreal.

He started toward her, not bothering to retrieve his hat—with her otherworldly beauty, he could tell she was definitely one of the Lore.

Shining red hair curled down to her waist. As he neared, he saw that her eyes were dark as night. A gown of the palest blue silk clung to her lush curves. When he spied the outline of her hardened nipples, he ran a hand over his mouth.

He was fifteen hundred years old. Had he ever been so instantly and fiercely attracted to a female?

She began sauntering along the road away from him.

"No, wait! Are you all right?"

She turned to him but continued to step back.

"I won't hurt you," he called, following. "Do you have a car out here?"

"I need your help," she said, her voice throaty.

"Of course." What would she think of his battle-scarred face up close? He hadn't cared much in the past, but with her . . . the idea of seeing her disgust made him hesitate. Until she turned and skipped down an embankment—farther away from him.

He hastened after her. "Do you live near here?"

"Need your help," she said once more, ducking behind a willow by the water's edge.

He joined her beneath the tree. "I have to get back to the city, but then I can come back to help you." *And get all your information so I can return for you once my duties are done*.

As he gazed down at her face, he began to feel dizzy once more, on edge even. His reaction to her seemed too powerful, her looks too alluring to be real. She had high cheekbones and the most flawless pale skin he'd ever seen. Her pink lips were plump and glistening.

Just when he began to draw back, she said, "Help me now." Grasping his hand in her two small ones, she kissed his palm with those smiling lips, then placed it over one of her full breasts.

Every muscle in his body tightened with want. Unable to stop himself, he kneaded her flesh with a low groan. The promise of pleasure blazed from her mesmerizing eyes, and he found himself lowering his defenses.

"This is what I need," she murmured in a siren's voice, arching to his hand.

"And the gods know that I want to give it to you, right after I've settled—"

"I need it"—she took his other hand and placed it high on her inner thigh—"*now*."

Rydstrom tried to shake himself. He had responsibilities. *But I've been so long without a woman*.

He hissed out a breath when she raised her hands to his horns, boldly grasping them to tug him down to her. "Kiss me, demon."

When a female steered a demon male like this . . . Rydstrom shuddered from the savage thrill, bowing his head as she bade him to with her sexual grip. Their lips met, and lust rocked him.

He felt a connection with her. Maybe even *the* connection.

With that thought in mind, he began taking her mouth hard. She was experienced, urging him on, meeting every thrust of his tongue, teasing him until his hands landed on her soft ass to rock her against his shaft.

Still, he somehow broke away from her. "I . . . can't do this now. I have to meet someone. Much rides on this."

"Make love to me," she whispered, now sidling closer to him. "Here. Under this tree, in the moonlight. I'm *aching* for you."

His horns were straightening, his cock throbbing. He could scarcely withstand the need to be inside her luscious body.

But he had to. *The kingdom's needs always come before the king's*. "No. I have obligations," he bit out, hating those obligations for the first time. Resenting them.

When he backed away, her brows drew together. "Then you leave me no choice, Rydstrom."

Just when he wondered how she knew his name, the road began disappearing, as though the earth had been draped, disguised. He twisted around.

An illusion all around him. Behind him, he heard a clang like the door of a jail cell slamming shut. As the chimera vanished, realization hit him.

"You're Omort and Groot's sister. Sabine, the Queen of Illusions." She'd opened a portal into a dungeon, then disguised it as just a continuation of the road.

"Very good, Rydstrom."

He'd warned Cade that their enemy would stop at nothing to thwart them in their quest to get that sword. Rydstrom hadn't known the sorcerer's sister was in league with Omort, or that she was this powerful in her own right.

And if the rumors were true . . .

Then she was even more treacherous than either of her brothers.

The most beautiful female Rydstrom had ever seen was the most evil. Or maybe this wasn't her true likeness at all. She'd probably given him exactly what he needed to see to become spellbound. "Show me your real form."

"This is." She smoothed her palms over her breasts and lower. "I'm so pleased by how much it arouses you."

Even now it did, and he despised her for it. "Why have you done this to me, Sabine?"

"It's not obvious?" With a flick of her pale hand, she directed his gaze to a bed in the center of the cell. It was uncovered and unadorned—but for the chains at the head and foot.

7

"You're a . . . *slob*," Holly murmured with a shudder, aghast at Cadeon's living quarters.

"Tell me how you really feel, Holly. No need to hold back."

Shirts hung over lampshades. The floor was dotted with old pizza boxes and crushed beer cans. DVDs were strewn everywhere, some with titles that had her flushing with embarrassment.

The chandelier that hung overhead had seventeen lit bulbs and ten bulbs out. She itched to knock out two more to make both numbers divisible by three. "This is . . . how can you . . . you live like this?"

When they'd first pulled up to this estate, she'd been impressed by the luxurious Garden District residence, one not far from her childhood home. They'd driven through wooden gates past the mansion to this pool house—which was also striking, easily twice as large as her spacious loft.

But inside, chaos reigned.

"Didn't know I'd be having company."

"Would you have cleaned if you had?" she asked.

With a shameless grin, he said, "Nah." Taking her by the elbow, he steered her to his bedroom, then into a bathroom that thankfully wasn't the biohazard she'd been expecting. "You've got five minutes. Clear?"

Holly nodded silently, still stunned by the disorder, shaking from the need to fix it.

"This is not the time to be peering at your new ears in the mirror or examining your claws." He turned on the water, adjusting the temperature. "Just get the blood and swamp water off."

He picked up a shampoo bottle, and must have found it empty, because he tossed it. "I'll be back." He jogged out.

When he returned, he had a towel and washcloth over his shoulder and his hands full of miniature shampoo and conditioner bottles. "My flatmate can't pass up anything free. There should be some you'll like."

He opened the glass enclosure and carelessly dropped them into the tub, where they scattered randomly.

Random. Holly hated random.

Tossing the towel and washcloth on the counter, he said, "I'll dig around, see if I can find you something to wear that won't swallow you. Call me if you need anything else."

When he closed the door behind him, she locked it. After tugging the filthy shirt over her head, she folded it and the towel as well. She grabbed the washcloth, then stepped under the steaming cascade.

All around her feet, bottles rolled with no order, no design. They taunted her.

She knew she didn't have time to arrange them into threes, but could barely resist the urge. *Just don't look down.*

Yet she had to in order to grab shampoo. Taking a breath, she plucked up a bottle.

Then she closed her eyes as she lathered her hair, trying to ignore her pointed ears with their sensitive, sharp tips and her longer, stronger . . . *claws*.

After shampooing her hair twice and rinsing conditioner through it, she scrubbed her skin till it burned.

Cadeon hadn't wanted her to gaze at her new features, but she had no inclination to. She just wanted out of this nightmare, wanted to get back to her ordered life, her ordered loft, her on-track career—

Oh, God, Tim!

Her boyfriend of over two years was even now in California presenting their research at a conference, working for their future. They planned for him to get a job at a local software security firm and continue his research, while she would teach.

How could she face him like this? How could she explain? *Well, I got struck by this bolt of lightning, and, voilà, I was able to kill a dozen demons. Did the lightning hurt? No, it felt great. Like a hug from someone you'd really missed.*

She had to get this condition reversed, would be willing to do just about anything not to be like this any longer.

Would I trust Cadeon to help me? The comforting presence she'd sensed watching her for so long—could it possibly have been him?

She remembered him from the day she'd won that award for differential equations student of the year. He'd stammered and flushed, behaving so differently from tonight, when he'd been confident and strong. And *cocky*. He couldn't have been more cocky. It was as if he had a separate personality or even a bolder twin.

Her eyes widened as she recalled him in the truck, touching her . . . privately. In all the chaos, she remembered that burning hand covering her between her thighs, his rough palm holding her up . . . his low growl that made her breath hitch.

When she turned under the water, the spray hit her breasts, and it felt delicious. Tingles of pleasure radiated through her. . . .

How could she be aroused after what she'd been through tonight? And after what she'd *almost* been through?

That man—that fiend—had been about to rape her on a stone altar. They all had. At the memory of all of them leering at her, thinking they would be inside her, she shuddered with disgust, any warmth dissipating.

Yet they hadn't hurt her, because she'd protected herself. She'd killed tonight. Viciously.

And I did it with joy in my heart.

At that thought, she gave a cry, her eyes flashing open, hands diving down to collect the bottles. The impulse to systematize the random couldn't be resisted. She bent down, collecting the eleven samples. Not a multiple of three, but it would have to do.

On the edge of the tub, she set out three groups of three with spaces between them, all labels out, of course. She leaned back and eyed the spaces, adjusting them for equidistance.

She set the two remaining bottles on the other side of the tub, on their tops. If they were upside down and separated, then they weren't part of the same set as the others. They wouldn't have to be included. She'd nullified them.

She rose, and her eyes immediately began scanning for something else to arrange—

A hand shot through the water, snatching her arm and yanking her out of the shower. The side of her face collided with a bared, muscular chest.

Just as she was about to shriek, Cadeon covered her mouth with a callused palm. "They're coming . . ." He trailed off, those green eyes dipping to her body as she futilely tried to shield her nudity. Seeming to give himself a shake, he produced a T-shirt.

"Here. Arms up!"

"Stop looking at me! I need to dry o—"

"Holly, put your goddamned arms up!"

Startled into complying, she did, and he dragged a man's T-shirt over her wet body. He smoothed the shirt down her, boldly, familiarly.

"I'm not looking, pet," he said, but his voice was huskier, and she could *feel* his eyes on her breasts.

She dropped her head in mortification, only to find that the button fly on his jeans wasn't all the way done, as if he'd rushed in here in the middle of getting dressed.

A line of golden hair trailed from his navel down his flat stomach to where only three buttons were fastened.

He wasn't wearing underwear. *Stop thinking about that. Stop thinking about it!*

She swallowed, averting her eyes once again. Her gaze landed on the table beside his unmade bed, visible through the bathroom door. Atop it was a book on psychiatry, of all things.

Cade dragged a still sputtering Holly from the bathroom to the den, then bent down amid all the belongings scattered throughout the room. "Two black SUVs just pulled up outside."

He didn't want to freak her out, but Cade thought some vampires had already broken into the main house.

"Here, take this bag." He tossed a prepacked duffel bag to her. Inside were his clothes, his lucky bush hat, cash, and gear.

"How can you possibly find anything?" She surveyed the chaos as if horrified anew.

"It's my system," he said absently, distracted by her wet T-shirt.

She followed his gaze, flushing violently, plucking the fabric away from her hardened nipples. But he'd already seen her in the bathroom.

Gods, how I saw her. Before, Cade hadn't known she was a true blonde. He hadn't guessed how pink and tight her little nipples were. And her breasts were much larger than they'd looked in the past, even when he'd seen her in her swimsuit.

They'd be a perfect handful for him.

He shook his head, needing to concentrate on getting her the fuck out of here.

"Cadeon, this isn't a system. This is the studied absence of one."

"Yeah, not as good as the one you were using for the shampoo samples. Agreed." He hadn't missed how she'd arranged them so precisely.

She had a disorder that made his disorder a special kind of hell for her. They were going to have to talk about her loosening up a bit.

Attention back to his task, he dragged on a black T-shirt, then snared a leather jacket from a chair. He spotted his flask of demon brew. "Catch." He tossed it to her without looking, but didn't hear it fall.

"Heads up," he said as he pitched a sat-phone in her general direction. Again she caught it. The Valkyrie reflexes were coming online nicely. Grabbing his sword and a sleeping bag, he turned to her.

She blinked at him, then down at the flask. "These are

the supplies we needed to get here? Twenty percent of our supplies is alcohol?"

"Good point. Twenty percent is seriously underprovisioning—" Sensing a change in the air, he tossed her the sleeping bag as well, and unsheathed his sword.

In a cloud of smoke, Rök appeared, bloodied sword raised.

Holly jumped back, but Rök didn't miss a beat, lowering his weapon and raking his gaze over her. Still staring, he addressed Cade: "You dress her in a wet T-shirt and make her carry the bags? Damn, Cade, I like how you roll."

In Demonish, Cade said, "She doesn't know she's mine. She'll get an idea when I tear out your throat for ogling her like that."

"Point taken," Rök said smoothly in the same tongue, turning to Cade. "You've got a slew of leeches on the street, waiting for you to pull out. And two dead ones in the main house."

Cade sheathed his sword. "Lucky thing there's a back way out."

"You meeting up with Rydstrom?" At Cade's nod, he said, "Good luck with that. Enjoy her while you can."

"Are you going to provide a distraction? Or maybe you'll just get summoned away right when I need you most?"

Rök was one of his best men, but the demon got summoned more than anyone Cade had ever known.

"Swimbos," Rök said with an aggrieved shrug. *Swimbos*—Rök's play on She Who Must Be Obeyed. "Can I help it?"

"Yeah, you can, Rök." Smoke demons formed temporary

pacts every time they had intercourse. Pacts allowed one to summon a demon at will. "Give celibacy a chance."

"Anything else you'd like me to do? Maybe something *possible*."

"Capture one of these vampires for info. Follow the trail and take out whoever ordered this. Also, get our crew to eradicate the rest of the Order of Demonaeus."

"Easy enough."

Cade took Holly's hand and dragged her toward the garage, but not before Rök let out a wolf whistle at her all too visible backside.

In English, Rök said, "Looks like you're getting a swimbo for yourself."

Cade yanked off his jacket, draping it over her shoulders. He bared his fangs at Rök, who merely gave a deep laugh.

"Who is that?" Holly whispered, cheeks flaming.

"Rök, a smoke demon. He's a mercenary in my crew. A fugitive. Lives under a terminate-at-will order in two dimensions." Cade took the bags from Holly. "As you can see, he's all broken up about it."

Inside the garage there was only one choice of vehicle. Rydstrom was driving his "normal" car, a rare Mercedes McLaren. And Cade had just hobbled his old truck.

All that was left was Rydstrom's pride and joy—which Cade and Rök were strictly forbidden to drive.

Desperate times, Rydstrom . . .

8

Cadeon popped the trunk of the most incredible vehicle Holly had ever seen, then hastily stowed their gear inside.

"What kind of car is this?" she asked, threading her arms into his jacket. It swallowed her. Though the bottom would probably hit him at the waist, it almost reached her knees.

"It's called a Veyron. It's my brother's." He unlocked the doors. "Quick—get in."

As she took her seat, he sank into his own, having to grasp his leg and drag it inside. At her look, he said, "The curse of the tall man in the small sports car."

She raised her brows at the plush interior. The dash was a brushed metal. The key looked like a minuscule USB drive.

Holly's dad had been a sports car enthusiast. She'd learned to drive in his Porsche Carrera and Maserati, and on many a Saturday, he'd taken her to auctions and shows. But Holly had never seen a car like this.

Cadeon pushed a button that said *start* and the garage-door opener at the same time. "Buckle up."

The seat belt was a four-point harness, a racing belt. As she hurriedly buckled it above her lap, he shifted into gear and pulled out.

The driveway from the garage split in two directions.

He veered left, and the cement ended shortly, turning into a tree-covered lane. Slipping from that alley to another backstreet, he said, "I think we've lost them."

She glanced in the side-view mirror. Nothing but deserted streets. Then she turned to him with a frown. "You're not going to put on a seat belt?"

"Why would an immortal need one?"

"The law says you have to wear it."

"Human laws don't apply to my kind," he said.

"They should, especially since you're driving on human roads, operating a vehicle that was built by humans."

"That you know of. Are you really going to get your panties in a twist about this—oh, forgot you aren't wearing any."

She crossed her arms over her chest. "You're not going to distract me."

"You're not going to get me to wear a seat belt." At her look, he said, "Imagine the oldest, most stubborn, most cantankerous dog ever to live. He'd learn new tricks better than me."

Seeing the mulish set to his jaw, she decided to let it rest, for now. "Who was back at the house?"

"Vampires. They're hot on our trail, for some reason. They'll break into the pool house, find it full of smoke, and then lose their heads to Rök's sword."

"I see. What did he mean about a 'swimbo'? I probably wouldn't want to be called one, would I?"

"Some demons can get summoned, most often by the opposite sex. *Swimbo* is a play on She Who Must Be Obeyed."

"But why would he call me one?"

"It's kind of morphed into a sexual term for a female you wouldn't mind being summoned by."

"Oh."

"It's a compliment," he added.

"Of course. Since it's also a play on *bimbo*."

"Hey, I don't make the words, I just use them." When the traffic opened up, he was able to put the car through its paces, upshifting for speed. The ride was as smooth as silk

As the engine purred louder, he seemed to go heavy-lidded. "That sound never gets old."

She hadn't driven a fast car since her dad had died—her own vehicle was a hybrid—and she hadn't ever thought she'd missed it until now. "I've never seen this make."

"That's because there are only three hundred of them. It's the world's fastest and most expensive car."

"How fast does it go?" she asked.

"Over two hundred and fifty. Zero to sixty in under two and a half seconds."

She tried to imagine that. Full acceleration would be like riding a rocket.

"It runs a thousand and one horsepower," he added.

"Twice as much as a Porsche."

He looked startled. "How did *you* know that?"

"My dad was a car buff, and I used to go to auctions with him. Don't you think this will be conspicuous for our purposes?"

"We'll take my brother's other car when we meet him."

"What is he driving?"

"A McLaren," he answered. "It's a Merce—"

"I know what it is." She gave a laugh. "Not exactly the optimal choice for vehicle concealment."

Cadeon slanted her a surprised expression. "I was thinking the same thing."

The chit knew cars.

Demons loved cars. And Valkyrie. He was doomed.

She chose that moment to uncross and cross her smooth legs, drawing his eyes, reminding him that she wore no panties. . . .

"Cadeon, eyes up!" She tugged on his jacket, but it had ridden up to her midthigh. "Clearly, I can't stay dressed like this."

"I've told you we can't go back to your loft."

"Then let me get a friend to meet us," Holly said. "I need to call her anyway to get her to stand in for my classes."

"Is she a good friend?"

When Holly nodded, he said, "Those demons knew enough about your teaching schedule to nab you easily. Would it be beyond them to keep a man on your friend's house?"

"But my glasses! She can bring my spare pair. I can't read anything without them."

Her glasses. Those small black ones that sat so sexily on her nose. They had the subtlest tilt at the corners, almost like cats' eyes, just enough to call to mind the fifties. The *bombshells* of the fifties.

He missed that decade.

"We'll get you new glasses. And we'll buy you clothes and shoes on the road."

"And we need to get my medicine refilled."

"What happens if we don't?"

She balled her hands into fists. "That's *not* an option."

"Some of these factions might think to check your

pharmacy records. This is a life-or-death situation, Holly."

"Though I understand very little about tonight, that fact has fully sunk in. But I'm not overstating the importance of those pills."

"We'll see. That's the best I can promise."

"Where are we meeting your brother?" she asked, letting the subject drop. He knew she'd come back around to it eventually.

"North of the lake."

"So we have about thirty minutes. Cadeon, will you kindly explain why I am the most popular girl in town?"

"You're a Valkyrie now, so that makes you a member of the Lore—it's a collection of mythical beings, except we're not mythical. Just about anything you've ever imagined or read about exists in some fashion."

"Like vampires and Valkyrie."

He nodded. "And werewolves and sirens and ghouls."

"What are Valkyrie like?"

Strange, eccentric. Beautiful to a fault. Holly would fit right in. "They're strong as hell. Fast, too, with good senses." He couldn't stop himself from saying, "But they're very docile, and happy to do a male's bidding."

She frowned at that, but before she could ask, he continued, "Now, about every five hundred years, an Accession comes, and—"

"What's an Accession?"

"It's a force that affects Lorekind by pitting species against each other. Some think it began as a mechanism to kill off immortals, or we'd never die, continue spawning, and overrun the earth. So every five centuries, unique things happen. And you're one of them."

"What do you mean?"

"With each Accession, a Lorekind female called a Vessel reaches sexual maturity. Her firstborn will be the ultimate warrior for either good or evil, depending on the father's inclination."

"That's why those demons wanted to . . . to . . ."

"Breed with you? Yeah. And the leeches wanted to kill you because they didn't know if the demons had already completed their ritual."

Her brows drew together. "Wait. I'm called a *Vessel*? Could there be a more derogatory term? By its very definition, a vessel is of no importance compared to its contents. Vessels are disposable. Couldn't these Lorekind have gone with *baby maker* or *bun oven*?"

"I lobbied for *cargo hold*, but just lost out."

Again, she recrossed her legs. They were toned, taut—all that swimming had done her right. He wondered what she would do if he reached over and put his hand on her knee, sliding it up her thigh. There'd be no panties to get in his way. . . .

As if she knew his musings, she pulled the jacket down with a glare.

Hell, he might have to turn her over to Rydstrom completely. *No*. As soon as the thought arose, Cade swatted it down. Call him a glutton for punishment, but he was going to take every second with her that he could get.

"All kinds of factions, both good and evil, will be searching for you," he continued, "wanting you either bred or dead. Even some of the good guys will seek to kill you."

"Why?"

"Because in the last seven Accessions, only one good offspring has been born. The rest are evil."

"So the odds are that mine would be, too."

"Exactly. They'd act for the greater good, or to ensure their own dominance."

"What if I got my tubes tied or something?"

"They'll kill you to make sure." And it probably wouldn't take anyway. She was too far gone into the transition to Valkyrie. If she had surgery, her body would simply "heal" it.

She was quiet for long moments. "This sounds really dangerous, protecting me. Are you doing it just for the pay?"

I've been protecting you for months. Because you drive me crazy, and I want you more than is right. "Yeah, just for the pay. I have a history of taking on tough jobs."

"How much are you getting?"

"Something priceless to my family."

"More specific, please," she said in a voice she probably used with unruly jocks.

Second rule of being a mercenary: Lie through your teeth—but stick as close to the truth as possible to keep it convincing and less complicated. "My brother Rydstrom—the one we're meeting—is king of our kind, the rage demons. But his kingdom was usurped by a dark sorcerer called Omort the Deathless. Like the name indicates, he can't be killed in the usual ways."

"Usual ways?"

"Most immortals can be killed only by an otherworldly fire or by beheading. Omort is immune even to those means. As you can imagine, he's hard as hell to defeat. But now, if I do this job with you, I'll get a sword that was forged specifically to kill him."

"A dark sorcerer." She pinched her forehead. "It just keeps getting better. I wonder that he doesn't want 'the Vessel' for himself, since everyone else seems to."

That supposition was a little close for comfort. A wicked sorcerer *did* want her, just not the one she was aware of. So Cade told her the truth: "Omort won't seek you. He can't breed with a Vessel. Because he was born of one."

But his half brother Groot hadn't been.

"So if Rydstrom is a king, then you're a prince?"

"Of a lost crown."

"Is he the one who dragged you away that day on campus?"

"You remember that?" On the one occasion he'd had to speak to her, for the first time in his life, he'd been off his game. Unfortunately, Rydstrom had been there to see it. "That's him. He's the good brother of the Woede. I'm the bad one. You'll see it as soon as we're together."

"What's the Woede?"

"That's what they call the two of us because we rarely separate." No matter how much they might want to.

"What was wrong with you that day?" she asked. "Why couldn't you talk?"

"Couldn't talk? It wasn't like that."

"You were babbling incoherently."

Funny, Rydstrom had described it as *blathering*. "I *never* babble."

"Why were you on campus anyway? Were you already watching me about this?"

"No, it was a coincidence." He exhaled. *A fated one . . .*

At the mention of Cade's brother, she noted the instantaneous change in him.

Clearly, he had issues with this Rydstrom.

She remembered the brother from that day of the awards. He'd seemed more reasonable. Maybe he'd be more inclined to answer her questions with direct, comprehensive answers. Every time Cadeon explained something, she got the sense that he was just treading the surface of the subject.

And yet again, Cadeon's gaze strayed to her bare legs. She hated this vulnerable feeling, going with no underwear, no hose, no bra.

Everything she'd ever learned about concealing her emotions she used now. She reached for her pearls to calm herself, but they weren't there. Nothing was as it should be, and she wanted to hit something in frustration.

This night was all wrong. A nightmare for someone like her. She didn't need a male like Cadeon casting her lustful glances—not now and certainly not when she'd been naked earlier.

Most times she endeavored to forget she had a body at all, much less one that could be sexy. Or could *feel* sexy.

No man had ever seen her completely naked before tonight. Now thirteen demons had.

But only one had lived to tell about it.

Oh, God, this is too much, too much to take in.

"All right, poppet, you've got to stop that leg-crossing thing, stat."

"I'm uncomfortable!" She'd never gone so long without undergarments. "I don't have my clothes, my jewelry. My laptop. Not even my shoes!"

"And now you've got me uncomfortable, too."

She could have sworn he'd *adjusted* himself. "You . . . you just touched yourself."

"I'm a demon. I'm not exactly shy about things like this."

She was appalled. "But you shouldn't . . . you can't just . . ."

"What should I do? You're an attractive female in my car who's not wearing panties. So to make you more comfortable, I should cut off circulation in my c—"

"Don't say it! I get the picture." Her nails dug into her palms. Not nails—claws. And for some reason they were now curling, her mind locked on that memory of his hard, tanned torso leading down to those unbuttoned jeans.

"I'm going to react," he said. "Even if you're not my usual type."

"Usual type? Oh, let me guess. *Swimbos* with more breasts than brains?"

He hiked his broad shoulders. "My kind prefer tarts with a little more meat on their bones so they can take a demon's lusts."

"Tarts?" Her jaw slackened. "My God, you're the most misogynistic man I've ever met. I bet you also like your *tarts* barefoot and pregnant."

"Nah, I like them barefoot, on birth control, and always available in my bed."

She sputtered. And then the truth of her situation hit her.

My fate is in the hands of a chauvinist demon, who seems to be trying *to exacerbate my condition.*

She'd never needed the medication more than now—when getting it seemed impossible.

Her mind was wracked with ideas and images that shouldn't be in there. She was unable to stop seeing that golden hair leading down from his navel. The more she endeavored not to think about it, the more the picture flashed in her head.

What would it be like to nuzzle that trail? To clutch his hips as she lowered her face to it . . . ?

Her heart thundered in fear of what she might do if she lost control.

The last time had been eight years ago. She'd terrified a young man, even . . . *hurting* him.

And he hadn't been the first.

9

"Rydstrom isn't here. He's *always* where he says he'll be."

They'd pulled over to the side of the gas station parking lot twenty minutes ago. Cade called Rydstrom's cell phone again, but got an out-of-area message.

"Maybe he got caught in traffic," Holly offered.

"No way." Cade rubbed a palm over one of his horns, then got out to pace in front of the headlights. Ten more minutes passed. *Something's definitely wrong.*

His brother had told him just tonight that Omort would be dispatching everything he had to stop them. Had Rydstrom somehow fallen victim to the bastard's powers?

Cade couldn't continue this job without Rydstrom—he didn't know where the first checkpoint was and hadn't been in contact with Groot himself. *I need Rydstrom for the directions.*

I need him to keep me in line with the asset.

Half an hour had dragged by when a red Bentley pulled up behind them, hopping the curb in an alignment-wrecking jounce.

"Well, if it isn't Nucking Futs Nïx," he muttered to himself as she parked the wheezing car. Never had Cade seen such an abused Bentley.

There were dings in the body, mud all over the tires, smoke tendrils rising from the hood, and at least two bullet holes. A Garfield doll was stuck to the rear window.

Surely Rydstrom had sent her to tell Cade about a change of plans. But this was a problem. Cade couldn't let Nïx near Holly without the chance of getting caught in his lie about reversing her transition.

He hastened to the car—and found the soothsayer shutting down the engine and the blaring music. "Where the fuck is my brother?" Cade demanded as soon as she opened the door. Sand poured from the floorboard.

Nïx gracefully stood, immediately strapping a sword over her back. She wore a T-shirt that read: *Keep Me Separated*. "Rydstrom's a bit tied up at the moment."

"What the hell does that mean?" he asked, studying Nïx's exotic eyes for lucidity. He'd seen them go blank with confusion many times and couldn't afford that now. "Nïx, did he send you to meet me?"

"No. I thought I'd drop by to see my niece." She peered past him in Holly's direction, and he stepped in front of her.

"Nothing is more important than this to Rydstrom. If you know where he is, then you must tell me."

Her tone casual, Nïx said, "Sabine, the Queen of Illusions, tricked him, capturing him."

Dread settled like a brick in Cade's stomach. "She's Omort and Groot's half sister." And rumored to be a hundred times more evil. "What does she want with Rydstrom?"

"I'm guessing she wants to be impregnated by him," she said blithely, while Cade's jaw slackened. "The last of the holdout rebels in your kingdom would be forced to recognize Rydstrom's heir—under any circumstances."

"But Rydstrom can't get her pregnant. Not unless she's his female."

"I'm sure with Sabine's powers, she could work something out."

"Is she in league with Omort? Is Rydstrom being held in Tornin?" *No one escapes the dungeons of Tornin.*

"I don't know if Sabine works with Omort or if she has her own agenda. And I can't see exactly where Rydstrom is imprisoned. All I know is that it's a shadowy cell."

"I need that sword even more now." He ran his fingers through his hair. "I don't know how to contact Groot or even where the first checkpoint is."

"I know where it is, but I don't see any further than that."

"What? That's all I need! Tell me."

"You just assume I'm going to allow you to ransom my niece to an evil sorcerer?"

"You're the one who set up this deal!" he snapped.

"But I hadn't seen that the Vessel would be one of our kind."

"You know what's at stake."

"What's at stake *for you,*" she said. "This is my kin."

"Then why are we even discussing this?"

She blinked at him. "Because I'm *mischievous*?"

Nïx started toward Holly, and short of violence, there wasn't a damn thing he could do to stop her. Cade was a lowlife mercenary, but he drew the line at hurting females.

Immediately, he thought of that vampire's Bride he'd killed. Or rather, Cade didn't hurt them purposely. *Block it out. . . .*

At the car, Nïx said, "Come, dearling."

Holly opened the door, pulling Cade's jacket tighter as she got out. She met Nïx eye to eye, almost exactly the same height as the Valkyrie soothsayer.

"Welcome to the family." Nïx kissed both of Holly's cheeks with loud *mwah* sounds, seeming not to notice Holly's startled expression. "I'm your aunt Nïx, the Ever-Knowing. I'm also the Proto-Valkyrie and Soothsayer without Equal."

"You're a Valkyrie?" Holly asked, her gaze on one of Nïx's uncovered ears.

"Only the oldest and greatest," Nïx answered.

Cade said, "She's a powerful prognosticator."

Nïx's eyes grew silvery with emotion. "And you are the spitting image of your mother. Strawberry blond hair and violet eyes."

"You were related to my mother?"

"Greta was my half sister."

"*Greta*," Holly said slowly, as if stunned to finally know her mother's name.

"She was a famous warrior. She died two decades ago, a glorious death in battle."

"Warrior? Battle? I thought Valkyrie were docile."

Nïx laughed. "Did the demon tell you that?" She made a tsking sound. "Cadeon Woede! For shame."

"Just having a bit of fun with that."

"What was Greta like?" Holly asked.

"She was part Fury—"

Cade made a strangled sound but covered it with a cough. "No way." The most fierce race of females in existence. Valkyrie were violent. Furies were . . . incomprehensible.

Hell, if Cade turned her over to Groot, Holly might off the sorcerer herself.

"Look at Holly's violet eyes, with the dark ring around the iris. A Fury's eyes."

"Why did she give me away?" Holly asked. "I know there must have been a good reason."

And there was Holly's signature confidence. She expressed no bitterness or self-doubt over the fact that she'd been given over.

"I've put together a welcome package with a letter that will explain more. But for now, you need to leave. It's dangerous for you here."

"Where am I going?" Holly demanded.

Nïx nodded in answer.

"Um, that wasn't a yes-or-no question."

"Indeed."

"I thought we were supposed to meet Cadeon's brother here."

"You were," Nïx said. "But he's not here."

Exhaling impatiently, Holly said, "Just tell me, how did I become like *this*."

"You make it sound like it's a tragedy."

"I . . . no, I didn't mean to, but I just want to go back to my old life. I'm a single code away from getting my doctorate, and I have classes to teach—"

"Yes, well, if I had students like your delicious football players, I'd be eager to return, too. Re-rowr."

Cade prompted Nïx, "Again, how'd she get like this?"

Nïx looked confused as if she didn't understand the question, then finally answered, "The seed was always there but was given water and sun with the lightning bolt." She turned to Holly. "And now you'll grow into the Valkyrie you were always meant to be."

"Cade told me that it's reversible?" she said in a tone tinged with disbelief.

"Did he, then?"

He pinched the bridge of his nose, prepared to be busted.

"He's right," Nïx said, shocking him, going along with his lie. "Only one man can reverse this. His name is Groot the Metallurgist. He's a powerful sorcerer. If you get to him before you become fully immortal, he can change you back," she said, though Cade knew that *she* knew that wasn't true.

Without a word, Nïx sauntered back to her car, leaving them no choice but to follow. "Now, I took the liberty of visiting your vampire-infested building and packing a bag for you. I know you'll want to change."

Nïx popped the trunk, displaying a large suitcase atop another pile of sand. She lifted the weighty-looking bag with a finger, setting it on the ground. "Oh, and here are your spare glasses." She pulled a pair from her jacket pocket, handing them to Holly. "Style name *Smitten Kitten*—love it!"

Enunciating every syllable, Cade repeated, "Smitten Kitten?"

Sliding him a discomfited glance, Holly donned them.

Nïx continued, "Of course the glasses will become redundant, since your eyesight should continue to improve each day. And here are your pearls." She handed over a strand that looked exactly like the ones Holly usually wore. Naturally, she would have backups. "These items are your talismans."

"Talismans?"

"Do you feel stronger when you wear them?"

Holly bit her lip and nodded.

"Then, yes, talismans. Now, those pearls have been bespelled. When you wear them, you'll be protected from scrying eyes."

Holly turned to Cade, as if for translation.

"It means, don't take them off." He collected the necklace from Holly and turned her around by the shoulders. "Pull up your hair."

When she piled up all those red-gold curls, he just prevented himself from kissing her slender nape. . . .

He shook himself and finished.

"You need to get dry," Nïx told her. "You're still a vulnerable little mortal. Oops, I forgot—you want to stay that way." She tittered behind her fingertips as if that inclination was so misguided it was *cute*.

Seeming dazed, Holly took the bag and turned toward the station bathroom.

"What do you think you're doing?" Cade snapped.

He tore into the bag and snatched the first pair of shoes he could find, shoving them on her feet. Then he took the bag and escorted her to the women's bathroom.

She groaned when he followed her inside and checked the stalls. Before he left, he pinched her chin. "Little bit, if anybody fucks with you in here, you give 'em a taste of what you gave the demons. Clear?"

Anytime someone asked Holly what she'd done the night before, she answered: "Studied, went to the library, swam."

Occasionally she varied the first two by doing them with Tim.

Tonight's activities? "Slew demons in horrific bloodbath, got shot at by vampires with machine guns, had a mad car chase through a swamp. Found out who—and what—my birth mother was. Learned about a secret world existing side by side with our own. . . ."

Too much to take in. She didn't respond well to change in even the most ideal circumstances. Now, she was just . . . numb, deadened to the shocks that kept coming.

At least, she hoped that she was numb. Otherwise that would mean she didn't particularly feel bad about her mass murders this evening.

Yes, those men were monsters, and, yes, Holly believed they'd gotten what they deserved, but shouldn't she feel a twinge of *something* that *she'd* done it? Revulsion? Fear?

She stood in front of the mirror and stared at her eyes. The rings that had always circled her irises were much more noticeable. *Because—don't you know—I'm part Fury.*

Whatever that was.

Nïx's eyes were also uncanny, but their golden color was breathtaking, while Holly's violet was merely odd.

Holly drew back her hair, unable to ignore her sharply pointed ears any longer. Again, ears like this looked great on Nïx—exotic and interesting—while seeming foreign and weird on Holly.

One of the most classic OCD symptoms was an unfounded fear of losing oneself. But Holly's fear wasn't unfounded. She truly *was* losing herself, one feature at a time. *If only I had my—*

Her eyes widened. If Nïx had picked up things for her, surely she would have noticed all the pill bottles Holly had left lined up on the counter.

Diving into her suitcase, she yanked the zipper open. Inside, she found the contents of the shoulder bag she'd dropped when she'd been abducted. Her wireless laptop and case, her cell phone, even her antibacterial wipes were all there.

But no pills. . . .

Nïx had somehow found that bag, then deliberately removed the two bottles. *Why, Nïx?* Holly leaned against the wall, tempted to run away, to escape all of this.

But Cadeon and Nïx were the only ones she knew who could help her get back to normal. Holly had no choice but to go along with their plans for her.

Plans that involved leaving town.

She hadn't crossed the borders of Orleans Parish in fifteen years. In fact, she rarely went anywhere except from her loft to the campus ten minutes away.

The campus really was her entire world—a regimented and orchestrated microcosm where things made sense. Days were divided into class hours, weeks into school days, and years into semesters.

Yet now she felt as if she'd been temporarily exiled.

Shaking away that thought, she collected her phone and dialed her friend Mei. When there was no answer, she left a message.

"Hi, Mei, this is Holly. I was wondering if you can take over my classes for a spell? Not a literal spell. Ha-ha. Um, I've had a family emergency crop up and might not be back for"—*how long will I be gone?*—"a week?"

Holly felt distanced from herself as she spoke, stunned by how normal she sounded when she was on the verge of breaking down. "Call my cell if anything comes up. I owe you big-time."

After she hung up, she exhaled unsteadily. *Need to get dressed, get moving.*

Crouching beside her bag, Holly checked the side compartment for her underwear, frowning at what she found. Inside were thigh-highs, thongs, and demi-cup bras, each still packaged or with the tags attached. They were all in her size, and they were . . . provocative.

Why on earth would Nïx swap out Holly's perfectly good high-waisted briefs and minimizer bras for these?

Left with little other choice, Holly smoothed on silky thigh-highs, and for the first time in her life, she donned a thong.

Once she was fully dressed with her pearls and glasses in place, she set about righting her hair. With angry strokes, she brushed the curls back, wrestling them into submission as usual, only now she made sure her weird ears were covered.

With the last hairpin in place, she studied her reflection. How could she look much the same as usual when she was such a wreck inside? Her eyes began to water, and she clutched the countertop for balance.

After all the madness of the night, she knew only two things for certain. *I have to get this condition reversed. And Cadeon Woede is dangerous for me to be near.*

The countertop cracked under her grip.

10

"Cade, you've got it bad," Nïx said as she hopped atop the Veyron's hood.

"What's new there?"

"You know Holly doesn't trust you?"

"She shouldn't! And apparently, not you either. So, don't leave me hanging. Why did you lie to her?"

"I wanted to see where you were going with this."

"I'm going ahead with the plan." He popped the trunk and opened his bag. Rooting for the flask, he snagged it, then drank deeply of demon brew. Unfortunately it had a delayed effect, but he would sow the seeds of buzz for the future.

"You believe you could turn Holly over to a wicked sorcerer, just when she can be claimed by you? You've waited nine centuries for her."

"I have to do this. I don't want to. Gods, I don't want to. But now that bitch Sabine has my brother, and I already owe him so much. This is the only way I can atone for what I've done. The kingdom and its people are now depending on me, and me alone."

The truth of that statement hit him like a stray punch. *Bugger me*. The fate of all Rothkalinians rested on the shoulders of the black sheep, the ne'er-do-well.

Speaking of which . . . "You told Rydstrom that the mortal Néomi died. Are you certain?"

"Abso-smurf-ly."

Cade hadn't realized he'd held out this much hope that she'd survived. *Block it out. . . .*

Nïx studied him. "I'm considering joining in with your deception of Holly. Mainly because I don't think you will be able to turn her over. And, no, I don't see that outcome. It's a hunch. And secondly, because I believe you have to be cruel to be kind. Holly needs to be educated about the world—bluntly and swiftly—and no one would be better at that job than you."

"What do you mean, educated? She's as educated as she can be."

"I want Holly to experience *life*. To take away the blinders she has so assiduously relied on. I think you're just the type of person to show her what she doesn't know and doesn't want to know. My niece is innocent in so many ways, and there comes a time in a woman's life when innocence is merely a euphemism for ignorance."

"How innocent could she be in this day and age?"

"She's avoided anything that could fire her Valkyrie tendencies—anything arousing or enraging. She has content controls on her computer, and no cable on her TV. She's lived a PG life. She's sublimated these tendencies so persistently that she's made herself ill at times."

"That's what the counting's about?"

Nïx nodded. "And anything she couldn't sublimate, she would medicate."

"She wants her pills now."

"Well, as her auntie, I say she can't have them. Now, other Valkyrie will have felt her energy emerging. They'll soon be searching for her themselves."

"Then you need to stall them."

After long moments, Nïx said, "I'll do it. If you vow not to fly any leg of the journey."

"You just want that because it'll give me more time to get attached to her, increase the odds that I'll just say fuck all and keep her."

"Yes."

"Damn it, the trip will take longer, possibly weeks. Groot's compound could be as far away as Alaska." Cade swigged from his flask. "And Rydstrom said the deadline was the full moon. What if we don't make it by then?"

"That's my condition."

"She'll be in more danger. Think of it—as soon as she's with Groot, she'll be hidden."

"Take it or leave it. But you won't get very far without the first checkpoint."

"Fine," he bit out. "I agree to your condition." More time with Holly. More time to get attached to Holly.

She emerged from the bathroom at that moment. With her hair pulled back in that perfect bun, she wore her "talismans," a nondescript sweater, and one of those skirts that hugged her plump ass—and made males like him wish they could be the one to unlock all the passion seething inside that outwardly prim female.

Her shoulders were back, her chin raised. Her signature confidence had returned in full force. That sexy *smart woman* confidence. Cade wanted to kiss her till her knees went weak.

"Where're we headed?" he absently asked Nïx. At that moment, more time to get attached to Holly seemed just the thing.

Nïx answered, "Mississippi Mile marker 775. You're

going north of Memphis to meet a demoness named Imatra. There are more detailed instructions in the welcome bag I put together for Holly."

"Uh-huh." He stumbled forward to get Holly's suitcase, vowing to stay silent until he regained his equilibrium around her—or until the contents of his flask finally took effect.

"I want to speak to my aunt alone."

Holly had expected Cadeon to argue. Instead, he'd donned a weather-beaten leather outback-type hat, muttered something about getting food for the road and updating Rök, then headed inside.

"Look at him in that hat," Nïx said. "Sex appeal that potent ought to be illegal." She watched him the whole way in, making a low growling sound and adjusting the sword strapped over her back in fitful motions.

Yes, Cadeon might be good-looking, but the fact remained that he was a demon—*with horns*.

"They don't make 'em like they used to." Nïx sighed, facing her.

Holly was struck anew by how preternaturally lovely—and peculiar—her new aunt was. "I wanted to thank you for bringing my things. But why was there new underwear and stockings?"

"Because I knew you would have serviceable underclothes." She gave a mock shudder. "Valkyrie like sexy, pretty things, and serviceable is rarely either. So I collected a few grand worth of lingerie for you."

Holly had needed that very unsexy underwear to make her feel, well, very unsexy. "Did you happen to pick up any of the pill bottles on the counter?"

"Ah, those bottles arranged in that perfectly straight line, divided into threes. Everything in your house was perfectly linear. Or in threes. Or at right angles," Nïx said, her golden eyes seeming to see through to Holly's very soul one minute, but going vacant in the next. "I delighted in disrupting each and every pattern."

Holly's stomach churned. The image of her sacrosanct home, perfect as she'd left it, had been helping her get through this night. She'd thought that once she got back there, she could slip right into her old life. "Disrupting?"

Just when Holly became certain she would throw up, lightning lit the sky behind her.

Nïx smiled at the bolt, seeming pleased with it. "You don't need the pills anymore. You used them to stifle your Valkyrie traits because you didn't understand them. But now you no longer need to."

"No, I want to reverse this. I need to. I hate change—I can't handle it," Holly said, clasping her forehead. "How long will it take to get to this sorcerer?"

"Anywhere from a week to a month."

"How long do I have until there's no chance for reversal?"

"You have roughly the same time frame before you're a bona fide Valkyrie."

"If the pills stifled my Valkyrie traits before, then would they slow this transition down? Could they buy me more time to get to this sorcerer?"

"It's possible." Nïx shrugged, flipping back her spill of long black hair, the silkiest Holly had ever seen. "Though I can't say for certain. I don't see anything predetermination-wise, and human pharmacology is beneath my notice."

"Nïx, please, I might not look like it, but I'm walking the razor's edge right now."

She nodded gravely. "I know. In the restroom, you had the urge to scream to the ceiling and pull your hair out. And really, dearling, they have someone to clean that area."

How did she see—

"Ever-knowing, that's how."

"Then tell me, is all this Vessel stuff true?" Holly asked.

"Yes, unfortunately it is. Best choose your babydaddy carefully."

"Why me?"

Nïx said, "A stroke of bad luck."

Holly's face screwed up into an expression of distaste. Bad luck was merely a random occurrence that didn't go in one's favor. "But if I get the Valkyrie change reversed, will I still be the Vessel?"

"I don't see how you could be. The Vessel must be of the Lore."

"So if I can get back to normal, people will stop trying to kill me?" Holly could nullify this chance event. She could take action to combat the random.

"Theoretically, it would follow."

So do the reasoning trail: Get Valkyrie change reversed, lose Vessel status. Stop having immortal assassins trying to kill me or demons attacking me. Break free from the finite solution set of dead or bred. Go back to being one code away from PhD and previous life. Eventually, have normal kid. No ultimate evil.

Nïx said, "But I think when the choice comes, you'll have grown to like your new self. At last you'll *have* a self."

"What does that mean?"

She pulled a curl free from Holly's tight chignon, irritating her. "Who are you, niece? You have no idea. You will soon, though." Nïx gave her a grin, as if Holly was on the outside of an inside joke. "Well, I must be off. Proto-Valkyrie and Soothsayer without Equal is a grueling, thankless job, but Nïxie must do it."

"Wait!" Holly followed her to her abused Bentley. "I have so many more questions. Did my mother die young? And who was my father? How will I get in touch with you? Are there more of our kind walking around? How can I recognize them?"

"All your questions will be answered in time."

This being already *had* all the answers. "Please, take me with you! You said I was family." And Holly felt that a few more hours with Cadeon might send her over the edge.

"If you want to stay a Valkyrie, then hop in. We have mayhem on tap for tonight," Nïx said, motioning to her backseat.

Holly glanced inside, then stared in horror. The space was piled with Pat O'Brien's cups, uninflated balloons, peanut packing filler, and boxes that read: *dangereux!* C-4 *plastique*.

She took an involuntary step back.

Nïx blithely continued, "But if you're set on the reversal, I can't take you to Groot's. His fortress is hidden, and you'll have to go through a series of checkpoints to reach him. It'll take at least a week, a week I don't have since I'm fighting an apocalypse. Just think, Holly"—she draped one arm around Holly's shoulders, and waved the other hand in an arc in front of them—"an *apocalypse*, the ultimate in disorder."

Holly shuddered.

"Would you want to take me from preventing that?" Nïx asked, releasing her.

"Well, of course not, but—"

"If you are adamant about having your gift overturned, then I'll arrange it so that Cade has to get you safely to the sorcerer to earn his sword. Is that what you want?"

"I want to go, but not alone with him! I don't suppose you could hire someone less . . ."

"Incredibly hot? With less lickable horns and a less sexy *Sith Ifrican* accent?" She shook her head, opening her car door. "No, Cade can keep you safe. He's strong, and he's ruthless."

Holly's lips parted wordlessly. *Lickable horns?*

"Oh, I almost forgot." Nïx fetched a weighty satchel from the passenger seat. "Here's your welcome kit. Must go now. Ciao!"

As Nïx started the car, Holly said, "One last question."

"Very well, dearling."

"Can I trust Cadeon?"

Nïx gave her a sunny smile with blank golden eyes. "As far as you can throw him."

11

I guess we're keeping the conspicuous car?" Holly asked when Cade pulled onto the highway, going north.

"For now. We've got to get out of town fast. Coincidentally, this car hauls ass."

"Where are we headed first?"

"Memphis. Nïx said she put the directions in your bag."

Holly reached into the backseat, grabbing the heavy satchel her aunt had given her. Inside, she found her passport, a handwritten letter, a map with an X right above Memphis, and two weighty tomes. One was called *The Living Book of Lore*, the other *The Book of Warriors*.

As she pulled out the letter, Holly asked, "Why did Nïx seem vacant at times?"

Cade sipped his Red Bull, never glancing her way. "She's so busy seeing the future, she spaces out in the present. You get used to it. Plus she's over three thousand years old."

That was mind-boggling. Nïx had looked the same age as Holly. "How old are you?"

"Nearly a millennium." Cade looked no more than thirty-four or thirty-five.

"You weren't kidding about being medieval. Why isn't your accent?"

"Lorekind adapt to evolving languages and dialects. It's unconscious."

When Holly cracked open the letter's black wax seal, Cade leaned over to scan the contents.

She turned down the corner of the letter until he shrugged and faced forward again. Then she read the flourishing script, or tried to—her glasses actually seemed to make it harder . . .

Dearest Niece,

Welcome to the family at last!

This letter will explain more that I didn't have time to. Inside your welcome package you'll find two books. One is the story of our origin and a record of the Valkyrie's noblest warriors. Your mother's history is among them.

Your father was a human civil engineer, the great love of Greta's life. He was killed in a revenge hit for one of her vampire raids before Greta even knew about you.

Revenge hit? Vampire raid? "Is Lorekind more violent than humankind?" she asked Cadeon.

Without turning to her, he said, "A lot more. We've got constant wars going on."

"Constant wars," she repeated. Why would someone like Holly ever want to descend into this new, even *more* tumultuous world . . . ?

Greta was heartbroken to give you up, but it's the Valkyrie way to relinquish human offspring. And we all thought you were mortal. She did it with love in her heart for you. Never doubt that.

Holly didn't. She now knew that her placement with the loving Ashwins hadn't been an accident.

The second book will explain some of the aspects of this new world you've found yourself thrust into.

Read both tomes. There will be a quiz.

Now, I know that you expressed some doubts about staying a Valkyrie. . . .

How could she know that? Unless . . . "She really is a soothsayer," Holly murmured.

Seeming to relax a bit, Cade said, "Oh, yeah."

But I ask that you at least give Valkyrism a sporting try. All the cool kids are doing it. And all you have to do is embrace everything you've ever feared and shunned for the last twenty years. Simple enough!

Lick Cade's horns for me, and, yes, you can treat him like a hireling if you wish, because that is certainly what he is—and what he's used to.

Lick his horns? Holly tried to act as if they weren't there at all, much less *licking* them!

Two tips: If you need to be certain that your erstwhile guardian is telling you the truth about anything, make him "vow it to the Lore." And if you don't want to get pregnant, don't eat. Valkyrie are infertile if they don't consume the fruits of the earth.

Warmly,

Nïx, Proto-Valkyrie, Soothsayer without Equal, Demigoddess, your loving auntie

Folding the letter, Holly sat stunned. *Too much to think about.* So much information, and she was only on the intro letter. Simply learning her father's occupation was momentous for her.

With a sigh, she pulled out *The Book of Warriors* and flipped to the "Origin of the Valkyrie" section—and found herself growing enthralled with the tale.

The Lore said that millennia ago, the gods Wóden and Freya were awakened from a decade of sleep by a maiden warrior's scream as she died in battle. Freya had marveled at the maiden's valor and wanted to preserve it, so she and Wóden struck the human with their lightning.

The maiden woke in their great hall, healed but unaltered—still mortal—and pregnant with an immortal Valkyrie daughter.

In the ages that passed, their lightning would strike dying women warriors from all species of the Lore—from Furies to shapeshifters to Lykae.

Freya and Wóden gave the daughters Freya's fey looks and his cunning, then combined these traits with the mother's courage and individual ancestry. The daughters were all half sisters, each one unique; but according to the Lore, one could always recognize a Valkyrie if her eyes fired silver with strong emotion.

Holly glanced up. "Did my eyes turn silver tonight?"

Cadeon nodded, finally giving her a glance. "It's how I knew you'd turned Valkyrie, or had begun to." He rubbed his palms on his jeans, briefly steering with his knees. "All Lorekind have eyes that turn a specific color." Cadeon's had been black.

Running her pearls along her lips, she pondered this new information. If Holly believed this legend, then that would mean that she was the granddaughter of Norse gods.

It was one thing for an adopted person to find out he

or she came from a family of wealth or fame. But this was ridiculous.

And yet, this information explained so much about herself that she'd never understood, things that a pompous psychiatrist had been all too ready to medicate away.

Her obsession with shining jewels? All Valkyrie had it, because they'd inherited their acquisitiveness from Freya.

Holly's captivation with lightning and her "uncontrollable urges" to run out into thunder storms? Valkyrie derived nourishment from electricity, taking energy from the earth. Lightning was how the species was first created—and how Holly was first turned.

She wondered if her "grandparents" had struck her with that comforting bolt, or if the lightning had been drawn to her during her emotional turmoil.

And Holly's freakish strength that she'd fought so hard to disguise? Valkyrie were preternaturally strong, fierce, and warlike.

As well as *amorous* . . .

She remembered the first time she'd been in bed with a male, a schoolmate named Bobby Thibodeaux. They'd been sixteen, and a few of Bobby's unpracticed kisses had made her crazed. She'd leapt upon him, overpowering him.

Holly had been so caught up, she hadn't realized how distressed he'd become. She'd eventually registered that he'd stopped kissing her back—and that her fingernails had been digging into his arms, holding him as he'd desperately tried to get out from under her.

As he'd gaped up at her in fear, she'd blinked down at him. As though someone else had inhabited her body, she'd throatily murmured, "I guess we should part ways here?" When she released him, he'd fled.

Once Bobby's tales had made the rounds at school, no boy would ask her out, so she'd buried herself even more in her studies.

In fact, she hadn't attempted to be intimate with another male until her first year in college. The only thing different about that encounter was that she'd grown more aggressive and even stronger.

Shaking away that memory, Holly turned to Greta's page in *The Book of Warriors*. Greta the Bold had been a master strategist and had led troops of Valkyrie, witches, and Furies in the great Battle of the Plains of Doom.

If the dates of that battle were correct, then Greta had gone to war when she'd been pregnant with Holly. Six years later, Greta had lost her life on the front line in the infamous Eighteen-Night Siege.

Holly was struck by the fact that if a new world existed, then she would have an entirely new history to learn.

Suddenly feeling exhausted, she dragged the weighty *Living Book of Lore* onto her lap without enthusiasm. Scanning the pages, she found encyclopedic entries on each of the "known species." After a brief intro, a more detailed history would follow. Flipping through, she found everything from wraiths and sirens, to Wendigos and demonarchies. . . .

"Do you want something to eat or drink?" Cadeon asked.

She wasn't hungry whatsoever. "Do you have anything to drink other than Red Bull?"

He pulled a bottle of water from the space behind her seat, handing it to her. *My favorite brand.*

"Thanks." She carefully twisted the cap, determined not to touch—

Crap! She'd touched the bottle rim. With a sigh, she put the cap back on and placed the bottle at her feet.

"Something wrong with the water?"

She debated not answering, but figured he'd encounter all her quirks over the next couple of weeks anyway—the eating difficulties, the germophobia, the endless arranging.

"I touched the rim." She put her chin up. "There was transference. I can't drink it now."

Instead of laughing at her, he reached behind her seat to grab another bottle. He opened it without contaminating the rim, then handed it to her. "These shorter caps must be a pain in the ass."

Her lips parted. She'd complained to Mei about the newfangled caps just the other week.

"So, you feeling overwhelmed yet?" he asked.

"A tad." She took a drink. She continued to feel as if she were reading fiction—as if all of this were far too fantastic to be true.

Even when a thousand-year-old demon sat a foot from her.

"Read the book to me, and I'll add details or explain things."

"How can I trust you? You said Valkyrie are docile. In *The Book of Warriors*, I read about Kaderin the Coldhearted, an assassin who strings up fangs collected from the heads of vampires she's decapitated. And then there is Emmaline the Unlikely, who slew her own father. Cut him up into three pieces." Three. *I like Emmaline already*. "Clearly, they are the picture of docility."

"Like I said, I was just having a bit of fun. It'd be like saying sirens don't like to sing."

She tilted her head at him. "So if I had questions, you'd answer them truthfully?"

"Yeah, if you answer questions about yourself."

She didn't see the harm. "Very well. I'll start. How many demonarchies are there? Where are they?"

"There are hundreds. Almost every breed of demon—from the smoke demons like Rök to the pathos demons—has a kingdom of some kind, usually in a separate plane."

"Separate plane? There are such things?"

He nodded. "There are more dimensions than can be mapped."

"What's your kingdom called?"

"Rothkalina." When he said it, his accent became more pronounced, as if even the mention of his home brought on keen feeling.

"How do you get there?" she asked.

"The most accessible portal is in southern Africa."

And that explained the accent. "So does it look like an alternate universe? Does it have purple skies and a green sun?"

"Nah. Rothkalina looks a lot like the west coast of North America."

"Oh," she said, feeling a bit silly. Then she frowned. "But if Omort is a sorcerer, why would he want to take over a demon kingdom?"

12

Clever chit, Cade thought. Few ever asked him that question, though it seemed one of the most material in his mind.

"The land is rich," he answered. "And the kingdom is strategically located."

But in truth, Omort had no use for the kingdom, and only kept it because he could. *The one who controls Tornin controls the kingdom.*

Omort desired what was within the castle.

Before written history, Tornin had been constructed around the legendary Well of Souls—to protect that mystickal font of power from sorcerers like Omort. And the rage demons had been dispatched to Tornin to safeguard the stronghold.

Yet they'd never been told exactly what the Well of Souls . . . *did.*

"Why are you called *rage* demons?"

"We get . . . enraged when we turn demonic. Mindless fury and all that."

"Turn demonic? Like when you fought tonight."

"Yeah, well, that was just a hint." In his fully demonic form, his skin would darken, reddening, while his body grew taller and larger. His fangs would elongate, and his horns would sharpen, reaching their full size. In that state, he could emit a toxin from the ends that could temporarily paralyze even an immortal.

She swallowed. "And how often do you get enraged?"

"It's extremely rare to turn fully. It happens only when a demon's life or the life of one of his family is in jeopardy." Or when he claimed his female for the first time.

"Why is Lorekind hidden from humans?"

"Historically, anytime some faction comes out of the closet, they get slaughtered."

"Like who?"

"For millennia, the witches kept outing themselves—until that last rash of burnings. And all those people in the past who were killed because they were supposedly possessed by demons? They *were* demons."

"But how do all these beings keep secret from humans?"

"It's easier than you think. We mainly stick to crazy cities, party towns. Most humans assume that anything *off* is a costume or, these days, part of an MTV prank." He grew more serious. "But every myth is an example of when some Lore creature boned up."

"What would you do if you got pulled over right now? What if you threw on your hat and a cop wanted you to take it off?"

"A lot of demons would run, collect a couple of bullets, then get out of sight to trace."

"Trace? I read about that. It means to teleport?"

He nodded. "But not all demon breeds can do it, and of those that have the potential, they have to work at it to master it."

"I assume you can't since you didn't trace us instead of going through the swamp."

"I used to be able to. For centuries I enjoyed that power. But Omort bound my ability to trace. My brother's as well."

"Will you ever get it back?"

He met her eyes. "As soon as that sword severs his head from his neck, we'll be free."

Cadeon's expression grew sinister, as if he was imagining beheading Omort right at that moment. Then his gaze slid to her, and he seemed to shake himself. "So questions about you now . . ."

"What do you want to know?"

"How did you find out you were adopted?"

"My adoption was never a secret. My mom used to tell me the story of the day someone left me on their doorstep. She always called me her foundling." Holly smiled softly. "They'd tried for years to get pregnant. When they couldn't and sought an adoption, the parish said my father was too old. And he outlived her."

Though not by much. He'd been so utterly in love with his wife of forty-five years that when they'd lost her to cancer, he'd wanted only to follow her wherever she'd gone. Her parents had had an extraordinary kind of love, the kind that you read about but rarely see.

Had her biological parents experienced it, too?

"I bet you never imagined your real mum as a warrior Valkyrie," he said, taking a deep swallow of Red Bull.

"No, we'd always supposed she was an unwed teenager." An unfamiliar scent hit her, and she sniffed the air. "Are you . . . tippling? Did you pour alcohol in your drink?"

"Maybe."

"You're drinking and driving!"

"If I were blotto, my reflexes would still be a thousand times better than a human's."

"You curse like a sailor and denigrate women, and now I find out that you drive under the influence." She peered over at the speedometer. "And you do it too fast."

"True, true, true. And you don't live a little, don't get the lead out, and never have fun."

"I do have fun!"

"You wouldn't know fun if it bit you on the ass."

Her chin jutted up. "You think I'm a goody two-shoes, a prude."

"I was going to say *preachy tight-ass*. But prude might fit. Especially after what Nïx told me about you tonight."

"What did she say?" Holly demanded.

"She said that you're innocent, and not just in body. I'd figured you were definitely a virgin, but—"

"How?" she interrupted. She wasn't secretive about her virginity, but she hadn't thought it'd be patently obvious to others.

"You've got it written all over you. It's like a flickering beacon for males like me."

"Please. Tell me. What do I have inscribed and flickering over me?"

"*Starving—for—it.*"

She glared at the roof of the car, grasping for patience. Because heaven help her, he might be right.

"So, I got that you were innocent body-wise, but the innocent-in-mind bit threw me. How is that even possible?"

"Why couldn't it be?" she asked.

"The media and such today. Sex is pervasive."

It was. But Holly had diligently trained herself to *Turn Away*. Somehow, she unfailingly forced herself to avoid anything that might make her lose control—anything erotic, passionate, moving, angering. . . .

A couple necking on campus? *Turn away*. A steamy scene on network TV? *Turn away*. "Can you accept that an alcoholic avoids the liquor store? Or that a dieter avoids the bakery?"

"A dieter still has to go to the grocery store."

"Unless he gets the groceries delivered," she countered.

"He?"

"Why would a dieter have to be a she?"

The corners of his lips curled. "Almost forgot what a little feminist you are."

"I guess everyone would be considered so, compared to a huge chauvinist such as yourself."

"Back to the subject. You're telling me you've never even seen people having sex in a movie?"

"Regrettably, my adult video collection isn't as extensive as yours."

He shrugged. "Not going to apologize for that. I'm currently between females. Flicks help to . . . pass the time."

Though she could scarcely believe she was discussing porn with an immortal in a million-dollar car, alas, she was.

"Answer the question," he said.

"No, I haven't viewed more than a glimpse."

"Before this trip is over, I'm going to get you to watch a flick."

"Never. I'm just not interested in seeing things like that." She was *dying* to see things like that. *Turn away* . . .

"Liar."

Now she shrugged.

"Do you even know the logistics?" he asked.

"Of course I do. I went to high school."

"And how does your boyfriend feel about all this?"

"Tim and I have decided to wait to have sex until we get married."

"He's onboard with that?" Cadeon met her gaze. "If you were mine, I'd give you a good seeing to at least five times a day."

This was why she avoided talking and reading about subjects like sex. Now all she could do was envision what a day would be like broken up by regular bouts of sex.

Would a male like Cadeon simply find her wherever she was and take her? She stifled a shiver.

He slanted her a heart-stopping grin. "Got you thinking about it, didn't I?"

"Got me thinking about what it'd be like with Tim five times a day," she lied.

Cadeon's knuckles went white on the steering wheel. Almost as if he was jealous. But why? Maybe demons felt possessive of females that were in their care?

"So tell me about *Tim*," he bit out.

"We've been dating for two years, and still, every day I'm struck by how perfect he is for me. He's caring and funny, and he's going to make a great husband and father. My parents both got to meet him before they died, and they liked him, too."

"Planning on *marrying* this bloke?"

"We're getting engaged as soon as we get our degrees."

In a brusque tone, he asked, "Aren't you a little young to get hitched?"

"Maybe, but when you find the right one . . ."

"And he's it?"

She sighed. "Yes. He's brilliant. One of a kind." When Cadeon snorted, she said, "How many men can discuss extremal combinatorics or how to use Mahalanobis distance in cluster analysis? How many know what a permutohedron or bipartite graph is?"

"Extreme combining?" He cast her a leer. "I'll discuss that any day."

"It's *extremal* . . . oh, never mind. You wouldn't understand. Tim and I comprehend each other on a different level."

"How smart can he be if he hasn't figured out a way to sleep with you in two years? I'd have had that locked up tight already."

Holly couldn't even manage a response. This male couldn't be more rude or overbearing.

He continued, "How're you going to know if you and Tim are compatible in bed if you don't do the deed before you get married? Come on, pet, you've got to kick the tires before you buy the car."

"I think that's a ridiculous"—*valid*—"argument. Sex can be taught just like any other skill. If there's something one of us needs, I'm sure the other will figure it out."

"You can't *teach* intensity. And who knows—you might discover a few kinks in your closet that old Tom might not be onboard with."

I know this. "*Tim* would do whatever it takes to make me happy," she insisted. But a full, abiding relationship between them would work only if she were normal sexually. Otherwise, how could he survive her strength? And how could they deal with her weird conflicting needs?

At once, she had the instinctive drive to overpower, and the instinctive need to be overpowered.

"What happens when things get a bit out of hand with you and Tim? How do you kids pull back on the throttle?"

Tim took so many herbs and extracts that she suspected his libido was chemically stunted. "We're strictly platonic right now." Yet even without his GNC stash, her boyfriend wasn't a very sexual person—which was perfect for her. "We're more cerebral than physical."

"Your cerebrum can't have an orgasm."

"We don't believe life has to be filled with orgasms to be meaningful."

He coughed on a swallow of Red Bull, then looked at her as if she'd spoken the vilest blasphemy. "You're killing me, halfling."

"I really don't want to talk to you about anything of this nature anymore. It's not an appropriate subject between us."

"A shame. 'Cause it happens to be my favorite one." Seeing she was unbending about this, he said, "Then ask about me more about the Lore."

"Very well. Do beings get married? Or form family units?"

"Some marry. Especially the species that are more humanized."

"Does your kind?"

"A lot do. More now than in the past. But not as a rule."

"Oh," she said, sounding as if his answer displeased her.

He hastily added, "Though we might not marry, we have something more lasting between us. A demon male has one fated female that he desires and needs above all others. He spends his whole life looking for her. A demon would be crazy to stray when he wants nothing more than to pleasure and protect his woman. Marriage is a little redundant."

"Have you found yours?" she asked, seeming fascinated with the idea.

"I . . . don't have mine yet."

"How do you recognize her?"

"You just know. A feeling. A connection. But, for my kind, we can't say for certain if she's ours or not without having sex with her. As they say, *In the throes, you know.*"

"How convenient."

"It's true. Things *occur* when you're having sex with her. Things you need in order to claim her." For the first time, the way would be opened, the dam breached.

"Like what?" she asked, then immediately added, "Wait—will your response be graphically sexual?"

To explain how a male rage demon could orgasm but never ejaculate until after the initial claiming of his female . . . ? "Odds are."

"Then please don't answer."

She gazed out the window, peering hard at the night, as if she desperately wanted to block him out. "Maybe I'll just rest for a while."

Minutes after she'd closed her eyes, she had nodded off. He kept glancing over at her, wondering what she was dreaming about with her brows drawn.

As he drove, he decided two things. If they were going to be on the road together for potentially weeks, then he would begin teaching her how to defend herself.

If I turn her over to Groot, she's going to have a sporting chance.

And second, he would be with her sexually. He could never take her completely—she may not be far enough into the transition to immortality to survive it. And if she did, once he'd experienced what it was like to be inside her, he might not ever let her go.

No, he couldn't claim her, but before he relinquished her, he would pleasure her. Cade thought she could be seduced—he'd seen a spark of interest in her eyes. She wasn't immune to him. Which meant he now had to coax her to trust him. Which meant he should be on his best behavior.

Except he had to admit that he kind of enjoyed baiting her like this. When her cheeks went pink and she grew flustered . . .

And Nïx did say she wanted her niece educated.

Cade wondered what his stalwart brother would think about his plans for Holly. Good money said he'd disapprove. Rydstrom was a fairly stand-up guy, with only a few skeletons in his closet.

Ah, but they were big ones.

Cade stilled. What if the Queen of Illusions discovered Rydstrom's secret weakness? What would she do to him then?

He also wondered if Rydstrom even now believed that their cause was lost because it rested on Cade's shoulders.

Cade wouldn't dwell on that thought. He was taking action, closing in on their goal.

Whereas Holly was plagued with unwelcome thoughts, Cade was mentally nimble, skirting disagreeable realizations with ease.

It was what would allow him to grow more attached to her with each hour—even as each second took him closer to the time he'd be forced to betray her.

13

Holly was at a ball, standing out on a terrace with Cadeon watching her from the shadows. He wanted her to join him there, but she was afraid to go into the darkness.

She kept looking over her shoulder back inside, unable to leave behind everything she'd ever known.

Yet his green eyes glowed from the shadows, and he held out his hand, beckoning her, promising pleasure more wicked than she'd ever imagined. . . .

"Good morning, beautiful."

Holly woke with a start, finding herself in Cadeon's arms in a dimly-lit room. He was staring down at her—with eyes that glowed.

"Didn't realize you had freckles," he said, his voice rumbling.

"Put me down." She squirmed to get free. She didn't need to be reminded of his deep voice, not when she'd just been dreaming about him—her subconscious telling her things with all the subtlety of a hammer's whack. "Where are we? What are you doing holding me like this?"

He set her on the edge of a bed with a soft comforter. "We're in a hotel for the day in northern Mississippi, and I was going to see if I could get you ready for bed without waking you."

"Ready for bed?" She rubbed her eyes and surveyed the

suite. It looked like they were in an upscale hotel, not that she'd been in many—or any—hotels in the last decade. The place might be nice, but right away she could see some things that needed to be rearranged to make sense. First, the chairs at the dining table—

"Yes, ready for bed," he said, plucking off her glasses, and setting them on the bedside table. Then he bent down to unfasten her heels.

"I'm sure I can manage the rest." She frowned at his sudden attentiveness. "I can do that," she insisted, but he wasn't listening.

He studied her shoe, with his lips curling as if he found it adorable. "You've the smallest feet, poppet." Once he'd removed her shoes, he said, "And now your top."

Before she could stop him, he pinched the bottom of her sweater and began tugging.

"Are you crazy?" She slapped his hands away, ducking under his arm to flee to the other side of the room.

"It's nothing I haven't seen before."

With her arms crossed over her chest, she said, "Just call me about thirty minutes before you're ready to leave tonight."

"I *will* be bunking here with you."

Holly tensed. Sharing a room with the husky-voiced demon she'd been dreaming about in the car? This wouldn't work at all. "How exactly would I explain this to my boyfriend?"

"How exactly are you going to explain any of this?"

Indeed. "I'm not going to tell him. If I can get this reversed, he never has to know."

"Good answer. It's against the rules of the Lore to tell humans about our world."

"But why do we have to share a room?"

"Because we're still too close to your last known whereabouts. There could be more vampires."

"I can take care of myself."

"That you can," he said easily. She was alternately discomfited and pleased by his ready confidence in her abilities. "But you'll have a hard time defending yourself when you're asleep. So that's where I come in."

Her stomach chose that moment of silence to growl loudly.

He grinned. "If you're going to be up for about twenty minutes more, I could go for some food. It's too early for room service, but there's a breakfast place across the street."

She nodded. "Can you just get me a bottle of orange juice? I don't like food prepared by others." *Or by myself*.

"We'll see. If you want to grab a shower, now's the time." At the door, he said, "And, Holly, do not take those pearls off. Or we'll be in deep shite."

She was still in the shower when he returned, which meant she was fair game. He grasped the bathroom door handle, gave a heft to easily break the lock, then swung the door open wide.

"The male's back from the hunt," he called, grinning at her outraged screech.

"Get out! Shut the door!"

Since he could only distinguish a vague shape behind the clouded-glass shower stall, he decided to comply with her requests.

Crossing to the dining table, he set down the plastic bag of food. Finding her something to eat actually *had* turned into a hunt—because she had such strict criteria.

He'd watched her enough to learn about her eccentric eating habits.

Cade had wondered why she hadn't hurried into the shower and been dressed by the time he returned, but now as his gaze swept the room, he realized she hadn't been able to drag herself away from rearranging everything not nailed down.

Three of the four chairs were neatly pushed in. With the fourth, she'd propped the chair's back against the table, leaning it forward on two legs. She'd clearly remade the bed and adjusted the pillows on the room's small sofa, which she'd also moved a few feet over.

The alarm clock on the bedside table was flush against the wall with no wire to be seen, and the remote control sat at a right angle to the center of the clock. The trash can was pressed directly against one end of the dresser, her suitcase against the other end. Her wireless laptop and cell phone sat perfectly parallel on the desk, charging.

Cade needed to check his e-mail and sports scores and map out their route for the day, so he opened her computer, and signed in as a guest. After routine Web stuff, he Googled a couple of things, unsurprised to find that she had the safe content filter on.

He leaned back in his chair, trying to imagine a life filtered of anything sexual.

Not worth living.

Hell, he was one to talk. He hadn't been with another woman since the day he'd met Holly, the longest stretch of celibacy since he'd first had sex. A few months ago, when he'd finally become convinced he could never have Holly, Cade had given a halfhearted try for a witch, but she'd wanted another.

Now he was glad of it.

He set the laptop back on the table, his attention drifting to her suitcase. Cade was itching to get a look at Nïx's letter. Thinking this a fine time to snoop, he crouched beside the bag, dragging it away from the wall so he could open the top wide.

After rooting through her folded skirts and sweater sets, he opened the side compartment, raising his brows at the contents. "*Hellooo, lingerie,*" he murmured.

Cade considered himself a male of simple tastes. He didn't need outrageous lingerie to turn him on. But the thought of prim Holly in those wicked scraps of silk sent blood rushing to his groin. . . .

She emerged then, wearing a bathrobe drawn up to her neck. "What are you doing?" she cried.

"Looking for Nïx's letter."

"You can't just go through my belongings!"

"I never would've suspected such naughty underthings from prim Miss Ashwin." He hooked his forefinger under the waistband of a thong, then spun it around.

"Give those back!" She snatched it away. "Nïx did this! She swapped out all my underwear and hose."

He didn't doubt it, but still said, "Yeah, *right*. Why would she do that?"

"I don't know—how could I possibly explain her actions?"

He snagged another pair of tiny panties, holding them up with both hands. "Then I bet a thong like this would still be feeling . . . *unusual.*"

"Ooh, give it!"

Before she could lunge for it, he rose, tossing it back

in the bag as if he'd grown bored with it. "Now I have to wonder what's under all that terry cloth." He pulled out another one of the chairs, then sank down.

She jutted her chin. "Regular pj's."

"Bullshite. Then let me see."

"I don't have to prove anything to you."

He leaned back with his hands behind his head. "I've seen all the goods, Holly. Not even half a day ago, so the memory's still fresh. No need to choke yourself with terry cloth," he said, but she wasn't listening, her sad-eyed gaze back on the pile of her now unfolded clothes.

"I'll have to redo everything." She looked so despondent that he decided to cut her a break on his teasing.

"What would happen if you didn't?"

"I would be a basket-case, unable to think about anything else." When she bent down to repack, her robe tightened over her ass, drawing his eyes like a magnet.

She shivered, then frowned at him over her shoulder.

"You can feel my eyes on you," he explained. "Immortals sense things more acutely. Sound, sight, even tactile perception. We call it *hypersensitivity*. You'll get used to it in time."

Once she was finished with her bag, she stood, no doubt scanning for more disarray. If her eyes had gone wild at the sight of him scrounging through her bag, then seeing her laptop open and out of place made her sway on her feet. "No . . . you . . . my *computer?*"

Holly cast him the same look he'd give a hellhound that had eaten his Super Bowl tickets. She secured the laptop, assessing it, turning it this way and that. "Your hands were *sticky*! Oh, God!"

He might've had a donut or two while he'd been waiting for his order.

She dove for her antibacterial wipes. Sitting on the bed, she turned from him, hunching over the computer, wiping it down.

He could only watch her actions in grim fascination, noting her shoulders rising and falling as she took deep, calming breaths.

Apparently reassured that nothing was screwed, she put the computer back on the desk, arranging it by the cell phone, then smoothed the comforter where she'd sat.

"Look, Cadeon," she began, but her gaze drifted back to the computer. She hurried back, adjusting it less than a millimeter to one side, then started again. "Last night I was too stunned to react to half the things you did. Now I'm not. You won't be able to treat me as you have been."

"Oh? Like with the saving your life and then driving you all night while you slept?"

"Like with the t-touching my computer. That was . . . bad. I'm not saying you can't use it—I don't mind sharing. But I need to sign you in and make sure you know how to treat it properly."

"I wasn't downloading porn or anything." *Didn't occur to me at the time*. "Just Googled some things and checked our route for tonight."

"Well, that's not the only area with you that has to change. There can't be any more planning to undress me as I sleep or bursting in on my shower and ogling me. Or even calling me those sexist pet names."

"You mean my endearments? What's wrong with them?"

"They're belittling to women."

He shook his head firmly. "None doing. It's just habit. This is the way males used to talk to females. And the endearments are female specific."

"Like how?"

"Like *pet* or *poppet*? I only call females I like by those." Only females he *really* liked. *Pet* was proprietary and *poppet* indicated affection. In other words, he'd never used those terms before. "If I'm not interested in a female, I'll call her *sweet*, *sweetheart*, or *dove*."

"Should I feel moved by this revelation? Honored to be deemed *poppet*?"

"I was going for charmed. But you're a hard one, pet."

"I'd be more inclined to be charmed if you had any respect for my privacy."

"We're going to be stuck together for at least a couple of weeks. Maintaining privacy would take too much effort, and would be futile anyway."

She pursed her lips, as if she couldn't argue with that. "Well, what about your cursing? Must you be so foul-mouthed around me?"

"I've been using those words since before humans decided they were *foul*." He began to set out food from the bag.

"Those kinds of terms are very jarring to people who were raised to avoid them. . . ." She trailed off. "Are those oatmeal pancakes?"

"They are."

"With honey?"

"Of course."

He knew her mouth was watering. "There wasn't any orange juice?"

"Oh, there was."

He dug into another bag and produced individually packaged cereals, a plastic spoon still in its wrapper, a sealed carton of milk and one of orange juice.

She narrowed her eyes. "All prepackaged. Exactly how long have you been watching me, Cadeon?"

"Long enough to know what you *like* to eat, and what you *will* eat . . ."

14

"I guess I wasn't that hungry anyway." Holly pushed her plate away after finishing only half of her breakfast.

"It's the change," Cadeon said. "Valkyrie don't eat."

"How is that even possible?"

"Dunno. How's it possible for shifters to change form, or witches to move things with their minds?"

After she threw the breakfast trash away, fatigue set in. It didn't help when he turned on a low lamp and pulled the heavier layer of drapes closed.

She sank down on the edge of the bed. Her body was exhausted, but her senses felt alive, humming. Hypersensitivity? She believed it. And now she was in a darkened hotel room, alone with a demon she'd had not-so-subtle dreams about.

Though she'd have thought his horns would be off-putting—not to mention his boorish behavior—she was actually feeling an inexplicable attraction to the demon. And she'd already had trouble controlling her urges.

Holly had experienced a variety of fears and idiosyncrasies and had been medicated for them. Now without her medicine . . . what would she do?

Somehow, she had to get her refills, not only to stifle these compulsions—but also to slow this progression.

Progression? Could she possibly get worse?

She recalled her parents taking her to Pompous Shrink,

the "best in the state." He'd droned on and on about her fragile mental health to her poor parents. . . .

"This is a classic case of obsessive-compulsive disorder. An OCD patient experiences a constant fear of transformation," he'd said. "She'll dread losing her sense of self, often experiencing impulses to act out of character. As these impulses can cause a great deal of anxiety, the patient will begin performing compulsive acts in order to suppress them. The stronger the urge, the more compulsive the behavior."

Oh, and there were chemical imbalances, too. "Most likely inherited from her mystery parents," he'd said with a resigned sigh, as if he'd seen this all before. "And exacerbated by Holly's insecurities over being adopted."

She'd never *had* insecurities about that. Her parents had been incredible—patient, encouraging, and loving. But they'd begun blaming themselves for her unusual behavior, looking for some fault in her upbringing, something they'd needed to provide for her but hadn't.

Her mom had apologized to Holly before she'd died. . . .

At that memory, she dropped her head into her hands.

"Whoa, halfling!" Cade quickly sat beside her. "What's the matter?" When she didn't answer, he said, "I'm not the type of male who's good at this sort of thing, this . . . comforting. But maybe . . . do you, uh, want to talk to me about what's going on in that head of yours?"

At length, she said, "It's all so bewildering. I mean, just last night, I was drugged and kidnapped, and then . . ." She trailed off.

"And then what? Tell me what happened to you."

Her voice had turned to a whisper. "It was horrifying. I woke up, and I was . . . naked, stripped for some kind of ritual. There were all these men watching me. I tried to reason with them, to beg them to let me go, but they just laughed and ignored me. Then, when it was about to begin, I shrieked."

"Valkyrie shriek."

She nodded. "Louder than anything I've ever heard. And the glass dome above broke. Then lightning struck me directly in the chest, and it went on and on. I don't remember much after that. I just recall feeling this rage, this uncontrollable need to do violence."

When had his hand rested on her back? It was big and warm, and he used it to gently rub up and down. "You've been through a lot. It's normal to react like this."

"Normal for a Valkyrie or for a human?" she asked, sniffling. "I don't quite have a grasp on either, since I've never been fully one or the other."

The truth of that sunk in at that moment. This meant Holly had to reevaluate everything. What was her personality truly like? She didn't recognize herself.

Just as Nïx had said.

And Holly knew that in the absence of a constant against which to measure, the introduction of new variables was a recipe for chaos. "I don't like my routine interrupted. I don't like surprises. On the best of days, I-I don't handle them well."

"Maybe you don't handle them well because you haven't had any practice with them."

"No, I have a condition—"

"So you like to arrange stuff. Where's the harm?"

She frowned. Holly had heard her dad say the same thing when he'd spoken to her mom about the drugs Pompous Shrink had wanted to put her on.

Holly shook her head. "You make it sound so negligible. But there were times when I couldn't leave my house for fear I would run out into a storm or get mesmerized by a shiny jewel. And now I have no idea how I'll react. Cadeon, what's normal for a Valkyrie cannot be normal for me." She knew she was being superficial, but she couldn't help adding, "And I don't want fangs and pointed ears!"

"Not that this will change how you feel, but I happen to love pointed ears."

She gave him a dubious expression.

"No, honestly. To a male from the Lore, they signal either fey or Valkyrie, and either species is renowned for its stunning females."

"Even if they didn't look freakish to me, they could prevent me from going about among humans."

"None doing. You'll just cover them with all this pretty hair of yours. I've seen Valkyrie plait braids over their ears or wear head bands over them. I've even seen them go with them uncovered and proclaim themselves extras on a movie set still 'in makeup.'"

Nïx hadn't seemed concerned about hers at all. "And the fangs?"

"They're so small, Holly." He grinned and laugh lines fanned out from the edges of his eyes. "Humans wouldn't notice anything was off."

"But I would be self-conscious, behaving differently."

"No, you'd learn to brazen it out. Evading detection is all about attitude." Had his voice grown rougher?

"If I get to this sorcerer quickly enough, then . . ." She trailed off, frowning. "Cadeon, are you smelling my hair?"

Uncaring now that he was caught, he took a handful and shoved his face in it, inhaling deeply.

"What is wrong with you?" she demanded, shooting to her feet.

"What? I just nee—wanted to smell your hair."

"You offer to talk to me, but you don't give a damn about what I'm feeling."

"That's not true, pet."

She huffed to her cell phone, unplugging it from the charger.

"Who are you calling?"

"The one I should be confiding in, instead of the mercenary demon who cares more about how my hair smells than my feelings!"

15

Visiting family?" Tim said, incredulous. "In Memphis? But you don't like to travel."

She moved the cell phone to her other ear. "A bit of an emergency cropped up. Everything's fine, but I thought I should be there." In a bid to change the subject, she said, "So tell me, how's the conference going? Is California nice?"

Cadeon prowled the room. *Okay, there's no way around it now.* The demon *had* been making advances toward her and now seemed jealous. But why?

Holly was exponentially younger than he was, and she wasn't a traffic-stopping beauty like Nïx. Holly was the cute geek. Not the immortal femme fatale.

She and Cadeon just didn't fit. She wasn't from his world and made no secret that she had no interest in joining it. . . .

"Our papers were well received," Tim said. "Very much so. I just wish you could be here."

Holly experienced a flare of annoyance that he'd enjoyed all the accolades. She was the stronger mathematician, and they both knew it.

She stilled. Where had *that* come from? She'd never felt so tetchy with him before. Here was yet another example of her transitioning into something she'd rather not be.

"I miss you," he said, making her feel even guiltier for getting irritated.

"I miss you, too," she said. At her words, Cadeon sat, then immediately stood, pacing again.

"Are you still working on your code?" Tim asked. "I didn't see anything uploaded." They shared an online account to backup their work and religiously uploaded every night.

"I'm starting back first thing tomorrow."

"The sooner you get it done—"

"I know, I know. The sooner I'm a doc." He was always so incredibly supportive, pushing her to reach her dreams.

In a lower voice, he said, "I can't wait to see you again, sweetheart."

Sweetheart. Why had she never noticed before that Tim often called her that endearment? "I know. I can't wait either."

Cade slammed into the bathroom, exiting short moments later looking like he'd splashed his face with water. "Hang up," he bit out before she could mute the phone.

"Who was that?" Tim said.

"A . . . cousin of mine."

"I didn't know you had any cousins."

"Me neither, not until recently. Finding branches of my family that I'd had no idea about." When Cadeon began striding toward her, she hurriedly said, "But I have to go now. Call you later?"

"Yes, of course. Be safe—"

Cadeon snatched the phone from her, braving her outraged slaps. "Holly's kissing *cousin* here," he said. "Sorry, Todd, the chit's going to have to ring you back in a week or two."

When he hung up on Tim, she snapped, "How dare you! All you're supposed to do is keep me safe—that's what you're getting paid for. Explain to me what kind of danger there was in talking to him!"

"No danger," he said, looming over her until they were toe to toe.

They were both breathing heavily. He was so imposing, seeming to take up the very air she needed, making it hard to concentrate.

"Then why?"

"Maybe I've watched the two of you together enough to know you'd be throwing away all your passion on him."

"That's not your place to say! Nïx told me you've been hired to transport me to the sorcerer—nothing more, and nothing less."

He looped his arm around her waist, holding her even when she beat her fists against his rock-hard chest. "That might be true, but it doesn't mean I can't let you know when you're making a mistake."

"Fine. Your opinion is noted," she said, keeping up her fruitless efforts to get away. "Now let me go!"

"I don't think you're getting the picture. Maybe I need to demonstrate what it's *supposed* to be like with a male."

Before she could react, he'd cupped her face and bent down, slanting his mouth over hers. The heat of his lips sent shivers radiating through her, stunning her. She was too shocked to move, to breathe. . . .

His tongue teased between her lips, coaxing her to open her mouth and accept his kiss. The sensations were unfamiliar, *pleasing*.

After a moment, she . . . did.

He used his tongue to stroke against hers so sensuously,

quelling her need to get free. She found her fists loosening, her palms resting docilely on his chest.

Holly never would have suspected the rough mercenary's kiss would be so erotic, so languid and hot. She couldn't stop herself from giving a tentative kiss back. He groaned against her mouth, so she did it again, getting caught up.

When she squeezed the muscles of his chest in fascination, he pressed her back against the wall with his body. Deepening the kiss, he effortlessly stoked her arousal to a fever pitch.

He broke away, but only to trail his lips along her neck. "That's it, pet," he rasped with a lick against her skin. "Let me kiss you. I'll do it till your toes curl."

They already were. And her nipples throbbed. She felt herself growing wet between her legs, aching to be touched there—

Without warning, he spread the top of her robe wide to her waist, revealing the black cami she wore. When he brazenly pinched her nipples through the silk, she nearly came out of her skin, jerking with a cry that turned to another moan.

"Silk's the only thing that should ever cover breasts this beautiful." His palms settled around her sides, his thumbs lazily brushing over her hardening nipples again and again until she was arching to his touch. She bit her bottom lip hard, struggling to keep from moaning.

"Sensitive halfling. I could make you come so quick. Do you want me to?" he asked, settling back into the kiss. As he licked her tongue so wickedly, she realized she did. So much.

Too fast . . . losing control. She couldn't stop kissing him.

Oh, God, I'm losing it. Why couldn't she stop kissing him?

Already, she battled overwhelming impulses to sink her claws into his body, to force him closer so he couldn't get away from her.

She was about to tell him that he could do anything he wanted when he pressed his erection against her, slowly thrusting.

Even as the rational side of her brain was reasoning that his size simply couldn't be right, the other side of her mind was filled with disturbing images.

She saw herself tearing off his jeans to get to the swollen shaft he rocked against her. Then, when he was lying back on the bed, she'd guide his erection inside her body, impaling herself on it as she squeezed the rippling muscles of his chest. . . .

When her hands dropped, claws poised to rip off his jeans, fear coursed through her. These urges weren't her own. Her eyes went wide and she broke away, shoving at his shoulders. "Stop . . . no!"

He pulled back, his chest heaving, his horns straightening. He looked dangerous and wicked and tempting.

"I figured you'd stop me." His lips curled in a smile that robbed her of breath. "But I got further than I thought I would."

Flinging herself away from him, she demanded, "What is this?" Her thoughts were scrambled, her body screaming for relief. "Why would you want to get far with me at all? What is the purpose?"

"I made a run at you."

She yanked her robe closed up to her neck. "A *run*? Why? Because you wanted to teach me a lesson, or because you're attracted to me?"

"Maybe a little of both."

"Why would you be attracted to me? It isn't logical."

"You're not just a nerd's wet dream, you know."

"What does *that* mean?"

"Means I find you sexy. I'm not going to lie to you about this."

"*Sexy?*" she said in a strangled tone. "But . . . but you like tarts. With more meat on their bones. That's what you said! And I've done nothing to try to attract this attention from you! I don't wear makeup or low-cut tops—"

"Do you think just because you don't try that you'll be unattractive?"

Well . . . yes.

"Face it, Holly, you're a natural."

This would not do. She pointed her forefinger at him. "No more kissing me, Cadeon. That's not part of this deal. I have a boyfriend."

"No, you don't. You've got a friend. The two of you don't sleep together, or do anything couples should do. And that's because you don't know better. You have no idea what you're missing."

She didn't have the heart to deny his words.

"In the short time that we're going to be together, I intend to keep trying to seduce you," he said. "Why not use me to ease your curiosity while we're stuck together? You can take a vacation from your boring life, get all this craziness out of your system, then go back to normal."

She hesitated, tilting her head . . . then railed at herself. Was she was actually considering getting lured into his sensual world? The dark side. Just like her dream.

When she parted her lips to speak, he said, "You don't have to answer right now. Just keep the offer in mind.

And one thing I can promise you: What happens with the demon, stays with the demon."

"How *considerate* an offer."

"That's me. Always thinking of others."

She squinted at him suspiciously, having the sense that he was excited, even . . . *happy* with her.

"I'm going to sleep." With her robe still firmly in place, she crawled under the covers.

"Ah, come on, halfling, you don't have to keep your robe on like a shark suit."

"I do when there are still sharks in the water."

"You can trust me not to do anything to you. I give you my word as a mercenary."

She glared at that. "Where are you going to sleep?"

He crossed to the couch and sank down, stretching his long arms along the back. "Here, unless you're wanting to share your bed with me."

"Ha!" She turned off the lamp. "In your dreams, demon."

"Admittedly, halfling," he rumbled from the dark.

16

When she woke near sundown, Cadeon was exiting the bathroom wearing only a towel, displaying far too much of that muscular body. Her lips parted with appreciation.

His tanned skin was taut and smooth over his rigid muscles, showing no signs of being shot just yesterday. His broad chest and back were damp from his shower.

Acting as if she still slept, she watched him moving about the room. She'd just been dreaming about him, the same vivid dream she'd had before. She swallowed, eyes riveted to that intriguing bulge behind his towel that swayed when he bent for his bag—

He abruptly turned, catching her staring at that part of his anatomy before she yanked her gaze up. He gave her a grin, and the blond stubble on his strong jaw glinted in the low light.

Even with the horns, he was too gorgeous for his own good. Worse, he knew it.

She resolved then that he'd never know that she found him handsome.

"Good, you're awake. I'm in need of your services."

"Pardon?"

"I need you to extract a bullet from me. I haven't been able to shed it."

She sat up, rubbing her eyes. "How would I do that?"

"Dig it out with your claws."

For all her phobias, she wasn't afraid of blood. But helping him would entail touching him. *No way*. It was too soon after their kiss this morning.

As she'd tossed and turned, trying to get to sleep, she'd decided that she would stay as far away from him as possible, biding her time until they stopped sharing rooms. "This is just one of your ploys to seduce me, isn't it?"

"Look, I wouldn't ask, but it's high on the back of my thigh and I can't easily reach it. Hurts like hell." He held her gaze as he said, "And, pet, I did catch it saving your life."

Guilt flared. He was in pain and needed her help. "You're right." She reached for her glasses, then tightened her robe. "Of course, I'll see if I can help." She hastily added, "But you have to keep your towel on."

"I will," he said, adding in a mutter, "but it won't do any good."

She frowned. Of course it would. He'd be covered.

When he stretched his massive body out on the bed, she sat beside him, trying not to stare at the muscled expanse of his back.

With a trembling hand, she eased the towel up, brushing it over the blond-tipped hair that covered his legs. "Where is it?" she asked, her voice unaccountably throaty.

"Farther up."

With a swallow, she tugged the towel higher. She glanced down to find that her claws were already curling.

Those thoughts began to suffuse her mind. She wanted to lick each droplet from his damp skin, to dip her tongue to the slight collection at the base of his spine. . . .

She shook her head hard, trying to jar loose the unwelcome images.

"Higher," he said.

"Yes, yes—"

When she uncovered the wound, she gasped. But not at the injury. His penis hung down between his legs. *Turn away. Turn—away. Turn away!*

Face burning, she finally did.

"Told you it wouldn't do any good."

She was furious, as much at his actions as at her own reaction—the mere site of his privates made her feel hot and flustered. "You could have arranged yourself differently!"

"You would've seen some or all. What's the difference?"

"I . . . there's a difference!"

Unable to help herself, she let her gaze flit to it again. Had it grown? Her lips parted. "You're . . . you're getting aroused!"

He looked up at her. "So?" With what sounded like a stifled groan, he adjusted himself until he lay on it. "Males do that." Seeming uncomfortable in that position as well, he turned to his back.

He'd gotten even bigger! "What do you intend to do about . . . with . . . Are you just going to walk around like that?" She'd wondered what he'd done with his previous erection as well.

"I'll grin and bear it, till my next shower."

"Next shower?"

He gave her a leer.

"Oh!" Her face flushed. He was utterly unembarrassed to divulge that he masturbated, and that he'd be doing it again at their next hotel stop.

Had he done it earlier while she slept? *Don't imagine that, Holly!* "You admit to it?"

"You don't?" he asked.

"No, I don't. . . ." She trailed off, that haze beginning to suffuse her mind.

As she stared, his breaths grew harsh, and his shaft distended under the towel even more. "You keep watching me like this, and my leg's not going to be the only thing aching." Their eyes met. "You've never seen a male aroused, have you?" he asked softly, with seeming tenderness in his tone. As if she'd charmed him.

Holly had caught maybe one or two stolen glimpses, but she'd never had *sustained* viewing. She couldn't, else she risked a loss of control. So why couldn't she turn away now?

She had for so long before . . .

With his hand at the edge of the towel, he said, "Do you want this off of me?"

She was shaking, she wanted it so badly. "Why would I?" Impulses were riding her hard.

"So you can see. You've got to be curious."

He took her hand. At first she thought he was going to place it on his shaft, and didn't know how she felt about that.

Instead, he put it at the edge of the towel. "Pull it off, Holly. Take a look. You don't have to do anything else."

One look. What would it hurt? Her curiosity goaded her. With a swallow, she tugged the towel loose. "That's it." His voice was husky, mesmerizing.

Once she'd uncovered his erection, it jerked as if excited to have her eyes on it. She stared, transfixed.

"Look all you like." He drew his knee up to give her a better view. "Or do you want to touch it?"

She did! So much. Her fingers itched to explore his length.

What would that smooth skin feel like? Earlier, she'd imagined sliding down his shaft, but hadn't known how to truly envision it.

Now she did.

I wonder what it would taste like? She flushed at her thoughts.

As her shaking hand reached forward, his stomach muscles clenched in sharp ridges.

When his erection pulsed again, a bead of moisture arose on the broad head. He gave a low groan, as if that had felt incredible.

How fascinating. . . .

She would rub the pad of her forefinger there and see how he liked that. *Inches away . . . about to feel it—*

Out of the corner of her vision, she spied his hand oh-so-subtly slipping toward her.

Comprehension hit.

The demon had baited a trap for her, using his erection as a lure for a gullible female.

She snatched her hand back as if from a flame, breaking her stare to meet his gaze. His eyes were growing black, yet somehow glowing. His horns were bigger and duskier than normal. His fangs were longer.

Oh, yes, this was clearly all about her—her *curiosity*. How could she be so naïve?

The demon was systematically breaking down her barriers. The dark side, lulling her, drawing her away. Everything was conspiring against her efforts.

Lulling me from what I know, from where I want to be . . .

Now she understood his words from earlier. He'd gotten further with her than he'd expected, and believed he'd get even further next time.

What was so bad—he probably would. And that made her fearful. If only she weren't so attracted to him, then she'd be safe. She'd never go into the shadows with him.

Reasoning trail: No demon, no temptation, no thinking about going to the dark side.

He planned to wear her down? "Cadeon, I believe you want services that aren't included." She stood, heading for the bathroom. Over her shoulder, she said, "But best of luck with that bullet."

17

When Holly emerged from the bathroom, dressed and ready for the drive, he'd still been battling his hard-on, scarcely able to haul jeans over his aching shaft.

It was probably a good thing that she hadn't put her hand on it before—because by that point, a weak breeze would've instantaneously set him off.

He'd been so close that he'd even given up a drop of semen, which had never happened before, a maddening glimpse of what spilling his seed would feel like.

Even digging out that bullet by himself hadn't put a dent in his need. His kind required release multiple times a day, or they were more prone to go into a rage state. For her sake, he'd have to take matters in hand soon.

Now, to see her with pink cheeks, dressed for in her smart clothes . . . He raked his gaze over her, as ever finding her effortlessly sexy.

Her heels weren't stilettos, but the way the thin straps hugged her trim ankles was arousing to him. The mere sight of her pearls could pain him, because whenever she ran them against her lips, one of his favorite fantasies always assailed him—the one of her wearing nothing but pearls and him riding her so hard that the strand bounced about her neck.

And her skirt . . . When he'd watched her in the past,

he hadn't understood why she would wear such conservative tops, then such provocative skirts. Yes, they went past her knees, but they also stretched so enticingly over her ass.

He'd finally figured it out. Holly didn't realize how those expensive materials molded over her generous curves.

Cade knew females liked to ask, "Does my ass look big in this?" But considering Holly as an example, he'd begun to suspect that women really couldn't determine what their asses looked like.

Oh, well. A question for the ages.

"Ready?" he asked.

She nodded, behaving as though nothing out of the ordinary had happened between them, while his balls were so blue he wondered if he'd ever get them back to rights.

If she wanted to act like she hadn't slowly licked her lips while her silver eyes were locked on his cock, he could play.

So, we pretend. . . .

After he took the bags to the car, stuffing them in the trunk, he remembered to open her door for her—*score one for the demon*—but just when he was about to slide inside, she got out.

"Oh, no, no," she said, eyeing the floorboard on his side—which was full of wrappers and crushed cans of Red Bull. "We can't start the drive out this way."

"It's fine, Holls. I'll dump the trash at the next gas station."

But she'd already retrieved her antibacterial wipes and crossed to his side, shooing him away. Setting out the wipes for afterward, she bent over in front of him to clear out the floorboard.

And he had to shuffle his feet wide to keep from falling over.

The skirt was so tight, he could discern she was definitely wearing one of those thongs. *Mental note: Always leave trash on the floorboard.*

When she'd been getting ready earlier, he'd had only enough time to do one of two things in private: contort naked, digging for the bullet, or take matters in hand with his hard-on. As he gaped at her skirt molding to her heart-shaped ass, he concluded he'd chosen poorly with the bullet.

He stifled a groan, beginning to pace back and forth.

A human male strolled by, then did a double take at her. The bastard's brows drew together with want.

Cade bared his teeth. *Don't mangle the mortal!* The human caught sight of him and wisely scurried away.

Once Holly had deposited everything in the hotel's trash bin, she used her wipes to eradicate innocent microorganisms.

"Are we ready, pet?" His voice was so hoarse it made her frown.

"What's wrong with your voice? Are you getting sick?"

He heard her asking the question, but his attention was already distracted. The evening was chilly, and her nipples were stiff under the beige sweater she wore. He absently answered, "Immortals never get sick."

She caught the direction of his stare, and her lips thinned. "Must you?"

I must. "First day in the new bra, yeah?"

As if calling on some inner well of reserve, she said in a long-suffering tone, "Yes, Cadeon, it is. . . ."

When they'd gotten on the road, she asked, "So tell me

about the checkpoint. Who's this Imatra woman? Do you know her?"

"Not personally. She's supposed to have been born of a sorcerer and a demoness, getting the strengths from both. Rumored to be a great beauty," he added truthfully, gauging her reaction. There wasn't a discernible one. "She owns a Lore tavern on the Mississippi River called the Sandbar."

"How *cute*." Had her tone been cutting?

Cade would be forced to take Holly with him there. The idea of leaving her vulnerable and alone in the hotel room was worse than what he expected at this bar. Besides, Groot's followers patronized the place.

Surely they wouldn't do anything to jeopardize what the sorcerer wanted so badly. . . .

"And then at the Sandbar, we'll get directions to another checkpoint?" When he nodded, she said, "Any idea where Groot's could be?"

"Some say it's in the north."

"What is he like? I feel as though I'm off to see the wizard."

"He's a blacksmith as well as a sorcerer, supposed to be able to enchant metal."

"Why so much trouble to get to him?"

Stick to the truth. "My enemy Omort wants him dead. So Groot lives in constant hiding."

"Because Groot can forge a sword that can kill Omort."

"Precisely."

"So then, Groot must be one of the good guys if he and Omort are enemies."

Vague it up. "Good or bad, you need to remember that all sorcerers have to be dealt with cautiously."

"How will he reverse the transition? Will there be a spell?"

"I don't know. I suppose."

"But only if we get there in time. Why didn't we just fly to Memphis?"

"Nïx made me vow not to fly any leg of this trip. She must have foreseen something bad."

"Do you always believe her predictions?"

"She doesn't get foretellings wrong—ever," he said. "But whether she tells you the truth about them is another matter."

"You seem to know her fairly well. Were you two ever . . . involved?"

"Involved with Nucking Futs Nïx? Not likely. In case you didn't gather Nïx is"—he twirled his forefinger at his temple—"addled."

"She's also beautiful."

"Never seen a Valkyrie who wasn't." He peered hard at her, making her flush and look away. "Speaking of Nïx—what'd you do with her letter?"

"I memorized and destroyed it while you were out for food."

"Then you knew I'd snoop through your things?"

"From what I know about you so far, it was a statistical probability."

Over the last three hours, they'd ridden in silence, with Holly working on her laptop, lost in thought—and him trying not to glance over at her more than twice a minute.

She had her computer stylus behind her ear, her glasses on, and she was now lazily fingering those pearls.

Don't do it . . . don't do—

And there she went, running them against her lips.

Maddening woman, with even more maddening ways about her! And she had no clue of the men she left hard in her wake.

Here he was, locked in a car all night with *his* female, knowing she needed to be pleasured. He had a driving demon instinct to please his female—and couldn't.

Cade was about to explode.

Just then her brows drew together, and she typed in rapid-fire taps. She paused, biting her bottom lip. When she hit *enter*, she glowered at the answer.

He wondered what proofs, theorems, or functions she was considering and then rejecting. What was going on in that incredible brain of hers?

But she hadn't only been concentrating on math over the last few hours. He knew she'd occasionally been thinking about earlier. Her face would flush, and she'd run her pearls against her lips, but faster.

Had she liked what he'd shown her? He'd been proud for her to see him hard, loving the feel of her gaze on his shaft, hoping to tempt her hands to it. And she'd been so close to touching him.

He knew he hadn't been on his best behavior at the hotel. But when she'd been talking to that tosser, Cade had been overcome with jealousy.

He tried to remember the last time he'd been so envious. Probably when the Lykae Bowen MacRieve had found his mate. Intense rivals, both Bowen and Cade had gone centuries without finding their females. Then the Lykae had gotten his in a pretty, funny witch—the one Cade had made a lackluster run at.

Now Cade had found his own female in a brilliant,

stunning Valkyrie, who was so confident she made him speechless at times.

But she was one he couldn't keep.

Another rapid bout of typing came, with another glare at her computer screen.

"Has anyone ever told you you're sexy as hell when you're mathematizing?"

She sighed, closing her laptop and removing her glasses. "Is sex all you think about?"

"It is when I'm in sore need of it. My kind need it three or four times on a regular day. And then after what happened between us earlier . . . ? You've got to be feeling the aftereffects, too."

"Hardly."

"Admit it. We had a *moment*." Though they hadn't even touched, he couldn't remember the last time he'd experienced anything so heated.

"It wouldn't matter if we did. I can control my baser urges."

"You said you didn't work things out for yourself. Which I know is a lie—"

"It is not!"

"It has to be," he said. "Otherwise the lust would just build and build."

"You're going to keep at this until I answer."

"You're beginning to understand me."

"No, I refuse this," she said, shaking her head. "We're simply not talking about this."

"Then talk about something else. You're due for a break from your work, and I need a distraction to take my mind from my aching thigh. Some Valkyrie refused to aid me in my distress."

"You deserved that."

"Probably," he allowed.

"Very well. What do you do as a mercenary?"

"I specialize in usurping thrones. They call me the king-maker." *Bragging now?*

"Then you're an insurrectionist."

"You're assuming that I'm taking thrones from their rightful owners."

She gave a nod in his direction, as if conceding his point.

"But mainly, I fight wars. The Lore is a violent place, good for business," he said, then snapped his fingers. "Oh, wait, I almost forgot . . . you're a *pacifist.*"

"That's not a bad word."

"It is when you're in the war industry."

She quirked a brow. Then seeming begrudgingly curious about his job, she asked, "How did you become a mercenary?

"I'd trained as a soldier to fight Omort." At nineteen, Cade had been thrown into a brutal training regime among Rydstrom's soldiers—who all despised him. For months, Cade had gotten his ass handed to him. Finally he'd learned he had to become faster, stronger, better than any demon in the army.

Ultimately, he had been, and people had taken notice. "In idle times between campaigns, I got offered some jobs." As Omort grew more powerful, crushing revolt after revolt, there'd been more idle times than not. "I had some success, and it snowballed. I've got a crew of forty-five under my command."

"All demons?"

"Mostly," he said.

"Do you discriminate against non-demons?" she asked.

"We don't discriminate. As long as the applicant is vicious, has killed before, and is willing to do so again, he's hirable."

"And how many women are currently in your crew?" she asked pleasantly.

"I walked right into that one, didn't I?" he said, but she merely raised her eyebrows, awaiting his answer. "No females have applied. Much. Hardly any at all. Hey, if you stay Valkyrie, I'll hire you. The PhD mercenary."

"That'd be a waste of study."

He grew still. "What's that supposed to mean?"

"It just seems like your occupation would utilize more brawn than brain."

"So the bigger your biceps, the better your military strategy and battle tactics? Is that what you think?"

She studied his face. "You're sensitive about this."

"What? I'm not bloody sensitive," he said, but his tone was gruff. "Back to you. You told Nïx that you were one code away from getting your PhD. What kind of code?"

"It's complicated."

Did she think he couldn't even follow along? That made his hackles rise. "The big, dumb demon has been known to understand a few things over his *thousand years* of life."

She gave him another studying look, as if he'd just proven her theory. "You really want to hear about my project?" When he nodded, she said, "I call it *barbed code*. I intend for it to be used in the private sector in computer applications to protect proprietary data. Eighty-five percent of all companies have reported data loss due to hacking or unauthorized access."

"You're telling me that many companies use codes?"

"*Everyone* uses codes. Or at least, anyone with a computer does. When you receive an e-mail, it's encrypted, until your e-mail program decodes it. An online banking transaction and even paying a speeding ticket online are code-heavy applications."

She turned, shifting her body to face him more fully, obviously loving this subject. Which disconcerted him.

If she was so keen on this stuff, then she'd want a partner who could discuss it with her. It pissed him off that she and that tosser spoke a language he could never know.

Once again—you can't bloody have her anyway!

"Cadeon, are you even listening to me?"

"What? Yeah, was just thinking about . . . how http always turns to https when I carry out a transaction."

"Exactly!"

Good save.

"Https provides an additional level of encryption." She eyed him with new interest. *Bloody good save.* "But every computerized code is still breakable. Every single one can be decrypted by brute-force computing."

"What's that?"

"Imagine a thousand computers working twenty-four hours a day on breaking a single code. That's BFC. So the general idea is to make a code so convoluted and complex that no one would have enough BFC available to crack it. But theoretically, it's still hackable."

"So what would your code do? Why call it *barbed*?"

"I want it to protect itself—by any means necessary."

"How would that be possible?" he asked.

"If it senses it's being decrypted, then it would cyberattack the decoder."

He gave a laugh. "Figures a Valkyrie would develop a combative code."

Her eyes flashed silvery. "This is very serious." He'd already known how devoted she was to her work, but had never seen her this passionate about it. "BFC won't work if my code takes out those thousand computers simultaneously. And imagine the implications for other uses."

"Like what?"

"Take, for instance, your antivirus software. It would no longer merely guard your computer against viruses, it could track the virus back to its origin, then send a mutated version to cripple the culprit's own system. Even e-mail applications would be affected. If you received spam, your computer would dispatch ten thousand spam messages directly back to the sender's real address, shutting down his system."

"I do believe that this is serious. It sounds like it could completely wipe out viruses and spam in no time."

"It totally could! The people behind them steal time from our lives, forcing us to defend against them or to deal with their fallout. And I resent it."

"So what's the holdup?"

She looked away as she said, "My code . . . attacks everything. Even friendly systems."

"The warrior code goes on the rampage."

She sighed. "That's correct."

"And you have to figure out how to make a code recognize a friendly from a foe."

With a nod, she said, "Imagine sending your coworker over in accounting a virus times one million. The results would be catastrophic to chance a friendly."

"So what are you doing now?"

"Trying to communicate with the code as a friendly to study exactly how it kicks my tail each time."

"Until I met you, I always thought codes were about words and riddles."

"Cryptology used to be the realm of linguists. Now it's dominated by the geeks." She said this proudly, as if she was one among them. "We're going to rule the world, you know?"

What Holly didn't understand was that when she said things like this, she didn't sound like a geek—she sounded like a Valkyrie.

18

I refuse!" she told Cadeon as they waited for the tank to fill up. "I won't do it!"

"You don't know what you're missing. Just a bite," he said, easing his hot dog toward her mouth.

From her perch on the hood of the car—where he'd insisted on lifting her—she eyed the offering with disgust and put up her hand. "Forget it. Gas station food is foul. Gas station hot dogs are beyond foul. Do you know how long it's been on those greasy rollers?"

"Long enough to taste *good*." He took a huge bite.

"You might as well be eating pickled pig's feet, fished from a jar."

His eyes went wide. "They had some? And you didn't tell me?" With a grin at her horrified expression, he said, "All right, all right. I had to give it a shot." He set down his dinner beside her, then bent to a plastic bag by his feet. "Here," he said, pulling out a bottle of orange juice. After painstakingly opening the top without touching the rim, he handed it to her. He also produced several packaged granola bars.

Cadeon could be unexpectedly thoughtful. For a demon. She took a drink. "Why haven't you made fun of me for my . . . quirks?"

He shrugged. "Everybody's got something unusual about them."

Holly tilted her head. He was wearing that broken-in, leather hat. Nïx had been right. He was sexy as the devil in it. She inwardly shook herself. "So what kind of gas mileage does a Veyron get?"

"At full speed, it can burn through a tank in twelve minutes."

She nodded slowly. "So basically this is a one-car solution to an unscathed ozone layer."

"Yeah. But it goes *fast*. Unlike that bladeless lawn mower you call a car."

"It's a hybrid! I drive it for the environment."

"But it doesn't go *fast*."

She rolled her eyes. "You said this was the most expensive car. How much is it?"

"One point two."

"Million?" she cried. She began scuttling off the hood, but he stayed her with his big hands on her hips.

"You don't have to get down. Always remember one thing."

"What's that?"

"This isn't our car."

His sat-phone rang then. "It's Rök. Need to take this." He crossed the parking lot for privacy. As if she could understand whatever that foreign tongue was.

She'd learned that Cade's phone had satellite access, which meant that it would work just about anywhere on earth. Which meant that she could patch her wireless laptop into it and have internet access anywhere on earth.

Once he returned, she asked, "What do you call that language?"

"Demonish," he answered. "You'll be happy to know that the rest of the Order of Demonaeus has been taken out. And Rök and my crew are on the vampires' trail even as we speak. You'll have two fewer factions out for you."

"Oh. Thank you. And thanks to Rök." How did one express gratitude for demon and vampire strikes? It wasn't like there was a card. "How did you meet him?" she asked, picturing the demon she'd briefly met. He was as tall as Cadeon with similar horns, though Rök's were more silvery. He'd had black hair tied back in a queue, and heavy-lidded blue eyes. Take away the horns, and women would find him gorgeous.

"We were adversaries, each with different strengths—he likes his spy intrigues while I like to whack things with swords. We kept getting hired by different factions to go after the same stuff or for our crews to fight. We eventually determined that we'd kill each other, and then no one would get the pay."

"And is it all about the pay?"

"Hence the term *mercenary*." He chucked her under the chin. "Try to keep up, halfling."

Mississippi Mile Marker 775

"I thought 'Sandbar' was just a cutesy play on words," Holly observed, pulling her lightweight jacket tighter. The air coming off the river chilled her to her bones.

"Nope. It's really a sandbar island," Cadeon said. After strapping his sword over his back, he began leading the way from the bluff where they'd parked down to the water.

She followed him along the dicey path, picking her way through roots and scrub, expecting to fall—or at least to get a run in her hose at every turn. "I still don't see a ferry."

"Then take off your glasses. See the beach? Right down there. Ferry."

She squinted, then stumbled, and a nanosecond later she was in his arms—his big, warm arms.

Startled by how much she liked it there, she said, "I can make it by myself."

"In heels?"

"I'll be buying more suitable footwear as soon as possible."

His voice was low and rough when he said, "I like you in your heels."

Why did she respond so readily to his mere voice, her body going soft against his? She'd never thought of voices as arousing, had never thought much about them at all unless they'd grated.

Tim's was pleasing. Cadeon's was . . . arousing.

At her ear, he rumbled, "I'd like them better digging into my back."

Of course, her mind went right to envisioning that.

"Got you thinking about it, didn't I?" Flashing her a look that said My *work here is done*, he continued down the path.

"Let me down, Cadeon. Now!"

He didn't, and there was nothing she could do about it because the demon was exponentially stronger than she was. She had no hope of overpowering him. . . .

Before, she'd never had sex for fear of losing herself—and hurting another. There was no way she could with Cadeon.

Which meant that technically, this lusty demon was a potential sex partner for her.

Holly tried to stem those thoughts. Even if he was possible from a physical standpoint, he still wouldn't do. Cadeon was uncouth, overbearing, and an unabashed chauvinist.

Case in point—he refused to set her down even when they reached the chunky yellow sand to meet the ferryman.

The man was a creepy sort, with bulbous horns that pointed ominously forward. Cadeon's were much better. At least she knew she wouldn't get an eye put out if they ever missed while kissing.

Not that they'd be kissing ever again!

"Only Lorekind allowed," the ferryman said.

Against her protests, Cadeon tugged up her hair from her ear. "Valkyrie," he said simply.

When she squirmed against him, needing to put her hair to rights, the ferryman said, "Is she here to fight?"

He expected her to fight more than he expected it from the mercenary demon?

"The Valkyrie's just here with me," Cadeon said, and the man allowed them aboard.

On the ferry, Cadeon finally let her slide down his body so she could fix her hair. Minutes later, they docked at a pier of questionable structural integrity, which morphed into an unbalanced walkway wending through a swamp.

A cabin was lit up in the distance, and music sounded from within.

"Stay close to me," he said. "We get in, get the directions, and get out, yeah?"

"Yeah." She heard something in the woods beside them. "Hey, what's moving out there?" She strained to see.

He plucked off her glasses, and she instantly spotted a family of deer. Okay, there was no getting around it—her eyesight was changing.

"Give those back!"

"People are going to wonder why you wear glasses. Immortals don't need them."

She snatched the glasses back, shoving them on. "Then let them wonder." At the door, she checked her pearls, sleeves, and hair. She always did this before she entered a building, one of her more pressing rituals.

"Suit yourself. Now, this is going to be a shade shocking for you. Just don't stare at any of the patrons. Clear?"

"I can handle myself."

"Now, that I'm aware of, halfling. And don't talk to anyone about our business either. Just assume everyone in here is out to do you wrong."

"Shouldn't be a problem. I do that with you all the time."

He gave her a tight smile. "And, Holly, remember what you're capable of. If things go south, don't forget that you can mete out some serious pain. Don't hesitate."

If he continued telling her how strong and powerful she was, Holly was going to have to reevaluate his status as chauvinist—

He opened the door; reality went on hiatus.

To a jukebox's tune of "Why Don't We Get Drunk and Screw," beings that she'd never imagined were socializing. The place was like a regular bar, except peopled with creatures from myth.

Two men arm-wrestled and an image of a beast flickered over each of them. Their eyes wavered from an amber color to the lightest blue.

Lykae: werewolves. She remembered reading about them.

Four tall males with pointed ears played darts—through

the crowd—from what had to be a distance of forty feet. *The noble fey*. Small, cherubic gnomes danced merrily. But for some reason, she sensed danger from them. Must be *kobolds*.

Sprinkled throughout were demons of all shapes and sizes and types of horns. She sulkily noted that Cadeon's were by far the finest of all of them.

Suddenly everyone stopped and stared—at her. She put her chin up. Cadeon drew her closer.

"Covering your unease well, halfling," he murmured at her ear, "but don't forget that a lot of these beings can still tell your heart is thundering. Calm it down."

Just then, the crowd parted to reveal a tall, shapely female traipsing toward them. "So this is the infamous Cade the Kingmaker," she said in a whiskey voice, eyeing him with obvious interest. "The rumors don't lie. You are the gorgeous half of the Woede."

"And you must be Imatra," he said, his tone inscrutable.

Just as Cadeon had heard, Imatra was a great beauty. And the woman obviously knew it. She wore a crimson silk robe over a leather miniskirt and a black bustier that pushed up her sizable breasts precariously.

Holly had on a twinset and a Burberry skirt.

Imatra sauntered around him, lazily trailing a finger along his shoulders. "Such a stunning male you are." She barely spared Holly a glance, then her attention was back on him. "You need to come with me to the back."

When Holly followed them, Imatra turned and said, "Just Cade. We've *business* to attend to." She winked at Holly.

Cadeon looked like he'd protest—Holly wanted him

to. But Imatra whispered something in his ear, and he said, "You stay at the bar, Holly. Don't interact with anyone. Just sit and stay quiet, or yell for me if you need me. I'll be back in fifteen minutes."

Then they were gone. And she didn't know how she felt about that stunning demoness flirting with Cadeon so aggressively.

Exhaling a breath, she sidled up to the bar and took a stool. This place reminded her of the Tatooine bar scene from *Star Wars*. What was the name of that place? Oh, yeah. The Mos Eisley Cantina. *I am such a geek to know that*.

"What'll you have?" the bartender asked her. One of his three eyes was missing. *Three not complete or two not nullified*. Either was bad. She tried not to stare, but the potential for three should be three!

She delicately cleared her throat. "W-water would be fine, thank you."

As she arranged the napkins stacked nearby in perfect squares, all around her males closed in. *Oh, yes, Cadeon. Don't interact, and I'll be dandy*.

"What business have ye here, Valkyrie?" the apparent leader asked.

She sensed a vague threat from these males. They were testing her. She recalled the last time she'd felt this way—her first day of class with thirty-three Tulane football players. She'd donned a façade of utter confidence, tolerating zero disrespect.

What were demons compared to freshmen jocks?

"I'm here enjoying the area," she said blithely. "Tell me, do you reside along the water?"

They all went wide-eyed. "Why do ye want to know

where I live?" the leader asked. "To take my head whilst I sleep?"

"Aye, Deshazior," another interjected, "that's the way of the Valkyrie. Creep in when you don't expect it, then, *bam*"—he slammed the bottom of his fist on the bar—"you're headless."

Be calm. Slow the heart. "While that might be the case, gentlemen, I was actually thinking that flood insurance must be a nightmare for you guys."

"She talks like a human," this Deshazior said. The demon, who himself talked like a Central Casting pirate, motioned to the bartender, and a shot glass appeared in front of her. "Drink, Valkyrie."

"I don't imbibe."

"It's rude to be turnin' away demon brew when it's offered to ye."

"Nonetheless, I never drink—"

"And bad luck to boot."

"Bad luck?" Her hand swooped up the shot glass. *A random occurrence that doesn't go your way.* "What can one drink hurt, yeah?" Great, now she was even talking like the oaf.

With her free hand, she collected a napkin, giving them a pained smile as she polished an area on the rim of the glass. To the accompaniment of Jimmy Buffet crooning, "They say you are a snuff queen, honey, I don't think that's true. . . ." she placed the drink to her lips, then turned it up.

The liquid burned like nothing she'd ever ingested, and she coughed, eyes watering. She placed the glass on the bar with its opening down, so they didn't try to refill it.

"How'd that treat ye?" Deshazior asked.

She couldn't yet speak, so she gave the only polite gesture that was applicable: a thumbs-up sign.

Everyone cheered, while someone slapped her on the back, much too hard.

"She'll have another!"

They lined up a second glass.

Oh, no. One down, one up. She would have to drink this and then one more to get to three. . . .

At number six, she felt surprisingly sober and wasn't as miserable as she'd thought she'd be, taking turns doing shots with demons in a sandbar bar. Indeed, she was quite relaxed.

And Deshazior was turning out to be a hoot. The storm demon had been a bona fide pirate, yet he text-messaged on his Sidekick faster than even she could. He was handsome in a grizzled way, and he also had an interest in mathematics since he'd been a navigator.

He'd told her the shots would hit her harder with each hour of the night. Holly was strangely looking forward to it.

She squinted at the Budweiser wall clock. Forty minutes had passed. Get in and get out, Cade had said.

"What is taking him so long?" she absently murmured.

A few demons smirked, and one said, "Imatra's a demanding one."

Demanding? *We're here for directions.* What did being demanding have to do with how long Cade was taking with the gorgeous demoness?

She scratched her head, got aggravated with her falling bun, yanked it down.

Her eyes widened. *Holly, you're an idiot.* Two demons in a back room, with their three-times-a-day needs . . .

"And it ain't like Cadeon the Kingmaker's not up for the challenge," another said.

Cadeon was back there having sex with Imatra.

All of the sudden, Holly understood why people cursed. Sometimes the emotion inside couldn't be vented with any known combination of tame words.

At least he was right about one thing. She *was* a preachy tight-ass and a hypocrite—because as she sat here getting increasingly *drunk*, all she wanted to do was utter the vilest oaths she could come up with.

He was an untrustworthy demon. She knew that. What had she been thinking even to imagine more with him?

Earlier, just before Imatra and Cadeon had gone back to her room, Imatra had flashed Holly that superior look, as if she'd taken something from her. In fact, Imatra had given her something.

Perspective where Cadeon was concerned.

Holly liked things ordered. Cadeon's bedding a sexy demoness the same night he'd made a play for Holly forever removed him from her consideration. By this act, he'd been nullified.

Yes. She'd wanted not to be tempted. To be unafraid that she might forsake her old life.

No demon, no temptation, no dark side.

Pasting a smile on her face, she asked the group, "Whose turn is it?"

19

I'm only here for business, dove," Cade said when Imatra poured drinks for them.

"You know it's bad luck to turn down demon brew. And it's rude to keep your sword on, like we're enemies."

He took the glass, none too subtly glancing at his watch. Ten minutes had already dragged past as she'd asked questions about the other factions out for Holly.

"Just need my directions, and I'll be off."

Cade couldn't imagine how Holly was faring out there. But he also had confidence in her, assured that she'd use that head of hers to stay out of trouble. He'd been impressed at the good job she'd done masking her amazement in the face of so many new Lorekind.

There'd been fey, demons, and Lykae, but fortunately, there were no Valkyrie. He knew all his plans could come tumbling down the minute she found out there was no turning back to human.

"Why the rush, Cade? Would it be so terrible to have a drink or two with me?" Imatra let her robe slink down her shoulder.

Cade believed most would think Imatra was beautiful, but he found her overblown and lacking compared to his halfling. "My asset's out there in a roomful of demons. She was human two days ago. There's a time element here."

"No one would dare hurt her."

No, but they might frighten her. "Then I'm keen to get to the next checkpoint, which should please your master."

"He wishes to inquire about the health of the Vessel."

Cade hated to hear Holly talked about that way, so impersonally. Groot would never see past what she could provide to discover what she was like.

"Holly's fine."

"We didn't expect you to be traveling alone with her."

"Wouldn't be. 'Cept for the fact that Groot and Omort's sister Sabine, that little bitch, captured my brother."

"We hadn't known if you were aware of that."

The idea of Rydstrom's imprisonment seethed inside Cade, but he strove to block it out, realizing that negotiating this checkpoint might not be as simple as he'd anticipated. Imatra seemed capricious. She could make trouble. He didn't want to blow this deal because he got impatient with her.

Imatra said, "I suppose everyone will know soon enough with the way Sabine's been bragging about her new plaything."

Cade ground his teeth. "Where is Rydstrom?"

"You expect me to tell you when you won't even take off your sword or share a drink in politeness?"

He dutifully shrugged from his sword sheath, laying it on a chair, then lifted his glass.

With a pleased smile, she sat on the edge of her desk, making sure the slit in her skirt rode up to her hip. This female was trying to be sexy—it was her whole persona, but it wasn't natural. She had to work at it.

And she still couldn't hold a candle to Holly, who couldn't care less if males found her attractive.

"Where's my brother, Imatra?"

"Likely in Tornin, but we can't say for certain. I'm sure more information will come to us—information we might share if this transaction goes smoothly."

"Why wouldn't it?"

"How can we know you won't sleep with the Vessel?" Imatra asked.

Good question. "The same way my clients have known I'd never fuck with whatever asset they've entrusted to me. Bad for future business. Besides, the chit is absolutely not my standard fare." My *standard fare was shite compared to Holly*.

The demoness studied him, as if determining whether he were lying. Were they suspicious? If so, how? No one but Rydstrom, Nïx, and Rök knew what Holly was to him.

"If you decide to get clever and try to have the sword *and* the girl, you will fail," Imatra said. "First of all, Groot is an incredibly strong mind-reader. You might be able to block his probes, but she'd have no chance. Secondly, the exchange will be made within Groot's fortress, which is mystickally protected, rigged with traps, and guarded by revenants. A forest of Wendigo surround it. You'll get her killed if she runs with you."

Cade hadn't realized until this very second that trying for the sword and for Holly had been an option in the back of his mind.

A favored one.

Now he felt his hopes plummeting.

"A lot of obstacles," Cade agreed. "How can I be sure that I'll even get out alive?"

"Groot has vowed to the Lore that you'll have safe

passage. If you vow as well that you will never reveal his location."

Swearing to the Lore was the most abiding vow an immortal could make. Even an evil sorcerer would feel compelled to keep it. "I vow it."

"Also, my master wants the Vessel fertile for immediate breeding. You have to ensure she continues eating," Imatra said, testing him, analyzing his reaction.

Cade just stopped himself from gritting his teeth. "Not here to play nursemaid."

"If she's not in the condition he wants her, then maybe your sword won't be as you'd prefer it."

Bugger all. "The *Vessel* has a mind of her own, but I'll give it a go with the food."

"One more thing—if she's not there by midnight on the next full moon, the sword will be tossed back into the forge, lost forever."

Cade had heard that Groot possessed a forge of unearthly heat in his hidden fortress. "He wouldn't want to give it to someone else who might kill his brother for him?"

"The weapon was forged for one of the Woede," she answered. "It would be useless to another."

"Understood. Now, if you don't mind, I'd like the second set of directions."

"I'll tell you . . . but only after you kiss me."

He narrowed his eyes, anger simmering. "Groot wouldn't like you imposing conditions to stymie me."

"He also wouldn't like to think that you and the Vessel are becoming involved." She slipped off her robe completely to pool on the floor. "Would it be a chore to kiss me, Cadeon?"

As a matter of fact, yes. Before he'd met Holly, this type of blowsy female would have appealed to him. He'd have kissed her and done a good deal more.

Now he'd only kiss her if he had to.

Had to? There was no future with Holly, and the sooner he got that into his head, the better. "Fine, dove," he grated. "A kiss for my directions."

"Just join me over here," she said, slinking to the bed, tossing the cover down with a practiced, sensual smile.

"None doing, Imatra." He grabbed her hand, pulling her back.

"So aggressive," she purred. "We'll have to do it standing, then."

"Whatever." He bent down and kissed her.

And it left him cold.

I better get used to this, he thought as he went through the motions. Cold is all he'd ever feel again without his own female—

"Excuse me," Holly said from the doorway. He broke away from Imatra. But Holly had seen.

His heart thundered as her gaze flickered over the unmade bed, then over Imatra's robe on the floor and his sword laid on a chair.

Ah, fuck. Now I've done it. His fated female had seen him kissing another. He'd never heard of this happening to a male of his kind. Because no one was this stupid.

But I can't have her anyway!

"I'd really like to get back to the hotel, but I don't wish to interrupt you two," Holly said breezily. She wasn't taken aback—or upset—whatsoever. The easy confidence was in force. Even Imatra seemed surprised. "Cadeon, I'll just catch a ride." She turned toward the door.

"Catch a ride?" he said in disbelief, striding the distance between them to snare her wrist. "Who the hell is going to give you a ride?"

Just then a chorus of males called that it was the Valkyrie's turn to do another shooter.

Her hair was free and curling about her shoulders, her glasses in her pocket. Her cheeks were pink from alcohol. Under his breath, he said, "Why's your hair down?"

"Because I'm in a bar?"

"You're drunk."

"You're astute. Now, really, I didn't want to disturb you. Just letting you know that I'm leaving."

Imatra donned her robe, straightening her clothes in an exaggerated manner. The bitch was trying to make it look like they'd slept together, and he couldn't deny it without appearing to give a damn about Holly.

"You're going with me," he told Holly, frowning at how utterly she *didn't* care about what she'd seen.

He'd thought she'd been attracted to him. Maybe even a bit proprietary after they'd kissed.

"Fine. I'll be waiting outside." With her little heels clicking on the rough-hewn floor, she sauntered out, leaving him confounded.

"I wondered about you two," Imatra said. "Now I can clearly see that Groot has nothing to worry about. You couldn't be more beneath her notice." Somehow the demoness had known Cade felt something for Holly and had suspected the reverse as well.

Then she'd been proven wrong by Holly's indifference.

"The directions?" he prompted.

"You'll be heading to Michigan."

"The *exact* directions?"

"In time, demon . . . One more drink first."

Cade heard male cheers as Holly entered the bar again. It was everything he could do not to charge out there and start brawling.

When Holly returned, Deshazior pulled out the seat next to him for her. With his brows raised in question, he made an okay sign and ran his other forefinger through it.

"Oh, yeah," she said, still unsteady. Just as she'd expected, Cadeon had been back there bedding Imatra, who'd relished being caught, giving her that superior look again.

No, this world wasn't for Holly.

But drinking might be. Secure in the knowledge that she wouldn't be led astray again, she decided to enjoy this very temporary vacation. She *would* get her old life back—ergo, she could do shots with demons in this new one for a bit.

"Did you see anything good?" Deshazior asked in a hopeful tone.

"No, I believe they were just finishing up."

"You think they'd only be doffing for a couple of rounds? I heard that Cadeon's a ladies' man."

"Oh, really?" she asked, her tone bored.

"I'm surprised he hasn't been sniffing around you," he said. "Demons love Valkyrie."

"Ah, but do Valkyrie love demons?"

"Aye. 'Cause we're the only ones ye won't kill in bedsport."

High-fives got thrown all around for that one. She forced a smile. Funny that they would touch on a fact that she'd just tonight put together for herself.

Afraid Deshazior would see something in her expression that surely wasn't there anyway, she asked, "Do you have a dollar for music?"

He handed her some currency she'd never seen, and she scuffed to the jukebox. Her mood improved exponentially when she found a Stevie Ray Vaughan album on tap.

This time when she returned, Deshazior patted his *lap* for her to sit. He wasn't hard on the eyes, even with his huge horns. She considered what the old Holly would do.

Determined to enjoy this bizarre night, she did the opposite, delighting the big demon. . . .

When Cadeon finally emerged from Imatra's lair, she was perched on Deshazior's knee, whispering in his ear, swaying to "Pride and Joy."

Her glasses were on Deshazior's nose, she believed she was wearing the pirate's sword belt, and she had a sinking suspicion that one of the smaller male demons was sitting on the floor beside her, lovingly rubbing his face against her free hand.

Cadeon's wide jaw bunched at the sides, and his eyes flooded with black.

In the background, Stevie sang, "You mess with her you'll see a man get mean."

20

My female's in another male's lap, her lips to his ear. . . .

Deshazior noticed him and jerked his chin in greeting.

And I can't kill him. The storm demon had made no move of aggression. Their breeds weren't at war. Hell, Cade thought he'd gotten drunk with him before.

If Cade did anything, everyone would know it was over a female. Through gritted teeth, he told her, "Up—now." She'd seen him kissing another and had seemed almost amused. Cade had merely seen her flirting with another, and he wanted to slaughter something.

"Problem, Cadeon?" Deshazior asked, studying Cade's face.

"That's my charge, and we're leaving."

"I'm going, I'm going." Holly stood unsteadily, removing a sword belt from her waist. Once she'd collected her glasses from Deshazior, she briefly patted his horns.

More than one male groaned, while she was oblivious, having no idea that for a demon, she might as well have fondled his crotch. "Perhaps I need one for the road—"

Cade hauled her over his shoulder. "Party's over, pet."

The others eyed him as if he was crazy for manhandling a Valkyrie, yet instead of growing furious, Holly blew her entourage loud kisses with both hands all the way out. "Mwah! Text me, Desh!"

* * *

"Cadeon, where are we headed?" she asked once they were back on the road, cruising down a dark, isolated highway.

He'd been silent for miles. As if *he* were mad at *her*. Without a word, he handed her a slip of paper that read:

The Laughing Lady Bridge on the Bloodwater River, Michigan's Upper Peninsula. A contact will be on the bridge at midnight on three consecutive nights beginning Friday.

"What the hell were you doing in there?" Cadeon finally said.

"I was just having fun while you were in the back, doffing Imatra."

"I don't have to explain myself to you."

"Certainly not." Leaning her head against the window, Holly gazed up at the sky. *Stars*. Brighter than any she'd seen in Orleans Parish in decades. *Neat*.

Cadeon said, "It's not like we have some kind of arrangement between us."

"No, indeed."

"What is this?" he demanded. "Some kind of reverse psychology?"

She sighed. "Cadeon, is it so incomprehensible that I'm not upset about this, because I'm not interested in you like that?"

"That's bullshite. You know there's an attraction between us."

"Attraction? You're kidding, right? I have *hypersensitivity*. You diagnosed it. Seems I'm not as discerning as usual. Even you can start to look like an option."

"Even *me*? What the hell does that mean? Women don't find me hard on the eyes."

"Nor conceited." His words brought to mind what the others had said about Cadeon—the ladies' man. "Those are women who probably have a thing for horns and fangs. I don't."

With his brows drawn, he rubbed a palm over one his horns, seemed to catch himself doing it, then yanked his hand down. "Don't like horns, huh? You were tickling *Desh*'s like there was no tomorrow. For future reference, you might as well have been giving him a hand shandy."

She didn't know what that term meant, but it sounded *bad*. "How was I supposed to know that? It's not like that little nugget of information was in *The Book of Lore*. And you're one to criticize my behavior in the tavern, Saint Cadeon."

"Damn it, Holly, it's not what it looked like back there with Imatra."

"I really don't want to hear your defense when there hasn't been an offense. I'm not really concerned about what it looked like. None of my business."

"Even after we just kissed last—"

"The kiss that I didn't want and told you we'd never repeat?" She frowned as a wave of dizziness washed over her.

"Do you not wonder *why* I would kiss you last night and then her tonight?" As if that was all he'd done.

"Because you're *a male*?" She shrugged. "Maybe you're like a lion in a pride, wanting any available female you see."

* * *

"She told me she wouldn't give me the bloody directions until I did it!"

"And that took an hour?" Holly said with more feeling. But then Cade realized she was laughing at him.

"An hour? You're drunk. . . ." He trailed off as he glanced at the dash clock. His brows drew together. "That witch! She must have slowed time in her room."

Now Holly laughed outright. "Slowed time. In her room." She hummed the tune from *The Twilight Zone*. "Just drop it. I don't care."

"I'd expect you to feel a shade proprietary after our kiss last night."

"I wouldn't feel proprietary, just as you wouldn't that I was flirting with Desh."

"*Desh.*" He seethed for long moments. "Your boyfriend's at a conference, you were kissing me last night and damn near handling me just a few hours ago, and then you were getting drunk and hanging all over yet another male. Lot of loyalty there."

"You pinned me. The disloyal virgin. Playing fast and loose."

"Why are you smiling?"

"Because I'm enjoying my first time ever being tipsy."

"That's what this is about," he said, relaxing somewhat. "When you sober up, you're going to be pissed at me."

She pinched her forehead and muttered, "Now I fully comprehend the term *buzz kill*. I never did before."

"You're calling me a—oh, now I've heard it all! The schoolmarm's calling the demon a buzz kill."

"Schoolmarm? Ha! You just dated yourself again!"

Cade felt compelled to do something to shake Holly up. He could stand anything but this indifference.

He parked the car on the side of the road, then reached for her, cupping her face and drawing her to him. But she shoved at him. Hard.

Valkyrie strength—definitely growing.

"Don't you dare," she bit out, her eyes flashing silver. "If I wanted to taste Imatra's lips, then I would have kissed her myself."

"Fine." He drew back. "I don't give a shite if you believe me or not." Shoving the car into gear, he sped off once more. . . .

After an hour of silence, she murmured, "Slow down."

"No. We've got time to make up."

"Cadeon, slow down. I don't feel s'good."

"How many bloody shots did you have? Two? Three?"

She gave a shaky laugh. "Bit higher."

"Did they tell you it takes a while to hit?"

"They did, indeed."

"Holly, how many?"

"I can say . . . with absolute certainty that the number was an integer, a multiple of three, and greater than or equal to nine—" Her head slumped forward.

It had taken Cade two uneasy hours to find even a somewhat decent hotel to stay in. Holly had been passed out, curled on her side in the seat, the entire time.

Just as he was carrying her to their new room, she blinked open her eyes, staring up at him.

So pretty. His anger had already ebbed, and now that mere look of hers made his heart punch his chest. He sighed. "Baby, after nine shots, you're going to be completely legless—"

She gave a moan. "I'm going to . . . *lose my legs*?"

He couldn't help but grin at her woeful tone. "You're going to be drunk, blotto."

When he set her on the bed, she lay back, but immediately cried, "Oh, God, it's spinning!"

He hurriedly dragged her leg to the side so she could touch her toe to the carpet. "Better?"

After a few moments, she murmured, "Better."

"Ah, the things I could teach you. Now I'm going to undress you for bed."

"I can do it," she slurred, appearing to reach for the top button of her sweater, instead shoving her knuckle in her eye. "Yow! That *hurt*."

"Let me do it—I won't look."

In a solemn tone, she said, "Yes, you will."

"Yeah, you're probably right." He peeled off her sweater. "But it's nothing I haven't seen before. . . ."

Oh, but it *was*, he realized by the time he'd gotten her down to her stockings and her black lacy underwear. He'd never seen anything like this in all his life. He exhaled a stunned breath, muttering, "*Ah, gods, halfling, I could come just looking at you*."

"Hmm? What'd you say?"

She was exquisite in her silky lingerie and thigh-highs. All that swimming had done her body so damned right.

Her arms and legs were toned, but she'd retained her softness. Her hips flared from her tiny waist. Creamy breasts spilled over that wicked half-cup bra.

She had a sexpot figure and would for the rest of her immortal life; he wanted to howl with pleasure just to be gaping at it. He reached for her breasts, his hands itching to knead them—

"Didya say something, Cadeon?" she asked softly.

He drew back his hands, making white-knuckled fists. Once more, he reached for her, again drawing back. He paced, struggling to blunt his hunger. His fantasy woman was laid out in the bed like an offering in silk—and he couldn't touch her.

Then he narrowed his eyes. If he wasn't going to take advantage of her, he'd at least get some answers. "Yeah, pet. Got a question for you. . . ."

21

"*Good morning, sunshine!*" Cadeon boomed by her ear.

Holly shot up, immediately clutching her head with a groan.

"Or good evening, rather," he said. "I let you sleep as long as I could, but we're on a schedule, you understand. And some of us like to keep a regimented schedule."

"Oh, God. I'm in hell."

"I've got the night all planned out. You're going to shower because you smell like a cask of hundred-proof, and then we're going to train. Once on the road, you're going to look up our destination. If you're not too hung over. Here, drink this." He opened a bottle of Gatorade, obviously giving care not to touch the rim.

She squinted at the bottle, then at her hands, which were both reaching for the drink. Soon she was chugging it down.

"Eat these," he said, handing her an unopened box of regular Saltine crackers, which she tore into.

For some reason, at that moment Gatorade and Saltines were *sublime*.

She began to feel better in minutes. "Thank you."

"I live a life of service. Speaking of which, do you need any help getting dressed? Like you did getting undressed?"

At his words, all the events from the night before flashed in her mind, and her eyes went wide.

Not only had Cadeon been with Imatra last night, he'd also taken advantage of Holly's first bout of drunkenness.

Through the haze of alcohol, she remembered him questioning her, coaxing answers from her about all kinds of things—*private* things. His voice had been so lulling, his demeanor relaxed.

Now she realized she'd been played.

Her face flamed as she recalled her disclosures: She didn't touch herself ever—because she swam laps when the need got too strong, or else she had vivid dreams and would wake up right in the middle of . . . she thought he'd actually supplied the word *coming*.

Shaming, but true. She'd often dreamed of vigorous sex to the point of physical reaction. . . .

Her hands clenched, anger warring with her abject embarrassment. And then, she'd admitted to him that she was curious about sex, but that any intimate situation she'd been in had always ended up with her hurting someone.

She shook her head hard. His behavior was beyond low. He hadn't taken advantage of her body, but of her mind—

He began drawing the cover off of her. "Fine, halfling, I'll help."

She yanked at the top sheet, irritably wrapping it around herself as she stumbled to her feet.

"Okay, now you *really* don't need to do that blushing virgin bit anymore—I got to ogle your body at my leisure for hours. Matter of fact, I had so long, I could have painted you, instead of just taking pictures with my satphone." He held up his phone with a wink.

"I loathe you," she said, precariously bending to collect

her toiletries and clothes. As she headed for the bathroom, she gave him the evilest eye she could muster. . . .

A long hot shower cleared much of the cobwebs from her head. And her stomach had settled. Once she emerged from the bathroom dressed for the day, she felt like a human being again.

She sighed. *Or not*. She couldn't truly say.

"How're you doing?" he asked.

"I'm perfectly fine." *I think I'm beginning to hate you. Which is good. I should be happy about that. It'll help me keep my eye on the prize*.

"You're pissed about last night."

"Shouldn't I be? You took advantage of me."

"I didn't touch you!"

"You know that's not what I'm talking about," she snapped. "You interrogated me."

"You're angry that I happened to ask you some questions when you happened to be drunk? I can't figure it. But that doesn't matter. At least you'll be jacked up for training time."

"What is this training you keep talking about?"

"I need to teach you how to fight. Sparring, self-defense." When she made no move to cooperate, he said, "Come on, it'll be fun."

She raised her brows. "I do believe I took down a dozen demons all by myself."

"You said yourself that you were in a rage. What if you don't go into that state again? Or what if you want to fight someone off without killing him? As long as your life's in danger, you need to be preparing."

Sometimes she found herself forgetting that assassins wanted to murder her. "Would this involve hitting you?"

"Maybe."

Nothing could be more compelling to her right now. "Then I'm in. What do you want me to do?"

"Take off your heels."

Once she'd removed her shoes, he motioned for her to stand facing him. "If you take nothing else away from what I'm about to teach you, remember two things: Never hesitate. If the instinct to strike is there, then do it. And second, don't be ashamed to run if you're outnumbered—but only if you think you can get away. Otherwise you're just wasting everyone's time and wearing yourself out."

She shrugged. "Okay."

"Now, how would you engage me if we were facing off? Say you had to get past me or you die."

"I'd try to hit you?"

"Unless you're battling another chick—which I wouldn't mind seeing if mud were involved—you shouldn't punch at all."

She pursed her lips. "I watch TV. What would a fight be without punches?"

"Okay, slug a haymaker at me." At her frown, he said, "You watch TV but *never* boxing? Forget it. A haymaker is an all-out, full-force hit."

The idea of battering his arrogant face had her clenching her hand in a fist.

"Do it now! Hit now—"

She did, aiming for his face; he turned so that the blow landed against his horn.

"Ow! That was unfair!"

"Don't ever strike a demon above the throat. He's going to use his horns in combat. And some of them can emit a poison from the ends."

"Can you?"

"Yeah, but only when I'm in complete rage form."

"So what you're saying is that you're toxic, and you can even be poisonous, too?"

He gave her an unamused look, then continued, "Even with other species, you should never go for the head. Think about it—most of it is covered by hard bone. The odds of hitting vulnerable areas like the mouth or nose aren't good. And if you land a hit anywhere else but those two spots, you'll likely hurt your hand more than your opponent. But that doesn't mean you can't attack the face. You can gouge eyes out, and rake your claws down a foe's cheek. Or you can give him a 'Glasgow kiss.' "

"What's that?"

"A head-butt. Say I've got your arms wrapped tight at your sides, and you can't get free. Just snap your head forward, aiming your forehead for the bridge of your enemy's nose."

"What about the old standby of kicking a guy in the groin?"

"Try it."

Love to . . . Without warning, she launched a kick. He caught her foot, forcing her to hop for balance.

"Cadeon!" she cried, and he finally released her.

"I could have tossed you backward. If you're going for the groin, use your hands. It only takes a little force to do a lot of damage there. And most males won't expect a small female to go for a grab. Now try to hit my torso. Charge me! Now! Do it!"

She did, but he snatched her hand. Using her momentum, he spun her around, looping his arm around her neck.

"That's all it would take, Holly. Your adversary could break your neck."

They were both breathing heavy, his forearm easing down to her breasts. She narrowed her eyes. He'd done this entire sparring scenario just to get her in a position like this.

At that instant, something snapped. Holly had officially had enough of Cadeon's tricks. She'd throw a few of her own.

She relaxed in his arms, acting receptive. As if pleased with her, he pressed his mouth to her neck. He was already growing hard against her.

Yet just last night, he'd been with another.

Don't think—just let instinct take over? She eased around in his arms. Gazing at his mouth, she whispered, "I want to kiss you."

His eyes widened, then narrowed. "*Holly* . . ." he said in a raspy voice, easing down.

Just before his lips reached hers, she jerked her head back to whip it forward into his nose. A *Glasgow* kiss. Distinct cracking sounded.

With his nose pouring blood, he squeezed her upper arms, "Holly, what the fuck—"

Using all her strength, she hiked her knee up between his legs.

His hands flew to cup his groin as his knees met the ground.

"You're right, Cadeon." She dusted off her hands. "That really *was* fun."

22

You broke my nose *and* my ballocks, and you're the one acting pissed off?" Cade said as he drove down the freeway, noting how nasally his voice sounded.

Without glancing up from her computer, she said, "You're the one who wanted to spar." Her tone was aloof, distinctly uninterested.

"I didn't know I was courting your feminine wrath. And I told you *not* to go for the groin. Doubtful I'll be able to reproduce after your knee-job."

"What will the world be like without little Cadeons to populate it?"

"If you were angry because I asked you some questions then you've gotten me back."

In that uninterested voice, she said, "Revenge is sweet." He'd never seen this side of her.

Yet even considering this animosity, he would still do the same thing again. He'd struck gold in his interrogation, having finally discovered why his female had remained a virgin.

She'd been too afraid of hurting another with her strength and aggression.

He'd also learned how she'd controlled her libido. With punishing swims and wet dreams. Thinking about the latter had even his abused manhood stirring.

"Is this how it's to be the entire trip?" he asked her.

"I simply don't have anything to say to you."

"Well, then I'm just going to talk. And talk. And say my piece. First of all, I didn't sleep with Imatra."

With a sigh, she asked, "Why do you care if I believe you or not?"

"Because if you think I got a leg over with that slag, then the chance of anything sexual with you will be drastically reduced."

Without looking up, she said, "Cadeon, a chance can't be reduced from zero."

"Gods, I love it when you talk mathy to me."

He wasn't going to charm her this time. She faced him with a blank expression.

"All right, so you don't think this is a jesting matter," he said. "I get that. But the fact remains that I didn't tup her."

Strangely enough, Holly had started to have minute doubts. Yes, she'd seen them kissing—which was bad enough, since he'd been making advances toward Holly the same night. But had they actually slept together? What if Imatra truly had withheld the directions?

Holly said, "You might be telling the truth about this, and I might come to believe you. But you're lying about *something*. I can feel it. So be careful what you convince me of."

Had something flashed in his eyes?

Whatever might have been there, he masked it quickly enough. "I don't think I can convince you. Of anything."

Interesting. He's backing down. . . .

"You believe I'm so wicked? I could have taken advantage of you last night, and I didn't."

This made her part her lips. "Do you honestly want credit because you didn't do anything to a helpless female?"

"No! Yes. No, damn it—"

"And you *did* do something to me! You had your petty interrogation, digging for my secrets." Struggling to get a rein on her temper, she said, "Look, we're stuck together for who knows how long. So let's just try to minimize the unpleasantness and get through this."

"Then use your laptop to get online, and look up our next checkpoint."

"Fine." She MapQuested it, saved the results, then Googled it.

"Well, what does it say about the bridge?"

"Officially, it's called the Bloodwater River Bridge. It's a covered bridge that was decommissioned thirty years ago as unsound. Only the locals call it the Laughing Lady, because it's supposed to be haunted."

"Then it probably is."

"You're saying ghosts are real, too?"

"Yeah. They're not of the Lore, though. We have phantoms—kind of the Lore equivalent of a ghost."

"What's the difference?"

"Phantoms can incarnate at will and travel the world. Not stuck in an attic rattling chains and such."

"Ever met a ghost?"

"Never seen one. Nor a phantom, either. They're kind of rare. So what's the haunt that's supposed to be here?"

What wasn't there? "The first death occurred during the construction of the bridge in 1899. A worker fell into one of the wooden casts used to set the bridge's piers. Unfortunately, it was already half filled with liquid cement. Before others could fish him out, he'd sunk deep. It hardened quickly, so the foreman decided to leave the body inside rather than explode the pier. After that, the locals said, the river got hungry for death."

"You mean the town wasn't named Bloodwater River until then?"

"No, it already was—there's a rare clay that turns the water reddish."

"So then what happened?"

"In the early 1900s, a serial killer disposed of bodies there. He murdered thirteen women and threw them off the bridge, allegedly because he wanted to feed the river. He was shot just before he fatally wounded the fourteenth victim."

"How did he kill them?"

This was where it got really creepy. "He chose victims who were sheltered, having dealt with little to no adversity in life. He'd kidnap them from their beds at night, take them down to the bridge, then stab them in the side of the chest or another place that wouldn't kill them. Then he'd tell them that he'd let them go if they could laugh at their situation. If they could stop crying and laugh, then he'd wouldn't slit their throats. Of course, none could. That's why they call it Laughing Lady Bridge."

"And he was shot? That was too easy for him."

"Why would we have to meet someone there specifically?" she asked.

"Don't know. But you shouldn't be afraid. I won't let anything happen to you."

"I'm not afraid. I'm more excited. I've always been interested in the supernatural."

"The supernatural's now the natural, halfling."

"Not for me. Not for long, it isn't. Now, if you don't mind, I have work to do."

And by *work* she meant *spying*—Cadeon had used her computer, having no idea that she had a keystroke program installed that would tell her what anyone had typed on it. *Duh*.

And the program had just finished collecting the data, allowing her to follow all his cyber-tracks.

After he'd looked up sports scores, he'd e-mailed someone with the message, "Pay up, sucker." He'd transferred a hundred thousand dollars to a *checking* account. But at the next entry, she felt an unexpected pang.

The demon mercenary had looked up . . . cluster analysis and extremal combinatorics.

Holly believed he'd had sex with Imatra, and Cade didn't know if he should try to convince his female otherwise. Holly had been bang-on with that "you're lying about *something*" crack.

They passed another car accident, crawling at a snail's pace. The drive from Memphis to northern Michigan was eight hundred miles—they'd gone ten miles in the last hour.

The palpable tension continued to build between them. She wasn't icy toward him, merely indifferent as she worked on her warrior code.

She was just letting him know how inconsequential he was to her. Kind of like the first time they'd met. He could play that game. He would ignore her right back.

He called Rök and checked in. "What's doing?" he asked in Demonish.

"We've followed the lead on the vampires," Rök said. "Tonight, we strike."

"Good news." Holly would be that much safer. "Hey, how long does it take to teach someone how to block mind reading? Could Holly learn in a couple of weeks?"

Demons had the ability naturally. Other Lorekind could be taught.

Rök gave a scoffing laugh. "Try a couple of years."

Once they hung up, Cade was left to his thoughts. *I'm ignoring her*. That stance lasted until she pinched her forehead, looking miserable. "You all right?"

She shrugged.

"Let me guess? Carsick—with a headache?"

She cast him a surprised look.

"You're carsick because you're reading when we're stopping and starting. And your head hurts because you're still trying to use your glasses when your vision has changed."

"I can't concentrate without my glasses."

"Look, let's knock off early tonight. I saw a sign for a mom-and-pop motel in a small town not far ahead."

"But we'll get behind schedule."

"None doing. At this rate, we'll get to the bridge just after midnight and be forced to wait around anyway. Besides, we're near Chicago, and I have some gear I need to pick up tomorrow."

"What kind of gear?"

"You'll see . . ."

23

"You're a masochist, aren't you?" Holly asked when he suggested more training.

"We can work with the sword tonight," he said. Though Cadeon had gotten two adjoining rooms at the motel, he insisted on lying on *her* bed. With his back against the headboard and his legs stretched out, he surfed channels, while she reconfigured anything not bolted down.

"You think I'll need to know how to use a sword before I get changed back?" She could swear he was watching her rather than the pay-per-view he'd been so delighted to find here.

"A lot of factions in the Lore carry them."

"Okay. Fine, let's sword fight."

"Good. Be right back." He rose and exited the room, returning a couple of minutes later with his sword and a broom. After snapping the end off the broom, he tossed the handle atop the bed, presumably for later sparring.

Then, with grave formality, he unsheathed his sword.

"How *old* is that thing? Have you had it carbon dated?"

He looked aghast, as if she'd insulted his grandmother. "Hey, no disrespecting The Sword. Besides, it's only three or four centuries old."

"Only? I would think that technology has improved since then. Why wouldn't you get a new one?"

"I'm on my way to, remember? Try to keep up, halfling."

She glared. "I meant in the last few hundred years."

"If it ain't broke . . . This weapon's saved my life many a time."

"How many have you killed with it?"

A shadow crossed over his face. "Too many." Seeming to give himself a shake, he held it up. "Now this is a double-edged greatsword. It's made to cut through armor and cleave a man in two."

"You really still use one of those?"

"Guns are pretty useless on us, as you saw when I was saving your life like a champ two nights ago." He handed it to her. "It's quite a bit bigger than most swords. So it might be difficult for you to maneuver—"

She easily lifted it with one hand, held it out at eye level to check its lines, then made an effortless circular slash.

"Ah, not too heavy, then. But pay attention to the handle—it's made for you to hold it with both hands, like in a batter's grip." He moved behind her, wrapping his arms around her sides to place her hands. "Like this."

"Are you going to smell my hair again?" she said sharply, irritated that she still reacted to his closeness.

"Can I help that your hair attracts males? Yet you act like it's *my* fault. Now choke up a bit on your grip. That's it. Get a feel for it. We're going to swing it slowly right, then left," he said, guiding her movements.

With each second she grew more comfortable holding the intimidating weapon.

"A little history while you accustom yourself," he said, his mouth right at her ear. "The word *sword* comes from the Old English *sweord*, which comes from the root *swer*, meaning to stab or prick." His voice was as low and rumbling as ever. "*Gladius*, the Latin word for sword, also means penis."

"It does not." She sounded unaccountably breathy.

"Do you want to bet me?" His chin rubbed over the point of her ear, the stubble tickling the sensitive tip, and she had to stifle a shiver.

Against her will, she found herself growing aroused by the heat of his massive body along her back. She could feel the rigid muscles of his torso flexing and relaxing as he moved with her.

"Since the first sword was forged, it's been a symbol of manliness and virility. You can see why when it's upright. Tell me, Holly, as you grip the hilt, does it call to mind anything you've seen recently?"

"Cadeon," she said warningly.

He continued undaunted, "And if the Latin word *sword* means *penis*, then you can imagine that the term for scabbard is its counterpart. That's right, halfling, a *scabbard* is called a *va*—"

"Stop! You're making this up."

"I'm not. If you read Julius Caesar's *De Bello Gallico* in the original Latin, you're in for a laugh, because soldiers are always dropping their *scabbards* or even using their *scabbards* to clod their foes over the head."

Another rasp of his chin over her ear. Did he know it was driving her crazy? Oh, of course he did!

"They say every sword has its perfect scabbard."

She refused to allow him to make even sword fighting sexual. "I'm going to double check everything you're saying."

"Be my guest."

"So you read Julius Caesar?"

"In the original Latin, Holls. Do you like me better now that you know I can read ancient languages?"

"I would have been impressed with proof that you can read at all."

"Sharp-tongued Valkyrie. Now here's your fighting stance. Feet shoulder-width apart." He tapped her ankle with his own to get her to step her foot out more.

"Should I stay on my toes?"

"Good question. Normally, no. To withstand hits, you have to keep your balance—which is more easily done on flat feet. You'd be amazed at how hard another sword can come down—it'll throw you. And to give hard strikes, again, you need both feet firmly on the ground. That said, the Valkyrie fighting style is different than most."

"How?"

"They rely on speed. They can get behind you before you even have time to turn your head. Their swords are usually smaller, rapier-like, made more for thrusting jabs than for striking. If one were to fight me, she'd try to prevent my sword from hitting hers at all. They most often kill with a blow to the back."

"That doesn't seem very sporting." It went against everything she'd been taught—or, at least, that she'd learned from westerns and movies with galactic honor systems.

"Sword fighting in the Lore isn't *sporting*. It's about keeping your head on your shoulders. Okay, now chest up." He placed his palm on her shoulder and pulled back. "Raise the sword in front of your nose and let the tip drop to about forty-five degrees from your face. This is called the middle position. From here you can block blows from the right or the left. Now let's modify this a little." He maneuvered her body so that she was standing with her shoulder in front.

He kept touching her, but she couldn't pinpoint an instance where it was unwarranted.

"If you turn to the side like this, it reduces the visible area of your body, making you a smaller target."

"Are you going to use your stolen broom handle, or not?"

He raised his brows. "You think you're ready to cross swords? Very well."

When he released her to collect the stick, she nearly swayed and was glad he didn't see.

Facing her again, he said, "I'm going to strike, and I want you to block." Raising the stick, he knocked it against the sword, and they began to spar.

As they circled each other, he continued his instruction. "Never hesitate. Never appear nervous. Elbows at your side. Keep compact."

His hits were slow enough that she could block them each time. "Avoid multiple combatants. Like in hand-to-hand, don't be ashamed to run if you're outnumbered."

As they increased in speed, adrenaline began to pump through her.

"Throughout history most sword fights have been decided with the first blow. Not like on TV. Every movement counts."

He was striking faster and faster, but she was still able to parry.

"No, no, no, you could have evaded that strike," he said, just when she'd thought she'd given a particularly good block. "Never block when you can evade. And remember, your surroundings are key. Always keep them in mind. Anything can be a weapon." He tossed a pillow at her, and she sliced it cleanly in two! Tufts of filler floated in the air—

He smacked her bottom hard with his stick. Which *infuriated* her.

"Don't like gettin' spanked? Then keep your eyes on your opponent."

Aggression flared, and she struck out with a yell. He shot out of the way, and the sword cleaved through the bed side table and phone.

Holly's eyes went wide. "Cadeon! I could have killed you! I'm sorry!" When he shrugged, she said, "You don't think this is noteworthy?"

"No. Slaying furniture is *fun*. I'm more concerned about the fact that we're sparring, and you're stopping to *apologize*. Where's the heart of the killer? Where's your merciless side? You're acting like a skirt."

"A . . . *skirt?*" she said in an incredulous tone.

"Hey, here's an idea. If you can draw blood before my premium pay-per-view show comes on in ten minutes, then I'll get you your pills."

She gave him a look that said *it's on*, then launched an attack. He deflected her next blow, but realized that she'd held back so she could strike a second time even faster. *Quick little female*. He barely got out of the way, letting a lamp die for him.

She's going to be one of the greats, he thought, but he said, "Is this all you've got?"

Lips thinned, she slashed diagonally upward with stunning speed; he had to block with his stick—she sliced the end off.

"Oh, dear, did I cut off the *tip* of your *gladius*?"

Cade winced. She was literally out for blood and was growing increasingly enraged. Again and again, they circled, with her striking and him dodging. Finally, he could say, "Your ten minutes are up, halfling. You lose—"

Her sword whistled down, missing his shoulder by millimeters. "Holly, back the hell down. We're done."

Eyes glowing silver, she said, "*I'm* just getting started."

He realized that if he couldn't hurt her, he'd have to fight dirty. When she charged once more, he spun around to get behind her. He lightly kicked the back of her knee, sending her off balance.

"Ooh!" Even as she staggered she swung a roundhouse slash. A picture on the wall fell victim.

"*Now*, are you done—"

Banging on the door sounded. A deep voice outside said, "Open up, this is the police."

Her face went white, her jaw slackening. The sword dipped in her limp hand. "*Oh, my God!*" she whispered. "What are we going to do?"

Cade himself was about to have a ball with this. "Duuude," he murmured. "You are going-to-*jail*."

24

What do you mean?" she cried.

"Jail, the big house, the two-legged zoo—"

"I know that! But why am *I* going there?"

Cade answered, "Your eyes are silver. And that demon brew gels in your blood *for days*. As soon as the cops break down the door, and see you amidst this destruction, you're off to roll call, baby."

"Oh, God, oh, God! I've never even had a speeding ticket!" Biting her claws, she said, "This is all your fault! You started it!" Her panicked gaze darted around the room. "Quick! Help me clean up—"

More banging.

"No time, Holly. But you know, I could probably fix this."

"How?"

"You let me worry about that."

He'd lived nine hundred years—surely he'd learned what to do in situations like this. *Yes, Cadeon will take care of this*. She gave him a grateful look.

"But you have to do something for me as well."

Her face fell. "It figures that you'd put a condition on this. What do you want?"

"You have to watch TV with me, a movie of my choice."

Where was the harm in that? She loved . . . "Oh! You mean one of *those* movies!" He'd told her he would get her to watch one before the trip was over. "Never, Cadeon. Not in a million years."

"Even when I can make this all go away?"

From outside, the policeman said, "Open up! We've been getting noise complaints."

"Oh, God!" she whispered. "One scene. I'll watch just one scene. If you can take care of this."

"Deal." He turned for his room, collecting his hat and an envelope from his duffle bag. At the doorway between their rooms, he said, "Try not to break the law again before I get back," then shut the door.

When she heard him exiting from his front door, she realized he was going to act as if he were merely a neighbor. Clever demon . . .

But what if something went wrong? What if they still demanded to see the room? She surveyed the debris in abject fear.

How can I get rid of the evidence?

Hitting on an idea, she began dismantling the remains of the table, breaking off legs and stuffing the pieces under the bed. Broken lamps and sliced pillows joined the collection.

Thirty nerve-shattering minutes passed before Cadeon returned. "What happened? Tell me!"

"Everything's taken care of."

She frowned. "You smell like beer."

He rolled his eyes. "Oh, yeah, Holly, like me and the cop were downing a beer together."

Of course, he and the cop had completely been downing a beer together.

They'd sat in a booth in the motel's lounge as Cade

spun tales that the man didn't hear because he was too busy staring at the stack of cash Cade offered him. The small town cop seemed an honest enough guy, but he had five kids and Christmas was coming. What was he supposed to do?

"No one's going to want to come in?" Holly asked.

He shook his head. "Not unless you start back up again. The room looks great, by the way." It was cleaner than when they'd first come—except now it had less furniture. "So, I did my part, Holls. Looks like it's showtime."

"I can't believe you are going to make me watch something I'm opposed to."

"You put it down, but you've never viewed it? The bra-burner's a tad hypocritical, no?"

"Though I've not yet tried drinking acid, I still put it down. And don't call me a bra-burner! There's no need to make fun of my feminism."

"First of all, I'm not *making* fun—I'm *poking* fun. And second of all, I'm doing it to your face."

"What does that mean?"

"If we bandy the subject, at least you know where I stand and you get a chance to persuade me to your way of thinking. Can you say the same about the other men in your life? The *yes men*?"

She narrowed her eyes. "Meaning Tim."

"He's not as perfect as you like to think." Naturally, Cade despised him with a deep and virulent hatred. But Cade had also gotten the feeling that Tim wasn't the lapdog he appeared to be.

"No, maybe he's not perfect," she said. "But I bet he doesn't consider women to be *tarts*, who should be in a man's bed twenty-four hours a day."

"I was jesting about that. Mainly. Almost totally."

She glared.

"For the record, male Lorekind have higher opinions of females than human males do. The playing field's more equal in our world."

"Ha! I find it hard to believe that men who've lived for centuries—and might even be *medieval*—believe in equality more than a human male raised in the Madonna era."

"The Lore is home of the Valkyrie, Furiae, Witches, and Sirenae. You underestimate females, and you find your balls nailed to the wall."

As she digested that information, he said, "You're not going to distract me from this. We had a deal."

"Made under duress. Did you ever think that I might be morally opposed to watching pornography?"

He snorted. "You're not the good girl you used to be. You get drunk and carouse with demons, sitting on their laps and giving them horn jobs in front of an audience. You went rock star on this poor mom-and-pop motel room. And just last night, you got me to show you my goods, though I was vulnerable and weak from a bullet wound." He shook his head sadly. "Face it, Holly, you're a *bad girl.*"

Her lips parted. Though his version of events was utterly skewed, the fact remained that all that had taken place to some degree.

He patted the bed so arrogantly. "I believe we had a date. Come on, this is just porn lite. If it costs six-ninety-nine, it's lite. Ah, the things I could teach you, halfling."

She gritted her teeth and sat on the bed as far away from him as possible. With her hands in her lap, she said, "Fine. I owe you one scene. . . ."

It started innocently enough. An attractive couple

began undressing each other while kissing. *I can handle this*.

But her face flamed when they were naked and stroking each other between the legs. Her brows drew together at how *hard* they touched. Surely that would have to be painful. . . .

By the time the man entered the woman, Holly's mouth was dry, her claws were curled, and she couldn't seem to get enough air.

Her scrambled brain was screaming *Turn away! Turn away now!* Just when she forced herself to close her eyes, the demon said, "Ah-ah, Holly."

She quickly faced him, and frowned. Cadeon hadn't been watching the movie.

His gaze was rapt on her.

"You're not even looking at it!"

"I'm a male—I'm going to watch whatever turns me on the most. . . ." As they stared at each other, moans, groans, and then finally yells sounded as the couple finished.

Once the scene had ended at last, Holly was wondering how she would ever be the same, but she refused to let him know how this had affected her.

"Well, that certainly was enlightening." Feigning a yawn, she stood, heading for her room.

"You sure you don't want to stay? *Buxom Babes: Volume Eight* is on after this."

"I'm going to have to pass." She closed and locked her door behind her, knowing that wouldn't keep him out if he wanted in.

And right now, if the demon wanted in, would she truly want to keep him out?

She flattened herself against the wall, digging her curling claws into the wallpaper.

25

Holly shot up in bed with a cry, clutching shredded sheets to her chest. She gazed around the room in confusion, surprised to discover what she'd just experienced was a dream.

The most erotic one she'd ever had. And yet it hadn't sent her over the edge.

She'd dreamed that the sword fight had ended with Cadeon tossing her to the bed and stripping off her clothes, then his own. Like the man in the film, he'd guided his erection between her legs, then held himself above her on straightened arms with his muscles bulging.

Once he'd entered her, he'd worked his hips, slow at first, but gradually building speed and power, until he was plunging inside her like a piston. She'd grown closer and closer under the onslaught of his teeth-clattering thrusts. . . .

Then she'd awakened.

Need to go swimming. Must find a pool. But she was in the north, in winter!

Here she was in this vulnerable state, and a pornophile demon lay in wait in the next room. She clambered to her feet, snatching up the ruined sheets to stuff them under the bed with the rest of the items she'd destroyed.

After making up the coverlet, she hurried to the bathroom to take a freezing shower. Yet even after she was dressed, she was still shaking, her hand tremulous as she tried to brush her hair. She repeatedly attempted to effect her perfect chignon. And failed.

She couldn't control her hair, her body, or her thoughts.

And the lightning firing outside seemed to mock her efforts.

Cade had woken, thrusting against the sheets, hard as rock for her.

The halfling's going to be the death of me. . . .

With a groan, he rose, staggering to the bathroom for a steaming shower. Under the water, he recalled her reactions last night as she'd observed people having sex for the first time.

As her eyes had gradually grown wider, her breaths had shallowed, making her breasts rise and fall until his hands itched to knead them.

Leaning his head to rest on his forearm against the tile, he gripped himself and began to stroke.

Her nipples had jutted so temptingly beneath her sweater, begging for him to suck—

A clap of thunder boomed outside. He shot upright when the lights surged on and off. His skin pricked, as if from electrical energy. *Holly . . .*

Dashing from the shower, he shook out his hair as he hauled on jeans. He stumbled toward the door between their rooms, barely able to fasten his fly over his shaft. After breaking the lock and entering, he found her dressed, sitting on the side of the made-up bed.

She seemed dazed, staring at nothing. Had she had one of *those* dreams? Where she woke up coming?

From her shaky breaths, it seemed his female hadn't got all the way there. . . .

He stifled a groan. She was in discomfort, aching for what he would easily kill to give her.

He moved in front of her and helped her to her feet. "You're trembling." He grazed the backs of his fingers over her cheekbone. Her breaths quickened from just that touch. "Ah, pet, you're about to go off just standing here."

She shook her head hard, eyes wide and flickering from violet to silver. Her tongue rubbed over one of her tiny fangs.

"Lie to me, but don't lie to yourself."

"This is why I need my pills, Cadeon!"

"That's not what you need." His instinctive drive was to use his body to pleasure hers, but he couldn't. As if she'd ever allow him to, anyway.

What would she allow?

"You're attracted to me, and you know I sure as hell am attracted to you. So I suggest we help each other out."

"What do you mean by *help*?"

Cadeon answered, "Not having sex, just giving each other a hand when one or the other needs it."

"Y-you're assuming a lot. *I* don't need release multiple times a day," she said, lifting her chin. "I'll be fine."

"Bullshite. You need it as bad as I do."

"That's simply not true. I don't even like you."

"You don't have to like me."

True. It's because he's such a cad that I can enjoy him. Holly already knew better than to feel more for him. She could just use him as he'd proposed that first night.

He began to maneuver her against the wall. And she let him.

No, this is madness. I would never think this way. . . . "It'd be wrong. I'd betray my boyfriend."

Cadeon laid his hand on the wall beside her head, leaning in. "Look at it this way. We can both release some pressure or we'll blow." At her ear, he murmured, "And when that happens, I'll be fucking you so hard to put out the fire. And you'll be loving it. When you moan my name, *then* you'll be betraying him." He pulled back, leaving her breathless—and dying of curiosity.

"Exactly how would we . . . do this?"

"You could stroke me off, and I could finger you."

She stifled a gasp at his coarse language, reminding herself that this was a very old *demon*.

If they did what he'd suggested, then he would see her naked, would touch her sex. A first.

Am I ready for this? No! No matter how much she might *want* to be ready. "You act as if we don't have control of ourselves."

He grazed one of her throbbing nipples, and she cried out.

"Does that sound like a female in control of her body? You need it so bad I could bring you off in three minutes."

She gave a shaky laugh at the absurdity of that. Then, of course, her mind seized on it. He was saying he could make her orgasm in one hundred and eighty seconds.

What if he . . . could? What would it be like to be brought to climax by another?

But if he did it to her, she'd only want it from him again and again. It was simple human nature.

I'm not quite human.

"Got you thinking about it, didn't I?" *So smug.*

"You know full well that you can't do it in three minutes. You're just saying that to initiate the contact and seduce me to do more."

"Then bet me. What do you want to win? Risk the touching. Get the reward."

Reward? Coincidentally, she needed something very badly. She hesitated, then said, "You let me refill my meds."

"Holly, you don't still want the pills—"

"And you have to go a week without cursing. Those are my terms. Take them or leave them."

"Fine. And when you lose, you have to go a week without panties. And you have to use your hands on me till I come, too."

The thought of fondling him till his big body shuddered and his semen released made her shiver.

No, that's not why she would do this—she would do it for her medicine. With a swallow, she said, "Would I have to be naked?"

He leaned in over her, surrounding her with his heat. "Not completely. Just enough that I could suckle your breasts and get my hand between your legs."

His mere words excited her. "I'll take the bet." *Wait . . .* "How will we know how much time has passed?"

He removed his dive watch. "It's got an alarm." He fiddled with it. "There. It's set to count down. You can start it," he said, handing it to her. "But we don't start counting till I have you in position."

"Position?"

Without warning, he lifted her into his arms and carried her to the bed, following her down.

"Lie back," he murmured as he lay beside her. Just his nearness on the bed was already arousing her—so she hit the timer.

Taking the watch from her, he tossed it to the bedside table. Then he grasped her wrists.

"Cadeon?"

"I'm going to hold your hands behind your back." He pinned them there.

"Why?"

"So you don't worry about hurting me. Try to get free."

Feeling a jolt of panic, she did, using all her strength to break his hold.

And she didn't gain an inch. She might as well have been held by steel.

"You can't overpower me. You can't hurt me."

Then this wouldn't be like the other times. He was an immortal warrior—not a human freshman. Holly found herself relaxing in his grip.

As soon as he felt her go soft, his free hand tugged her skirt up past the tops of her stockings until her panties were exposed. She started to tremble as he eased them down to her knees.

"Part those pretty thighs for me."

As she hesitantly did, he drew her sweater and bra up, completely exposing her breasts.

"Wait . . . I think I've changed my—Oh!" she cried when he fastened his lips around one of her nipples.

He sucked the peak inside his mouth, licking it there, making her moan, "*Oh, my lord.*"

She thought he might make her climax just from his insistent suckling. She was still reeling from the delicious heat of his mouth when he ran his fingertip along her sex. She gasped a shocked breath.

"So hot and slick." His voice sounded pained. "Even more than I imagined." Using her own moisture, he began to rub his forefinger over her sensitive clitoris.

Holly had never been touched like this, had never imagined . . .

She struggled to hold on, to think of other things, but she yearned for release, getting closer with each clever caress of his finger and firm tug on her nipple. She dimly realized her hips were arching wantonly to his finger, but she couldn't stop them.

"Spread your legs more."

Every second of every day in the past, she'd fought not to think about the needs of her body. Now it seemed there was no fight, there *could* be no fight.

Her knees fell open wide.

He groaned around her swollen nipple. "That's it."

Losing control . . . those impulses arose.

Yet she was helpless to act on them. He'd seen to that. "*Cadeon . . .*"

Faster, faster, he rubbed his finger over her now throbbing clitoris, dipping it to her sex to rewet it. "I'm going to put it inside you, okay?" he said against her breast, beginning to delve that finger.

With a moan, she accepted defeat. This was too delicious, too overwhelming for her to resist. "Don't stop . . ."

Inch by inch, he filled her until it was all the way in. At the same time he stirred that finger deep inside her, he began slowly circling his thumb over her clitoris. He rasped, "Does that feel good, baby?"

Mindless, she thrashed her head on the pillow. "*Yes, yes!*" He was going to do it, would make her climax. The first man ever to. "Just don't stop, please . . ."

"Not until you've come for me."

"*Oh, God,*" she cried. "Oh, yes!"

"That's it, Holly. I've wanted to see this for so long. . . ."

Her climax overtook her. Her eyes flashed open in shock at the almost frightening intensity—stronger than anything she'd ever felt before. Wet, clenching, going on and on, until she arched her back and screamed with pleasure. . . .

Seeing her coming was the hottest thing he'd ever witnessed, making him so hard he feared he'd join her before he even got his cock out.

As he wrung every ounce of pleasure from her, her tight sheath squeezed his finger, milking it so hungrily over and over again.

Lightning flared outside, the thunder shaking the room.

Finally, she whimpered, "No more," and pushed his hand away—just as his watch alarm went off.

Leaning up over her, he snatched it from the bedside table, crushing it in his fist to silence it.

When he turned back to her, he saw that she hadn't rushed to cover herself as he'd expected. Her hair had come loose. Her sweater, skirt, and panties remained where he'd left them.

She was beyond caring. This was how he'd always wanted to see her—unlaced, drugged with passion until her prim façade shattered. She was panting with heavy-lidded eyes, her swollen nipples wetted from his mouth.

Those blond curls between her legs were damp from

her orgasm, and his cock strained for them. He ran the heel of his palm along his shaft, asking, "Will you ease me, Holly?" His voice was hoarse.

When she bit her lip and nodded, he yanked open the button fly of his jeans, shoving them to his knees. His cock sprang free, pulsing between them.

Eyes riveted, she sat up, murmuring, "But I don't know how. I don't want to hurt you."

"You can't hurt me more than I do right now. Just touch it."

Holly tentatively raised her hands to his shaft. At the first contract, he hissed in a breath, and involuntarily bucked. All he could think over and over was, *My female has her hands on my cock*.

She began to run her soft, soft hands over his heated flesh. When his cockhead grew slick like it had last night, he groaned in bliss. Using her forefinger, she daubed the moisture, spreading it in circles on the crown. "That's so good, baby," he rasped. "Now, just stroke it for me."

She didn't, instead continuing to explore with whispery touches when he needed fast friction. When she dipped her other hand to cup him, hefting the weight of his ballocks, he yelled out in fresh agony, hips rocking uncontrollably.

"Wrap your fingers around it! I'll do the rest." He attempted to calm his tone. "If you understood the pain . . ."

Taking her hand, he had her grip his shaft. "Ah! *Better* . . ." he groaned once he could grind into her fist for relief.

He reached down to rub her tight little clitoris. With his other hand, he kneaded her breasts, one then the other.

She ran her face against his torso, moaning as she kissed him there. She had the sexiest moans—short, sharp, each one laden with need, making him crazed to sate her.

I could take her . . . He could be fucking her in seconds. *She'd let me.* Though he desperately wanted inside her, he couldn't do it. He would change, going fully demonic.

And then he would know for certain that she was his.

So he bucked harder, reaching farther down to cup her sex, fondling her with his whole hand. She squeezed his shaft, beginning to pump it until his hips stilled, and she took over.

Stroking his female while being stroked. *Nothing has ever been this good. . . .*

Her eyes slid shut as she started coming again, giving him more of those maddening moans.

His demon instinct recognized her as his own, roaring within him to claim her. As she quivered on his palm, he began to turn but fought it.

"Holly, you're going to make me come so hard . . . keep going." His breaths heaved, his body tightening like a coil. "Keep—ah, fuck!"

Release . . . He roared to the ceiling in a blinding surge of pleasure. Though he didn't ejaculate, the orgasm continued on and on, relentless, until he had to shudder away from her grip. Falling back on the bed beside her, he stared at the ceiling in amazement. For nine hundred years, he'd been waiting to pleasure his female.

And then to be the first to show her this . . . ? He felt a pure masculine thrill recalling how her silvered eyes had gone wide with surprise right before she'd gone over the edge.

At last, to have this shared experience between them—it felt destined, momentous.

When he faced her, she said, "Cadeon, you didn't . . . ?"

"Rage demons don't ejaculate, not until we claim our fated female."

"So that's what you meant by how you would know." When he nodded, she said, "I didn't do anything wrong?"

"No, love." He leaned over to nuzzle her ear. Even after his mind-numbing release, her scent had him stiffening again, his cock distending against her pale thigh. "Of course not."

"Very good, then." She pulled her clothes into place, then rose with a firm nod. "That was pleasant, Cadeon." She might as well have dusted off her hands. "I'll just freshen up, and then we can get on the road."

As she sauntered into the bathroom, all he could do was blink in disbelief, lying on the bed with his damned pants at his knees. He felt . . . used, finally understanding how he'd made nine hundred years' worth of females feel before.

This feeling sucks. He snatched his jeans up. Hell, he *had* been used. And worse, he'd gained no overall ground with her, which angered him.

When she returned, he tossed her back to the bed.

"What are you— Stop this!" she cried.

"Looks like I won the bet, poppet." Taking her slaps, he shoved up her skirt, then yanked off her panties, stuffing them into his pocket. "I'll be taking my prize."

26

"Can't get my mind off earlier," Cadeon murmured, his knuckles white on the steering wheel.

No kidding, she thought. For the last two hours, she'd kept reliving the things he'd made her feel—and made her do.

Twice.

And she kept seeing the pained look on his beautiful face before he came and the way his thick flesh had pulsed as she'd stroked him. His brutal yell had given her shivers.

Going without her panties wasn't helping. Knowing they were in the demon's pocket was surprisingly erotic to her. "Well, you're going to have to try harder."

Just as she would. If only she weren't so *aware* of him. She definitely had hypersensitivity. His scent was mouthwatering to her, lulling her to get closer to him whenever they sat near each other, which incidentally was every minute in the car.

Like a man's voice, a man's scent had never been particularly noticeable to her, unless, of course, it was unpleasant.

But Cadeon's scent made her claws curl for him, for his body heavy and hot atop hers.

"If I had my way," he continued, "I'd hole up somewhere with you for a couple of weeks and do nothing but—"

"Give me a good seeing to?"

"Yeah."

"Well, that's not a possibility. You need your sword, and I fear every day I'm getting closer to the point of no return with my transition."

"I know, I know."

"We're just going to ignore this."

Until now, she'd never truly comprehended the term *sexual awakening*. Now she did. He'd done things to her that she could never forget. Holly would never be the same again—because a line had been crossed. She'd had a taste of something, and she wanted more of it.

Which wasn't possible. So how did she get everything to go back to sleep?

"Ignore? Yeah, let me know how that works out for you," he said as he turned into the entrance of an exclusive-looking shopping plaza, what appeared to be one of those über luxury malls. "We're here."

"This is where you're getting gear?"

"Where *we*'re getting gear. You need some warmer clothes. Things you can move in."

Actually, she wouldn't mind a new turtleneck or two. Maybe a heavier jacket.

Once he'd parked in front of an upscale department store, she got out, absently shutting her door behind her. Again, her mind was a tangle of thoughts. . . .

For so long, any arousal she experienced had always been accompanied by the fear of hurting another.

Earlier, the fear had vanished—because she'd been unable to hurt him, helpless to do anything more than have her body expertly petted to orgasm. She felt a flutter in her belly at the memory, but then frowned. *Expertly*.

He was, after all, a ladies' man. Had he brought Imatra the same kind of pleasure . . . ?

"Hey, you forgot your computer," he said, negligently waving it at her.

Her eyes went wide as she hastened to him. She'd almost left behind her laptop? It was the one thing that was absolutely indispensable in her life, so critical to her she'd often wished she could have a hard drive implanted in her hip.

"Your mind's occupied, then?" he asked in that arrogant tone. "So much for ignoring what we did."

"I was thinking about something else." When she reached for it, he held it over his head. "Give it back! You might drop it!"

"I'll give it back, if you admit that you were thinking about me."

"Fine. I was. All about you. Now give it!"

He eventually did, looking surprised by how easily she'd capitulated. But this was her *computer*, the source of all that was right and good in the world.

Once she'd looped the strap of the case over her shoulder, he placed his big hand on her lower back. She gave him a pointed glare, which he ignored, whisking her inside. In the ladies' department, he even held up jeans to her hips, eyeing them for size. *Highhanded male!*

Through gritted teeth, she asked, "Exactly how do you expect me to try on jeans without underwear?"

He patted his pocket. "You want them back? We might be able to work something out." He shoved a few pairs of jeans into her arms, snagged some cashmere turtlenecks, then marched her to the dressing room.

She'd thought he'd wait in the sitting area outside. No such luck. "Cadeon!" she snapped when he followed her in, shutting the door. "You can't come in here!"

He planted a hand on the wall behind her and leaned in. "I need to be in here. Because you're about to kiss me."

"Is that so?" She'd tried for an arch tone, yet only sounded intrigued.

"Uh-huh. If you want your panties back for tonight."

"Fine. I'll go without jeans."

"Going to get chilly running around in skirts with nothing on but thigh-highs."

She exhaled impatiently. It *was* nippy. "I'll kiss you, but only if I'm freed completely from the bet. Not just for tonight."

"Then you have to French kiss me. Not a peck on the cheek."

There went that plan.

"Very well. But I don't exactly know how to begin." Would he be inwardly laughing at her inexperience? Comparing her to Imatra?

Holly wished she were a better kisser than that demoness.

"You won't be needing this," he said, tugging her bag off her shoulder to set it on the bench behind him. "Now, you're going to have to go on tiptoe to reach me."

"You won't meet me halfway?"

"*You* are kissing *me*, remember?"

She placed her hands on his shoulders for balance, then rose up on her toes.

"Even on tiptoe, you'll need to pull my head down to yours. Cup the back of my head."

When she accidentally touched the tip of his horn, he groaned. She quickly moved her hand higher, but he said, "It feels good when you touch them."

"You really can feel with them?" she asked, recalling what he'd said about her behavior in the bar.

"Of course. Male demons love to have their horns stroked."

She filed that away for later.

"Next you're going to put your opened lips against mine, then lick my tongue. And once you've gotten to that point, you just do whatever feels good for you."

She swallowed, unable to tell if she was giddy or nervous or both. Then on her toes, she drew him down, putting her lips to his.

As if to encourage her, he gave one flick of his tongue to hers. Then he let her take over, never rushing her as she began to explore him with tentative licks. Finally, he met her tongue again, but allowed her to control the pace, slowly tangling it with hers.

The kiss was languid, but unmistakably carnal. She couldn't seem to stop herself from deepening it—

Girls' giggles sounded in the dressing room next door.

Holly broke away with a gasp, trying to quiet her panting breaths and gather her wits. But then her brows drew together as she gazed at Cadeon's face.

His eyes had gone black, and his horns had straightened and thickened. Just like each time they'd been intimate.

Yet she'd seen none of these reactions when he'd kissed Imatra.

Was it because he'd already been satisfied? Or not at all?

"There." She ducked out from under his arm. "I've done it."

His voice hoarse, he said, "That you did. Glad I brought this." He donned his hat. That weather-beaten, leather one that made her heart thud. Once his eyes had cleared, he said, "I'll sneak out now. To go and sit like the other perplexed males who don't know how they got here."

"Wait!" She pointed at his pocket.

He chose to misunderstand her. "It's at—your—service, m'love."

She rolled her eyes and mouthed, "My *panties*."

He handed them over with a shameless grin. At last, she had the dressing room to herself. Yet as she zipped up a pair of three-hundred-dollar jeans, she stilled. *I can hear the whispers from the girls next door*.

Holly could tell they were whispering right at each other's ears, likely with a cupped hand, but she could clearly distinguish their words: "He's frigging *hawt*. Like the hawtest ever. Go act like you're getting me another size and see for yourself."

And Holly could hear their hearts clamoring each time they returned from walking past him.

Which meant he could hear them as well. No wonder he knew he was gorgeous.

"Come out so I can see," he called.

She checked herself out in the mirror and hardly recognized her reflection. She hadn't worn jeans since she was in her early teens. Because her chignon kept falling down as she tried on the turtleneck sweaters, she'd ended up plaiting her hair in two braids that would cover her ears. She wore no glasses, because she didn't need them. Her cheeks were pink, her skin seeming to glow—like Nïx's had.

She pursed her lips, hating to admit that there were advantages to being a Valkyrie.

"Come on, then."

"Just a minute!"

And then he was just outside her door. "Getting greedy to see you, pet."

At that, one of the girls in the next room sighed.

"The jeans don't fit." Though the waist was gaping, the back was too tight. She turned in the mirror, frowning over her shoulder. She'd never really noticed how big her backside was. No wonder Cadeon was always riveted to it!

"Then I'll get another size," he said.

"No, they're too big and too small."

"Let me be the judge of that."

"Fine." She opened the door.

His lips parted. "Turn around." Once she made a self-conscious circle, he said, "Well, then. I'd thought your ass in one of your skirts was earth-shattering, but your ass in jeans tops even that."

When the girls next door giggled anew, she glared. Undaunted, he reached past her for her computer case, then started dragging her out. "What are you doing?"

"We're done."

"But they don't fit," she insisted.

"We'll get you a belt."

"Wait, this is only one outfit!"

"None doing. We're getting you five pairs of these earth-shattering jeans, and that sweater in every color, and then we're finished, yeah?" Out in the store, he said, "Damn, that was close. I got you out of there just in time."

"What are you talking about?"

"You were about to claw out the girls' eyes for their interest in your demon. It was imminent—lives held in the balance."

"You're not *my* demon."

"No? You sure kissed me like I was."

"Ooh!" she muttered under her breath.

He snagged a black leather belt, coiled on a display table. "Try this." He looped it around her waist, taking his time with his arms around her, lingering. Ten to one odds said he was smelling her hair.

"It's fine," she said, so he got her a few more, then set about collecting all the jeans and sweaters.

When it was their turn to pay, Cadeon told the lady at the register, "Good evening, dove."

The woman stared speechlessly at him, unable to do more than fuss with her hair.

"Ma'am," Holly prompted, more sharply than she'd intended.

Once she snapped out of her daze and began scanning the tags, Cadeon murmured at Holly's ear, "Another close call. These silly chits flirt with death."

Holly kicked his shin. In response, he gave a deep chuckle.

When they'd finally gotten their bags and had taken the tags off the clothes she wore, he told Holly, "Go try on some hiking boots downstairs." He handed her a Centurion American Express card.

Apparently the demon was rich. "You need some expensive ones that you don't have to break in. With Gore-Tex for snow."

"Where are you going?"

"Getting a coat and some things. Stay in this store till I get back. . . ."

In the shoe department, she picked out two types of boots. One pair was sturdy, with a Gore-Tex coating, because she needed them. Yet she also chose a pair made of sleek, black leather with higher heels—because her claws were curling for them and she was helpless not to.

When the saleslady returned with her size, Holly tried them on, walking around the area. Did everyone walk differently in boots? Maybe with a little more strut?

Holly bought the two pairs, wearing the black ones. Her task complete, she sat and waited for Cadeon to return. With no activity and no one to talk to, her mind began mulling recent developments. . . .

She'd officially been unfaithful to her boyfriend. And that just wasn't her way. She'd never cheated on a test, had never even broken a promise. Tim was too nice a guy to deserve this—

How well do you really know Tim?

The thought came out of nowhere, making her frown.

He was perfect for her, a steady, even-tempered guy, who was incredibly driven in his career. As driven as she was. He was tall, slim, and handsome in an affable, nonintimidating way. And as she'd told Cadeon, Tim would make a great husband and father.

Which was more than she could say for a male like Cadeon, who would be unfaithful to her and most likely an absentee father to any children he might have.

Yet earlier with Cadeon, she'd had a realization. There were things about a man that could be learned so much more easily when in a sexual situation, when the walls were down.

Cadeon's eyes had been lustful, hungry, but his touch had been tender, almost as if he'd been savoring or even . . . awed.

Holly hadn't expected that gentleness from the rough mercenary and never would have seen it if not in bed with him.

What would she discover about Tim in a like situation?

She tried to imagine doing the same things with him. Yet she couldn't—because she kept seeing the demon.

No, no! This was a perfect example of her new, foreign thought processes taking over. *The ones that reason why mutual petting with a demon makes sense: because I can learn—wink, wink—about him. As a person.*

She was doubting Tim only because she wasn't herself. *Not* because of any faint suspicion that she clung to him as a personification of her old life—the one she feared leaving . . .

Her thoughts went blank when she spied Cadeon coming for her, his long-legged stride eating up the distance, his shoulders back, cocky half-grin in place.

Maybe Cadeon had a good point, she thought dazedly. Maybe she should have one last adventure before her normal, ordered existence resumed. A little sexual experimentation, a little excitement . . .

When he reached her, he swooped down and gave her a kiss before she could react. "You missed me, didn't you?"

She was sputtering, having been kissed for the first time in public. "Hardly."

"Huh. Then I wonder why your eyes went all silvery when you caught sight of me."

"They did not!" Her gaze darted. "What if someone saw? Oh, God—"

"Relax, halfling. Humans will just think it's a trick of the light. If you brazen it out. Now let me see what you've got."

He raised his brows at her new boots. "Very nice. But you only got two pairs? I was expecting credit card abuse and retaliatory shopping from you."

"Sorry to disappoint." He had several bags. "What did you get?"

"I'll show you over dinner."

"Dinner? Do we have time?"

"I have to nourish my halfling, else she grows irritable. Besides, it'll take us five hours to drive, tops, and it's only six o'clock."

"What do you expect me to eat in a restaurant? You know I have to have things prepackaged."

"I've already put in an order. Just trust me."

27

For fifteen years, Holly had been overdressed for fairly much everything. Now the demon had put her in jeans, then taken her to a posh restaurant.

As they sat waiting for their food, she wondered what he'd ordered for her. A tin of green beans? Maybe fruit cocktail? Or since this was a seafood restaurant, she'd probably get a can of tuna.

"So check out my loot," Cadeon said as he dug into one of his bags. He'd removed his hat, shaking out his hair to cover his horns, and now looked insufferably gorgeous.

"Here." He handed her two packages. "I got you a watch. You used to have a nice one."

He'd noticed even that small detail?

"I got one, too," he said.

Oh, yes, because he'd pulverized his in his fist earlier. "They're not . . . matching or anything, are they?"

"Holls, I'm a demon; I'm not a tool."

"Oh, of course." She accepted the box, raising her brows. *Cartier*.

She'd always steered clear of that brand because many of the watch styles were diamond-intensive. Not so good for her since she'd get entranced with each glance at the time.

When she opened the package, she almost smiled. Not a diamond in sight. Platinum, simple but elegant. Why was he being so . . . thoughtful? "Cadeon, it's lovely, but really, this is too nice. I can't let you pay—"

"I'll expense it. Now, close your gab, and open the next one."

She glowered, but did. Inside were . . . her glasses. Smitten Kitten. She blinked at him. "You're giving me my own glasses?"

"I had the lenses changed to clear. You said you couldn't think without them on, and you were getting headaches."

Her lips parted as she donned them. Who was more supportive? Tim, who verbally encouraged her, or Cadeon, who made her work possible?

Stop comparing them! Tim also didn't go and doff bar owners of the sexually insatiable demoness variety.

"They feel perfect. But, Cadeon, I'm turning back. My eyesight will go bad again."

"Then get them changed again later. But for now, you've got work to do," he said, adding gravely, "Holly, it's not like codes write themselves." He handed her another bag. "Now, check out the coat I got for you."

Reaching into the bag, she pulled out a small, formfitting ski jacket. "It's red."

"It should be. You don't own anything red." Again, he'd noticed.

She was surprised by his good taste, but still said, "It doesn't look very heavy."

"New technology, halfling. This will keep you warm when it's twenty below. Just trust me. Besides, you're not feeling the cold as you used to, are you?"

"No, I guess not. . . ."

The server came with their drinks then: a beer for

Cadeon, and for her a chilled bottle of Perrier—unopened per Cadeon's request.

Once the man left to check on their order, she said, "Why are you always concerned about me eating?"

Cade exhaled, hating this part. *Because I'm not a good man, and I'm about to betray you in the cruelest way imaginable. . . .*

It seemed to him like every moment of satisfaction with his female cost him another lie, digging himself deeper, ensuring there could be no forgiveness.

Block it out. "Maybe your transition can be slowed if you held onto some human traits?"

She sighed. "I'm hungry less and less. I could easily see myself forgetting to eat altogether."

"The change has already taken a foothold in you. I don't think you even realize how much stronger and quicker you're getting."

She grew quiet for long moments, folding and refolding her napkin with her thin, nimble fingers. The ones that had been wrapped around his shaft mere hours ago. He shifted uncomfortably in his seat.

"Cadeon . . ."

"What's on your mind?"

"I was just wondering . . . what's it like to live forever?"

Wearying. Without a mate and family, it was so damned wearying. But he answered, "Living forever has it perks. Such as the not dying part. Are you thinking about signing on for immortality?"

"I don't know how to answer. I definitely see advantages to being a Valkyrie. But I don't want to be the Vessel.

I don't want to be *dead or bred.* And I don't know how I'd reconcile my current life with the change. What if I flashed an ear in class?"

"You'd be amazed how many Lorekind live among humans, and they never know it."

She tilted her head. "Honestly, I'm not certain that I'd want to live forever. . . ." She trailed off when the server returned with their dishes.

For Cade: a twenty-ounce porterhouse. For her: bananas unpeeled and boiled eggs with their shells intact, accompanied by plastic ware, still in the wrapper.

She looked from her meal to his, her expression growing forlorn.

"You want some of my steak, don't you?"

She shook her head hard, clearly wanting some of his steak. "I still have . . . issues."

"I know, I know. You like things untouched and still packaged."

She frowned when the server returned with another plate for her, filled with lobster tails and uncracked crab legs.

When they were alone again, Cade said, "Behold, the ultimate in untouched and packaged foods. You can crack the shells yourself without any transference, then eat the meat with the plastic fork."

She blinked at him. "Do you know how long it's been since I've had fresh seafood?" Then her lips curled into a smile.

Score another one for the demon.

"I'm a good date, aren't I?"

"If only you weren't so modest," Holly replied outside

the restaurant. In truth, he *had* been a good date, creatively working with her quirks. And the dinner had been phenomenal.

He crossed to a garbage can, throwing the watch boxes away. From that distance, he turned and tossed something to her. "Think fast!" he said.

Was it shining?

A *diamond* ring.

Her wide-eyed gaze locked on it in the air, her hand shooting out to snare it.

She opened her palm, shivering with wonder. "What is this for?" she asked in a daze.

"Aversion training. Now you have to look away from it," he said at her ear. When had he moved so close to her?

She hastily hooked her finger into the ring so he couldn't snatch it from her, but she couldn't look away.

"Break your stare."

She shook her head irritably. He'd thrown it at her, but expected her to take her eyes from it?

"Look away, or I'll toss your laptop into that public trash bin over here. Imagine the germs teeming in there. You think the hard drive will even be salvageable?"

Holly started quaking with the effort to look away. "Don't . . . please!"

He covered her hand, then wrenched the ring from her clutching fingers.

The trance broken, she glared at him. "That wasn't funny!"

"Not meant to be. You need to practice with this, ten times a day if you have to. You have a vulnerability, poppet. A big one. You've got to overcome it."

Though he was brusque and abrasive, he did seem to have her best interests at heart. She nibbled her lip. "The diamond was real, or I wouldn't have seized on it." When he nodded, she said, "How much do mercenaries like yourself make these days?"

"I've got a fortune in gold. Ah, was that a flicker in your eye? Do you like me better now that you know I'm rich?" He curled his finger under her chin. "Because I'm all right with that."

He gave her a brief kiss on the lips.

"Stop doing that!"

He kept sneaking kisses, treating her as if she was *his* girlfriend. Which flustered her. It did *not* excite her.

"Now, prepare yourself," he said. "It's time for you to drive a really fast car."

28

"It's ideal for our purposes," Cadeon said, gazing down the length of the highway.

It was deserted, looking like an abandoned airstrip through the forest, and was visible all the way to the mountains in the far distance. Old snow lay in clumps off to the side of the road, but the pavement was clear and dry.

"You're really going to let me drive?"

"Whose car is this?"

She answered, "Not ours."

"Good girl."

As he pulled over, she surveyed the area. The forest was lit by the waning moon, the sky clear. "I can't believe I'm all the way up in northern Michigan, and there's no real showing of snow."

"Maybe so, but now you get to see the northern lights."

"No way! Where? I don't see them—which way are they?"

He pointed to the left, just above the tree line. "There's your Aurora Borealis."

Her gaze followed, and she gasped. Shimmering violet lights danced against the black sky. As they swirled, they alternately obscured, then highlighted the moon and stars.

Seeing this made her heart sing, and she murmured, "So lovely."

"Legend held that the Valkyrie created the lights."

"What was the legend?"

"The early northlanders believed that when the Valkyrie rode from Valhalla to choose brave warriors for eternal reward, their armor cast a strange flickering light over the sky."

"Really?" When he nodded, she said, "You know a lot."

"You think?" he asked nonchalantly, but she could tell her comment pleased him.

She was inclined to be nice to him, still delighted over her dinner, and excited about finally driving this car.

"You ready?" He turned a knob to the left of the driver's seat.

She could feel the car sinking lower and heard a whirring behind her. "The spoiler in the back—"

"Retracts into the body of the car. So do the front flaps. And here's something you'll like to hear. These changes reduce the drag coefficient by .05 percent."

She quirked a brow. He was speaking her language. Once they traded places, she sank into the driver's seat, adjusting the mirrors.

"You know how to drive a stick, right?"

"I cut my driving teeth on a Carrera, thank you very much."

"Good. Then put on your seat belt."

She fastened the harness. "You, too." At his mulish look, she said, "Please?"

"Fine, fine," he said, startling her by conceding so easily. "Now just pull out real slow."

Though he had yet to drive slowly, she dutifully slipped the gear into first and eased out onto the road.

"All right, get her up to the speed limit."

Steadily giving gas, Holly shifted to second, then third.

"That's it. You're doing good. *Really* good. What do you think?"

By fifth gear, she was convinced the clutch was the crispest on earth, the accelerator the most sensitive. The engine was responsive, like nothing she'd ever driven. "Incredible. It maneuvers so easily. All-wheel drive?"

"You know it."

"It's hugging the road." Like a bullet on a magnetized rail.

"Believe it or not, this car is as heavy as a tank. A full two tons."

"No way."

"If it's so easy to drive, then let's see you open her up."

So Holly accelerated, feeling a thrill when she saw she'd broken the highway speed limit.

"Faster, pet. Come on, kick 'er in the guts!"

"You asked for it." She nailed the accelerator, and the car shot forward, plastering them back into their seats. *One hundred miles per hour*. The tiniest correction on the wheel caused the most precise adjustment in the direction. *One forty*. The power, the thrum of the engine, the control—all so heady.

The road was indeed like a runway. And Holly felt like a different person—a boots-wearing, seafood-eating, thong-clad driver of million-dollar cars.

When she peeked at the speedometer again, they were doing a hundred and eighty.

Her heart was racing, her adrenaline pumping. But she also felt something she never expected.

She was getting really aroused.

By the time she was flirting with two hundred miles per

hour, there was no ignoring it. Her breaths grew shallow, and she wriggled in the seat. *Still getting worse.*

Two hundred ten. She licked her lips. Speed. Seductive. *Sexy.*

He'd grown quiet. She darted a glance at him.

He was staring at her, his eyes dark and inscrutable. "Pull over," he said.

"What? Did I do something wrong?"

"Just stop the car."

As soon as she'd pulled over and put the gear into park, his hands shot for her, cupping her face, drawing her in for a searing kiss. With a cry she responded, crushing her lips to his, flicking her tongue.

Her hand shot for his erection. She wanted to touch it like before, but she couldn't reach it. He put his palm between her legs but she couldn't spread them enough because of the steering wheel and console.

"Bugger this," he growled, snapping off his seat belt, and slamming out of the car.

Just as disappointment swept over her, he opened her door and freed her seat belt as well. His big hands grasped her sides, lifting her from the car to set her on her feet outside.

"Cadeon?" When he started on her zipper, she cried, "Someone will see!"

"No one's driving by."

When he shoved her jeans and panties down past her knees, she cried, "What if— *Oh.*"

She didn't have time to resist before he'd placed her on the top of the car, spreading her legs to open her bared sex.

"What are you going to do?"

"Show you something new." He nuzzled her thigh with his cheek, his stubble rasping her tender skin. She could feel his warm breaths. . . .

With a start, she realized what he intended. But she couldn't make herself protest. Everything he'd shown her so far had been amazing. Why would this prove any diff—

"*Oh—my—God,*" she gasped when he licked at her clitoris with his strong tongue.

She fell back on the car, overwhelmed, spreading her legs even wider in welcome. Unimaginable pleasure assailed her, and she couldn't bite back a sharp moan.

He spread her flesh between two fingers, licking her, ravenous on her sex. "Pull up your top over your breasts."

"I'll freeze . . ."

"You won't."

"Why—"

"My hands are busy. Do it, or I'll stop."

Where was his other hand? Comprehension came. "*Oh* . . ." The idea of him masturbating as he kissed her like this sent shivers all over her skin.

With a swallow, she tugged her sweater and bra up as he'd done in the hotel. She hadn't perceived a breeze from the forest before, but now it brushed over her sensitive nipples, hardening them even more. She moaned anew.

He reached up and placed her hands on her breasts. "Play with them," he said, before returning his mouth.

As she began to cup her breasts, she gazed up at the sky with heavy-lidded eyes. Above her the stars were feverish, the northern lights glimmering from violet to red and punctuated by her growing lightning. *A dream*.

Already, the pleasure was about to overwhelm her.

"Your nipples"—he sounded in pain—"pinch them."

As he set back in, she did, shocked by her own touch, arching her back sharply. More breeze, more stars, more insistent licks.

"Are you ready to come?"

"Yes!"

"Me, too," he rasped, then he sucked her clitoris between his lips.

She screamed, shooting upright as her orgasm ripped through her. He was licking, groaning, using lips, tongue, and teeth to wring more from her.

When he gave a harsh growl against her flesh, she knew he was about to come right after her. Even when she was finished, he continued his kiss, as if it heightened his own pleasure.

Once he was spent, he lay his head on her thigh, catching his breath.

Eventually, she sat up on her elbows.

After staring at her uncovered breasts with his brows drawn, he met her eyes. "Every five hundred miles?"

She shook her head. "Four twenty."

29

Laughing Lady Bridge,
Bloodwater River, Michigan

This is the place. Pull over on the shoulder." Cadeon motioned for her to park beside a rock ridge just in front of the bridge.

Holly put it into neutral, engaged the parking brake, then surveyed the scene.

And she'd thought the Sandbar had been in the middle of nowhere.

For the last several hours, the Veyron had prowled along winding roads through fog-draped woods, ever downward to the Bloodwater basin. The area was mountainous, the roads seemingly etched through escarpments.

She and Cadeon had spoken little. He'd been quiet, lost in thought. She'd still been reeling from what they'd done. And what they might do in a hundred more miles . . .

He glanced at his new watch. "Twenty till midnight. We're early."

"Well, it's certainly atmospheric," she said.

Mist blanketed the river, trapped between the towering cliffs that bordered the water. It was so thick, she couldn't even see across the bridge—which looked as if it led straight into nothing. . . .

Still, she was more excited than uneasy. This could be a real-live haunted bridge.

"I don't suppose it'd do any good to ask you to stay here?" he asked.

Getting out, she said, "None!"

"You seem in a fine mood."

"I'm wearing new clothes, new boots, a new jacket." She felt jauntier, younger.

"Do you really think it's the clothes that are affecting you so—or the three orgasms you enjoyed today?"

Well, there was that. Yet she tapped her chin as if pondering his question, then answered, "No, it's definitely the clothes," making him scowl.

They set out toward the bridge. The Laughing Lady used to be fully covered, but now parts of the wooden roof and siding had rotted in places, exposing the skeleton of trusses beneath.

That rusted iron groaned with each fog-stirring breeze.

When she spied the water, the tiny hairs on her nape rose. In the foggy moonlight, it looked exactly like blood.

After skirting the roadblock, they started across, with her avoiding the cracks between the boards. About twenty feet in, she glanced back, hesitating when she couldn't see the car.

"Stay closer, Holly."

She caught up with him. "Is the bridge . . . swaying?"

"Yeah. The deck gives a little, so it won't break. Here, hold my hand."

She raised her brows. "I'm getting an eighth grade vibe here. Taking the girl to the spooky place? So she'll be *fwightened* into necking with you? Am I getting warm?"

He gave her a smug grin. "After what we just did on the roof of the car, necking seems quaint, yeah? Besides, you want to hold my hand." He took hers in his. "Admit it."

Arrogant demon. "No . . . I *don't*." She withdrew it. "Just because we've been *intimate* doesn't mean I want to be *affectionate* with you." She needed to try to keep some distance between them. For all she knew, the next checkpoint could be another bar, with another demoness. . . .

And Holly could finally admit to herself that catching him with the beautiful Imatra had . . . hurt. She often had to struggle not to picture them kissing.

Though Cadeon had been considerate at times, she knew that deep down he was still a cad.

"What we did changes nothing between us," she said. "I still have a boyfriend, and you still have your *chits on your jock* or however you view your conquests."

Well, that appeared to piss him off.

"And you count yourself among *that* number?" He snared her hand again.

"Why wouldn't I?" She pulled away, but he held her firm. Through gritted teeth, she said, "Let—go."

A dangerous light glinted in his eyes. "I'm holdin' it, or you're going back to the car."

"Screw off. Don't talk to me like I'm a child."

His tone derisive, he said, "Holly Ashwin said *screw* with no one else but me to witness the occasion. I'll let go as soon as you admit that what's between us is more than just physical for you."

"You're the one who suggested that I use you to ease my curiosity, to take a couple of weeks to get all this craziness out of my system. Then when I do, you're not happy until I admit to something I don't feel."

"You think you're just going to use me and not be affected in turn?"

"Why not? Like you've never done the same!"

"I've always done the same!" he thundered, his words echoing in the weathered enclosure.

Suddenly, eerie laughter sounded, women's laughter, from no apparent source.

Cadeon yanked Holly behind him, as they peered around in the thick mist. "We're starting back. Now."

"Is it the ghosts—"

His body shot up from hers into the air. As she screamed, some invisible force hurled him into one of the trusses, shaking the entire bridge with the impact. His back bent the iron girder he smashed into, one of his horns embedding into it. With a yell of pain, he wrenched his head forward to dislodge it, dropping to his feet.

More laughter sounded.

"Cadeon!" The ghosts. It had to be them. "Oh, God, they're real."

"Stay down!" he roared.

She crouched, but she hadn't been touched. Why hadn't she been?

When he tried to reach her, invisible hits struck him from every direction until he was flung down the entire long length of the bridge. Furious, he bolted to his feet.

Again and again, he grappled to reach her, each time propelled back. "Get to the car! Drive off!"

When they lifted him once more, he struggled to fight back but couldn't. His foes weren't substantial.

Realization hit her. She shot to her feet, charging through the mist for him.

His eyes went wide as she neared. "*Holly, no!* Get the fuck away—"

"Wait!" she cried out to the night. "He's not hurting me."

At length, the force dropped him to the ground.

Holly knelt beside him, helping him sit up. She sensed they were surrounded, menace seething all around them. "He's with me!" She took Cadeon's hand and placed it against her face. He cupped her gently, as she'd known he would.

The attack abruptly stopped.

"What the hell's going on?" he grated, running his sleeve over his bleeding lip. His cheek was cut deeply, his shirt nearly ripped from him.

"I think they believed you were hurting me, or forcing me to the bridge," she said. "They're probably sensitive about aggressive males dragging females around out here."

He surveyed the area warily. "Thanks for the save, pet." When he tried to stand, he gritted his teeth in pain, his hand clamping his ribs. "But with that big brain of yours, you couldn't have figured this out sooner? Preferably, before they broke a slab of my ribs?"

"Oooh! I should have let the ghosts—the *female* ghosts—spank you like a moppet some more!"

An arrow lodged into the iron between them, vibrating there with a loud *twang*. Their heads whipped around in the direction of the car. But she couldn't see who'd fired it—

"Go! Into the fog!" Within a split second, Cadeon had her hauled up and running in the other direction, putting himself between her and the enemy.

"I thought some more factions would want to breed

with me!" she cried as she ran. "Where are they, Cadeon? Huh? Because it seems like most just want to kill me!"

"If they'd wanted to kill you, they wouldn't have missed!" A torrent of arrows flew at them. Two plugged into his back.

"Cadeon!"

"Keep—running!"

Just before they reached the other end of the bridge, two more hit him. He tossed her behind a boulder on the side of the road, then ducked down with her.

Twisting around, he gave her his back. "Pull them out!"

"Oh, God." They were so deep. She grasped one of the shafts as far down as she could. With a swallow, she yanked until it tore free. Blood dripped down from the wound, and for an instant, she thought there was a bluish cast to it. She blinked her eyes, and it was gone. "Who are they?"

"Fey archers."

"I thought they were the good guys," she said, pulling the next arrow free.

"They are." He glanced out from behind the rock, then jerked his head back just as an arrow whizzed by his face. "And they believe we're the bad guys. Remember? You're possibly the source of the ultimate evil, and I'm a demon mercenary."

She wrapped her fist around the third arrow and yanked. Nothing. "Cadeon?"

"It's stuck in the bone. Pull harder."

Glancing out again, he murmured, "How the hell did they find us?" He craned his head over his shoulder, giving her a narrow-eyed look. "You took off your pearls, didn't you?"

"I'm not an idiot." She wrested the arrowhead free, and blood welled.

With his jaw clenched in pain, he grated, "Not sayin' you're an idiot. But how else would they find us? No one's followed us."

Arrows began to hit the boulder—some bouncing off, others actually implanting into the solid rock.

"Just fess up, halfling. You made a mistake. It happens. Even to the best of us. But I need to know if—"

"I didn't freaking take them off!"

If possible, his expression darkened even more. "Then you called your fuckwit tosser of a boyfriend and told him where we were going!"

She took hold of the final shaft. "If I was going to reveal that to Tim, I would have told him in our own code."

Sounding gruffly hurt, Cadeon said, "You two have a code?"

"Maybe your female, Imatra, threw us under the bus. Huh?"

"Imatra's *not* my female!"

"Hmm. You sound pretty sure of yourself. Yet you said you couldn't be one hundred percent certain unless you *attempted* her. *Finally*, you come clean!"

"I did not attempt her! *Finally*, you're jealous."

She pulled on the arrow shaft—nothing. "Not jealous, just sick of you lying to me. What else would you have been doing in there for an hour?"

"Damn it, Holly, to the gods, you frustrate me. She bloody slowed time!" he bellowed so loudly, even the shots paused before resuming. His fangs were lengthening, his eyes darkening.

"Awfully convenient! Just admit it." When she snatched the fourth arrow free, a plug of skin came out with it, making him growl in pain. "You're so sure because you gave her a try—"

"I know she's not my bloody female—because you are!" He turned to her.

"Oh, like I'm . . ." She trailed off at the look on his face.

The volley continued. Bow strings sang in the distance. The fog swirled, and yet she and the demon stared at each other.

"Cadeon?" He was being serious. "When . . . how . . . You've known this?"

He exhaled and gazed away. "From the day I first saw you. Been watching over you ever since."

As if a final puzzle piece clicked into place, her mind saw the whole picture clearly. He *was* the comforting presence she'd felt for so long. He'd been jealous of Tim right from the beginning. The first night when Cadeon had saved her, his big fingers had patted her face, comforting *her* as he'd taken bullets for her. *"Shh, female,"* he'd said.

"I don't know what to say." *This immortal warrior's wanted me for a year?* Holly could scarcely believe it.

And he hadn't been with Imatra.

An arrow sailed from above, plummeting down to jut from the ground between their legs.

"Bugger this. It's about to rain them." His eyes and horns grew darker, his fangs shooting longer. "Listen to me. You're going to follow directly behind me. I'll push the archers back so you can reach the car—then you get the hell out of here!"

"What are you going to do?"

He stood, looking brutal—like a demon backed into a corner. "Going to protect my female."

30

As Cadeon loped forward into the thick fog, she ran behind him, flinching at the *thunk* sound the arrows kept making as they hit him. Again and again, he pulled them free of his body, casting them away to clatter on the wood.

With each second, he was turning more demonic, those corded muscles growing larger. Though he was injured, he was still using his body to shield hers, just as he'd done that first night.

Not merely for money. But because he believed she was his.

He motioned for her to break away and dash for the car. She would get it started, but there was no way she could ever leave him behind—

With an unholy roar, Cadeon charged the archers. Just as he was about to lunge over their boulder cover, Holly heard a female cry, "*Cade?*"

He skidded to a stop, and a woman popped up, demanding, "What exactly are you doing with the Vessel?"

Cadeon knew this female, too? She had long, flowing brown hair, pointed ears, and a trim, perfect figure. She was ethereal, her face luminous.

And they knew each other. Again, a preternaturally lovely woman was linked to Cadeon in some way. Nïx, Imatra—wait, not Imatra . . .

What is it with him and gorgeous women?

He snapped, "What the hell were you shooting me for? After what we went through, I'd expect different, fey!"

"I didn't see it was you!"

They'd gone through something together. How special.

Cade glowered at Tera, who raised her chin unrepentantly.

"Who is she?" Holly asked from behind them.

Never taking his eyes from Tera—her bow was still drawn with a nocked arrow—Cade said, "Tera of the noble Fey. In the last Talisman's Hie, I saved her life at least a dozen times."

Tera raised her brows. "I believe I had your back as well, demon."

"You competed in the Talisman's Hie?" Holly said, sounding admiring, which meant his shoulders decided to go back of their own accord.

And clever Tera noticed.

"How've you come to be here?" he grated, frowning when a wave of dizziness hit him. He shook it off.

Tera answered, "I'll feel more comfortable speaking about that when we know what you plan to do with her—"

"Switch to Demonish," he interrupted in that tongue.

Tera knew all languages, and answered him in the same. "You're taking the Vessel to an evil sorcerer, Cade. Factions are going to take notice."

He narrowed his eyes. "Will you kill me to take her?"

"What is she to you?"

"She's . . . mine."

Tera's eyes briefly widened. "I told you to give up on the witch! Didn't I tell you?"

"Yeah, yeah," he said, wondering why his tongue felt thick in his mouth.

Tera cast a studying glance at Holly. "Hmm. I sense she's a much better fit for you anyway. Well, you must have a plan up your sleeve—it would be impossible for you to relinquish her."

So it would seem. Why did all these chits keep thinking that he'd be unable to turn Holly over? Nïx, Imatra, and now Tera.

Because they didn't know how far his back was against the wall.

Instead of answering her question, he said, simply, "I've waited nine hundred years for her, Tera."

"I remember," she said. "And am happy your wait is over. Is it possible your female could already be carrying your babe?"

Those words made his body go still, even as his heart began to thunder. *His* female carrying *his* babe. "She could be," he lied.

Tera visibly relaxed, motioning the four bowmen behind her to stand down. "Then the warrior will be for good."

He couldn't help but ask, "You really believe that?"

"You've done some . . . questionable things, and you can be menacing and violent. But you're not evil. So what's your plan for Groot?"

"I can't divulge it. Not when it could put my female in jeopardy."

"Very well," the fey said. "Do you need our aid?"

"Yeah, get the word out to the good guys that Holly's not fair game."

"I will, gladly."

"And you can tell me how you knew to come here."

"We had an informant at Imatra's bar," she said.

"Could others have gotten the information you had?"

"Probably. Our contact wasn't fey. His loyalty was to currency."

Cade ran his hand over his forehead, frowning to find it dripping with sweat. "I've got to get Holly out of here." He would return alone at midnight tomorrow. Switching to English, he said, "Come on, halfling. We're leaving!"

Guardedly, she made her way toward them.

To both Holly and Cade, Tera said, "Then we part ways here, hopefully with peace still between us."

Cade shrugged. "What's a few arrow wounds among friends, yeah?"

With a wince, she said, "About those arrows, Cade. They were dipped in poison—"

"Poison!" Cade bellowed. "Ah, come on, Tera!"

Holly gave a cry behind him. "What poison? You're poisoned?"

Cade turned to her. "No, I'll be fine. It'll just hurt like—"

From out of nowhere, fire hurtled down at him with the force of a rocket. Flames engulfed him as the impact sent him flying.

Just as Holly screamed, "*Cadeon!*" one of the archers yelled, "Fire demons on the cliffs!"

The blast that hit Cadeon looked like a cannonball shot from a flamethrower. His burning body slammed into a ridge, crushing solid rock before falling to the ground still ablaze.

At once, she sprinted for him, yanking off her coat.

"Bows up—shoot to kill!" Tera ordered, her delicate voice now booming as her own bow joined the salvo.

As Holly ran, she chanced a glance at the cliff above the bridge. Through the wispy mist, she saw four demons. Liquid fire danced in their palms.

When she reached Cadeon, Holly spread her coat over him, shoving the material against the flames. Once she'd put them out and drew her coat back, she stared in shock at the damage to his upper body.

His hands were . . . gone, melted to stumps from where he'd tried to ward off the flames. On the right side of his head, his face and hair were burned completely away. That eye was missing, and she thought she could see bone.

Tera yelled to her, "Get out of here!" A stream of arrows flew at the demons, the fey launching them with supernatural speed. "We'll stall them!"

Holly nodded, even as she had no idea how she'd get Cadeon to the car. She stooped down to drape his damaged arm over her shoulders as she'd seen people do on TV, then heaved upward.

What the . . . ? She'd easily lifted him to his feet.

Cadeon grated something that sounded like "Can't touch me."

"What?"

"Poison—"

"We'll talk about this later!" She'd heard what Tera had said and was aware that they faced a subset of problems—but she really couldn't think about that right now!

At the car, she slung him into the passenger seat, then stuffed his long legs in, trying not to freak out about all the damage he'd sustained.

As she yanked open her own door, she spied the fey's truck just around the bend, parked sideways, blocking the road between rock faces.

Holly swung her head in the other direction. A flimsy roadblock, a questionable bridge, and a demon-filled ridge awaited.

Reasoning trail? *This car can fly. Bust through the roadblock, gain more speed on the bridge, then jet right under the demons. . . .*

If the bridge held. Hadn't Cadeon said this car was heavy as a tank?

Don't hesitate . . . follow instinct. Inside the car, she pushed the start button. *Need momentum to hit the roadblock. Oh, God, oh, God . . .* She shifted into reverse, then floored the gas.

"I'm going to get you out of here, Cadeon. We're going to lose them."

Another blast landed just behind them. The demons were on the run from the feys' arrows, but still firing from their vantage. She slammed on the brakes, skidding to a stop inches from the new column of flames.

Cadeon flew forward, cracking his forehead on the metal dash—but this actually seemed to rouse him. "Fuck! What're you doing?" he yelled.

"Trying to get us out of here!" Holly shifted into first gear, then stomped the gas again. The tires peeled as the car surged ahead. Never looking away from the road, she said, "Hold on!"

"Watch the roadblock—"

The front bumper crashed into it, torpedoing the wood. Pieces of lumber bashed the windshield like baseball bats. A split second later, the car ramped down onto the deck of the bridge, the entire structure wobbling dangerously beneath and around them.

Another demon blast struck the bridge's roof. Streams

of fire sieved through the gaps, or oozed from the roof, dropping in her path . . . She steadied the wheel, righting the car. *Almost out, almost to the gauntlet below the demons. I can do this!*

The car stalled.

As she gaped in disbelief, they crawled to a stop in the middle of the bridge, a mere hundred feet from where she'd initially started.

"No, no, no!" She hastily shifted to neutral, pushing the start button again. Nothing.

"Battery's out . . ." Cadeon rasped. "No juice."

"Why?" she cried.

"Don't know. Run, Holly! Get to the forest . . . follow the river back."

"I'm not leaving you."

He squinted at her with his remaining eye. "Why not?"

"Because . . . because I'm just not! So tell me how to get this thing started—"

Another explosion above them. Fire had eaten through most of the wooden roof, leaving the skeleton of rusted trusses. A glance at the churning river below, and she knew their next move. Her stomach roiled along with the water. "Cadeon, our only chance is the river . . ."

She trailed off as writing began to appear in the fogged glass on her side window. One of the ghosts was communicating with her! Holly swallowed, whispering, "Cadeon, are you seeing this."

"Still have . . . one eye."

"Numbers? It looks like latitude and longitude." They had to be the directions to the next checkpoint! She quickly memorized them, then asked Cadeon, "You ready to swim?"

"We'd never make it down," he rasped with a jerk of his chin toward the end of the bridge. A demon had appeared. He raised his flaming hand, about to shoot at them dead on.

Her gaze flew up to the rearview mirror. A second blocked the other end.

Now there was no way to escape, nowhere to run . . .

Suddenly the demon's neck snapped to the side, his head at a right angle to his body; he dropped to his knees, then fell face down, the flame in his hand snuffed.

The one behind them suffered the same fate. The ghosts!

"Thanks for that!" Holly said to the unseen entities, then tried the start button once more.

Nothing.

Timber began to whine beneath the car, unable to bear the weight. One board snapped, then another. The burning structure shuddered and pitched all around them.

More writing on the window, quick and shaky. *EXORCIST. Free us.*

"Oh, God, of course," Holly said, nodding frantically. "Yes, I'll bring one back here as soon as I can!" she vowed.

At once the engine purred to life. Her eyes widened. *In gear.* "Hold on, Cadeon!" *Floor the gas.*

They didn't move an inch.

She shot a glance to her side-view mirror. The back tire was spinning at the edge of an iron underpinning. In the other side-view mirror, she saw the back wheel was spinning furiously—on nothing.

"More gas," he grated.

"You said this has all-wheel drive!" She flattened the accelerator. Smoke billowed from the front peeling tires.

"That's why we're . . . not in the drink yet."

Traction caught; they were thrown back against their

seats as the car lurched forward over booming, cracking supports.

A wall of flames appeared at the exit.

"Oh, God, oh, God," she muttered, clenching the wheel.

"*Do it.*"

"Cadeon, if you're the praying type," she murmured, "now would be a choice time."

31

Fire buffeted the car, roaring all around them. Then came a split second of clear night before the next two blasts landed.

Holly swerved around one, drove through another, then floored it, unbridling the engine on the curving road.

She chanced a glance at Cadeon, but almost wished she hadn't. Panic hit her hard. He was burned over most of his upper body, some of the wounds so severe, there was no physical resemblance to whatever feature had been there before.

Most of his visible flesh looked as if it had melted.

A minute passed. "They're not giving chase." Another minute. "They must have parked on the other side and can't get across the bridge. Or maybe the archers got the last two?"

A noxious smell arose, like burning rubber. Was smoke rising from the back rear tire? She couldn't tell in the fog.

Four minutes passed. "We did it, Cadeon!" she said, determined to keep talking to him. "My God, that was wild! Did you feel the bridge shaking? The deck collapsed like a line of dominoes behind us!"

Headlights shined from down in the basin.

"They're coming again! Why won't they *die?*"

"Outrun . . . them. You can do it . . ."

"On it!" She downshifted for speed up a straight section. "Let's see what this baby—"

A loud bang sounded. The car wobbled. "What—just—happened?"

"Blown tire. Now . . . will you please . . . fucking leave me?"

Ditching Cadeon was simply not an option. She kept her foot on the gas, fighting to steer the car, fighting for inches . . . All those criminals on *Cops* could go for miles with a busted tire!

Think, Holly, think!

She'd just driven on a considerable straightaway and a sharp bend lay up ahead. The road was flanked with ridges on both sides. A nebulous idea arose.

"Cadeon, whose car is this?"

He rasped, "*Not . . . ours.*"

"Just checking."

From his position, propped up against a birch above the ridge, Cade watched Holly snagging the last of their gear from the car, finalizing her trap.

Surely, this couldn't work. But it had to . . . her life depended on it.

Because for some reason, she refused to leave him. And he was helpless to protect her. The poison from those arrows was eating away at him inside, and when his body tried to sweat it out, the chemicals were like acid on his burns, keeping them from healing.

Dizziness was constant. Black spots swarmed in front of his eye as he struggled to stay conscious. Every movement was grueling.

She trotted up the rise, dumping their stuff to the ground

except for his sword, which she unsheathed. Crouching beside him, she laid the weapon over her knees. In readiness.

Could she consciously kill a demon, or possibly more? Could she mindfully make the decision to take a life?

"What are our chances?" she asked.

He grated, "One in fifteen. Don't know if . . . I'd take them."

"You would if there's zero chance otherwise."

The truck was flying up the winding road, headlights going from visible to concealed to visible once more. Tires screeched around the hairpin curves before falling silent when the driver reached the straightaway and gunned the engine.

"Here they come," Holly murmured. "Five . . . four . . . three . . . two . . . *one*."

The driver slammed on the brakes at his first glimpse of her improvised Veyron roadblock.

Too late.

With nowhere to turn, the truck t-boned the heavy car; the sole demon catapulted through the windshield, hurtling through the air.

On his landing, bones cracked audibly, then the momentum sent him scraping over the skin-eating pavement. Eventually, he stopped, sprawling unconscious.

"And that's why even immortals need to wear seat belts." As lightning began to fire all over the valley, Holly rose, wielding Cade's sword. He heard her absently say, "Sit tight. I'll be right back."

Holly advanced to where the fire demon lay, looking like a boneless lump of tissue on the road.

She was about to kill a defenseless being, but there was no help for it. He was already beginning to heal, had ignited the tiniest flame in his lacerated palm.

She quickened her pace. Now she could see why Cadeon had taught her to finish an adversary without mercy. Within moments, this mangled being could be a threat again.

Once she stood over him, she raised the sword above his neck. *Don't hesitate!* With a yell, she swung it down, sending up a shower of sparks against the pavement as she severed the head.

Done, then. That's behind me.

Forcing herself not to look back, she ran for the demon's truck, praying that it might be drivable. Through the smoke from the collision, she saw that it was still running! The engine had been protected by a weighty winch attached to the front bumper—the winch that had cleaved the Veyron nearly in two.

But now it was locking the vehicles together in a tangle of jagged metal. She set down the sword, then grasped the contraption to see if she might budge it.

She pulled up on it with all her might, bewildered to see that she was raising the freaking truck—

The winch tore free in a rush. Pain lashed across her arm as she dropped it. "Damn!" Her gaze shot down. The serrated metal had sliced her arm to the bone.

She tore off the hem of her sweater, knotting it over the wound. She'd definitely need stitches, but couldn't worry about that now. . . .

When she returned for Cadeon, he was unconscious. Her heart lurched, even when she knew he couldn't die like this.

Or could he?

Had some immortal out there actually tested poisoned fey arrows for a contraindication with limb-melting burns?

After she'd gotten him and their things into the truck, she climbed in. Putting it in reverse, she eased back, extricating them from the frame of the million-dollar-plus car.

Without the prop of the truck, the Veyron folded in on itself like one of Cade's Red Bull cans. . . .

32

Taking the demon brew away from the demon when he was burned, poisoned, and laid out naked in a bathtub was clearly ill-advised.

"Give me back my goddamned flask!" he bellowed, his words echoing in the motel room's tiny bathroom.

Wringing another wet cloth over him, she said, "You don't have any fingers to hold it with anyway."

Like a little boy, he shoved the two wrinkly fingers he'd managed to regenerate in front of her face.

"Fine," she sighed. When she handed the flask over, he snatched it to his chest. "You had better be careful," Holly began in a serene tone, "I've heard that stuff takes a while to hit."

"Bugger—off."

She let that slide, knowing it had to be killing a proud male like Cadeon to be vulnerable like this.

"You should've left me . . . in the goddamned truck."

"You are officially the surliest male I've ever met."

"And you're treating me like I'm really hurt," he said, an inane statement, considering that half of the flesh from his waist up was still gone.

On the way to find a nondescript motel where she could hide the stolen truck, Holly had noticed that his skin would seem to be on the path to regeneration, but then he would sweat out more poison. His waxy flesh would well up again.

Once she'd secured a room, she'd ignored his grumbling as she'd removed what was left of his burned clothing, then led him to the bathtub.

After filling the room's ice bucket with both ice and water to dip a cloth in, she knelt beside him, gently wringing the chill water over his skin. She kept her eyes averted from his privates—almost without fail.

The poison had a bluish tint to it that rinsed away easily enough. If only it didn't keep coming back.

The pain must be agonizing.

"Why're you being . . . so nice to me?" he asked gruffly, raising the flask, drinking deep.

"Because you *are* hurt, and you need help."

"Not 'cause of what I told you?" he said.

Well, there was that. His admission had thrown her. It brought a whole new layer to whatever they had between them, an aspect of permanence to a flirtation.

All his advances hadn't been merely because the job had put her in his path. He'd sought her out, then had volunteered to protect her.

"Not only because of what you said." She dipped the cloth again, wringing it over his chest.

By the time the flask was empty, his skin was finally free of any blue tint and had begun regenerating before her eyes. By morning he should be completely healed.

Reminded of her own injury, she unraveled the makeshift bandage over her arm. Then stared in astonishment. The skin was already mending.

If I chose to stay a Valkyrie, I could keep this healing ability. . . .

She frowned. *Or I could be burned alive by demons because I'm the Vessel.*

"I think you're all clear," she said. "Let's get you to bed." She helped him stand, then held his swaying form steady as she wrapped a towel around his waist—not that he was modest. The only thing he seemed discomfited about was being injured.

"Can you sit upright?" she asked when they reached the bed.

"One of the first things . . . I learned as a pup."

"Okay, I'm going to get a compress for your forehead." Yet, as soon as she released him, he collapsed back on his burns, hissing in a breath. "Cadeon! Here . . . ," she said, helping him stretch out over the length of the mattress, then drawing a sheet to his waist.

When she returned with her ice water and cloth, he was mumbling in Demonish, seeming out of his head.

Was it the delirium from his injuries making him this way, or the demon brew taking effect? Or both? "Cadeon, are you drunk?"

"Blot—to."

She wondered how he'd feel if she took advantage of *his* drunkenness. Her eyes widened. *I should!* She had so many questions about this male. The more she thought about it, the more she realized he'd divulged very little about himself.

And he had done this to her first. *Turnabout's fair play.*

She sat beside him. "Cadeon, can you hear me?"

He didn't open his eyes. "Nothing wrong . . . with my ears."

"Of course, not." She laid the cloth on his forehead. "So . . . you and Tera seemed close."

"Been through a lot."

"Was she your girlfriend?"

He gave a laugh that sounded more like a grunt. "Not at all."

"And you really didn't sleep with Imatra?"

"Bloody hell, noooo, I didn't . . . She's a slag."

"Then why did you kiss her?" Holly asked.

"Directions . . . and to see."

"To see what?"

"That it wouldn't be all that bad without you."

This was interesting. "Did you make a determination?"

He gave a bitter laugh. "It'll be all that bad."

Oh, Cadeon. "You've known I was your female for a year?" He nodded. "Why would I be chosen for you?"

"Fate decides . . . who I can be most satisfied with."

Nibbling her lip, she asked, "Have you slept with anyone else since you knew it was me?"

"Gave a halfhearted try for a witch . . . she wanted a werewolf instead."

There was no getting around it—Holly was jealous of the witch.

But then Cadeon said, "And I wanted you."

She dipped the cloth, then gently returned it to his head. "Why did you never approach me, or tell me even days ago?"

"Can't have a human for my own . . . forbidden. They never survive the claiming."

"Claiming? You mean the first time for sex?" He nodded. "What happens that's so dangerous?"

"I'd go all the way demonic. I'd bite you . . . stun you. Keep you steady while I come in you."

"Oh." She didn't know if she was horrified or titillated

by this information. Again, she was reminded that he was a demon, a different *species* from her. "Then wouldn't you want me to stay Valkyrie? So I could survive it?" Why would he be helping her reverse the change?

He grew quiet. "Not going to claim you anyway. Know this."

"Why do you know this?"

"Only in my mind."

Seeing he wouldn't reveal more on the subject, she asked, "Were you jealous of my relationship with Tim?"

"Wanted to kill the prick . . . not good enough for you."

"But you are?"

"Nah . . . wish I was," he said. "You can do better than a mercenary."

"But aren't you also a prince?"

He went motionless. "Of a lost crown . . ." In a derisive tone, he said, "I can put any king on a throne, 'cept for the one I lost."

"What throne did you lose?"

He exhaled a long breath. "Rydstrom's."

Her eyes went wide. "How?"

His voice grew hoarse and even his accent changed when he murmured, "My fault. Mine own doing."

"How could it be your fault?"

"Mistake. *The one who controls the castle . . .*"

"What does that mean?"

"They all *died*."

"Who, Cadeon?" No response. "Does Rydstrom blame you for losing his throne?"

"He does . . . always has. He should."

Anger flared within her. Had his older brother—the king—been making Cadeon's life miserable for nine hundred years? "Why do you still talk to him? Why live on his property? Why be half of the Woede?"

"Guard the king."

"Yes, yes, but you don't have to forever!"

" . . . be easier if I just could hate him."

Her previous ire gave way under the weight of sympathy she felt for this male. "You want to hate him?"

"Can't manage to."

"Why?"

"He's m'brother. If he gets hit . . . I feel it, too. Weird." He tried to give a shrug, then gritted his teeth in pain as his new skin pulled tight. "Holly?"

"I'm right here."

"Proud tonight . . . my female's brave," he murmured, his breathing deepening.

Holly had been brave—she'd proven her mettle, getting Cadeon and herself to safety.

That didn't mean she *ever* wanted to have to prove herself like that again. There had been so many close calls. At any given point in that battle, her life could have ended. . . .

He slept now, his broad chest rising and falling steadily. She bit her lip, her gaze falling on his horns.

The temptation proved too great to resist, and she tentatively felt one. It was smooth, and her fingers glided over its length.

When had her wariness over this part of him turned to fascination? She felt a clenching in her stomach when she gazed at him. *Want* . . .

No! No *want*. She didn't trust her emotions or even her thoughts.

She finally dragged herself away to take a shower, but

once she was clean and dressed for bed, she was still wide awake. So she straightened the room, then fired up her laptop to map the next checkpoint.

When she was online, she saw Tim was connected as well, though it was midnight in California. She was surprised by how much she longed to talk to him, to have a taste of the normal. *I need a fix of normal.*

Should she call him this late at conference? As she debated, she thought to herself how lucky she was to have him. Never would she have to worry about hearing another woman in the background or Tim's voice slurring from drunkenness.

That certainty was comforting.

Holly liked certainty. She liked living her life in predictable, regimented hours, backed up by the campus class times. Just thinking about her old life soothed her now.

So far, in the Lore, the only thing certain was that nothing was ever certain. Why would someone like her ever want to join this chaotic, violent world? Much less having to worry about what her child might be like, or if she'd be attacked by demons. . . .

Need—fix. She reached for her cell phone and rang him.

"Holly?" Tim quickly answered. "Is something wrong? I saw you were up, and it's two in Memphis. Is everything all right with your family?"

"Um, good." *Liar. Liar.* "Everything's working out. How's the conference?"

"It'd be better if you were here."

"Maybe I'll go next time." How difficult could a conference be compared to what she'd done tonight? She'd evaded fire bombs. She'd killed. . . .

"I'd love for you to come with me," he said. "Will you be back in New Orleans by the time I return?"

That depended on where the next checkpoint was. The one based on the coordinates that a *ghost* had given her. Holly felt like giving a hysterical laugh. Instead, she said, "I'm not sure, but I'll know more tomorrow."

"I noticed that you haven't uploaded anything to the storage drive. Are you blocked?"

She sighed. "Yes. And it's miserable."

"I'm sorry, Holly," Tim said. "I'm here if you need an ear."

"I know. You're always there for me." Reliable, steady Tim.

"You sound . . . different. Are you sure everything's okay? It seems like something's on your mind."

Actually . . . "Tim, what would you say if I wanted to work off campus? Maybe get a corporate job after graduation?"

"You know that I'd support you in anything you wanted to do." He hesitated. "It's just that . . ."

"What?" she asked.

"Sometimes, you don't . . . do so well, um, off campus."

A nice way of saying that she'd occasionally been incapacitated. "What if I could do better?"

"I'm sure you can do anything you put your mind to. But I also thought you wanted to have kids."

"Well, lots of women work in the corporate world and have kids."

"That's true," he agreed, but for some reason, her ear twitched.

"Do you not think they should?"

"Of course, I do." He sighed. "Holly, it almost sounds

like you're spoiling for a fight. Did I do something wrong?"

She pinched her forehead. She was the guilty party here, the one who'd been unfaithful on top of a sports car, and yet she was feeling aggressive and irritable with him.

Even though she recognized this within herself, she still couldn't stop from asking, "Why have you never pushed for us to have sex?" When he began to sputter, she knew her unusual bluntness was throwing him.

Finally, he answered, "Because you were so staunchly against it."

"But you do *want* to make love to me?"

"Of course I do, sweetheart." There was that endearment again. Did it sound insincere? Cadeon only called women that if he *didn't* want them.

Tim continued, "You're beautiful and desirable."

Then why haven't you locked that up?

Where were these thoughts coming from? She'd made a commitment to Tim, and now she was rethinking it only because her life was in such upheaval.

Decide nothing until back to normal. Keep the constants constant.

Tim was a good man. Any girl would be lucky to have him. Even her parents had liked him.

Or had they merely been delighted that she had a boyfriend?

"I'm sorry, Tim. I don't know what's wrong with me. Maybe I can call you tomorrow?"

"It's okay. We all have days like this."

Tim never did.

Once they'd hung up, she gazed vacantly at her computer screen.

Even if she did decide to break up with Tim, the alternative was *not* Cadeon. The demon might be thrilling and sexy and . . . *fun*, but a relationship with him would never work. He was too implusive, his moods too mercurial. She didn't know if Cadeon was even capable of a deep and lasting love.

And Holly wanted a love like the abiding one her parents enjoyed. She'd always hoped that something approaching that could grow between her and Tim.

Then why hasn't it in two years? You're clinging because you're afraid.

Shut up, dark side!

Holly wanted steady and normal. She would not succumb.

Which meant she had to get to Groot. Her mind back on the prize, she opened Google Earth. After determining that the longitude was just around the tip of Idaho, she eased the pointer north, frowning that she wasn't near the latitude yet.

Farther, farther . . .

When the pointer rested on their destination, her lips parted on a stunned breath.

33

Cade shot up in bed, drenched in sweat, heart thundering.

He'd dreamed of the blustery night mere weeks ago when he'd killed the mortal Néomi. The night he'd ruined their chances with the vampire.

Cade took his dreams very seriously, and he'd had this one before. He must be feeling more guilt about this than he'd thought. Yes, the death had been an accident, but it had been caused by *him*—not by Rydstrom or even Rök, who'd both been there.

He shuddered, recalling the sickening feeling as his sword had sunk into her. Her pale face had looked as shocked as he felt. Blood had bubbled from her lips as she'd tried to scream.

When she'd slipped from his sword to the ground, Cade had caught his brother's gaze. Through the rain, Cade had seen that same look Rydstrom had given him nine hundred years ago—pity mingled with contempt. . . .

Cade blinked down, surprised to find Holly in the bed with him, though she was on the outside of the cover, dressed in her robe and curled under a blanket. Her pink lips were parted, her lashes thick against her cheeks. Shining against the pillow was a riot of red-blond curls.

He leaned over and plucked up a strand, rubbing it between his thumb and forefinger. As he gazed down at her, memories from the night began to arise. He remembered how brave she'd been with the fire demons, and how she'd refused to leave him, instead managing to drive them out of danger.

She'd talked to him the entire way to this motel, seeming to know how much he'd needed to hear her voice. All night she'd cared for him.

Cade remembered being so damned proud of her, of the way she'd taken everything in stride, rising to the fore.

He'd also realized that what he felt for her was more than the pull of fate. . . .

Releasing her hair, he eased from the bed, then he scuffed into the bathroom. He checked his face in the mirror. Healed.

Even after he'd finished showering and dressing, she still slept. She must be exhausted from the night.

He saw her laptop was open and on. She'd already researched their next direction, mapping it. Where would they be going . . . ?

"*Bugger all,*" he muttered. *The Northwest Territories*. Just under the Arctic Circle.

They would have to cross the border, then travel nearly the entire length of Canada while heading ever northward. She'd determined sixty-seven hours of driving time—if the weather was perfect.

As usual, her cell phone was lying parallel to the laptop. He frowned, vaguely recalling her voice lowered, as if in conversation. Had she made a call? He checked the log. *Son of a—* "Holly!" he bellowed.

She shot up in bed, shoving her curling hair from her face. "*Whaa?* I'm up!"

"You called the tosser last night?"

"You checked my phone?" she cried, scrambling to her feet. "How dare you!"

"Even after what I told you at the bridge?"

"I needed someone to talk to." When she saw he was about to crush her phone, she snatched it from him.

Wait . . . More memories emerged. She'd questioned him! Cade cast his mind back, trying to recall everything he'd told her. "Seems like you talked to me quite a bit! Interrogating me!"

"Now you know how it feels to be taken advantage of. Turnabout's fair play."

"It's hardly the same! You were drunk, while I was poisoned and burned."

"And drunk," she added.

"You called him even when I was hurt? While I was lying unconscious, you talked to him?"

"Yes, Cadeon, after I tirelessly saw to your healing, and then determined that you were going to be fine, I did make a call."

Cade's eyes widened. "To break up with him?"

"No! Just because you told me I'm your female doesn't make the corollary true. We still don't have a relationship."

"In other words, the square root of fuckall is fuckall."

"You don't want me to be with Tim, but you're not offering anything else."

"What's that supposed to mean?"

"You told me I'm your female, but you have no plans to ask me for any kind of commitment."

He ground his teeth. *Because I can't!* "Would you say yes if I did?" he asked, noting that he'd gone still, awaiting her answer.

"No, Cadeon," she finally said. "I wouldn't."

A fear skittered up his spine—something he'd considered, but dismissed. "Are you *in love* with that human?"

With an unflinching gaze, she said, "He's what I want."

They'd made the cab ride from the motel to the closest car dealership in stony silence.

Now, as a bemused salesman escorted them about the lot, they bickered over what to buy for the rest of the trip. She wanted a new, smaller SUV, and Cade wanted a used "gas-guzzling behemoth," as she put it. Though he'd calmly pointed out the various merits of his choice, she refused to see reason.

He kept his cool until she said, "But that manufacturer doesn't have environmentally conscious policies."

Enough. "Oh, like I give a shite! I just want to get a truck and get the hell out of here."

At that, the wide-eyed salesman excused himself.

Clearly grappling with her own temper, she said, "But a new one will be less likely to break down."

He shook his head. "Trucks today aren't made as well."

"I don't agree," she said. "And I think we'll be more comfortable and safer with the options offered in newer models."

"More options means more things that can break. Now, there's not a damn thing wrong with that white Bronco—"

"Oh, *please*," she snapped. "O.J. called, wants his car back."

"Were you even born in time to see that car chase? Or did you have to catch it on YouTube?"

"I saw it live. I was already *twelve*, cradle-robber! Now what's wrong with the little Range Rover?"

"The dealer might frown on me paying for an eighty-thousand-dollar car *with cash*. Besides, after you offed our seven-figure ride last night, you'd think your mind would be on economizing."

"You know whose car I offed last night? *Not—mine*. Is this the gratitude I get for saving your life? Don't count on me to come rescue you again. I'll let you fricassee the next time you're on fire!"

Cade's sat-phone rang then, like a ring-side bell. "I'm taking this call. Hey, I've got an idea. While I'm gone, why don't you try to see reason? If you can recognize it."

He stormed across the parking lot. "What?" he barked in answer.

"You sound like hell," Rök said.

"Any word on Rydstrom?"

"My spies in Tornin are almost certain he's being kept there."

Cade said, "And no one escapes from Tornin." The thought of that sent his foul mood plummeting.

It was time for Cade, the master of blocking out unwanted realities, to analyze some pretty grim fucking realities.

His brother: being used by an evil sorceress for impregnation.

His female: stubbornly clinging to her relationship with the fuckwit, and approximately two weeks away from hating Cade bitterly anyway.

Himself: in full-on identity crisis. The killer for hire with no conscience was finding that lies to Holly tasted like soot in his mouth. The big, bad mercenary was having nightmares about an accidental death. . . .

"But I do have some news," Rök said. "You know that mortal you skewered?"

Speak of the devil. Cade scowled. "Néomi. What about her?"

"I just saw her singing karaoke at the Cat's Meow."

Cade's jaw slackened. "*Singing?*"

"Yeah. There were a few pitch problems in the beginning, but in the end she really worked it out—"

"Rök! Are you saying she survived?"

"Unless she has a twin . . . But my gut tells me that was the vampire's Bride I saw."

Rök's instincts had saved their lives more times than he could count. If this was true . . .

Néomi's male knew of another way to kill Omort—an alternative to the sword. If Cade could get his hands on that information, he wouldn't have to betray Holly.

"Why didn't you abduct the mortal? You know how valuable she is."

"She's quick. She seemed to have just . . . disappeared out from under us. But I'll find her again. I've got a good lead."

If they had Néomi, the vampire would do anything to get his Bride back, even divulge how to kill a sorcerer. . . .

"Capture her at all costs, Rök."

"We're already on it. But you're still continuing on—in case we don't, right?"

He exhaled. "I am. I have to. But you *will* find her. Use any means necessary." Once they'd hung up, Cade gazed over at Holly, and his heart thundered in his chest.

Hope—a way out. A way to have *everything* he'd ever wanted.

He'd held himself back from her because he'd known he would be forced to hurt her worse than she'd ever been. But this development gave him the possibility of a future with her . . .

Yes, *possibility*. Before, anything between Cade and Holly had been doomed because there were so many epic obstacles: betrayals, ancient vows, dark lies, the wills of evil sorcerers.

Now, if the only thing between them was a fucking mathematician . . . ?

And one she hadn't been able to say she loved.

This is as good as locked up. Cade would simply have to convince her why he was the better male for her.

He looked forward to it, he thought as he strode across the lot toward her. She caught sight of him and nibbled her lip, studying his expression. She'd worn her hair in that bun, but it was looser, pretty. She was so beautiful she made his chest ache.

In Cade's absence, the salesman had ventured back, but now looked nervous at his approach.

When Cade reached Holly, he swung her into his arms and kissed her.

"Cadeon!" she sputtered when he released her lips. But he kept her in his arms as he told the bewildered salesman, "We'll take whatever the missus wants. And quickly." Cade met her eyes. "We've got exactly *four hundred and twenty miles* to drive tonight before she'll be satisfied."

34

Their new vehicle was barreling down the highway.

Earlier, she'd been so disarmed by Cadeon's dramatic change in mood—which he'd refused to explain—that she'd compromised with him. They'd bought a brand new truck that had an SUV-like compartment over the bed.

And now the demon was continually glancing at the odometer as he drove well over the posted speed limit.

She sighed. "Look I know I said we could be . . . intimate every four hundred and twenty miles, but I've had second thoughts after what happened last night. I don't want to lead you to expect something that can never be."

"Can never be because of your boyfriend? The one you couldn't tell me you loved?"

"It's not just that. You have to understand that all I've ever wanted was a steady, dependable partner and a normal life. You're not . . . normal." Her gaze flitted to his horn, and he saw it, rubbing it with a scowl. "It's not just you. It's this entire world. The Lore."

"What's wrong with the Lore?"

"Hmm, it's—oh, I don't know—exceedingly *violent*? As evidenced by last night."

"That was pretty extreme even for the Lore," he said, then added, "And for the record, I'm *not* ungrateful about your saving my ass. I know what kind of shape I was in.

Poison does a number on demons. We're really susceptible to its effects."

"Why?"

"Species that can emit poisons are vulnerable to others," he answered. "So did you mean what you told those spirits last night? About returning with an exorcist?"

"Of course. I'm going to ask my aunt to help me find one. Why were the ghosts used as messengers for the coordinates anyway?"

"They were perfect for it. They can't be bribed or tortured for the information. After that checkpoint, anyone thinking to find us will be stymied." He added, "As long as you keep those pearls on."

"How would the spirits know the coordinates?"

"One of Groot's followers would have given them the information well in advance."

"Why would they agree to become involved?"

"Maybe Groot promised them the exorcism they wanted."

She frowned. "If he promised, then why would they ask me for it?"

"Uh, probably just being sure. So, what all did I tell you last night?"

"You mean other than the fact that I'm your female chosen by fate?"

"I think fate made an excellent choice for me. The best."

He could be so charming when he wanted to be. "I also learned that you have *issues* with your brother Rydstrom."

"You have no idea," he said dryly.

"Why?"

"We're polar opposites. He's rational, always looking at things logically, whereas I follow my gut more times than not. He's educated, well-spoken, and . . . kingly. I'm irresponsible, the notorious ne'er-do-well," he answered with a shrug, as if this was just a carved-in-stone fact of life. "What else did I say?"

"You told me you would *bite* me, to stun me during the claiming. How? Is it some kind of venom, like from your horns?"

"No, I'd sink my fangs into a muscle between your neck and shoulder."

"And go fully demonic?" When he nodded, she said, "What's that like?"

"My skin would darken, reddening. It's supposed to be an attractant to females. My body will get bigger, my horns and claws growing to their full length. And my face will change. The planes will get sharper."

She bit her lip. "You also said that the only place you'll claim me is in your mind. What does that mean? Have you fantasized about me?"

His lids grew heavy when he said, "Oh, yeah."

"Like, you've imagined me . . . *naked?*"

"Ah, halfling, I've stripped your body a thousand times. I've taken you when you were wearing only your pearls, so hard they bounced on your neck."

She stifled a shiver.

"You're quite lusty in my fantasies. And you have a predilection for going down on me at every chance."

Her cheeks heated. "Going down on you . . . that's exactly what it sounds like, isn't it?" Was her voice breathy? She couldn't help but try to picture what that'd be like.

"It is, but I don't want you to imagine doing that to me. At all. Just get it out of your mind, before you start seizing on the idea, and then that's all you can think about. . . ."

Central Saskatchewan
Canada

"You ready to review self-defense techniques?" Cadeon asked, as he drove along a desolate stretch of highway.

She nodded. "Just let me upload and power down." She was having to use sat-phone internet access in this isolated area, and it was glacially slow.

Not that she had much progress to upload. Though she'd plugged away at her code, she still had yet to make a significant break.

As she waited, she thought over the last three days. Canada had flown by in a blur.

That first night when they'd been about to cross the border from Michigan, she'd been a wreck, certain that they'd be found out as Lorekind, but Cadeon had been cool, so relaxed. The entire process had taken all of half a minute.

Because darkness lasted so long at this latitude, they were driving most hours out of the twenty-four. Cadeon only needed about four hours of sleep, and she'd found that she didn't need much more.

As they'd traversed the country, they settled into a comfortable familiarity. After so long together in the truck, the rest of the world seemed cut off from them. They'd begun finishing each other's sentences. He regularly pointed out things he thought she'd like to see, getting her to glance up from her work.

Early on, they'd reached an XM radio compromise. Blues rock played when she was working, and any other time, they listened to the fast-paced ska music he liked. She hadn't admitted it to him, but it was growing on her as well.

They collected supplies as they needed them, and as they could find them. He'd bought her a new coat to replace the one lost the night of the bridge and also a sat-phone for her, in case they somehow got separated.

Though they hadn't been intimate again—she had somehow resisted his advances—he'd been putting on the full-court press with her.

And it might be . . . working.

She thought of Tim less frequently, and she sometimes found herself resenting the guilt her relationship with him brought her. But then she'd feel guilt for the resentment. A vicious cycle.

It wasn't fair to him. Over the last several days, she'd reached a decision. She might not end up with Cadeon, but she didn't necessarily think she belonged with Tim either.

She recalled the injury to her arm. It had healed without a mark by that next morning. Holly had begun to believe that it was too late for the reversal anyway. And she wasn't as broken up about that as she'd thought she'd be.

In truth, she'd begun seeing herself with Cadeon more and more. She'd grown accustomed to his abrasive, low-brow humor. He made her laugh and made sure she didn't take herself too seriously. She could stare at those green eyes of his for hours.

And he'd proved considerate, always seeing to her needs, working with her quirks. She never opened a bottle when he was near.

He was also tirelessly teaching her, making her spar whenever they stopped at a hotel for a few hours. Then back on the road, he quizzed her on what she'd learned. . .

When she finished her upload, she took off her glasses and closed the computer. "Okay, ready to drill."

"All right. What's the first thing you do with multiple assailants? And why?"

"Count them, because if I decide to run, they'll likely split up. It'll help me determine whether I'm being surrounded."

One nod. "You've encountered a foe—where's the first place you look?"

"The eyes. They'll change color if he's enraged. After that, I'd look at the hands to check for weapons."

"Say he's enraged and carrying. What's your facing-off position?"

"I narrow the target, with one foot in front of the other, one shoulder outward." Before he could ask, she said, "My *left* shoulder. Because I'm right handed."

"Utilizing your environment—two examples."

"Put obstacles between me and my attacker," she said. "And use the lighting to my advantage—shadows distort perception."

"How many pounds of pressure does it take to break a knee?" he asked.

"Only twelve."

"And what do you do if a human male threatens you?"

"Clean his clock, and teach him the time of day."

"That's my girl." He gently chucked her on the chin, and she flushed with pleasure.

"Why do you keep preparing me?"

"Because we're not finished yet. You've still got people trying to kill you, and we've still got at least one more checkpoint. It could be as dangerous as the last."

* * *

Cadeon was out on the hunt for uncracked steamed shellfish, leaving Holly back at the hotel to work, "because codes don't write themselves."

But she was blocked, unable to get anything done. She decided to call Mei to make sure everything was going all right with her class. The boys could be . . . boisterous.

"Everything's fine," Mei said, but didn't elaborate. "How are things with your family?"

"Getting better. A lot better. I think everything's going to be fine."

"That's good."

Holly's ear twitched, and she frowned. "Mei, do you want to tell me something?"

"Look, I wasn't going to call you because I know you've got a lot on your plate, but there might be a time element involved with your work, and I'm sick of women being passed over for these jobs anyway."

Holly's stomach began to churn. "What are you talking about?"

"You know Scott was at the California conference, right?"

"Yes, he went at the last minute." Scott was Mei's boyfriend, a well-respected mathematician and all around nice guy.

"This morning he called me with some disturbing news. . . ."

"Just tell me, Mei."

She took a deep breath, then said, "Tim's been stealing your work—and passing it off as his own."

35

As Cade waited for food, he checked in with Rök. "Any word on Néomi?"

"Again, we were closing in and she just seemed to . . . vanish," Rök said, sounding like he was scratching his head.

"A *mortal* is evading you? Come on, Rök—we're running out of time! I need you to be on this with everything you've got."

"I have a really good lead. I'll get her this time."

Rök sounded confident enough, but once they hung up, Cade was uneasy about their prospects.

And Cade had begun mulling another idea—a way for everyone to win. It'd be extremely dangerous. Riskier than anything he'd ever attempted.

If his plan failed, everyone would *lose*.

In life, Cade's season record wasn't all wins. And when he fucked up, he tended to go big.

He should stick with Rydstrom's wishes, carrying out this operation the way the king intended. Cade would put his idea out of his head.

But what if . . . ?

"What?" Holly cried.

"Tim's been taking sole credit for the papers he's presented," Mei explained. "So Scott figured that he'd just spaced and forgot to mention you. But then later, Scott heard him talking to the recruiters from Lockheed Martin. Tim was downplaying your involvement in all of your past co-projects. And I knew that with your background you had to have carried a lot of them."

"I carried all of them," Holly absently said.

"I shouldn't have told you till you got back."

"No, you did the right thing. I appreciate your letting me know."

"What are you going to do?" Mei asked.

"I don't know." Surely Tim wouldn't screw her over like this.

How well do you really know him . . . ?

"Holly, if you confront Tim, you can tell him where you heard it from. Scott's livid."

Stealing research was about the worst thing one could do in their small community. Everyone toiled too hard not to be fiercely protective of their projects. Not to mention the fact that in their field, research could be worth millions—or even billions.

Scott was well-respected among all his colleagues. If he said Tim had done this, then Tim was going to get crucified. . . .

Once she and Mei hung up, Holly sat on the bed, dumbfounded. She'd always felt confident that her boyfriend wouldn't betray her sexually. Had he betrayed her academically? Had that been why he'd been pushing her for her new code?

No, no, she was sure there was a reasonable explanation for this. This was merely hearsay, at best. Maybe Scott had overheard incorrectly.

Tim was a good guy. He was *normal*.

She called his cell phone. He answered before the end of the first ring.

"Tim, I'm glad I caught you. Do you have a minute to talk?"

"Absolutely. My next presentation's not for an hour."

"So Mei just called me . . ."

"Oh? What did she have to say?"

Holly's ears twitched again. There was something different about him, a treble in his voice that was altered. *He's nervous*. She could perceive it so clearly now. *Valkyrie senses*.

The benefit of the doubt went out the window. "When you presented our work, did you take sole credit for it?"

"What are you talking about?"

"Did you downplay my role in our projects with the Lockheed recruiters?"

"I wouldn't do that! Of course not. I know better than anyone how hard you've worked on our project—"

"Just cut the bullshit. I know you're lying. I can hear it in your voice."

Quiet. Finally, he said, "I might have played up my role in the work, but I did it *for us*. You know the big firms usually hire men in our field. I had the better shot at getting that job. And then, just think, I could buy us a house. You wouldn't even *need* a job."

She sucked in a breath. "Who *are* you? Need a job? I *already* don't need one—I love what I do. Was this your play all along?"

"There was no play. We work better as a team, with me as the front man."

"What the hell does that mean?"

"We need to stick together, to keep the work together. We could be unstoppable."

Here was a man who actually wanted her for her brain. Or, at least, he wanted to use what it could do.

"Be realistic, Holly. You can barely get to classes without me. How well were you going to do in the corporate world?"

"Oh, my God." Red covered her vision. What had Cadeon called Tim? *Oh, yes . . .* "You know what, you fuckwit tosser—you can have that goddamned work." Lightning struck outside, and it felt right. "I'm on to something so much bigger. Something that's going to rock our industry."

"Holly, just wait—"

"Don't ever contact me again. Or I will nail your balls to the wall over this." Click.

Deep breath, deep breath. She waited for the tears to come. And waited.

Yet all she felt was a sense of relief. *How freeing . . .* She was done with guilt, free from indecision.

Holly had no obstacles now—if Cadeon tried more, she wouldn't rebuff him. The idea gave her a giddy thrill of expectation.

Actually, *she* might try for more. Even more than Cadeon would expect. . . .

"The male's back with food . . ." He trailed off when she stood before him, wearing only that black silk number she sometimes slept in—the one that guaranteed he'd be wide awake and hard as rock for hours.

"I'm not hungry." The lights were low and the bedspread was drawn down.

"But you need to eat," he said absently as she sauntered up to him.

Her eyes had begun to grow silvery. "Maybe I'm hungry for something else." She took the bag of food from him and tossed it away.

His brows drew together. "Uh, what happened between the time I went for food and now?"

"I broke up with Tim."

Cade's heart began to thunder, and damn if she didn't notice.

"You really like that news, huh?" She smiled.

"What's not to like? But why now?"

"He stole credit for my research. And he was after the code I'm working on now."

Cade went still, fury spiking through him. "Holly, I'm going to give you his throat for this."

"Aw, you say the sweetest things, demon." She stood on tiptoe and pressed a gentle kiss to his lips.

Deciding he'd kill Tim for her anyway, he relaxed and said, "I know how to play those heartstrings, yeah?"

She unbuckled Cade's belt. "I called him a *fuckwit tosser*."

"That's my girl." He stripped off her top, then his shirt. "Are you coming on to me to get back at him?"

"Probably." Down went his zipper.

"I'm okay with that."

And if he'd thought this couldn't get any better, she bit her bottom lip and said, "You told me you'd fantasized about me, um, going down on you. What if I wanted to try it?"

Trying to keep his cool, he grinned down at her. "Then you'd be my *best* girl. . . ."

Once they were naked in bed, and she'd begun kissing down his torso, he swallowed hard. Would she lose her nerve? *Don't lose your nerve, Holly. . . .*

She took him in hand. A first halting lick was followed by another. Soon she was circling all around the head with wet flicks of her tongue.

"*That's it, Holly,*" he groaned, "*just like that.*"

"You taste so good," she murmured in a delighted tone.

He struggled not to thrust to her hot tongue, but the instinct to move his hips was so powerful. "Suck it inside your mouth," he rasped. She did, making him arch his back sharply. "Ah! What are you doin' to me?"

Hastily pulling back, she said, "Am I doing something wrong?"

"Everything's too right." Hand palming her head, he pressed her back down. "I fear I'll come before I'm ready."

With a satisfied smile, she rubbed her cheek against his shaft, then continued. He pulled her hair out of the way so he could see his female pleasuring him like this.

A fantasy made flesh. After so long.

Bending his knee, he raised his leg so she straddled it, her wet sex against it.

She moaned around him, one of those sharp, yearning cries that made him frenzied to pleasure her. Immediately, he reached for her hips, pulling her toward him.

"Cade? I liked that. . . ." She trailed off when he repositioned her, settling her knees by each side of his face, her mouth at his cock.

"Then you'll love this," he rasped before he lost himself in licking strawberry blond curls. Her sex was so hot, the flesh exquisitely tender. He licked in bliss.

But she froze. "Cadeon?" She sounded stunned. He dug

his heels into the bed and thrust up. After a hesitation, she took him between her lips again, her mouth soon growing greedy. The shy virgin was gone, replaced by a hungry, demanding Valkyrie who expected to give and get pleasure.

With his hands splayed over her ass, he gripped her, holding on to her as she wickedly rocked her sex against his mouth.

When he worked his finger into her sheath, she spread her knees wider with a cry. She was losing control. Thunder boomed all around the building, quaking the walls.

He wanted this to last forever, but he was already on the verge. *She needs to come first.* As he withdrew and thrust his finger, he sucked her hard little clitoris between his lips, snaking his tongue over it.

She screamed, then took him deep. Her moans around his shaft sent him over. As she came, he groaned and licked, joining her. . . .

She rolled off him, sprawled beside him as they caught their breath.

"Who knew demons were so delicious?" she asked as he dragged her to his chest.

"Demon. Singular. Don't be getting any ideas."

36

The Northwest Territories
Headlands of the McKenzie Mountains

The sixtieth parallel was the last one before the Arctic Circle.

They'd passed the sign marking it several hours ago.

For the last four days, they'd headed ever northward toward the Canadian Rockies. The land grew starkly beautiful, the temperature holding steady at a balmy fifteen below. The sun never ascended much higher than the spruce tops, and it both rose and set two hours outside of noon.

Now she was waiting for Cadeon in the parking space—singular—at the White Tail Lodge, which promised to be the final outpost before serious, isolated wilderness.

In other words, their final destination.

The "Lodge" itself was a strange hybrid of trailer and cabin. On the gray siding, antlers were nailed to the side, spelling *Wh te T il Lo ge*.

Holly thought it should spell: *We gave our lives for this??*

As Cadeon bought supplies, she patched her laptop into her sat-phone to upload all of her day's work into a Tim-free account.

The only lingering fallout from Tim's betrayal was her anger and a burning desire to complete her code. And without the obstacle of her ex-boyfriend, Holly had few defenses against Cadeon's appeal.

She was reminded of her last look at the Veyron. Without the prop of the truck, it had helplessly crumpled. Now without the guilt and sense of obligation, Holly was doing a free fall for the demon. . . .

She and Cadeon indulged—often. He happily allowed her to explore him, drawing a knee up, telling her to "Have at it." They slept in the same bed. Each time, he wrapped his body around her so tightly, tucking her close to him. She wondered if he was following some innate demon instinct to protect her.

They showered together—one of the highlights of each day for her.

But he never tried to make love to her, even when she'd hinted that she'd be amenable to losing her virginity. Though she could tell how badly he wanted to take it, he still made no move to.

Was it only that he didn't want to hurt her? Every day he noted how strong she was becoming. Did he doubt that she could handle the claiming?

Or was there another reason he resisted . . . ?

When he'd returned and finished loading up the back, she asked him, "What all did you get?"

"Food, staple goods—apparently eggs and butter are like gold if we do happen upon anyone north of here. And as many tanks of gas as we can ferry. I also found out that we're going to have to cross a winter road."

Winter road—a euphemism for ice beneath tires and possibly not much more. "No way around that?"

"Only way to get from here to there, love."

* * *

"This is the checkpoint? It's adorable!" Holly hopped out of the truck, gazing at the snow-covered cabin. "It's straight out of a winter wonderland calendar!"

His female's mood had certainly improved since the ice road. The normal—but loud—shifting of ice had terrified her, and she'd held on to the dashboard the entire way.

When a fox bounded by in the foot-high snow banks, she clapped her gloved hands in delight. "Cue the fox. How perfect!"

Cade found it *too* perfect with its blanket of snow on the roof and quaint chimney on the side.

She asked, "Are you sure this is the exact location?"

"GPS says we're here."

"I guess someone will meet us?" she asked, starting for the door.

But he swooped her back. "For all we know, this is an elevator to hell. I'm checking it out. Do not come in until I tell you to."

He found the door unlocked and cautiously entered it. The pinewood floored creaked beneath him. The cabin was so spotless, even Holly would approve.

"Do you see any directions?" she called from outside. "I wanna come in!"

"Not yet," he called back. "Still looking around."

The interior was simple, with sparse wooden furniture throughout. There was a bathroom, a back bedroom, and a kitchen with a wood-burning stove and a well pump above the basin.

A claw-footed bathtub was situated out in the main room in front of the sizable fireplace.

The idea of seeing Holly bathing there, in front of a fire . . .

With each of their encounters over the last few days, he'd found it increasingly difficult to resist claiming her. His mind was constantly filled with thoughts of being inside her, his reasoning clouded by want.

She'd been regularly tiptoeing around the subject of sex, a question here or there, and he thought he knew why.

Holly wanted him to take her. Completely. He was humbled by that, yet at the same time, he knew he couldn't. Even if he didn't trade her to Groot for the sword, the fact remained that Cade had deceived her over and over. He'd already done more than she'd likely forgive, done more than enough to earn her hatred. Taking her virginity under these circumstances struck even him as wrong.

And he wanted more than merely sex from her. He wanted *everything.* Claiming her should be the beginning of something more—not a guilty, fleeting act.

Cade shook himself, and began searching the cabin high and low, checking the two closets and few cabinets. He crossed to the fireplace. Up the chimney was about the only place he hadn't looked. He crouched beside the opening, reaching up blindly—

And felt folded, waxed paper attached to the chimney flue. He pulled it free.

A map to Groot's fortress.

They could start for the sorcerer's today. Holly would surely want to, fearing the approaching transition. But Cade needed to buy Rök time.

And even if Rök failed, every second Cade could stall would allow her to transition more fully to immortal, gaining strength, and losing vulnerability.

Deciding to hide the map, he tucked it into his coat pocket—

"What you got there?"

She was right behind him. After the slightest hesitation, he said, "A map to Groot's."

"So when do we leave?"

"We still have almost two weeks to get there. Maybe we should stay put for a day or two to rest up from the drive."

"Okay," she answered, surprising him. "I'd love to have a bath."

He ran a hand over his mouth.

Though Cadeon had been so gung-ho to get up here, now he was dragging his feet to begin the final leg. But Holly was fine with staying at the adorable cabin.

In a closet, she'd found thick quilts, clean bedding, and a fur hearthrug neatly stored in bags. Once she got everything arranged to her liking, it'd be perfect.

After he'd brought in their kerosene lantern and supplies, he'd set off to chop firewood. He'd collected just enough to start heating her bathwater and warming the cabin for her, then returned to cut more for the night.

As Holly unpacked their gear and food, she gazed out the window at him, losing track of time. As she watched the magnificent male laboring in the snow, she felt a pang. She loved the way he moved, with such surety and presence. Now that she knew every inch of his body, she appreciated it more than she ever had.

Holly wanted all of him, but he refused to give in. He'd called himself *her demon*. But he wasn't, not yet.

Want. She wished she had someone to talk to about all this, someone to ask—

She frowned when her sat-phone began to ring. The

only one who knew the number was Cadeon, and she could still see him outside. "Hello?" she answered.

"You wanted to speak with me?" Nïx asked.

"How did you— Scratch that. Do you know where I am?"

"I know it's snowy and cold. Perfect for snuggling up with your demon. Have you decided if you'll keep him? Or is he too big to be an inside demon?"

Holly sighed. "I like being with him, and I think I do want to keep him. But that means I would have to keep my immortality."

Unfortunately, if she remained a Valkyrie, she remained the Vessel. And events like the Laughing Lady Bridge would continue to happen.

"And which way are you leaning?"

To be with Cadeon . . . "I think I'm sticking with the program."

"I knew you'd succumb to peer pressure! A good thing, too. Since you've already completed the transition."

Holly had suspected as much for days. "But how does this affect your deal with Groot? Cadeon will still get his sword, right?"

"Of course. So when should Auntie Nïx be expecting a little vamon from you two?"

"Vamon—oh, I get it. A Valkyrie and a demon. Ha-ha. Don't hold your breath. He won't . . . well, he refuses to have sex with me."

"Why on earth? That doesn't sound like Cadeon, *at all.*"

Holly glared at that. "He doesn't want to attempt me, to bring out the demon full force."

"Yes, but what do *you* want? Listen to your instinct. What is it telling you?"

Again, she gazed out the window at him. *Want!* "It's not *telling* me anything—it's *screaming* for me to be with him. But it's not like I'm on the pill. And he can't exactly run up to the gas station for condoms."

She was already late with her period, doubtless because of stress, so she wouldn't be ovulating. Right? She'd even double-checked online. She didn't think it possible she'd get pregnant, but if it happened . . .

"Would it be so bad to have a baby vamon?"

At first, the idea had struck Holly as out of left field, but the more she thought about it, the more comfortable she became.

Why should Holly possess all this strength and have no one to protect? Why control her family's fortune and have no one to share it with?

The idea of waiting until certain life events had transpired before having a child no longer applied. She was going to live potentially forever. If she wanted to undertake something exhaustive and demanding for herself, she could do it in eighteen or nineteen years as easily as she could now.

"It doesn't matter anyway," Holly said with a sigh. "He won't do it." He'd proved he could stop himself already, in each of their encounters.

"I'm confused. He's a demon with an instinctive need to sate his female. You're his female. He'll do anything you desire."

"What do you mean?"

"Dearling, it's time for you to take the demon by the horns."

37

"We got up here just in time. Storms are blowing to the south . . ." He trailed off when he found Holly reclining in the tub, wearing nothing but her pearls.

She crooked her finger at him. "It's big enough for two in here." Steam was rising all around her and firelight flickered over her skin—just as he'd imagined earlier.

"You don't have to ask me twice." He dropped the firewood he'd been carrying and stripped off his clothes.

"Is that enough wood to keep us warm tonight?"

Easing into the water behind her, he drew her up between his legs, until the smooth curves of her ass cradled his stiffened shaft. "I'll keep you warm. Don't you worry about that," he said, brushing his lips against her neck until she shivered.

He leisurely skimmed a hand down her body to her sex, slowly stroking for long, long moments. When he slipped his finger inside her, he found her already nice and slick. With a moan, her legs fell open against his.

With his other hand, he pinched her nipples, one then the other, rolling them between his thumb and forefinger. Her arms fell back, her fingers lacing together behind his neck.

When he pressed the heel of his palm against her clitoris, she started rocking on the finger inside her, so he gave her another.

She arched her back, her pert ass flexing against his cock. His hissed in a breath as the swollen crown rubbed over her curves. He could draw his fingers away and be inside her so easily, impaling her on his length. And he knew she would happily accept him. . . .

As if she read his mind, she murmured, "Cadeon, I want you to take my virginity."

This was straight out of his fantasies—where it should remain. But how many more times could he resist before he lost control? "I can't. I never want to hurt you." He didn't only mean physically. Cade might not have had a way out of lying to her, but he had a choice about this.

Gently nudging his hand away, she rolled over between his legs, her slick breasts rubbing over his chest. "Is that the only reason?"

"You're not on the pill, and you're the Vessel . . ."

"It's not the right time of the month for me to conceive. But even if I did, it wouldn't be the end of the world."

"It might just be if I'm the father. Remember the ultimate evil part?"

"You're not evil."

She wouldn't feel that way for long. "Holly, you have no idea." He set her away, then got out of the tub, snatching a towel from a nearby chair.

"You can't convince me of that so don't even try. It's because of the pregnancy thing, isn't it? I know this is a lot to think about. But I wouldn't hold you responsible—"

His shoulders shot back, and he narrowed his eyes. "You think I can't take care of my female and my kid?"

As soon as he'd said those words he stilled—just as he had on the bridge talking to Tera. *The sheer obviousness of it.* Why did something feel as if it had just shifted into place?

"Of course, you can. I was just—"

"That has nothing to do with it. You haven't even seen me at my worst. Holly, I could kill you."

"No, Cadeon"—she reached from the tub, and plucked up a large splinter of wood—"you can't." She dragged it over her forearm.

"Holly! What are you . . ." He trailed off when the cut began healing instantly.

"You *can't* hurt me. I'm an immortal now."

"But the change—I thought you didn't *want* this."

She rose and sauntered up to him, water drops trickling over her sleek body. "I want to stay like this." Her eyes were silvery. He couldn't look away, couldn't pull back, even when she reached under the towel and started stroking his cock.

"What changed your mind?" *Say I did. Say it was me!*

"You. I want to be with you, completely. I want to make love with you."

Everything he'd dreamed of hearing from her. And still he forced himself to say, "It won't happen, Holly."

She'd tried reasoning with Cadeon, but he'd held firm. It was time to play dirty. "You win." She ran her fist up and down his length, stripping his towel. "Then let's just release some steam."

She kissed down his chest and torso, nuzzling the trail of hair below his navel before kneeling in front of him on the fur hearthrug. Hands flat against his chest, she took his shaft between her lips, licking the broad head.

"Ah, Holly, that's it . . ." Threading his fingers in her hair, he guided her head. "Gods, it's so good when you do that . . ."

Soon he was subtly thrusting as he did when on the verge. His body tensed, his erection pulsing.

Her hands eased down to his ankles. Grasping them tight, she wrenched upward with all her might.

Caught off guard, he dropped flat on his back. "Holly!" he roared. "What the fuck—"

But she was already straddling him.

He tossed her to her back on the fur. "Is that how we're to play this?" he grated. He didn't recognize his own voice.

When he pinned her arms over her head, his cock slipped against her damp sex, making him shudder with want. She rolled her hips at the same time, almost dooming them both—because for one perfect moment, the crown had nudged right at her entrance.

His gaze trailed from her face to her breasts, rising and falling with her hectic breaths. With a groan, he dropped his head to suckle her.

As his tongue swirled around one of her nipples, he couldn't stop himself from rocking his cock against her folds again, hunting her wetness for that connection again.

She was looking for it, too, undulating her hips. "*Cadeon . . . please*." She didn't know how to ask for what she needed.

"Does it ache inside?"

"Yes!"

He drew his hips back to slip up and down . . . again that tightness began to glove him, giving him a maddening glimpse of what it could be like. "You need my shaft in you?" Why was he teasing her like this? When he had no intention of taking her fully? "But are you wet enough to take it?"

"*I am . . .*" she moaned.

At her ear, he whispered, "You want me to mount your little sheath? Ride you till you clench for my seed?"

At that, her head thrashed, her hair tossing on the fur. "*Cadeon, why?*"

He didn't know why he was goading her, pushing her. He needed something from her. As he suckled her breast, he tried to read his own instinct. An ache, a need for more than just plunging inside her.

No! The only thing he needed was the will to stop this.

But why? He couldn't permanently hurt her. She was an immortal. Wanted to be one because he was.

"*Please . . .* "

Holly, wet for him, begging him to take her . . . he tried to recall all the reasons this was a bad idea. But he'd wanted her for so long.

"Let my hands go," she murmured. "I'll be good."

He released her, his own hands trailing beneath her to cup her ass. "Ah, gods!" he bit out, when he prodded right at her soft core again. The scent of his female's need, those beseeching moans . . . they were triggers he couldn't fight. He was turning. "I'm going to . . . lose control."

Suddenly he *wanted* to bite her, to pump his seed inside her body, marking her as his own.

No! I can't have what I want . . . He began to draw away from her—

She seized his horns, clutching them tight.

"*Uhhh . . .*" he groaned, his eyes rolling back in his head. *Too stunned to speak, to move.*

She guided him back down to her body. "I need you inside me." When he tried to pull back, she gave a decisive yank.

Which meant—it was over.

38

"*Release me . . .*" His voice was a hoarse rasp.

When she'd first clutched his horns, he'd gone wild, shuddering his massive body over hers. Now his eyes appeared almost dazed as she held on to him. "Cadeon, I want you."

Using his knees to spread her thighs, he loomed over her, his breaths in her ear. "I didn't want to hurt you."

"I'm hurting right now!"

At once, he gripped his shaft to guide it into her. "*Holly . . .*" he groaned as he wedged that broad head inside. "I need to fuck you so bad."

"Then do it," she cried, arching her back.

Inch by inch, he pressed into her, stretching, filling her. "You're so little . . . so tight." His forehead was beading with sweat. His brows were drawn as if he was suffering pain, but his eyes slid shut like he was savoring it.

Holly needed this, was desperate for him, but it did hurt. If she'd done this before she'd become an immortal, she probably would've passed out from the pain.

Now she gritted her teeth, willing her body to accept his. To get this out of the way so she could have pleasure again.

He began to change above her, his horns lengthening in her grasp. His skin was altering as well. He'd said it would act as an attractant.

He hadn't told her it would make her crazed.

As his flesh slickened with sweat, it darkened into a burnished red color that made her feel frantic to lick it, to taste it.

She released his horns to caress his magnificent body, leaning up to flick her tongue against his chest and nip it. She grew wetter in a rush, and the pain began to ebb.

"That's it. I feel you taking me in." When he opened his eyes, they were black, staring down into hers. "You're goin' to be mine?"

"Yes!" This was more than sex, more than taking her virginity. He was claiming her, and she wanted it.

Possession—she read it lit so clearly in his burning gaze. "*I'll never let you go now.*" His voice was low, almost frighteningly rough.

"I never want you to," she whispered.

By the time his shaft had delved as far as her body would allow, his appearance had altered utterly.

Firelight flickered over his seething muscles and his taut, dark skin. In this form, his face was harsher, more brutal but still starkly beautiful to her. His eyes were filled with hunger and promised wicked things. That armband above his bicep glinted in the light.

A demon with immortal need was seated deep and tightly within her. She was unafraid, wanting him for her own with a desperate ache.

At last, he drew back his hips and plunged forward, rasping, "*Mine . . .*"

She gave a cry in pain. Yet she heard herself saying, "Do it again!" After another long withdrawal, he thrust even harder. Pleasure began to drown out any discomfort as he drove into her again and again.

Holly didn't understand half of what was going on, just that everything was happening so fast. She was changing—her claws curled as she sunk them into his muscled ass, urging him on for more. She began panting as electricity charged the air.

He was changing—not only in appearance. His aggression was spiking, his manner with her rougher, more demanding. "Need you . . . to take more of me. Need deeper inside you." He was earthy, animalistic, making her want to be as well. "More!" He shoved harder.

She cried out in bliss.

"Arch your back."

As she did, he lifted her hips and wrenched her along on his shaft.

"Ah, yes!"

He tangled his hands in her hair, cupping her head with one hand. He looped his other arm around her back, clutching her ass tightly, holding her flush against him as he rode her. At her ear, he rasped, "You're goin' to take me good and deep . . . then I'll come for you."

She moaned at his words, writhing in his arms. "*Cadeon . . .*"

The pleasure was so intense, it bordered on pain.

But it was also unfamiliar, as if he'd never had sex before.

He'd never known how heavy and aching his sack could feel. He'd never had to grit his teeth from the throbbing pressure as his semen rose in his shaft.

The moist clench of her sex seemed to demand it from him. *The heat of her . . .*

As he lunged his body over hers, his chest rubbed

against her stiffened nipples. Her back arched to him, her breasts jutting.

Elemental drives ruled him. His gaze was drawn to the tender flesh between her neck and shoulder, just under the line of her shining pearls.

"Holly . . . can't stop myself."

"Don't stop!"

"Mine." He sank his fangs in her.

Her arms fell limp over her head, her body quiescent as he rutted over her. She screamed with pleasure as she helplessly came.

Her sex clenched around his cock, milking it for the seed he could finally give her.

Mindlessly snarling against her flesh, he plunged into her again and again. The ache, the pressure, the throbbing inside . . .

He was crazed with the need to ejaculate, thrusting, grunting, driving. He released her neck, throwing back his head to roar as his come began to shoot from him. His back bowed from the force of it, jetting out in wave after wave.

He'd claimed her. *Holly's mine . . . at last.*

He collapsed over her, heaving his breaths against her marked neck.

Once he'd begun to gather his wits, he leaned up to see how badly he'd hurt her, an apology on his lips. "Holly, I . . ." He trailed off at her expression.

She looked even hungrier for him.

"Is that all you've got?" she said, her voice a purr.

His eyes went wide, then narrowed. "Oh, I've got more, baby." He clutched the back of her neck. "A lot more."

"Then let's see it." Her claws sank deeper into his ass.

He hissed in a breath, and his cock pulsed inside her. "Later, I'm gonna do you nice and slow, but right now I just need to bend you over things and see what this sexy little body of yours can do. . ."

"Try to keep up, demon."

39

He'd exhausted her. Holly lay sleeping soundly beside him, her slim arm stretched over his chest as he sifted his fingers through her hair.

Cade had been merciless with her, making her come over and over. But he wanted her to remember this night for the rest of her life.

He kissed her shoulder where he'd bitten her, glad to see it was rapidly healing. Her transition was indeed complete. She was an immortal. *His* little immortal.

He'd claimed her. There was no going back, even if he wanted to. And he did *not* want to.

In the morning, he'd remember why this had been unwise, but for now, he blocked out all doubt, allowing himself this night.

Awash in satisfaction, he'd been grinning, or on the verge for the last half hour. Prim Miss Ashwin had thrown one over on him, making the ancient demon feel like a weak-kneed lad. She was a wanton, holding nothing back from him.

Even as she wore her dainty pearls.

He'd never imagined a sense of completeness like this. And what if he'd gotten a babe on her? Again, he grinned. *My female and my kid.*

If Holly thought that Cade could try her patience, imagine what his demon spawn would be like.

Maybe Valkyrie daughters and demon sons . . .

His phone rang, casting him back to his much bleaker reality. He dragged himself from the bed to answer it, knowing who it would be.

Rök had been checking in several times a day. And never with good news. . . .

Cade asked, "What do you have?"

"Not a lot. It's like they're being tipped off, every time we get close to Néomi."

The deadline was drawing near. With every night that his crew couldn't find the vampire's Bride, Cade's hopes dwindled. Should he keep his crew scouring the city?

Or begin planning his riskiest idea ever: an assault on a sorcerer's fortress.

"We'll give it seven more nights."

"I'm . . . *happy?*" Holly said aloud, with a frown. Yes, for the last week at the cabin, that's what she'd been feeling. Contentment.

As she straightened up, waiting for her computer to charge in the car, she found it hard to concentrate on cleaning. *That's a first.*

And she might even be more than merely happy.

Holly's parents had had that kind of love so rare that one only read about it. Maybe it happened more often than Holly thought.

Maybe it's happening . . . to me.

Her demon had only been gone an hour—he was out ice fishing—and already she missed him, missed his booming voice and heavy footsteps. She craved his addictive scent—cold and pine and Cadeon.

Earlier, he'd said, "If I go through the trouble of catching, cleaning, and cooking fish, then you *will* go through the trouble of eating it."

For him, she was going to . . . try.

The last week with him had been incredible. She regularly experienced what a day was like broken up with bouts of sex. In fact, Cadeon did just find her wherever she was and take her.

He was insatiable. Even in sleep he grew aroused. His erection would stiffen against her backside, and as he softly growled in her ear, he'd rock it against her.

She'd woken him more than once for *a good seeing to*, which clearly delighted him to no end.

The strangest thing about sex—she didn't have any bizarre quirks with it. This was the one area in her life where she was *normal*.

Well, if you could call her need to be overpowered by a demon normal.

Cadeon had also continued her training, working with the sword—and with the diamond. She could break her stare three out of ten times, but only if he threatened her computer.

They played hunting games and hide-and-seek. Her night vision was nearly perfect, and she could leap twenty feet into the air with the ease of an afterthought. He'd taught her to rub pine needles over herself to mask her scent, and she'd become so stealthy that she could actually stalk him from the trees.

And she continued her own work, pushing to finish her code so that when this quest was over with, she could do nothing but enjoy her demon.

Only two things marred this time. The first was his secretive calls. Outside, she'd hear him snapping in Demonish, pacing back and forth amidst the spruce trees. Then when he returned, he was always distant with her, taking time to relax again.

The second was his attitude about the future. His full-court press across the country of Canada had . . . cooled.

Even after she'd been *claimed*, he didn't speak about the future, evading the subject if she brought it up. At first, she'd had insecurities, wondering if she'd done something to disappoint him or put him off.

But that was ridiculous. They were good together, better people than they were apart.

No, she felt confident that he wanted her as much as she did him.

Puzzling . . .

"Did you miss me, halfling?" he asked from the door.

She ran and leapt into his arms. "Terribly."

"I've got a surprise for you."

"Lemme guess—it's a *fish*?"

He nipped the tip of her ear, which always gave her shivers. "Get your gear on and meet me outside. The weather's nice."

The surprise was a burlap sack filled with snow, hanging from a limb.

"Gee, Cadeon. I didn't get you anything."

"It's for sword practice."

She collected his sword with a long-suffering sigh, though she secretly enjoyed this training.

As he cleaned his catch, he instructed her. "Thrust, parry, counterthrust, twisting block, strike. Nice. That's it, halfling."

Even in the dry, arctic air, she was working up a sweat. Her sparring was improving. He'd even said that she was better than some warriors he'd faced on the battlefield.

Holly didn't know if that was true, but she knew she wasn't laughable anymore.

"Underhanded sword fighting techniques," he said. "Give me two."

As she continued working on slashing attacks, she said, "Obscure my enemy's vision by throwing something like my jacket over his face or sand in his eyes. And second, I could wound my opponent's advancing leg."

"Why?"

"To take blood any way I can—because blood equals strength."

"Very good. Here's a new one. Sometimes you can take a hit in order to see what your opponent's got, or to let them think you're weak," he continued. "They'll get overconfident, 'specially with a tiny chit like yourself."

She nodded.

"Or you can fake an injury. Like dragging your leg to lull a predator. So you give a little to get a lot."

She froze, her mind whirring. "Oh, my God, that's it!"

"What's it?"

"My code—how to identify foes from friendlies. Give a little! In quantum cryptography no measurement or detection can be done to a two-party dialogue without disturbing the system, thereby giving the outsider away. . . ."

"Uh, yeah?"

"If you know the hacker's there, you let him in! You let him take information! He'll get more aggressive, then come with BFC, and you shut them all down. You don't have to have an unbreakable code. You just have to infect your own data, designing it so that when it leaves your system's environment, it can't survive. It will wipe itself out, along with everything around it."

"Go!" he ordered. "Stop gabbing and get it into your computer then."

With a laugh she ran for her laptop.

"But remember," he called, "clearly, sex helps math. Ergo . . ."

Later that night, they lay bundled up in the small bed together. Running her fingers up and down his chest, she said, "You're dragging your feet to get to Groot's."

"I was rushing for your sake before. We've got days before the full moon deadline. And it'll only take a day of hard driving to get there. Now that you want to stay a Valkyrie, we have time."

"Then talk to me. Tell me more about yourself, such as why you would think you'd lost your brother's crown."

He liked how she worded that—as if *she* didn't believe it. "I was supposed to go to Tornin, Rothkalina's capital, to stand as head of state until Rydstrom returned from war with the Vampire Horde. I didn't. I was content with my foster family, and they needed me."

"*That*'s why you got blamed?" she asked in disbelief.

"Omort saw this as a sign of weakness and attacked." Cade had tried to shed the guilt, telling himself that there had been a thousand factors in play. Yet over these long years, he continually saw examples of catastrophes caused by the smallest choice or action.

"Wait, you said your foster family? Did you have foster brothers and sisters?"

"I did." He swallowed. "But they were all murdered by Omort's army."

"Oh, God, Cadeon, I'm so sorry."

"Revenants attacked our farmstead."

"I read about them. A sorcerer reanimates a corpse, raising it from the dead, right?"

He nodded. "Since the creature's already dead, it can't be killed."

"How do you fight them?"

"Only when you kill the sorcerer can they be destroyed. Which is a problem since Omort can't be killed by beheading or unnatural heat."

She asked, "Do you blame yourself for your foster family's deaths as well?"

He gave her a grim nod.

Her eyes were sad when she said, "You've been carrying around all this guilt for nine hundred years? What about the saying *time heals all wounds*?"

He met her gaze. "That one's a lie."

"I want to fight," he told Rök after she'd fallen asleep. "Get mobilized."

"Are you sure? Think of how many ways this attack can get botched up. You'd be risking your brother's life and your kingdom's freedom for a woman."

"Not just a woman. My woman." He'd realized tonight that if Holly got hurt on his watch, then he would have done the same thing he'd blamed himself for a thousand times—failing his own.

"Give me one more night," Rök said. "We can get to your coordinates in fourteen hours if we have to."

Continue to search for the mortal, or go forward? "No, we're out of time," Cade said. "I can't chance it. We're going to war."

After he hung up, Cade joined Holly in bed once more, gazing down at her, sleeping peacefully.

What was going on in that incredible mind of hers as she turned to him so trustingly? Was she dreaming about warrior codes and formulas?

Could she be dreaming about him?

Holly slept deeply, assured he would keep her safe. Stroking the backs of his claws over her arm, he murmured, "*I'm going to fight for you.*"

40

What the hell do you mean, *can't get up here?*" Cade bellowed into the phone. The deal expired tomorrow. "You're fucking mercenaries; I'm ready to go to war."

"The ice road is completely blown out," Rök said, having to yell over what sounded like gusting wind. "That's the only way from here to there."

"What about heading west, then coming up north?" Cade paced in the snow, winding around spruce trees.

"We could, but we'd never make it in time."

"Trace the distance—"

"We can only trace as far as we can see, which is about two feet right now," Rök said. Cade heard a door slam, and then the background noise dimmed. "The snow drifts have killed visibility. And I've already checked on a chopper. It'd take a day just to get one up here."

Cade punched a tree.

"I'm sorry, friend, but you're on your own. You've got to take your female to Groot to get that sword. You don't have a choice."

I do have a bloody choice. Fuck nobility. Fuck selflessness. *This isn't my life*. He would turn his back just like before. *I want to run with her*.

Cade could find another way to free Rydstrom from Sabine. Then his brother would finally just have to learn how to live without his crown.

Rök said, "I'm not suggesting that you should actually turn Holly over."

"If I even bring her near Groot, I risk her life. I can't jeopardize her like this. I *won't*—"

"Look, I didn't want to tell you this, but there's more on the line than you think. News of Rydstrom's disappearance and your quest has gotten out. Demons in the kingdom are awaiting your results. Cade, they're ready to war again."

"What do you mean?" Their people had been so brutalized that they had no heart for revolutions.

"If you can claim that sword, they'll view it as a sign that a revolt could be possible. The sword has become symbolic now, a rallying point. They want to see that if one half of the Woede is compromised, the other can still take care of business, as it were."

As if there weren't enough pressure . . .

"And I have to tell you—the betting's rampant over whether the black sheep will come through. So here's the strategy: You'll have to convince Groot that you're only there to drop off the goods, get your pay in return, and get out, or he won't give the sword to you. So convince him, then smite him with his own weapon."

"Do you know how many things can go wrong with that plan?"

"All right, say he gets suspicious and has his guards escort you out," Rök said. "You'll be able to go fully demonic now, changing to protect your female. In that state you could take on an army. You'd be able to get her out of there."

Act like I'm making the trade, get the sword, kill Groot—it sounded so easy. "And if any of this goes south, Holly's going to be the one to pay for it," Cade said, scrubbing a hand over his face. "You would do this in my position?"

"You shouldn't ask me. I can't really comprehend what you're feeling for her that would make you even think about choosing her over a kingdom of people—much less over your brother's life."

Cade had been born to protect her, and yet he was considering placing her directly in harm's way. He was debating the ultimate betrayal.

To persuade Groot that this was merely one business transaction among many, Cade would have to act like a callous mercenary. One who'd tricked a naïve young woman.

Which was true in many ways.

Rök added, "Since your exile, you haven't returned to Rothkalina, but I have. It's . . . not good. There are a lot of people counting on you."

Cade swallowed. *Now, at last, after all these years, is my chance to atone.*

"Rydstrom's counting on you, too. Right now your brother's somewhere secretly praying that you'll come through. Even as he's certain you won't."

Unbidden, a memory arose in Cade's mind of a night so long ago—a night of anguish and guilt, of pain as he'd never known.

When Cade had been burying his foster family, Rydstrom had found him. Without a word, he'd taken up another shovel. Shoulder to shoulder, they'd worked together.

Cade had just cost Rydstrom his throne, and yet his brother had silently helped him get through the hardest thing Cade had ever had to do. . . .

* * *

When Cadeon returned, he stretched out behind Holly, wrapping his warm, naked body around hers.

He tucked her tightly against him as he always did. Outside, the winds howled down from the Arctic, whipping over their cabin, but she felt so safe, protected by her big demon.

She couldn't imagine ever sleeping without him again. Before she drifted off, she thought, *I'm in love with Cadeon Woede*.

41

They'd started out early in the morning, speaking little over the first couple of hours they'd been slogging north.

"What's wrong?" Cade finally asked her. "You've been quiet." He wondered if she suspected anything. She'd been wary of him in the past. But he sensed that she'd jumped in with both feet with him, deciding to trust him completely.

Which would make this all the more devastating to her.

"I'm just sad to leave," she said. "Maybe we can hole up here for another week on the way down? You can teach me to ice fish."

With his eyes averted, he said, "Yeah, maybe so. Did Nïx ever give you a way to contact her?"

"No, why?"

"Wouldn't mind some Monday morning quarterbacking, except in advance." His gut was tied in knots as he wondered if this was the right move. *Was* there a right move? At any turn, Cade would fail someone. It felt wrong to deceive and hurt Holly, wrong to risk his brother's freedom, wrong to ignore the needs of an entire kingdom.

He could already see the betrayed look on Holly's face. Would he be able to keep up the charade of indifference, when he wanted her more than he'd wanted anything in his entire life . . . ?

Whatever road there had been initially deteriorated into a primitive trail as the terrain grew more mountainous. Every few miles, Cade had to drag trees out of their way.

He'd cut this journey so close that anything could set them back. Part of him wished they would miss the deadline, hoping for something, anything, that would prevent him from having to turn her over—to take the matter out of his hands, so it wouldn't be his decision either way.

Then Cade would think of his brother, and the guilt would assail him.

Holly perked up. After hours of grueling four-wheel driving deeper into the mountains, the trail had finally begun improving.

By the time it actually resembled a road, the dense forest of spruce opened up into a small valley.

It was just before two, which meant that the sun hadn't yet set, so they were able to see some of the spectacular scenery. A whitewater river etched its way through the valley. Mist swirled above them, like a gossamer lid over all.

Cadeon leaned forward on the steering wheel. "This area should be bare, the river frozen."

Instead birch and aspen trees still had their leaves, and there was not a single patch of snow.

"Maybe it has its own microclimate? I've read that hot springs can melt the area around them."

"Yeah, that's probably it," he said, but he was distracted.

They followed the road as it ran parallel to the river. "Look, it's a little town," Holly said, then frowned. "A *ghost* town." And she didn't use that term lightly anymore.

"It's an old coal mining village. I saw the entrance to a shaft a while back. Groot must have set up here so he could have fuel for his forge."

They passed a startlingly well-preserved sign that read: *Prosperity, NWT, est. 1902, pop. 333.*

Along the water stood forty or fifty abandoned buildings, each appearing to be from the early nineteen hundreds. They had wood shingles for the siding and roofing and were austere, built in that creepy, unadorned Quaker style.

Though there was no snow, a crystal clear sheen of ice covered everything, like a varnish. "This place literally looks frozen in time. Why did the residents leave? Did the mine go bust?"

"They didn't leave," he said quietly, turning onto the main street.

It was then that she noticed doors were wide open, or hanging at odd angles, attached to stretched hinges. She spied a pair of antique-looking bicycles, turned on their sides in the middle of the street, as if they'd been abandoned in a panic.

"Cadeon, what is this?"

"Wendigo. They attacked here. I've heard these mountains are teeming with them. They act as a natural boundary for Groot."

"I read about them. They used to be humans, but were turned into cannibals. They eat corpses. They even . . . eat people alive."

He nodded. "Cousin to the ghoul, ravenous for flesh and highly contagious—even to other immortals. All it takes is one bite or scratch."

"How?"

"A toxin emitted from the claws and fangs."

"How long does the transition take?"

"Three to four days," he answered. "Long enough for a victim to realize what's happened, to come to terms with it, and then to decide what has to be done."

"What? What has to be done?"

In answer, Cadeon pointed off to the side of the street to a towering birch tree. Tattered nooses swayed from its limbs.

"Are the Wendigo still here after all this time?"

"Probably. They can survive on animal flesh if they have to."

They neared the town's church. "Is that what I think it is on the chapel?" The building was still eerily pristine—on its sides. Across the front, ruddy spatter stretched in distinct arcs at least fifteen feet high.

He nodded. "It's blood."

"Oh, God . . ."

"The villagers still living and uninfected probably barricaded themselves in that church. The windows are boarded on the inside."

The front doors hung askew. Just past them, Holly spied stacked pews. She could imagine the scene all too clearly. Once the front blockade had fallen, the people inside had been trapped by their own defenses. The Wendigo likely dragged out screaming villagers, tossing them to the waiting pack. . . .

"Cadeon, even if I'm not interested in being human again, I'm glad you brought me."

"How could you be?" His tone was almost sharp.

"Just in case you need me to get your back," she said,

frowning when she saw his knuckles go white on the steering wheel.

Just as she parted her lips to ask him what was wrong, he said, "There's Groot's fortress."

As the mist began to clear, she glimpsed a magnificent waterfall, at least four hundred feet high. Directly atop it was . . . a castle, built at the fall's edge.

Five towers all conjoined to a central keep over the water. Above it, a stone smokeshaft billowed gray smoke. Even from this distance, the mighty forge was visible.

"That's why the river isn't frozen and why there's so much mist," he said. "It heats the water—"

"Cadeon!" She swallowed. "Down a side street. I think I just saw something running!"

42

Cade had spotted them, too. Wendigo hunted in packs—and they were stalking them.

"Are they still following us?" she asked, eyes darting.

"Yeah."

The road continued up the escarpment, taking them ever higher and closer to the keep. He turned on the wipers when mist from the falls became as thick as rain, until they climbed above it.

The sun had set, and the full moon had begun to rise by the time they came upon a perimeter fence. Metal spikes pointed outward like old-fashioned bulwarks, yet he could see that they were fastened to gears. Cade suspected that they would move if disturbed.

The front gate was towering and complex. One section rolled on a rail to the side, and another could be raised and lowered. When the truck was directly in front of it, the two components opened to allow just enough space for him to ease through, then both closed inches from his back bumper.

They were in. *Minutes till show time*.

"There's no way Wendigo can get past that gate. You can relax now," he said, inwardly wincing.

This part of the drive seemed endless to Cade. His hands were damp on the steering wheel, and at every instant, he was tempted to turn around.

But he didn't turn around, instead parking in front of two colossal entry doors. Made of iron, they stood at least a couple of stories high and were flanked by flaming torches the size of a man.

When Cade grabbed his sword sheath to strap over his back, she raised her brows. "Just in case we have to depart quick-like."

The noise from the waterfall was deafening when they got out of the truck. Immediately, those doors groaned open, seeming of their own accord.

"You ready?" he asked, having to raise his voice over the sound.

"Ready to get this over with!"

When he and Holly entered the empty hall, no one greeted them. The doors eased shut behind them, just as another opened across the bailey. They had no choice but to follow the path available, leading them deeper toward the heart of the castle. Their footsteps echoed on the stone floor.

As much as Cade despised Groot, the military part of Cade's mind couldn't help but be impressed with the design of the castle. The layout was a defensive dream.

Five baileys had been built in an X formation, all connected to the largest tower in the center by narrow walkways. Only one bailey was on land. The other four were constructed on man-made piers or natural pediments in the water.

If Groot were attacked, he could destroy the walkway from the land bailey, and the others would be unreachable.

Even if an enemy decided to approach by water, at least two of the baileys would prove unassailable because they lay at the direct edge of the waterfall. The strength of the current would make them impossible to near.

An attack by air wouldn't work. The forge vented smoke so dense it would cloak the castle from above.

When they passed through the far door, it led them outside to a walkway over the water, connecting to the forge. Cade glanced over the stone balustrade. Beneath them, the silt-laden water dropped at least four hundred feet down, churning in monstrous eddies and spitting up foam. The din was so loud he would have to yell to be heard.

In the main tower, the forge had large bay doors that opened up like a warehouse. The area was filled with blacksmith tools: tongs, pincers, and an anvil as big as a car. An immense furnace blazed. Directly across from the forge opening was a crenellated parapet wall.

Inside the main keep they entered a long, dimly lit hall. All along the walls, he saw glowing white eyes, like penlights covered with a milky film. He smelled the stench of rot.

"What are they?" Holly whispered.

"Revenants," he grated. Imatra had said they'd be here. His jaw clenched. She'd neglected to mention that there would be *hundreds* of them.

"I thought only *evil* sorcerers raised them from the dead," Holly said.

"Standard sorcerer issue," Cadeon answered. "They all use them."

The revenants' skin was putrid, their bodies in varying stages of decomposition, and they each had a disgusting metal spike shoved into their temple. "What's with those spikes?"

"I don't know," Cade murmured. "I've never seen that before."

The opening and closing of doors finally ushered them into a study with plush rugs, rich wood paneling, and an inviting fire. The cozy room looked as if it was missing an Englishman with a pipe, reading classics aloud.

Still, she said, "I thoroughly don't like this place."

"Me neither, pet."

Minutes later, a towering, muscular man strolled in, followed by six revenants.

"Groot?" Cadeon asked in an incredulous tone.

She understood his disbelief. Holly had pictured Groot as a fragile, white-haired wizard, straight out of *The Lord of the Rings*.

Instead, he was hulking, his muscles bulging under his old-fashioned trousers and tunic. His smith work must have developed his physique.

His skin was shiny and sallow, as if the only light he'd seen for years was from a fire.

"And you're the infamous Cadeon the Kingmaker," the sorcerer said. Then his deep-set, pale eyes darted to her. "Welcome to my home, Holly. I am Groot the Metallurgist."

He had an unctuous demeanor, eyeing her intently, even . . . *smugly*? She unconsciously took a step closer to Cadeon.

This entire place was wrong, unnerving. She knew down to her bones that this man was evil.

"You have the sword?" Cadeon asked.

"I do."

"And it will kill Omort?"

"I vow it to the Lore and wish you much success with

it. I *want* you to succeed." His mincing way of speaking seemed out of place for such a burly male. "I would like to leave this compound once in a century or so." Groot smiled in her direction. "To take my new bride out."

Why is he looking at me?

"Cadeon . . . ?" she murmured. When he didn't answer, she met his gaze.

And saw a man she didn't know.

No longer merely cocky, he now looked *cruel.* "What is this?" she asked, dread tightening her stomach.

"It's a trade. Sorry, pet. I need that sword, and Groot needs a Vessel."

Her lips parted. "A Vessel," she said dumbly. *This isn't happening. This can't be happening.*

"Have you made her eat?" Groot asked.

Cadeon answered, "Three squares a day."

She remembered all those times Cadeon had urged her to eat. Now she knew why.

To make sure I'm nice and fertile for the evil sorcerer.

She couldn't get enough air. "There's no reversing my change to Valkyrie?"

"Nah. I just needed your cooperation to get you to my employer here."

Oh, God . . . oh, God. Breathe. "I was part of a . . . business transaction?"

"Yeah, that's about right."

Groot chimed in. "Your guardian sold you over. For a weapon." He snapped his gnarled fingers, and those foul, rotting soldiers seized her arms. "Put her in my room."

"Cadeon?" As they began forcing her out, she cried over her shoulder, "You don't mean this!"

* * *

Cade gritted his teeth, battling not to go to her with every ounce of will he possessed. When he felt Groot studying him, he forced himself to shrug. "Never trust a demon, love. . . ."

Before, he'd wondered if she'd suspected him. At the look on her face, he knew. *She'd really believed in me*. She'd trusted him utterly.

She began struggling against the revenants, seeming shocked when she couldn't budge their grip. When tears welled in her eyes, pain stabbed him like a knife to the heart.

Keep it together, five more minutes. As long as the sorcerer was with Cade, he wasn't hurting Holly.

Groot's going to give me the sword, I'll kill him, then come for you. We'll take our chances together. . . .

The door closed behind her. Cade forced himself to breathe.

"She's exquisite," Groot said with sigh. "It will make this process that much more enjoyable."

Cade had never wanted to kill anyone so badly in his life. This sick fuck thought he would have Cade's female, was already envisioning it.

And Groot was brother to the sorceress who had Rydstrom. At that instant, Cade decided he'd kill every single member of that family with the sword Groot was about to give him.

"The revenants look stronger than before," Cade said, his tone deceptively casual.

"The metal spike. I'm able to infuse them with a hundred times more power, and control their actions even more precisely. They're handy to have around. They're stronger than even, say, a rage demon."

Holly might not have suspected Cade of anything, but Groot did. "I'm not here to make trouble. I just want the sword. Get in, get out."

"Very well. I have it here," Groot said, crossing to a weapons cabinet. Once he'd collected the sword, he unsheathed it.

The weapon was a thing of beauty to behold, glimmering in the light.

Groot started across the room toward Cade, then faltered. "Actually, I'll keep my distance, if you don't mind." He made a motion like he was about to toss the sword. Once Cade raised a hand in readiness, Groot pitched it to him.

When Cade caught the handle, he felt the smallest prick in his palm. Changing hands, he darted his gaze down and found what looked like a silver thorn embedded into the skin. He plucked it free, and a drop of blood welled. "What the fuck is this, Groot?" But he knew . . .

"Relax, demon. It's just a little toxin to make you sleep. Your kind is so susceptible to it. You'll wake up unharmed a few hundred miles from here with no memory of how to locate this place."

Blind panic . . . rage . . . Cade charged the sorcerer, bellowing, "You goddamned bastard! I'm going to feed your heart to—"

The world went black.

43

As the guards led her away to yet another bailey, Holly felt numb with shock. She willed herself not succumb to the tears that threatened.

Holly thought that once she started crying, she'd never be able to stop.

Cadeon had deceived her. He'd lured her into this trap by telling her she could have her transition reversed. And then he'd made sure she was fertile for another man.

Holly had loved him, and he'd feigned the same only to get her here. Had he ever cared about her at all?

When the guards forced her into a bedroom, she fought them, but even with her new strength she could gain no ground. The entry doors audibly locked behind them.

The chamber was dominated by a large bed with black silk sheets, a vile reminder of what this madman intended to do to her.

How could Cadeon betray her like this . . . ?

No, get it together, Holly! She swiped her sleeve over her eyes. She needed to take note of her surroundings. Yes, she'd been wrong to trust Cadeon, but that didn't mean his training didn't make sense to her—or that she wasn't about to need it.

Holly surveyed the area for escape. Besides the main entry doors, there were two other sets. She ran to the first, a narrower door, finding it locked. She tried the next. Also locked. But it felt colder to the touch. It had to lead outside. She *thought*.

The layout of the castle confused her, and she'd been so dazed as they'd brought her here that she hadn't paid enough attention.

No escape? Then she'd fight. She scanned for weapons. Her gaze landed on two battle-axes crossed high above a fireplace. Just as she'd tensed to leap for one, Groot entered.

The door automatically locked behind him. No keys to steal. "You look upset."

Trying to make her voice steady, she said, "I just didn't see that one coming." What an understatement.

He gave her a disbelieving look. "Not even *a little?*"

She gritted her teeth. She recalled how she'd never fully trusted the demon in the beginning, always having that niggling doubt. But she'd forced herself to ignore her apprehension.

"Well, I'm sure he made you very earnest promises to win your trust. Did he give you the fated female song and dance?" When Holly averted her eyes, he exclaimed, "Oh, he did!" With a sigh, he said, "I'm afraid you fell for the oldest trick in the Lore."

Wait . . . She faced him again with her chin up. "There are ways to tell if I was truly his female. I had proof."

"And who informed you of what that proof might be?"

Oh, my God. Her heart fell. Cadeon had obviously lied about certain aspects of rage demon physiology as well. *I'm an idiot!* How he must've laughed behind her back.

"Every single thing he told you was a lie. They come more easily to his tongue than the truth."

"But Nïx also told me—"

"Nïx? You trusted that mad creature? She plays with fates. It amuses her. When you live that long, I suppose you take entertainment where you can get it."

Betrayed by Nïx as well.

"Now, we both know why you're here," Groot said. "Are you going to make this more unpleasant than it needs to be?"

Think! Play along. Buy time. "No. I'm tired of running. I'm tired of being shot at. Anyone who can keep me hidden and alive looks very good right now."

"Precisely. I'll keep you protected here. You're much better off without Cadeon."

"And I'm *sick* of being betrayed. At least I know at the outset that you can't be trusted."

"Smart Valkyrie. Now, I just need to make sure the demon departs." He crossed to the thin door, and it opened automatically. He entered a small anteroom that contained what looked like a master control booth, with two rows of TV screens and monitors, multiple keyboards, and at least four whirring CPUs.

Keep him off his guard. "Nice system. You know the way to a geek's heart." She saw all the screens were security camera feeds. "But paranoid much?"

His tone amused, he said, "It's not an easy thing when the most powerful sorcerer in the world wants you dead."

"Why the technology? Why not use magick?"

"I use both." He pointed to one of the second row monitors. "That outer gate is mystickally protected. You could run a tank into it, and the gate wouldn't budge an inch. It can only be opened from this control."

She raised her brows at the screen. "Those are Wendigo." The ones that had followed their truck.

Their faces were long and haggard, as if their normal human ones had been stretched like putty. Stringy hair grew in patches all over their graying skin. They had hunched backs and emaciated bodies. Some still wore scraps of clothing.

Their red eyes glowed with an unearthly hunger.

"Yes, my barbarians at the gate. They are excellent guards, viciously protecting the valley," he said, sounding admiring. "A few follow the rare vehicle, craving fresh meat. Most stay in the town."

Fresh meat. Holly stifled a glare, her anger rising. She couldn't stop thinking about those villagers trapped in that church. Their last sight had been these horrific beasts. . . .

Her thoughts were interrupted by a display on one of the many screens. "Is that . . . is that the cabin I just stayed in?"

"Oh, yes."

Don't throw up, don't gag. "You *spied* on us?" She had never hated anyone so instantly and so violently as much as she did this bastard.

"Did you think there was no reason for such an innocuous checkpoint? It looks so rustic, you never suspect the cameras. Initially, I'd had them installed to make sure you two weren't plotting against me. But then, there were other . . . benefits." He reached his gnarled hand toward her, and she forced herself not to recoil as he brushed her cheek. "The more I watched, the more I wanted you."

The humiliation and disgust she felt were overpowering.

"I could scarcely wait for you to be delivered to me, but the demon wanted to enjoy you for himself first."

Once her eyes stopped watering, they focused on his

face. "Then you know there's a chance I could be pregnant with the demon's baby."

"I suspected as much. He's probably just as likely as I am to spawn evil."

"Is he?"

"He's known in the Lore as a brutal killer. But I do want the babe to be *mine*. If you're pregnant, I'll take care of it."

"Take care of . . . ?" It dawned on her what he meant. "Why would you want a child at all?"

"To possess the warrior of ultimate evil. I want to mold it, shape it."

Looking away, she studied the screens, trying to determine the layout of the castle, to find an escape route. She felt as if she was in a video game. Level one, defeat pervert. Level two, engage army of revenants. Level three, steal vehicle and evade Wendigo.

Another screen drew her attention. She squinted. "Is that a . . . female revenant? I thought only men were raised from the dead."

Groot gave her that disturbing smile. "It gets lonely out here."

That's it. She retched in her mouth. "You know what? I can't do this. No subterfuge. You're just too revolting for me to pretend."

The demon she'd thought she loved had delivered her to a monster who slept with reanimated corpses.

Tim's *math* betrayal was laughable now.

"In that case, I'll have to insist that you accept my welcome gift immediately." He opened a drawer and withdrew a felt-lined case. Inside lay a shining spike, looking like a new, polished railroad tie.

"What is that for?" she demanded.

He rose, starting for her. "It replaces your will with mine."

The spikes in the revenants' heads. "You think you're going to put that in my temple?" Her claws sharpened like daggers. She would use them to slit his meaty throat. *Never hesitate*.

"It will only hurt for a few months, until your head grows around it permanently."

"Over my dead body, Groot. I'll fight you to the death over this. I'll—"

Suddenly the biggest diamond she'd ever seen appeared.

From behind his back, he'd produced a brilliant stone the size of his palm. "Look how it sparkles, Valkyrie."

Faultless light, cylinders of brightness. She stared, riveted. *Have to look away. Or I greet a fate worse than death*.

Panic made her heart thunder. *Break away! I can do this. . . .*

"Your eyes have grown silver," he said, his voice getting thick. When he was directly in front of her, he raised the spike. "Just relax for me, Valkyrie—"

Her hand shot out to snatch him between the legs.

She broke her stare just as his eyes widened. He dropped the diamond and the spike to pry her loose. She wrenched down with all her strength, hissing, "This will only hurt for a little while. Just relax for me."

When he doubled over, she used her free hand to shove his face down as she hiked her knee to it.

Crunch. Once he collapsed with a muffled groan, she whirled around, about to leap for a battle-ax, but revenants stormed in. He must've sounded some kind of silent alarm.

"Hold her down!" he ordered from the ground, wiping

his palm over his bloody face. With a grunt, he swooped up the spike, then lumbered to his feet once more.

The guards started for her. She counted twenty with swords and armor. Multiple combatants coming for her. She needed to run, but the main exit was blocked. The second door led to the control booth. Her head swung in the other direction. Only one option.

Charging to those doors, she barreled her shoulder into them with a yell. They burst open.

She surged forward onto a balcony—directly over the edge of the falls. The doors had indeed led outside.

Trapped. In front of her, revenants blocked her way back in. Behind her . . . a four-hundred-foot drop.

When Groot elbowed through the guards, looming with that spike in hand, she leapt atop the slippery stone balustrade.

"Come down, Valkyrie," he yelled over the thunderous falls. "You don't know what you're doing."

Have to run. And there was only one way to go. Down.

Reasoning trail: Jump into the waterfall, possibly lose head, which will kill even an immortal. If I survive, float directly into Wendigo lair to be eaten alive.

Or accept the spike.

Could she actually force herself to make this leap?

"You won't survive it," Groot bit out. "And if by some miracle, you do, you'll wish to the gods that you hadn't."

44

Her scream had ripped through the darkness of his mind, beginning to pull him back from the abyss. *Fight . . .*

Her electricity pricked his skin, as if refusing to let him stay under. Thunder boomed insistently all around him.

She's in danger. Needs me to fight . . .

His demon instinct began to stir within him, rousing him to consciousness, grappling against the effects of the poison.

Two guards were dragging Cade away from her. Farther away from her with each step that he didn't resist.

Somehow he slitted open his eyes. His blood began pumping faster, fueling his muscles, feeding his wrath.

With a bellow, he lunged to his feet, shoving the two guards free from him. When they brandished their swords, he unsheathed the one at his back, frowning for the briefest instant.

It was Groot's. The bastard had actually kept the terms of their bargain, putting his sword in Cade's case.

Raising the sorcerer's weapon against his own guards, Cade slashed at the two. Before they could rise again, he charged past them only to halt in his tracks at the walkway to the forge.

Dozens of them converged, choking the narrow path.

And there was no way Cade could get to Holly without passing through the forge.

Though the poison was dissipating, it was still blunting his change, preventing him from turning completely.

And his enemies couldn't be destroyed. He slew them again and again with the sword, but they rose each time. The weapon was useless against them.

Cade sheathed it at his back once more. Surveying the scene, he realized what he had to do. He charged them, heaving the revenants over the side of the walk into the water. He thought the current would catch them, sweeping them away. *Corpses . . . meet the corpse eaters*.

Instead, they sank like rocks with their heavy armor.

Throwing them bodily, he plowed his way to the forge. Inside were three walkways to different towers. *Which one to choose?* More revenants appeared. *Where had the bastard taken Holly?*

His question was answered when he caught sight of her.

She was atop a balcony rail—at the direct edge of the falls.

As he frenziedly battled to get to her, she slipped, waving her arms for balance, robbing him of breath. "*Holly!*" But she couldn't hear him over the falls.

With her hair whipping in the wind, she swept a glance over her adversaries. *Trapped. She knows she can't fight them*.

"*Holly, no!*" Cade roared, charging for her. "*Don't do this!*"

She swallowed . . . then stepped off the ledge.

Ah, gods, no! Heart in his throat, he sprinted to dive in right behind her. He dimly heard Groot yelling at him. *Almost to the railing, tensing to hurdle it—*

Like a shot, his body flew across the space, crashing into the wall of the forge, pinned there by a dozen swords.

She hit the water with shattering force, a scream ripping from her chest.

Eddies churned, keeping her submerged. *Can't get air*. The roiling power of them.

Kicking desperately, she stretched her arms up to the surface that she could see—but couldn't reach.

The underwater current seized her, shooting her down the river like a bullet in a rifle barrel. The force slammed her into a boulder; she clung to it with her claws, scrabbling up from the deep.

Finally, she broke to the surface, sucking in air, but the waves soon pried her from her sanctuary, tossing her like dross.

A fallen tree ahead. She swam frantically for it. *Can't miss it*. Just ahead . . . almost there . . . *Got it!*

She used it to haul herself in, then crawled on hands and knees up the rocky shore.

I made it. With each ragged breath, she coughed, an agony on her ribs. *I survived. I—*

Her ear twitched. She dragged her gaze up. And met red eyes glowing with an unearthly hunger.

For her.

"If you don't release me, she's going to die!" he bellowed as Groot approached him. Cade had never wanted anything so much as he wanted over that ledge. With all his might, he writhed, slicing his skin on the swords, biting at his own flesh to get free.

"She probably wouldn't have survived the falls," Groot

said, pinching his nose and snapping it back in place. "But if she did, would you really expect me to let you go with the female, the sword, *and* my secret location?"

"*Fuck the sword!*" At last, Cade was turning completely. "Keep it! And I'll vow to the Lore . . . not to tell of this place."

"Even if the Valkyrie lived, she'll be infected or eaten before anyone gets to her. Besides, there'll be another Vessel in a few centuries. And all I have is time."

Cade roared with fury, his horns straightening, sharpening, his fangs and claws lengthening.

"I'd really hoped you would kill my brother, but now I see you can't be controlled."

You have no idea.

Groot sent another sword flying straight for his neck. In a rush of blood, Cade tore free, ducking under the sword with an inch to spare. Once more, he lumbered toward the railing, almost to the edge . . . Thoughts grew hazy in his rage state. *Get to my female . . . Protect her . . .*

Groot himself sacked Cade with the force of a freight train. He looped a thick arm around Cade's neck. "I can squeeze the life out of you, demon . . ."

I want over that goddamned edge! Cade's head shot back, his sharpened horns sinking into Groot's face like a viper's fangs.

The sorcerer collapsed, instantly paralyzed; at once, revenants descended upon Cade.

He mindlessly slashed at them with claws, horns, fangs. But they couldn't be slain as long as their master lived. Cade swung his gaze on Groot, then wrestled to get past more guards to him.

The sorcerer lay with his grotesque muscles clenched,

his eyes wide, registering everything, but unable to move.

Snatching up his great body, Cade battled to get to the forge, taking sword thrusts, growling in fury with each strike. At the edge, he lifted Groot overhead.

The bastard had recovered enough to beg, "*Please . . .*"

With a roar, Cade heaved him into the fire.

Flames consumed Groot's body, then flared, too large to be contained in the smoke stack. The entire castle shuddered.

Mortar cracked, stones beginning to plummet. Cade faced off against the revenants standing between him and the water. The next one that he slew stayed down. But the fortress never settled, continuing to quake on its supports. He felt heat building all around him . . .

Cade fought ever closer to the ledge, to Holly, to protecting her.

So close—

The furnace erupted, exploding the forge, spewing boiling metal. The blast engulfed him, hurtling his seared body into a wall. He slumped down.

The ground began to disappear beneath him, the castle giving way.

45

The explosion in the distance distracted the Wendigo just long enough for Holly to bolt to her feet and sprint past them. The sky rained embers as blast after blast rocked the castle, towers collapsing.

Holding her ribs, she raced down the riverside, slipping on the rocks. The Wendigo gave chase, running with a lumbering, uneven gait, their long, knifelike claws bared.

More emerged from the shadows before her, forcing her to dart back toward the town. She realized they were maneuvering her, but there was nothing she could do about it—

Once on the main street, she scanned the area. Their eyes glowed out from around the corners of buildings, from roofs, from inside homes. Dozens of them.

Need a weapon . . . anything.

There! Behind a home. Her gaze fell on an ordinary wood ax, wedged into a stump. She limped to it, tearing the ax free. Getting a good grip, she swung it, growing accustomed as she sized up her foes.

Wendigo stalked closer.

Monstrous. Up close she saw they had dripping fangs and smelled like rotten meat.

There would be no hacking with the ax—she couldn't afford to have her weapon get stuck in one of their bodies.

No, she would use full-forced swings, taking their heads cleanly off their necks.

Just when the larger ones tensed to leap at her, night turned to day. The last mighty tower erupted in a plume of fire, bathing the valley in light.

The nocturnal, north-dwelling Wendigo shielded their eyes. As they hunched with wet hisses, she raced past the line of them.

She chanced a look behind her. *I'm outrunning them!* They couldn't catch her.

By the time she neared the edge of the town, she'd left them in the dust. Free! Still running, she passed the sign.

And slowed . . .

Prosperity.

Three hundred and thirty-three villagers had sought to make a life here. There'd been no prosperity awaiting them—only terror, then gruesome, agonizing deaths.

They'd been lured here by a promise that was far different from the reality. Just like her.

Lured by the hope of a better life, or by the love of a demon—what did it matter?

She stopped, breaths fogging in the growing chill. The Wendigo thought another meal was here for them. A piercing fury bloomed within her. How would they like to be the prey for once?

Furies are predators. Valkyrie are warriors. I'm both.

Something inside her . . . *clicked*. Things became clear.

She turned back, surveying the town. Without the heat from the forge, flurries began to swirl.

The old Holly would be screaming that this wasn't rational. But she wasn't the old Holly.

Briefly setting down her ax, she wrung her clothes and hair out, then bashed the ice off an evergreen limb. She rubbed the needles all over her, disguising her scent.

She doubled back, creeping around buildings as she made her way to the chapel. At the entrance, she stole inside, her calculating gaze flickering over the boarded windows.

Ax in hand, she leapt up onto one of the exposed rafters. Crouching there, she slowed her breaths, calming her heart. Awaiting.

One by one, they entered, hunting, sensing her. She tilted her head, dispassionately eyeing her quarry as her foremothers had before her.

When the chapel was filled, a bolt of lightning flashed over the valley. The largest one finally craned its head up.

With a shriek, she dropped down between them and their only escape.

She lives.

Cade forced open his eyes once more. She'd screamed, not in fear but in fury.

The blast had catapulted him all the way down to the valley. The impact mangled his body, splintering bones out from his thighs and forearms.

But she lives. And she was in jeopardy once more. Gritting his teeth, he began to shove bones back under his skin, as he gazed around him, wary for his enemies.

Why hadn't he been attacked by the Wendigo? Why weren't they attracted to the scent of his blood?

Though he couldn't yet stand, he would reach her somehow. *She'd believed in me.*

He'd fucking crawl to her if he had to.

Just as he was about to shove his femur back into place, he stilled. *That goddamned sword . . .*

It was still strapped to his back.

"Where do I go now?" she whispered, as she closed the church doors behind her. There was no answer, nothing but echoing silence.

She'd swept death over this place. Yet she felt little of the satisfaction she'd expected, only gut-wrenching sadness from Cadeon's betrayal.

So alone . . .

By the time she'd reached the edge of the town once more, her clothes and hair had frozen. Ice formed on her eyelashes.

As Holly turned in dazed circles, shuddering from cold and shock, she felt warmth from above. She raised her face in confusion.

The northern lights.

They waved and floated so peacefully, calling to her, beckoning like opened arms.

Without thought, Holly ran headlong toward them, into the darkest wilds, with no other thought than to follow the lights. . . .

46

Holly had eluded him for four days, but Cade was fast on her trail, hauling ass down a frozen road toward another mining town. He had even more of his crew scouring the countryside for her.

Cade had lost her in Prosperity that night. After finding a scene of carnage, Cade had realized the reason he hadn't been attacked by Wendigos was because she'd slaughtered every last one, unwittingly saving his life.

After that, she hadn't headed south as anyone else in her position would have. Had she gone in that direction, then she would've been trapped in the same bottleneck that had blocked his men.

Nor had she headed east, following the river or the road toward easier terrain.

She'd cannily headed northwest, straight into the heart of the mountains.

By chance, he stumbled upon her direction, having spied a miner with a black eye and a broken arm. The man had grown cagey when given Holly's description.

Apparently, she'd cleaned his clock. *Good girl . . .*

Cade had broken the man's other arm for her trouble.

Once on her trail, Cade had been able to readily trace her movements because the men in the Territories remembered her. In the dead of winter, not many females were about, much less beautiful ones.

At the portage where the miner had previously stayed, Cade had been directed to the next town to the north. There, Holly had sold her watch for a single meal and a pair of snowshoes, then made her way on foot to another camp. Once she'd bunked through the worst of a storm, she'd begun hitching to the mining town Cade now sped to.

He believed he was only hours behind her—he'd find her there. The thought made him increase his speed even more.

She was out of money and had no one to call. She wouldn't contact her human friends and didn't have Nïx's number. Not that she would call her aunt anyway. Holly had to know that Nïx had been in on the scheme from the beginning.

The scheme . . . Cade's gaze flickered over the sheathed sword propped on the passenger's seat. Cade hated the mere sight of it, a constant reminder that he'd been forced to choose yet again.

Before, he hadn't really gotten the term "hollow victory"—*a win is a win, so what's not to like?*—but now he understood.

The ne'er-do-well had finally done well.

And he'd never felt more like a failure.

Because of him, Holly was in constant danger, no doubt afraid and confused. Yes, she was stronger, but she was still so young and had hardly ever left New Orleans, much less hitched across the Territories in the winter.

The worry for her was punishing. In his lifetime, Cade had been tortured many times. He'd been a sinew away from being beheaded. None of those ordeals came close to the constant ache in his chest . . .

Cade was in love with her. Damn it, he wanted his halfling back.

* * *

Holly huddled down in a side alley, sitting on a mound of dirty snow. More of the vile stuff was coming down wetly. If she never saw snow again . . .

She had no idea where she was. Yet another barren mining town. They were beginning to blur together.

Unable to sleep for the last four days, she was nearing mental and physical exhaustion. The hunger she hadn't felt in weeks now redoubled, making her dizzy.

She was out of money, her watch long since sold, and there were no banks for wiring funds here. There wasn't even a regular post. Not that she had anyone to contact for help.

I am utterly alone—

The pay phone at the corner began to ring. As a girl who worshipped technology, Holly didn't want to be in a place where there were still pay phones about. Pay phones equaled somewhere she oughtn't ever be.

Eventually it stopped ringing.

So what to do now? *I can keep moving, or I can sit in the dirty snow till I freeze.*

She actually *could* sit in the dirt. No longer was it incapacitating for her. Of late, fate had enrolled Holly in a comprehensive immersion therapy. She hadn't showered for days, had no way to brush her teeth. She'd slept in unwashed sheets, bunking in portages that smelled of men's feet and cooked onions.

What is my next move? She could only hope to hitch another ride—

The ringing began again, and this time the sound grated on her frayed nerves. She shakily rose, then crossed to the phone, intending to take it off the hook. But once she picked it up, curiosity compelled her to answer.

"Hello?" Her voice was hoarse.

"Look for us!" Nïx yelled over blaring music. "We're vibrating with bass." Click.

What—the—hell? Holly hung up the phone, staring at it for long moments, as if it held the answers as to how and why Nïx had just called her.

Minutes later, a red thumping SUV skidded to a stop in front of her. A Valkyrie with a glowing face and a wry expression was behind the wheel. Nïx was in the passenger seat, waving for Holly to get in.

Holly flipped her off, returning to burrow in her dirty snow.

The two women followed her.

"Wow, you look like a bucket-o-fuck," the glowing one told Holly.

In a cheery tone, Nïx said, "This is your aunt, Regin the Radiant. We don't believe she possesses verbal governors of any kind. Now, come along, dearling. We're late for the airport."

Holly's brows rose. "I'm not going anywhere with you."

Nïx blinked in confusion. "Why ever not?"

Holly gaped before she could finally find words. "Maybe because you lied to me, tricking me to go off with an evil demon? One who turned me over to a sorcerer who planned to impregnate me with the *ultimate* evil!"

Nïx tapped her gloved finger against her chin. "I guess you couldn't throw Cade very far."

I'm going to sack her. I'm going to shove her face into the yellow snow over there.

Nïx chided, "Now, dearling, that's not nice. . . ."

"I want to talk to Holly alone," Regin said.

With a shrug, Nïx turned for the car. Once she and Holly

were alone, Regin said, "There are four reasons why you should come with me now. Firstly, there's food in the car, and apparently, you're still a masticator. Second, a warm shower and a clean bed can be had in less than two hours. Thirdly, Nïx is bat-shit crazy, and you're not the first one of us that she's sent on a freaky vision quest. And the last reason you should come with me? *I* didn't fuck you over."

Holly kind of liked this Regin. After all the duplicity she'd dealt with, a straight shooter might be nice to be around.

Yet then, even Regin resorted to trickery. "Very well. I didn't want to have to do this, Holly." She sighed. "But you're leaving me no choice." From her pocket, she pulled out a cache of antibacterial wipes, waving them enticingly. "Look what Auntie Reege has. Who's your buddy? Who's your favorite Valkyrie?"

When Holly somehow resisted, Regin sighed, "Fuck this noiseage," then swooped Holly up under her arm, pinning her to her side. Though Holly fought, she carried her to the truck. Once Nïx reached back to open the door, Regin tossed Holly in the backseat.

Holly was still sputtering, dragging her matted hair from her eyes when the truck took off, heading out of the city.

Nïx turned to face her. "Well, did you have fun on your adventure?"

I'm delirious. This is what it feels like to be in delirium. "Oodles of."

"Good." Nïx handed her granola bars. Holly gorged on them without even taking off her filthy gloves.

"Soon we'll be in New Orleans, where you can meet your coven. We have your room all set up—you're to live with us at Val Hall now."

"New Orleans?" Holly sputtered, choking on granola. "You sent me across the entire *continent* when I'd been in the same city as my own kind?"

At her nod, Holly gave a weird, high giggle. She started laughing outright and couldn't seem to stop, even after she'd also begun crying.

"There, there," Nïx said. "If I hadn't sent you on this trip, then you wouldn't have your own page in *The Book of Warriors*!"

"We're here," Regin said, turning into what looked like an airfield.

"Seriously, dearling, you need to chillax."

"Why, *Auntie* Nïx? Why do I need to do *anything*?"

"Because in minutes, you're going to see the demon at the chopper pad."

Two things registered in Holly's addled brain. She was about to ride in a helicopter.

And she'd be damned before Cadeon saw her crying. She ran her crusty sleeve over her face.

"Why is he coming here?" she asked as they parked next to a sleek, silver helicopter with blackened windows.

"Because he's after you," Nïx said, hopping out of the car.

When her aunts jogged toward the chopper, Holly followed. "*Why* is he after me?" she asked Nïx, having to yell over the rotors.

Regin got there first and slid open the door. "I love the smell of napalm in the morning!" She ushered Nïx in, shoved Holly up, then climbed inside behind her. A female pilot began pressing buttons and flipping switches. The rotors sped up, growing louder.

Holly cried, "Nïx!"

"Oh, yes, of course. What was I thinking? Holly, this is your aunt Cara the Fair."

The pilot gave her a two-finger salute against a helmet that read *Fly Me Friendly*.

Nïx continued, "She's part Fury, as well. She's flying us all legs on the way home, and then she's off to . . ."

"Colombia," Cara finished for her.

"Nïx, damn it! Tell me!"

Her brows drew together. "Tell you what, dearling?"

"Let it go for now," Regin said. "She's spaced."

They'd just lifted off when a truck skidded to a stop, and Cadeon jumped from the cab.

She frowned when he charged for them, with his eyes black, pumping his arms for speed, looking more determined than she'd ever seen him. But why? Seller's remorse?

Or worse?

What did he think the Vessel would get him now? A magickal bow and arrow? An enchanted shield?

Regin slapped her knees. "Oh, my gods, look at him running like his life depended on catching us." She slid open the door. "Is this straight outta *Platoon*, or what? Willem!" she cried, holding out one hand. "Run, Willem!" Then she choked on her laughter.

"Why would he be doing this?" Holly whispered to herself, but even over the clamoring rotors, Regin heard her.

"Why do you *care*? Historically, whenever a prick serves me up to a skeevy sorcerer to use like a brood mare, I stop analyzing his motives. Historically. Now give him a nice New York State bird, and get him out of your head."

47

Val Hall—home of the New Orleans coven of Valkyrie—was a nightmare.

Wraiths clad in ragged red cloaks circled the old antebellum mansion, the yard was filled with lightning rods and charred trees, and dense fog wafted with no deference to the breeze, as if it were alive.

At Holly's first sight of the place, she was tempted to turn on her heel and get back into the car, heading for snow country. Except she couldn't because Nïx had dropped off her and Regin, chirping that she'd be back *in a week*, but there were "snacks in the fridge."

On the flight to New Orleans, Holly had learned little about Cadeon's actions from her aunt. All she'd been able to glean from Nïx's ramblings was that Cadeon had had pressing reasons for what he'd done. Not what those reasons were, or how he could so callously abandon Holly. She'd thought she'd have all the time in the world to question Nïx. Now Holly was left just as confused as before with no relief in sight.

As Regin led her inside, Holly saw some Valkyrie were sitting on the roof, while others rocked in wicker chairs on the second-story gallery with a TV in front of them and what looked like Wii controllers in their hands.

Inside the manor, Regin pushed even more Valkyrie out of the way. "Make a hole, clear out. She's new."

Most of them eyed Holly with curiosity, some with suspicion. And then the mass questions for Regin began:

—"You sure she's fully one of us?"

—"Is this the one we get to haze? Dibs on her clothes!"

—"Can she play pool?"

—"Is she any good at video games?"

"*Good* at video games?" Holly asked the crowd. They were sizing her up, just as her jocks once had, and just as the Sandbar denizens had. So she said, "I can *make* video games."

Apparently, those were big words for this crowd.

"You heard her," Regin said. "She's already a creature with which one doesn't fuck."

—"How?"

"She's getting a page in *The Book of Warriors*. She tagged a pack of Wendigo and culled the membership roster of the Order of Demonaeus by a quarter. And that was just this *month*."

This is what you are, Holly. A killer. A creature even violent Valkyrie admire.

Holly was overwhelmed, perspiration beginning to bead above her lip.

"So let's have a little boo-yah respect for Holly the . . ." Regin trailed off with a frown. "What should your Valkyrie name be?"

They were all too close, making her dizzy, unsteady on her feet. She put her hand to her forehead and muttered, "I feel nauseated. Maybe I should lie down."

—"Dude, told you she wasn't a Valkyrie. We don't throw up."

Now Regin studied her with her brows drawn. "What's doing?"

What's doing? The first day Holly had ever seen Cadeon, he'd said that to her. Reminded of the bastard, Holly retched, throwing up the contents of her stomach.

The crowd backed away with a collective gasp.

"Well, the good news is that I got your trailing name," Regin said. "Welcome, Holly the Preggers."

Five days had passed since Holly had been smuggled into Val Hall. Cade had been seconds too late at the chopper pad, and now she was in the hands of the Valkyrie. "I can't believe the men you sent didn't keep her from getting inside," he said to Rök as the two of them lay in wait among the burned trees on the property.

"This coven has a three-thousand-year-old soothsayer and witches batting on their team," Rök said. "They've got sneaky covered. They probably have a portal we can't see."

"Now Holly's with her family," Cade said, taking a slug of demon brew. "They won't exactly be arguing my case."

"Not to put too fine a point on it, but your chances were pretty much blown with or without the Valkyrie's interference. In my experience, nothing says *we're taking a T.O.* like getting the finger as a helicopter dusts off."

When Cade scowled, Rök continued, "I put too fine a point on it, didn't I?" He snapped his fingers for the flask. "So tell me what it's like."

"What's what like?"

"You know—this." He waved at Cade's face then in Holly's direction.

"A two-demon siege of Val Hall?" He knew what Rök was talking about, but wouldn't make this any easier.

"You're going to make me spell it out, aren't you?"

"If I have to cop to it, then yeah."

After another swig, Rök said, "What's it like to care for someone more than for yourself? I only ask because this is the first thing you've done that I haven't."

"The way I'm feeling now, I would recommend staying the hell away from it."

At Rök's raised brows, he said, "Imagine you got lanced straight through the center of your chest."

Rök nodded gravely. "Happened more than once."

"Then imagine how you'd feel if that huge hole never mended."

"Not good."

"Not good at all. If I could just talk to her once before we leave for Rothkalina." The grim reality of his situation was that even if he could somehow win Holly over, he'd immediately have to leave her.

"You *have* to talk to her before you can leave. Face it, you wouldn't be any good to us right now. You don't eat or sleep. You're obsessed with something, and it's not victory against Omort. That's how leaders get their men killed."

"Holly could stay inside for months working on her code." Cade ran a hand over his face. "Still no luck with Nïx?"

"I've got the entire crew beating the streets for her—"

"Who are we looking for?" a voice whispered from behind them.

Cade and Rök both scrambled back. Nïx had been crouched directly behind them, peering at the manor along with them.

Neither had heard her approach.

Cade recovered first and said, "I've been searching for you."

"I've *never* heard that before." Nïx looked as mad as ever but she also appeared . . . tired.

"How is Holly?"

"Splendid. She's settling in nicely. She even has a date next week with someone name Desh. He's a demon. Maybe you know him?"

The news felt like a kick in the teeth

"So what did you want with me?"

"I want to see her before I have to leave for Rothkalina. I don't care if it's just for five minutes. Can you arrange a meeting?"

"Where?"

"Where-bloody-ever!"

"You'll have to do better than that," Nïx said. "Holly told me just the other day that she wished she had a great, big house."

"She truly did?" he exclaimed. He'd get her the biggest, best—

"No, she didn't truly," Nïx added with a sigh. "Maybe? Sure! I can't remember. Anyway, the fact remains that Holly might actually somehow forgive you, and then what will happen? Do you expect my niece to live in your pool house man-cave with you and the smoke demon?" She waved a negligent hand toward Rök, and he saluted her with the flask. "The days of your unplanned, rolling-stone existence have ended, Cade. Having a female all of your own is a big responsibility."

"I'm on it. Just get me the meeting."

"I'll help on one more condition: You and your crew stop searching for Néomi and the vampire."

Néomi was indeed alive. "How did she survive?"

"After you so rudely gutted her? She's a phantom now. Long story. But witchcraft was involved."

Rök exclaimed, "A phantom! No wonder I couldn't bloody find her. I never had a chance, did I?"

Nïx shook her head sadly. "Especially not when I was tipping her off to your every move . . ."

Both males were stunned silent by that. Finally Cade said, "You knew she lived? Yet you told us that she'd died. You lied—"

"Yes, and people who lie are *bad*. Oh, but I didn't mean *you*." Her eyes going vacant, she said, "I did tell a fib, but only so the fates would align to get you here, skulking around Val Hall at midnight tonight—with Groot dead, with you in possession of a mystickal sword, and with Holly . . ."

"With Holly what?"

"Nothing." She gracefully stood. "I'll get started on our plan," she said, sauntering off, leaving his heart thundering at the idea that he might win Holly back. "By the way," she called over her shoulder. "Your brother's back in town."

48

"How are you liking it here at Val Hall?" Nïx asked.

"I like it fine," Holly answered, wondering if her aunt was lucid.

Nïx was a font of information. But to get to it, one had to first catch her. Then one had to catch her when she was lucid. Over the last two weeks, Holly hadn't had much luck with either.

"You're settling in?"

This put Holly on edge. *What's Nïx getting at?* "I am," she answered slowly. In fact, she was getting on with her new life quite well, all things considered.

Since she couldn't return to the loft, she'd accepted the room the Valkyrie offered her at Val Hall. Regin had taught her how to survive at the manor—how to steal others' clothes and defend her own, how to know who'd just gotten dry cleaning back for the really good takes, how to anticipate and avert pranks.

Holly was expected to train with weapons several times a week—especially with the Accession nearing. Regin had helped her try out swords to pick the one she liked best. "Anything but a greatsword," was all Holly had requested.

She was also expected to practice Wii because the witches were winning even when drunk, and were getting overly cocky about their abilities.

In her free time, Holly could work on her code, which

everyone mistakenly believed was a video game, so they left her alone.

"And what about your school?" Nïx asked.

"I found out last week that I can finish my PhD from here." When Holly had called her doctoral advisor and described her project, the woman had told Holly that her code would be more than enough to complete her degree. No more classes, to be taught or taken. Mei had taken over jock duty—and she'd gleefully related that Tim was facing an ethics panel and lost grants. . . .

Holly had known her code would be enough to finish her doctorate. Universities owned their students' research. Her code could earn the school untold riches.

But she didn't care that she would lose out. The school had been good to her.

Nïx asked, "But you know you can go out every now and then?"

She nodded. "With a buddy." Holly was in much less danger now that Cade's crew had in fact taken out two factions, and Tera the Fey had spread the word that Holly was not to be touched.

Plus, Holly's reputation as a slaughter-happy Valkyrie would make enemies, as Regin put it, "a jot leery" about attacking her.

Still, she wasn't to go anywhere without another Valkyrie.

"I'm glad to see that Regin has taken you under her wing," Nïx said. "Though I wonder about that, since she isn't exactly the most giving of Valkyrie."

Holly said, "She's already admitted that she's using me for distraction and advised me not to look too deeply into it." *Straight-shooting Regin, telling it like it is.*

Regin was even going to help her find an exorcist for the Laughing Ladies—though she wouldn't accompany her to the bridge. Fierce Regin was terrified of ghosts. So Holly was still looking for a buddy to go with her to Michigan in the winter.

Yes, Holly was settling in. Life was almost dandy. Except for the fact that she was pregnant with an evil demon's spawn.

In a rare bout of lucidity, Nïx had explained that Cadeon could've "double bagged it," and Holly could've been on the pill, a sponge, *and* an IUD, and he still would've "slipped one past the goalie."

The Vessel was hyper-fertile at all times for the first pregnancy. A virile male could have blown her a kiss, and Holly would've been calling him in nine months.

Good to know. *Now*. Score another one for Nïx, who could've divvied that little nugget of wisdom, but hadn't.

Holly didn't actually believe Cade was *evil*. But her general attitude about having a demon baby was: *Meh*. She couldn't get worked up about it one way or the other, and waited each day for it to sink in, hoping to feel some kind of excitment.

She'd forgiven her aunt for the most part. Without Nïx's interference, Holly would still be stubbornly clinging to her old life, when this one suited her far better.

Holly had realized that being with Cadeon wasn't the sole reason she'd been happy. And though it didn't feel possible now—even after everything, she still missed him terribly—Holly believed she could be happy once more.

All she'd ever wanted was to feel normal. In the Lore, she did. Even with her lingering quirks and compulsions, Holly fit in.

Nïx had told her that she would finally get a sense of herself on her journey, and in fact, Holly had discovered who she was: Holly the Bright.

It was her new Valkyrie name. She kind of liked it. Especially when compared to her coven's first few ideas: Holly the Spawner, Holly the Plucky Single Mother, and Holly Crocker.

Nïx said they'd chosen her name because of her intelligence, but also due to the fact that she'd followed the northern lights to get away from danger.

"Any thoughts on Cadeon?" Nïx asked. "You can't put him off forever."

He actually hadn't lied about Holly being his by fate. And Nïx had told her that the demon would be wanting his female back.

For the first week, he'd continued coming to Val Hall every night. Initially he'd acted as if he owned the place, striding right up to the front door—or at least intending to. The wraiths had caught him and tossed his towering frame into an oak so hard the trunk had split from the impact.

The Valkyrie playing Wii on the porch had cackled with glee.

If he yelled for her, her aunts slapped headphones on her ears, then sicced the wraiths on him even harder.

But then, five nights ago, he'd stopped coming. . . .

Now that Holly had time to think things over, she'd recalled all of Cadeon's tireless training. She'd begun to suspect that he really did have feelings for her and had been counting on Holly to free herself when he turned her over.

His "pressing needs" had consumed him. He'd had to make a choice, and she'd lost out.

Holly could almost understand that. But what she couldn't understand was *how* he'd given her the kiss-off at Groot's. Holly had been terrified, numb with shock, and he'd been cruel, callously indifferent.

He'd sure fooled her. She'd never forget the look on his face when he said, "Never trust a demon. . . ." The ease with which he deceived still stunned her. She couldn't even count how many times he'd lied to her over the course of their journey.

Holly couldn't look back over their relationship and know if anything was real. *How could he have left me behind—*

When Nïx cleared her throat, Holly realized that she'd spaced as badly as her aunt usually did.

"Something on your mind, dearling?"

"Um . . . no, everything's great. Thanks for checking on me."

"I'm really glad you like it here." Nix smiled blankly. "But now you have to move."

49

He was nervous as he pulled into Rydstrom's estate. Why hadn't his brother called anyone to let them know he'd escaped? Cade's mind ran riot with theories.

Had Rydstrom been tortured? Had they done something to him so horrific that he was unable to face others?

Cade parked his old truck—which still chugged along despite water damage and bullet holes. With a glower, he collected the sword. He despised it, and was happy for the chance to get it away from him.

As he approached the main house, he noticed that all the shades were drawn. But as soon as Cade went to unlock the side door, Rydstrom cracked it open. He wore no shirt or shoes and was buttoning up his jeans as if he'd just slung them on.

Cade's brows rose at the sight of him. "Rydstrom?"

His brother was . . . changed.

There was a mean set to his clenched jaw that had never been there before. The rigid muscles in his neck and shoulders were bunched with tension. His eyes were narrowed, and they looked *crazed.*

Four thin lines of blood ran down his chest and across his scarred cheek—as if someone had raked nails over his skin.

What the hell was going on? *And what was done to him to make him like this?*

"Are you going to make me stand out here all afternoon? Open the door."

His brother made no move to, only glanced back over his shoulder into the house.

"Rydstrom, you're worrying me, man. Let me in, and tell me what happened. The last I heard was that you'd been captured by Sabine."

No response.

"Were you taken to Tornin? Did you fight Omort to escape?"

Rydstrom finally shook his head.

"Then how the hell did you get free? No one escapes Tornin."

"I had an ace in my pocket," he said, his voice rough.

"You don't sound good. Are you all right?"

"I will be." Rydstrom looked back over his shoulder again. "Soon."

"I got the sword," Cade said, offering it to him. "Killed Groot, too."

Rydstrom nodded, accepting the weapon without interest, barely sparing it a glance.

Cade was confounded, saying slowly, "That's the *sword* that will defeat *Omort*."

"We go to war in the spring," Rydstrom grated. "Be ready."

"That's all you've got to say? So much for abject gratitude, or even a pat on the back." Cade's temper spiked. "If you knew what I went through to get to that goddamned thing, what I put my female through . . . Oh, and if you haven't noticed, your Veyron's missing, and it's never fucking coming home—"

"*Is someone out there?*" a woman suddenly screamed from inside. "*Oh, God, help me!*"

Cade distinctly heard a mattress squeaking.

And the rattling of chains.

"I'm being held against my will!"

His jaw dropped. "Is that . . . *Sabine?*" Had Rydstrom used his captor to escape? "Was she your ace?"

"*Please help me!*" she shrieked at the top of her lungs.

Rydstrom peered at him hard with those crazed eyes, as if he dared Cade to do something.

Striving for a casual tone, Cade said, "So, you've got an evil sorceress chained up in your bed, then?"

And he'd had no clothes on earlier.

"She's *mine*," Rydstrom seethed. "I'll do whatever the fuck I want to her. And it's nothing that wasn't done to me." His massive fists clenched.

"Hey, hey, no need to slug me, brother. To each his own, yeah?" Had Sabine done such a number on the noble-minded, kingly Rydstrom that he considered *this* a good idea? If so, then maybe a little tit for tat was in order.

"Once I'm done with her, I'll contact you." When Rydstrom shut the door, Cade stared at it for long moments.

At length, he turned for the steps. "*Fuckall*," he said on a stunned breath. *Does this mean I'm no longer the bad brother . . . ?*

"You're really kicking me out?" Holly asked Nïx.

They were on their way to look at a home for sale, one that would be "perfect for Holly and the vamon."

"You can't raise a kid at Val Hall," Nïx said. "The lightning danger alone would make it mortally prohibitive."

Holly had gone along with her, too wearied to put up a fight. She'd even agreed to ride in Nïx's Bentley, which was still a mess. Though the clutter still affected her, it didn't bother Holly quite as much as before. "You got rid of the C-4?"

"Oh, gods, yes. That same night, too." She sighed. "*Good times*."

"How much farther is it?" Holly asked. It was late afternoon, and the winter sun would set in an hour. "We're already twenty minutes out of the parish."

"And we're already here," Nix said, turning into a gated entrance that opened at her approach.

Lined with oaks and magnolias, the drive was winding—and long. "How many acres is this?"

"I dunno. I'm thinking plus-or-minus lots and lots." When the drive opened up, Holly's lips parted. The estate was breathtaking.

Rich landscaping surrounded a three-story, cream-colored mansion. Built in the French Colonial style with steeply pitched slate roofs and arched dormers, it had galleries that ran along the front and sides, with ornate wrought iron rails in glossy black. Three-story-high Doric columns flanked the front entrance.

"It's called Nine Oaks." On each side of the mansion were three ancient oaks, with presumably three in the back. "It's got twelve rooms. Several potential nurseries."

It was weird to talk about things like nurseries. Weirder still: the fact that Holly actually *needed* one. *Meh*.

"What do you think?" Nïx asked, as she parked in front of the entry walk.

"It's amazing," Holly said honestly. A crisp breeze was blowing, fanning the damp banana trees and palms. "But don't you think it's a bit grand for me and one kid? The loft would be better."

"This feels like a great place to raise a vamon, no? Well, we're here, we might as well look around."

With a shrug, Holly followed her up the bricked walkway. It split, curving around a fountain—that had nine sprays of water.

They climbed up the six stairs to the porch and found the door was unlocked. "We can just walk in?" Holly asked.

"We're expected."

The furnished interior was just as appealing to Holly as the exterior. It seemed everywhere she looked, things were in threes or multiples of.

Six bar stools, three track lights per strip. Twelve rooms and three stories . . . All the numbers were working for Holly.

But the office upstairs sealed the deal. The room was spacious and airy and had a huge window that overlooked *a pool.*

As usual, her attention was drawn to the computer, and she wondered what the owner of this place was packing. It was fired up, with the specs pulled up onscreen. Holly's brows drew together. "This platform isn't due out for another year. No civvie has a system like this. Whose is it?"

From behind her, she heard a rumbling voice: "It's yours, halfling. Because codes don't write themselves."

50

Oh, come on, Nïx!" Holly glared. "You set me up again? I can't believe you told him!"

"I told him nothing about *that*."

"About what?" Cadeon asked cautiously.

"None of your business!" Holly snapped. "What do you want?"

"You."

"Play nice, kids," Nïx said. "I'll be in the car. Which may or may not remain here." Then she abandoned Holly.

Holly gave him a bitter smile. "You working with Nïx to trick me—why, that's original!"

"You wouldn't have seen me otherwise, and I have to talk to you."

She noticed then that he'd lost weight. His face was leaner, and he looked weary. *Like I care!* "I think anything that needed to be said was. I believe it went along these lines: 'You were part of a transaction.'"

"I had to do that. I had to act like I didn't give a damn, or Groot wouldn't have given me the sword."

She grew still. "You have a lot of nerve mentioning that sword to me."

"I came back for you to get you away from him—"

"Really? You see, I wouldn't know that because I only stuck around for Groot's *first* attempt to hammer a railroad spike in my temple!"

"What did he do to you?" Cadeon strode forward, reaching for her arm.

But she jerked back with a hiss. "Don't you dare touch me! I got *myself* away before Groot made me his unthinking sex slave and brood mare—no thanks to you."

"I know. I saw you jump."

He truly *had* returned for her.

"I was diving in right behind you when Groot skewered me with flying swords. I would've been there even sooner, but he poisoned the hilt of the sword, drugging me when I grasped it."

"Why did the castle blow?"

"I threw Groot into his own forge. Unfortunately, I got caught in the blast as well, or I would have been by your side in the village against the Wendigo. Not that you needed my help."

"So had you always planned to come for me? Or did you have a change of heart over bartering me?"

"The plan was to get the sword, kill Groot with it, then get you the hell out of there as quickly as possible."

"Then why didn't you tell me about it?"

"I couldn't. Groot is a mind reader. Demons have blocks, but he would have read you like a book. And I tried to teach you to fight to prepare you in case something went wrong."

"How about not taking me there at all? How about not betraying me? You lied to me the entire time, telling me that I could change back."

"I did, Holly. I lied through my teeth. But I didn't feel like I had a choice. Look, you knew why I needed that sword, but you don't know how badly."

"Oh, but I do. You'd searched for nine centuries for a

way to kill Omort, you think it was your fault that the entire kingdom of Rothkalina fell, and you blame yourself for your foster family's death." As she listed these things out loud, it struck her anew how monumental each truly was.

"And there's even more to it. That first night my brother didn't show, it was because he'd been taken by Omort's sister. Tricked by her sorcery and trapped in her dungeon for her to . . . use."

"What do you mean?"

"Sabine wanted to have Rydstrom's child to take over our kingdom forever. The idea of him in that situation . . ." Cadeon ran a hand over his face. "For Rydstrom that would have been a fate worse than death. And I thought the only way to free him would be the sword."

"Thought? Past tense?"

"He somehow escaped and got back here. But he's . . . different. I'm worried about him."

When Holly tilted her head, Cade said, "Will you walk with me?" He was surprised he was able to speak so evenly.

His female was lovelier than he'd ever seen her. Her long blond hair was loose, curling about her shoulders. Her skin was glowing, her eyes bright.

Seeming as if her curiosity got the better of her, she walked beside him.

"I understand why you would feel like you had to do anything for the sword," she said. "I get that, Cadeon—I really do. But understanding your motives doesn't make me feel better that I was the collateral damage. How can

I believe in anything that happened between us when you were bent on betraying me the entire time?"

"Not the entire time! I'd had another plan. And then when that fell through, I ordered my men to meet me in the Territories. I'd planned to storm Groot's fortress."

"What happened?"

"On the day before the deal expired, I found out that they couldn't reach us. The ice road was blown, and they couldn't chopper in because of the weather."

"The storms to the south . . ."

He nodded. "That's why I was always on the phone with him. I was scrambling to do *anything* besides what I ended up doing. But I didn't see another way out. In my situation, what would you have done?"

When she nibbled her lip and glanced away, he knew she was thinking she'd do the same.

"You don't know how hard it was to act like I cared nothing for you. Or what it's done to me since."

"What's it done to you?" she asked.

"Made me gut-sick from wanting you." Cadeon eased closer. "From missing my Holly."

She could feel his heat, and his addictive scent tickled her nose. *Want*. God, she'd missed him.

"What was Nïx talking about earlier? What didn't you want me to know?"

Why not tell him? He'd find out soon enough anyway. "You're going to be . . . a father."

He seemed to choke on a sharp inhalation. "A father? Me? *We* . . . " Then after a moment, he laughed, swinging her up in his arms.

She was stunned by his reaction. "I didn't think you'd be this happy." Had she never realized how momentous this was until she saw Cadeon's utter delight? His excitement began sparking her own. *Not so meh.*

"Are you kidding me? I've got an ally on the inside now, who'll be wearing down your defenses against me. It ups my chances of getting you back." Then he stilled. "Are *you* not happy?"

"I . . . could be. It's been hard to come to grips with." She quirked a brow. "You're not worried about your *ally* being the ultimate evil?"

He tenderly brushed a curl behind her ear. "If I were evil, I couldn't love you this much."

Breathe, Holly.

"If you give me another chance, I'll never lie to you again."

"But how can I trust you? Tell me. Because you've just waltzed back into my life with more words, more promises. . . ." She trailed off with a frown. "Cadeon, where are your horns?"

He shrugged. "Ditched them. You need normal. And I need to give you everything you've ever wanted. Like this house. It's got a pool in the back. And it's freakishly neat and everything's in threes. I searched high and low for it."

So that's where he's been. "But your horns," she cried. He'd once told her how excruciating losing one was. And they were part of his identity, part of what made him a demon.

Yet Cadeon had cut them off for her.

"If you don't mind them, I can regrow them in a couple of weeks."

"Were you just going to keep cutting them?" she asked, thinking of the pain.

"If that's what it took to make you happy, then of course I would."

At that, her defenses crumbled. *Want!* She'd missed him too much, needed him too badly.

"You're folding, aren't you?" He gave her one of his heart-stopping grins. "You can't stay mad at me because you know I'm going to get it right this time. Plus, you need someone to go with you to see some ghosties."

For some reason, she *did* believe he would get it right, believed it with all her heart. "I might be folding a *tiny* bit. But only because I need a ride to Michigan."

"Gods, I've missed you, halfling." He cupped her face. "But Holly, I have to tell you—I'm leaving for Rothkalina in the spring. We go to war."

She drew back. "If you want us to be together, then we *stay* together. None of this *the male goes off to battle* crap."

"You think I'll take my pregnant female into a war-torn plain?"

"You will if you want to keep her. My mother went to battle while carrying me."

He exhaled. "I never want to put more lies between us, so I'm saying at the outset that I will do everything in my power to dissuade you from this."

"And I'll fight hard to be by your side. Looks like it's on."

His lips curled. "Oh, it's *on*." But then, he grew serious once more. "Did you hear me when I said I was in love with you?" His voice was hoarse, laden with feeling.

"I heard you."

He brought his mouth down to hers for a searing kiss

that left her knees weak. When they broke away, catching their breath, he said, "You're in love with me, too?"

"I might be," she murmured. "Are you going to use sex to try to seal this deal with me?"

"Oh, yeah." With a growl, he trailed his lips down her neck.

She smiled up at the ceiling, her eyes sliding closed in pleasure. "Because I'm okay with that. . . ."